The Photograph

Neil White

Copyright © Neil White 2023

The moral right of the author has been asserted. All rights reserved. No part of this book may be reproduced, stored in a retrieval system, or transmitted, in any form or by any means, without the prior permission of the author, nor be otherwise circulated in any form of binding or cover other than that in which it is published and without a similar condition including this condition being imposed on a subsequent purchaser.

All characters and events in this publication, other than those clearly in the public domain, are fictitious, and resemblance to real persons, living or dead, is purely coincidental.

www.neilwhite.net

Cover design by Ken Dawson

ABOUT THE AUTHOR

Neil White has been a practising criminal solicitor in the north of England for nearly thirty years, where he lives with his wife, Alison. Aside from a legal career, Neil has written thirteen thrillers. These include the Jack Garrett series, published by HarperCollins, the Sam and Joe Parker trilogy, published by Sphere, and the Dan Grant series, published by Hera. His fifth book, *Cold Kill*, was a number one bestseller, and his books have been translated into a number of foreign languages.

As well as writing thrillers, in 2016 Neil published *Lost In Nashville*, a heart-warming tale of a father and son who seek to rediscover their relationship by travelling the life of Johnny Cash.

When he isn't writing or speaking in a courtroom, Neil can be found ploughing through his Netflix list, or his to-be-read pile, or watching rugby league.

For more information, check out his Amazon page, or his website at **www.neilwhite.net**

BOOKS BY NEIL WHITE (in order):

Jack Garrett series
Fallen Idols
Lost Souls
Last Rites
Dead Silent
Cold Kill

Stand-alone
Beyond Evil

Sam and Joe Parker trilogy
Next To Die
The Death Collector
The Domino Killer

Dan Grant trilogy
From The Shadows
The Darkness Around Her
The Innocent Ones

Other fiction
Lost In Nashville – A Father. A Son. The Open Road. And Johnny Cash

FOR ALISON

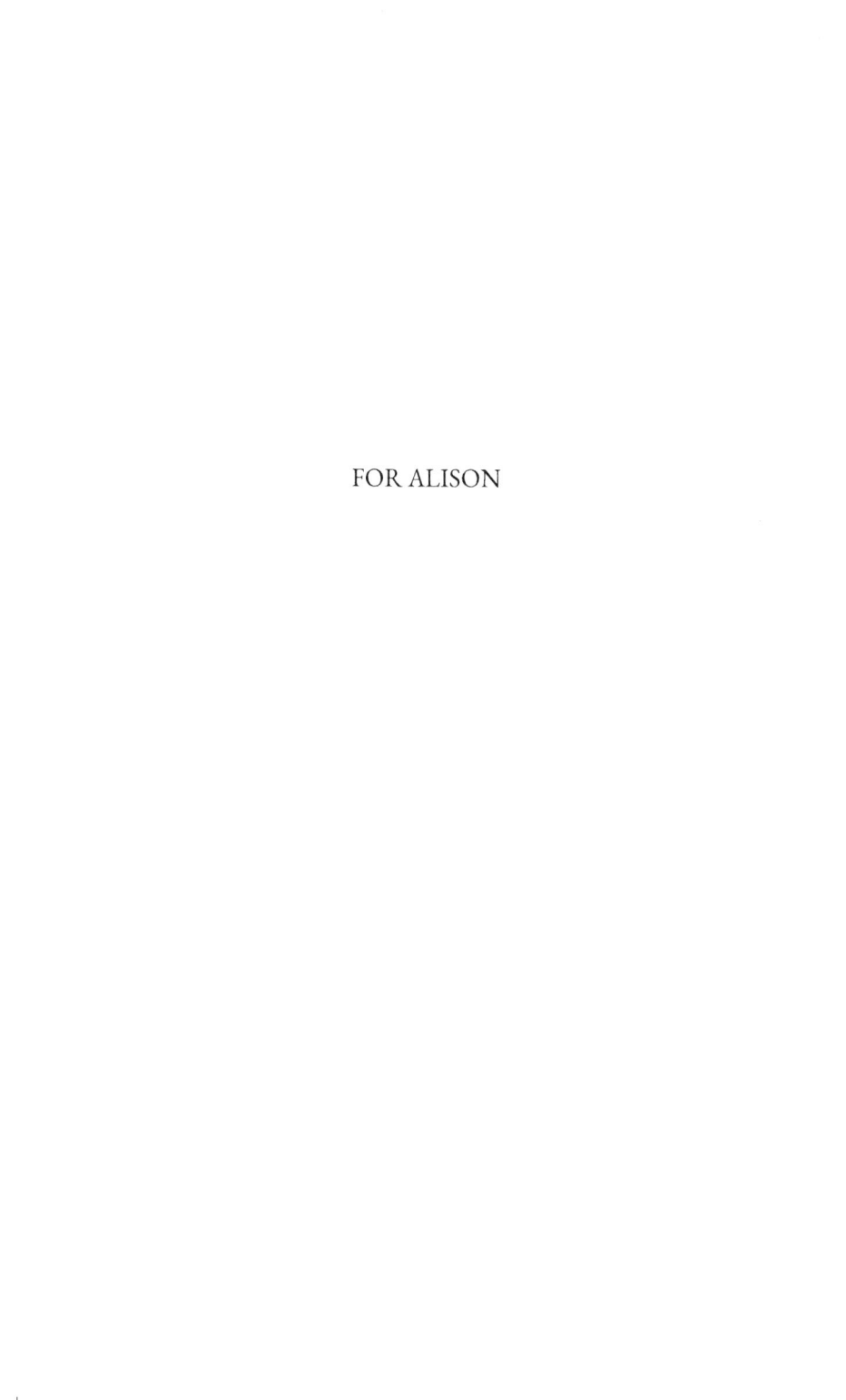

One

Amy ran towards the beach, the air sharp, the night colder than she expected. Whatever the season, the sea chilled everything.

She'd rushed out, the call coming in a few minutes earlier from Rob, a uniformed copper not long in the job. As her feet pounded on the concrete slipway that led to the beach, an access for the boats carried there on trailers. she wished she'd gone for more than just jeans and a jacket.

Rob was in the distance, leaning forward, his hands on his legs. There were shouts and whoops further along, by the glow of a campfire. Someone was having a party, the silver tips of breaking waves as the backdrop, lit by the lighthouse that swept the bay. Four turns, then a break, then four more. It would go like that all night, a rhythm familiar to everyone who'd grown up in the town.

She looked towards the flicker of the campfire, and wondered how long their fun was going to last.

Rob straightened as Amy got close.

Amy stopped and tried to catch her breath. 'What's going on?'

He pointed towards somewhere behind him before putting his forearm over his mouth, as if to stop himself from vomiting.

'Take a breath, talk to me.'

'I came here for those,' he said, then pointed towards the flickers of the campfire as he sucked in some night air. 'Someone called from one of the houses, complaining. My sergeant told me to have a look.'

Amy knew they'd get a premium service at this end of town. Money equals power equals influence in Cookstown. If the rich locals get worried, they get a police visit.

'You haven't got me out here to close down a party,' she said.

Rob sucked in more large breaths, his eyes bright dots against the uniform of black polo shirt and cargo pants, his dark hair cropped short.

'I'm sorry,' he said. 'I shouldn't have called you. I can deal with this.'

'I'm here now.'

'It's against the breakwater, just down there,' and he flicked his hand towards the rolling tide.

'What's against the breakwater?'

'A body. A woman. At first, I thought it was a shop dummy or something. It looked broken.'

'How close did you get?'

He shrugged and let out a long breath.

Amy knew what that meant: not close enough.

'Christ, Rob, you might be able to save her.'

Amy sprinted towards where Rob had been. He lagged behind. Amy told herself not to get angry with him. He was a young copper, and the first dead body was always the worst, but preservation of life trumps everything.

Amy jumped over the gnarled board that connected the battered wooden posts that stretched into the tide, the sand higher on one side. Seaweed trailed over some, slippery and gleaming. It went against her every instinct, but she hoped, for Rob's sake, that the woman had died a long time before. If she'd died as Rob tried to keep his supper down at the top of the beach, his career would end before it ever really got going.

The sand was sodden and hard, sculpted into ridges by the receding tide, already busy with wormholes. The woman was sprawled on her front, her legs twisted, jogging bottoms pulled partially down, although Amy guessed that was from the rigours of the sea rather than from any human act. Her jumper looked over-sized, drenched and stretched out.

As she reached the body, Amy used her phone to illuminate the scene. There was no hope of resuscitation. The woman's face was pale and grey, her eyes closed, the pallor of death.

Amy turned to Rob and waved him over. 'You need to see this.'

Rob stalled.

'Don't make it about you,' Amy said. 'It's about her. She's the victim.'

'Okay, I'm sorry,' Rob said, before he took a deep breath and trudged towards her.

When he reached her, she asked, 'How did you spot her?'

'It was the skin. I don't know if it was the moon that caught it, but it seemed to shine.' Rob looked down and clenched his jaw. 'If I could have saved her, I would have done, I promise. I called you because I couldn't be seen like this. You know, shaking, puking.'

Amy reached out to put her hand on his shoulder and softened her tone. 'It'll get better. I can guarantee that all those who give you grief now were once shaking, trembling little men. But if you ever get into trouble, they'll back you. Cops stick together when they need to.'

'Thank you,' he said. 'Do you think it's her? Sarah Marsh.'

As soon as Rob said the name, Amy realised he was right.

Sarah Marsh had been reported missing by her husband the day before. It hadn't generated much activity, wives are allowed to run away from their husbands, and there were rumours of tensions within the marriage, but the description fitted.

'Possibly,' she said.

Rob stepped forward. 'The bulletins mentioned a tattoo on her shoulder, two tennis rackets crossed over each other,' and he bent down as if to move the woman's clothing.

Amy grabbed his wrist. 'Don't touch anything.'

'But she's been washed up.'

'Are you sure about that? Can you rule out that she was dumped here to look like that?'

'Do you think that's a possibility?'

'Everything is possible until you discover otherwise. And even if the sea did wash her up, that doesn't mean that all the forensic traces have been scrubbed. Let the forensic team do their work. Mr Marsh will find out soon enough.'

Or perhaps he already knows, Amy thought, but she decided not to voice it.

'Sorry, I wasn't thinking.'

'It's a learning curve,' Amy said. 'Have you touched her anywhere?'

'No, I didn't, I swear.'

'Good.' Amy took some pictures with her phone, the flash bright, the images so stark, much worse than a twisted, dark shape wedged against a breakwater. Straggly blonde hair. Pale skin. Nail varnish.

That's what stood out. The nail varnish.

The rest of her was a corpse thrown up by the sea, but the nail varnish was something she'd done when she was alive, an evening spent with a small brush, something mundane. Done when she was a living person.

Their attention was diverted by the distant strobe of blue lights. The scene was about to get busier.

Amy stepped back and winked at Rob. 'This is where you turn into the hero.'

Two

No one paid any attention as Amy walked towards the campfire.

The crime scene investigators were on their way, and Rob had gone back to his squad car to wait for them. Amy had made him walk a long way around, not wanting to disturb any potential footprints in the sand more than they already had.

Embers drifted upwards and danced around as the wood crackled in the fire, casting part of the beach in an orange glow. The dunes were behind them, spiked by clumps of long grass. It was a youthful scene. Some stared into the flames, the shadows flickering, whereas others were sitting and drinking, or lying on rugs, teenagers kissing and fondling.

Enjoy it, she thought. The world will ruin them soon enough.

From a distance, she'll have looked like a curious neighbour, perhaps coming along to ask them to quieten the party. As she got closer, someone on the other side of the fire spotted her and gestured with a beer bottle. She pulled out her police ID.

They were just kids, no one more than eighteen years old. Clean clothes, good skin, straight white teeth. These were the kids who saw their life away from Cookstown. Not for them the slow life, working in the arcades or waiting tables. A couple had teased their hair into dreads, but their university futures were written all over them.

'No one leaves,' she said.

There were moans of dissent, so she held her hands out. 'I'm not here to arrest anyone, but we've found something over there. A whole ton of police cars will be here soon, and they're going to want to speak with you. It might be bad news if your parents don't approve of you being here, but this is how it's going to be.'

A voice further along said, 'What have you found?'

Amy ignored the question and asked instead, 'Are you all accounted for?' There were murmurs as she added, 'Look around. Is there anyone not here now who was here earlier?'

More mumbles, until someone said, 'No, I think we're all here.'

She softened her tone. 'No one is in trouble. We just need to ask you what you've seen tonight. The party's over, but you'll get a story to tell.'

'What if we just leave?' said a female voice next to her. 'How are you going to stop us?'

Amy pulled out her phone and began to take pictures, people shrinking back at the flashes. 'There, you've all become traceable now. If you leave, we'll come to your house, because I'll ask myself why you wanted to go and be all suspicious. And if I turn up at your house, it'll be with a search warrant. I'll be seizing everything. Your laptops, tablets, phones, all of them, and we'll go through the lot. Messages, pictures, those nudies you don't want anyone else to see. Trust me, don't make yourself a suspect. Do the decent thing and talk to us.'

Some of the kids looked behind them as the blue strobes of police cars got closer.

Amy looked around the group. 'Trust works both ways. I don't care what you smoke or snort, so if you've got something on you that you don't want to be found, get it on the fire now. Just don't leave it in your pockets.'

There was a pause as that sunk in, and then a few rooted in their clothes and wallets and threw small packets of whatever into the flames.

Amy smiled. 'Thank you. You're good people, and when you find out the full story, you'll know you did the right thing.'

A stream of cars pulled onto the road that ran by the seafront.

'Wait here,' Amy said, and set off walking.

She marched towards the closest squad car, squinting at the flashing lights. Car doors were opening. A cluster of people had gathered around the first car in, some in uniform, some in suits. She recognised a chief inspector, Mickey Higham, a Cookstown stalwart who could drink most under the table, and over the years had got into scrapes that would end the careers of most. The years had softened him though, his swept-back hair turned silver and showing more of his pink scalp than when he was younger.

As she got closer, he turned and said, 'What is this?'

There were traces of irritation in his voice. Maybe she'd ruined a good night.

Amy pointed back towards the breakwater, a thin black shadow further along. 'Evening, boss. There's a woman on the beach. It looks like she's been washed up, but it could be a ruse, dragged to the waves and left there. We're thinking Sarah Marsh as a maybe.'

Higham swallowed.

Amy guessed the reason. Sarah Marsh was an architect, rich and successful, so being found washed up on the sand would make for a good press story, which would then examine what they'd done after she was reported missing.

'Can you be sure?'

'Just a guess, but her description fits.'

He gestured towards those stood around the fire. 'And these people?'

'Just kids, hanging out. I told them to wait there. Someone needs to get their details and find out what they saw.'

Higham stood and gazed towards the corpse on the beach, then hung his head and muttered, 'fuck.'

Three

'You better be bloody joking,' Charlie said, turning away from the window, putting his mug on his desk. 'Seriously, this is a bad idea. The worst I've ever heard.'

Monica held out her arms in protest. 'You said we need to generate work. The police aren't making enough arrests, you said that yourself. We could just nudge them a little.'

'Grassing on your own client is too far.'

Monica stepped closer and spoke in a whisper. 'It's not *grassing*. There'll be drug arrests, there always are. It's just making sure the police turn to our clients, not someone else's. Come on, Charlie, we're a defence firm. We defend people who've done horrible things, so there's no point in getting squeamish. There's even an up-side, with one more drug dealer off the streets. Everyone wins.'

'Do you think you're being original? Do you think it's never been done before?'

'Well, I don't know.'

'You don't, because you're my receptionist.'

'And law clerk.'

'And billing clerk, and everything else.' He turned to Eleanor, who was leaning against the window, opened to let out her cigarette smoke. 'You got anything to say about this?'

She flicked her cigarette out of the window, following Charlie's rule that if she smoked in his office, there can be no after-effects.

Approaching fifty, Eleanor was Charlie's police station rep and crown court clerk, twenty years as a detective giving her the clout. The cigarettes had taken their toll though, with harsh lines that puckered her mouth and a voice that growled.

It would have been a longer police career, but it was brought to an end by an incident at a Christmas party that made the national papers, when she punched her inspector after he made a move on a young constable who was too fearful to tell him to get lost.

She never stopped loving the law though, so she worked for Charlie, the only person willing to hire her.

'We used to get some solicitors trying to do the same,' she said. 'Selling out their clients to make sure they went to court.' She shook her head. 'We all remember Peter Taylor. Had a good little practice on King Street.'

Monica frowned. 'Yeah, I've heard of him. Closed his business and retired.'

'Not the dream finish he wanted,' Charlie said. 'That isn't the whole story, because we know what happened next.'

'I'm not going to like this,' Monica said.

'He tried to get some work in,' Eleanor said. 'Just like how you're saying, tipping off the police about one of his clients, just so that he could be the hero in the police station when the cops did the raid. It was a great plan, until his client was told where the information had come from. Guess what, wonderkid, the best dealers have contacts in the police, those who'll give them the wink when a raid is due, things like that.'

Charlie sat down and leaned back in his chair until it creaked. 'So, Peter Taylor, well-known Manchester solicitor, starts to make offers to the police, just to get the work. He thought he was untouchable, because lawyers think like that, as if it's all some game played out with rules and etiquette.' He wagged his finger. 'Not at all. One day, Peter is bundled into a car and is taken to some place out of town, an old warehouse or something, and they tied him to a chair. Now, Peter thought he was a smart man, could handle himself because he worked with crooks, but he found out that having the nerve to stand up in a courtroom doesn't count for anything when you've got your feet in a bowl of liquid that they tell you is petrol.'

'Alright, I'm sorry,' Monica said. 'It was a stupid idea, I get it.'

'It was. And it might not have been petrol, but are you going to take that gamble when they're lighting matches next to your ear, singeing your hair and threatening to drop lit ones into the bowl?' He shook his head. 'Peter Taylor learned pretty quickly that he was dealing with dangerous people.'

Monica blushed. 'I didn't know. Is that why he retired?'

'You think that's the end of it? No, not by a long way, because they made him do what they do, deliver drugs into our city, into Manchester. They made him one of them. Told him that if he didn't, they'd do to his kids what they'd done to him. He had to drive to an address in Liverpool and collect the stuff, a sports bag full of it, and drive it to his client's house. Once he'd done it, Peter Taylor was a drug runner, the lawyer who got too close to his clients. He sold up and moved on.'

'I'm sorry, I didn't think.'

'No, neither did Peter. It's why we do things legit, by the book, because it's only by keeping on the right side of the line that we stay out of the gutter that most of our clients are in.'

Monica cocked her head. 'How do you know all this?'

'The dealer told me. I got the case Peter had tipped off the police about, and he couldn't wait to tell me.'

'How do you know he wasn't bull-shitting?'

'Because it wasn't a boast. It was a threat, aimed at me. Do your job, be a lawyer, and things stay civil, but I had to remember whose side I was on: his. This quiet patch we're in?' He shrugged. 'All we can do is sit it out. Something will turn up.'

'What about doing some PI work?' Monica said. 'I've got a friend in a firm across the way, and they've got a bank of holiday claims they don't want.'

'There's a reason they don't want them.'

'We've got lower overheads. We could make them pay.'

'If a Manchester firm wants rid of files, they're not worth having. I can bet they're all people claiming holiday sickness, and the insurers have turned up Facebook pictures of them having their best holiday ever.' He smiled. 'Monica, we'll be alright.'

'Okay, if you're sure,' Monica said, then backed out of the room.

Eleanor watched her go before saying, 'She's young and stupid. She'll learn.'

'I know,' Charlie said. 'I was the same, but it's a job where it's too easy to make nasty enemies. Or do things wrong and people go to jail who shouldn't, and they remember that and bear grudges.'

'She's right though, we need to do something. And The Law Society are still on your case. I saw the letters, wanting your response.'

'I wasn't drunk. I was hungover, and I can handle that.'

'Charlie, you went to court stinking of booze and your client went to prison. He said you weren't with it, was still slurring.'

'That's bullshit.'

'Yeah, but you gave the guy an open-goal. He wants to blame you for going to prison, so he finds a reason for it being your fault. You need to focus more.'

Charlie sighed. 'Can you sweet-talk some custody sergeants, persuade them to nudge punters towards us?'

'Let me see what I can do,' she said, and left Charlie alone.

He put his head back and groaned.

Being a lawyer was supposed to be better than this. When the partners in the firm all retired at the same time, Charlie took over and rented office space close to Chinatown, above a sports massage clinic.

The notion always made him smile. He didn't like to judge, but some of the men who visited didn't look that sporty, although the noises that filtered up to his floor told him that they enjoyed the massages.

The partners had let him keep the name though.

Not for the goodwill, but because Charlie liked the name: Greenhalgh, Banks and Houghton. They thought it had some old-time grandeur, but Charlie shortened it to GBH. For a while, it adorned the back of buses around the city. *Get GBH for your GBH.* Any crime-related pun he could think of, until it became too expensive to continue.

His office had a view though, if you counted looking along the blank stare of the buildings in a city centre back street.

There was a promise of a better life further along, with the glass and steel of the new Manchester visible over the rooftops, banks and fashion houses proclaiming the new northern powerhouse.

It was bullshit. It was still the same grimy city he'd grown up in, with the homeless sprawled in every spare doorway and redbrick mills dominating the distant skyline, barren moorland hills beyond. Dirty canals and rain-washed alleyways. Hair worn too long by men too old to wear it, a city brought up on music and football, all done with a snarl.

Some of the London swagger had infected the place though, with a new breed of office workers who preferred to conduct their business over a latte in a chain coffeehouse, giving the impression of being always on the go, a life of perpetual motion.

'Shoot me now,' he said to himself, before rubbing his eyes awake.

He ought to get better lighting. The Venetian blinds and piles of paper he never got around to clearing made it dingy, but redesigning the office meant an outlay he couldn't afford.

Monica came back into the room.

She had a law degree, and was sitting the Legal Practice Course as a part-time evening class. That's how it was now, that wannabe lawyers had to chase every way of getting a job. Places on law degree courses had increased in the last decade, in the hope of creating opportunities. It just meant that there were too many students for too few jobs, so that the only people who got jobs as trainee solicitors were those with connections in a firm.

Some, like Monica, sat on reception desks, hoping to be discovered like an actor waiting tables in Los Angeles.

'I'm sorry, Charlie, I know there's no one in your diary,' she said, 'but there's a man in reception who says he needs to see you.'

Debt collector was Charlie's first thought, but before he could say anything, Monica added, 'His name is Gerard Williams, and he said he has a problem.'

Four

Amy stood at the window of the police station, a coffee in her hand, the lack of sleep dragging her down. The incident room behind her was getting noisier as people waited to be given their orders and the investigation given some structure. All leave had been cancelled and overtime had been authorised. The Major Crimes Unit had loaned a few, the department that travelled the county whenever a murder happened, although they didn't seem keen on taking it over.

Or, at least, Mickey Higham didn't seem keen on letting go of it. This story was heading for the nationals, slain architect washed up on a beach. Amy guessed that Mickey had spotted his time on the courthouse steps, speaking into the microphones, the hero of the hour.

The sun was brightening outside. Two fans on opposite sides of the room were blowing hard, but struggling to keep the room cool. Shirts were open, ties pulled down. So different to the normal routine of a small station in a small town in a forgotten part of the country.

The station was on a narrow side street in the town centre, attached to the courthouse, with a dank subterranean corridor running from the cells to the small cage below the courtroom. An old blue lamp was still attached to the wall over the main entrance, although the steps had been replaced by a ramp, and the heavy wooden door had given way to an automatic glass entrance.

Cookstown seemed like a long way from anywhere, grown into a town by the Victorian seaside boom, then left behind as the trend disappeared, declining to just a dot on the map.

Summer brought some promise, when there were more jobs and more people. The boards came from the shops that sold seaside rock and postcards and beach-balls, and the locals no longer had to wrap up against the harsh North Sea winds.

It was a strange mix though, because the locals grumbled about the influx, with the roads and pavements more clogged, the pubs noisier with strangers. After dark months spent drinking and brawling with each other, the local hotheads banded together and took on the visitors instead.

That was what policing was about in Cookstown, splitting up fights. It was a town where people felt safe, with windows and doors left open, the drug-fuelled crime of the big cities a distant problem.

Then, cases like this one happened. Less than once a year, but they still happened, because people are people, and human beings have always shown a passion for killing other human beings.

The main hope for the squad was that it was a suicide or accident. It would dial everything down, all postponed until the Coroner made the decision on why or how Sarah Marsh had died.

Amy turned back to face the crowd as Mickey Higham went to the front of the room.

He perched on the edge of a desk, his arms folded. Like her, he hadn't slept, but he bore it more heavily, with a flush to his cheeks and his eyes red. The responsibility of rank. People spoke in quiet murmurs.

'The post-mortem tells us she was murdered,' Higham said, which quietened everyone. 'It's not complete yet, but there was a skull fracture caused by something heavy and small.'

'What, like a hammer?' someone said from the back of the room.

'We don't speculate. We find the weapon and test it. But this is going to get big. Sarah Marsh was an architect. Well-respected, well-liked, but,' and he shrugged. 'Architects make mistakes and people lose money, or spend their lives staring at some glass cube next to their lovely brick house. They have neighbours they fall out with. They have affairs they keep secret. Architects are like all of us.'

'Boss?' Amy stuck up her hand. 'Don't we start with the husband before we spread the net?'

Higham bristled, his eyes narrowed. 'You earn the stripes, you get to tell me I'm wrong. Until then, it's my show.'

Amy returned Higham's glare, before she shrugged and said, 'Just remember I said this if we get swamped and it turns out it was the husband all along,' ignoring the collective wince that went around the room. 'Like you say, it's your show.'

A young detective, with cropped hair and a lilac shirt and tie, raised his hand. 'Was she washed up? Or was she dumped there, in the hope she'd be taken away by the tide?'

'Only preliminary findings at this stage,' Higham said. 'We'll know more when we get the full report.' He pointed to Amy. 'You want to look at the family? You do that. Dig into Sarah's life. I want to know where she went, who she'd been speaking to. Rebuild the last twenty-fours of her life.'

'What about the Major Crime Unit though? I know they've loaned a few bodies, but why not let them take it over?'

Higham sighed, heavy with sarcasm. 'But we've got you, Amy Gray, the daughter of super-cop, Jimmy Gray.'

Amy's cheeks flushed. Her father had been the senior detective in Cookstown before he retired, and Mickey's boss. 'That's unfair.'

Higham held her gaze. 'Lodge a complaint.'

Amy gripped her pen a little tighter and resisted the urge to throw it, but instead she stared at her notepad.

Once Higham had given out the jobs, he pointed at Amy and said, 'You're not ducking the tricky stuff though. Come with me.'

'Where are we going?'

'It doesn't matter where. You're following orders.'

As she turned to leave, a young officer in uniform blushed and said, 'Got a man on the phone, wants to speak to someone on the squad, but he didn't say what it was.'

'Okay, thanks,' Amy said. 'Put him through to my phone,' and she left the incident room to her own desk, in the furthest corner of the next room.

By the time she got there, her phone was ringing.

'Hello, Detective Constable Gray. How can I help?'

There was a beep, then a voice said, 'It's not what you think.'

Amy faltered. 'Why, what do I think?'

'You'll look at the family, that's how it always goes, but it's not how it seems.'

There was a slur to his voice. His number was displayed on her screen, so she jotted it down before she asked, 'Can I have your name?'

A pause, then, 'Not yet. Don't waste your time with me.' He hung up.

She looked at the phone in disbelief before muttering, 'What the fuck?'

Five

'Gerard Williams?' Charlie laughed. 'Where has he been caught this time?'

'He didn't say,' Monica said. 'Should I ask him?'

'No, don't. He'll enjoy telling me.'

Gerard was one of Charlie's stranger clients. And one of his favourites.

Like most criminal lawyers, Charlie had a mixed client base.

Some were wracked by addiction and fed it with petty crime. They were the steady earners, with regular court appearances, but they never did anything serious enough to net the big cheques. Most often, they'd plead guilty and pray for a short sentence, although that might depend on the time of year. Like Christmas. Not many hardened lags pleaded guilty in December. Put it off until the new year and enjoy the festivities.

And there were the the *occasional slip-up* clients, like the Saturday night fighters and drink drivers, people who led decent lives but came unstuck every now and then.

It was amongst the hardened criminals that the real money was made. The drug dealers and professional scammers, white-collar fraudsters and thugs for hire. Their files are filled with huge amounts of electronic data, or pages and pages of bank statements or phone printouts. More pages meant a higher fee.

Bigger cases meant longer sentences though, and it was a dirty truth that Charlie needed the worst people to stay on the streets for as long as possible, spreading misery around, always another undeserving victim waiting to have their lives ruined.

But he was a criminal lawyer. If he didn't like it, he should have chosen something cleaner, like conveyancing or personal injury work.

Gerard was a rarity amongst his clients, in that he had the money to pay Charlie's bills rather than relying on legal aid. That made him a popular client, because Charlie could charge four times as much and Gerard never complained.

That wasn't the reason Charlie liked him though.

Gerard was a shoplifter by trade, known by all the security guards in the city, his early successes based on the unlikeliness of his habit. And it didn't seem to matter to him what he stole.

Most shoplifters are marked out by whatever drove them to do it, often caught when making a poor attempt to steal booze to get them through one more empty night.

Or they will steal to sell on. Batteries and bacon were the most popular. Batteries because everyone needs batteries, and bacon because the shape is perfectly suited for sliding into a thief's waistband.

Charlie rarely bought bacon for that reason, because the bacon always went back on the shelf when the shoplifter was caught, even if it had just been lifted out a thief's underwear.

Gerard Williams was different, because he did it for the thrill, not the fix. He had the money to buy what he stole, but where was the fun in that? Gerard Williams was the only shoplifter Charlie had represented who stole books, always for his own use and pleasure. Even antiques at some point, trinkets concealed in his pockets.

Charlie made his way to the reception area, just a collection of armchairs he'd rescued from a house clearance, the cloth worn out, stuffing showing in places. Gerard was sitting patiently in one, one leg crossed over the other, staring straight ahead.

'Gerard, good to see you.'

He turned and peered over his glasses. 'Ah, Mr Steele, a delight as always. I'm looking forward to the day when we meet in less perilous circumstances.'

Charlie had to hide his smile.

There were no traces of Manchester in his accent, his voice deep and cultured, everything said with a flourish, the final word of each sentence drawn out as if to emphasise a point. He wore corduroys and a shirt, his neck shielded by a cravat, yellow with black dots.

The refinement was just a first impression though. His fingernails grew too long and his hair was swept back and greasy. Although Charlie knew he was only in his mid-forties, he seemed older, his cheeks gaunt, cheekbones like ridges.

'Come through,' Charlie said, and turned to lead the way.

Gerard groaned as he stood but Charlie didn't slow. He got to his door and held it, watching as Gerard shuffled towards him, a supermarket bag in one hand.

'I do apologise,' Gerard said. 'Gout, I think.'

As he went past, Charlie caught the scent of stale booze. He gestured to a chair. 'Take a seat.'

Gerard grimaced as he sat down.

Charlie sat opposite, his elbows on his desk and leaning forward. 'Where have you been caught this time, Gerard?'

'Nothing like that, Mr Steele. With this, oh, whatever it is, gout or arthritis, I'm not as fast as I used to be. Not that I was ever one for sprinting from the guards, but you've got to have some speed and dexterity. It's all about the distraction, you see, making a play with one hand as the other works its magic. I should have been a conjuror, but I don't seek the roar of the crowd. Rather, the thrill of the chase.'

He waved his hand. 'I haven't come here to indulge you in that way.' He tilted his head. 'Can I trust you, Mr Steele?'

'I don't understand.'

'Whatever I say here will stay a secret between us?'

Charlie frowned. 'It depends on what you say. If you tell me you're about to kill someone, I can tell the police about that. In fact, I'm obliged to tell them. But generally, yes, this discussion is confidential.'

'I worry, you see.'

'What about?'

'Power corrupts, Mr Steele.'

'Yeah, yeah, and absolute power corrupts absolutely, but Gerard, you're talking in riddles.'

He held up his hand in apology. 'You're a lawyer,' he said. 'I've got a legal problem.'

Six

Mickey Higham was staring straight ahead as he drove, both he and Amy heading for Sarah Marsh's house. The atmosphere was strained, Higham showing no inclination for small-talk.

As they got close, Amy broke the silence. 'I had a phone call before, at the end of the briefing. A man, but it was strange.'

He didn't shift his gaze when he asked, 'Strange, how?'

'No introductions, no hello. Just told me that things aren't what they seem.'

'Cryptic. Did he say what he meant?'

'It must have been connected to Sarah, because he asked to be put through to the squad, but how does he know anything? We haven't released Sarah's name yet.'

'News travels fast in Cookstown. Did he identify himself?'

'No, but I got his number,' and she pulled a piece of paper from the top breast pocket of her suit.

Higham took it from her and put it in his own pocket. 'I'll take care of him.'

'But what the hell did he mean?'

'This sort of thing comes up all the time in murder investigations. People get a perverse kind of pleasure out of it, derailing us. Ignore it.'

'But what if it's important?'

'And what if it isn't? Just leave it alone. I'll sort it out, and you go back to doing what you were told to do. If he rings again, keep him talking, but consider it a crank call.' He swung into a gravel driveway that curved towards a double-fronted redbrick house. 'Focus on Sarah's husband.'

He stepped out of the car and slammed the door. Amy set off walking.

As he caught her up, she glanced towards Sarah Marsh's house, the next one along the lane, another sprawling redbrick, except that yellow tape blocked the way, the crime scene technicians just white blurs through the windows. Roland Marsh was in a neighbour's house.

She'd expected the Marsh house to be more modern, with strange angles and wood cladding, because of Sarah's profession as an architect, but perhaps she just wanted to preserve a beautiful house.

Amy said, 'I hate this part of the job.'

'You're taking the lead, so you better grow to love it,' Higham said, and banged on the door.

The door was answered by a woman with hair sprayed to a stiff wave. Bright pearls hung across a jersey made from wool finer than anything in Amy's wardrobe, as if she'd dressed for the TV interviews that might come later.

'Mrs Richardson? Is Mr Marsh through there?' and Amy gestured to a room that overlooked the well-manicured front lawn.

'No, officer, he's at the back, so that he can't see the CSI people next door.' She grimaced. 'It makes it too real somehow. Come in.'

Amy followed her, past a staircase of varnished walnut and through a kitchen that glistened its expense, with polished granite and modern white cupboards. It led to a conservatory that provided views to the garden at the back, shaded by trees.

Amy turned to Mrs Richardson and lowered her voice. 'When was the last time you saw Sarah Marsh?'

'It was the first question I was asked when the police called round.'

'Humour me, because I haven't been told.'

'I haven't seen her for a couple of days, but I thought I saw headlights on Friday. Whenever they back out of their driveway at night, they flash through our curtains.'

'What time do you think that was?'

'Ten o'clock, perhaps. It had just gone dark, and it had been such a lovely day, and I wondered where the dear thing might be going, with Roland being away. I never imagined anything like this. That poor man.'

'Do you know if it was Sarah's car?'

'Well, I can't say for sure. I didn't look out from behind the curtains. Not that we're unneighbourly, you understand, but we keep ourselves to ourselves. I'm not that type, you know, to pry.'

Amy swallowed the retort that it would be a damn sight more helpful if she was. As she was guided to the conservatory, Roland Marsh was sitting and staring out of the window.

As he turned to greet her, Amy was struck by the hollowness of his gaze, the shock of the recently-bereaved that is hard to fake.

His skin was unnaturally smooth, barely any stubble showing, so that his cheeks looked pink and scrubbed, wearing a pastel V-neck and cream trousers.

'Mr Marsh, good morning, and I'm so sorry for your loss. I'm Detective Constable Gray.'

Roland Marsh ground his jaw.

Higham stood in the doorway as Amy took the chair opposite.

She leaned forward, to close down the space, and said, 'I just need to ask you about your wife's movements?'

Roland was framed against the sunlight that beamed through, putting his face in shadow and turning his hair into a halo.

'She wasn't just *my wife*. She was Sarah. And why weren't you asking on Saturday, when I called you? Why did you leave it until now? You might have found her alive, not washed up on the beach. And do you know what's the hardest thing? I can imagine it. How she'll look. What you'll do to her. How you'll all stand around her naked body and point and comment and mutilate her. I can picture it all. And I wish I couldn't.'

'That's why it's important that we catch this person. We need to know all about Sarah. Her private life, her secrets. Your secrets.'

His eyes widened. 'Am I a suspect?' Then, he scowled. 'Of course I'm a suspect. I'm her husband.'

'Where were you before you reported her missing?'

'At a conference in Leeds. We both were, but some of the other architects were chaps I knew from when I first started out, so Sarah came home and I decided to have a last night with old friends. Got here just after one on Saturday. Sarah wasn't in, but I thought she'd gone on a shopping trip. When she hadn't come home by the evening, I called you.' He paused as he swallowed back his tears. 'Sixth-sense, call it what you want, but I knew something was wrong. She didn't answer her phone on Friday night or anytime on Saturday. That isn't her. And her car was still here, so she couldn't have gone far. But you didn't do anything. You took the call, made a note, and that was it. I called again yesterday, but still no response.'

Amy tried to soften her tone, because she knew there were tough questions to ask.

'How was your marriage?'

She scrutinised him as he said, 'You ask me this, today of all days?' He jabbed his finger on the chair arm. 'We loved each other.'

He stopped. He stared down and his bottom lip trembled.

'Mr Marsh?'

He took a deep breath. 'She seemed distracted this last couple of weeks, as if something was playing on her mind.'

'And she didn't tell you what?'

'No. I asked, but she said it was nothing, so I left it alone.'

'Tell me about Sarah,' she said.

He blew out. Tears jumped onto his eyelashes and his cheeks flushed.

'We got together at university, in our final year, both wanting to be architects. She'd just come out of a messy split from her first serious boyfriend. Engaged, all the works, and I was there to pick up the pieces. We just, you know,' and he clicked his fingers. 'We could talk all night. Sport, politics, books. She was an intelligent woman, but funny and sweet and pretty and mischievous all at the same time, and just about everything I wanted. And me for her. She wanted to move back to Cookstown after university, where she grew up. I followed, and we've been here ever since.'

'Did Sarah have anything planned for the weekend?'

He thought about that for a few seconds, until he shook his head. 'Not that she told me.'

'Her car was seen leaving the house at around ten on Friday. Did she tell you where she was going?'

'I wasn't tracking her. If she went out, she didn't tell me about it.'

And if it had been Sarah that her neighbour had seen pulling away from her house, Amy thought, she was keeping secrets. And secrets are suspicious when the person with them ends up dead.

***

Charlie frowned. A legal problem was a billable problem, and Gerard had money, but Charlie knew his own limitations.

'Is it a criminal legal problem, Gerard, because that's all I do?'

'Sort of, in a roundabout way, but Mr Steele, you're a lawyer, so you deal with the law.'

'It's not as simple as that. We all specialise.'

'And you chose crime. Why is that?'

Charlie thought about that, a question he had asked himself many times. 'It just seemed the right fit,' he said. 'When I was a kid, I used to love the old American stuff, because my Dad watched them all the time. *Ironside. Petrocelli. Cannon. Columbo.* I got hooked. When I was doing my law degree, I never imagined myself pouring over contracts. I pictured myself in a courtroom, or a police station.'

'We are quite the same,' Gerard said, smiling, revealing teeth that had once been gloriously straight and clean but had been stained brown by lack of attention.

'The same? How?'

'We do what we do for the adventure. Isn't that just the best thrill?'

Charlie sighed. 'Gerard, I don't want to break it to you, but you're a shoplifter. I love you for it, because your habit is my income, but it hardly makes you a master criminal.'

'Cutting, Mr Steele, but you work from a tiny office over a brothel, so we are both, shall we say, at the lower end of our professions.'

'It's a sports massage clinic.' Gerard raised an eyebrow, which made Charlie laugh. 'Okay, okay, you might be right. Don't ask, don't judge, provided they keep the noise down. Tell me how I can help.'

Gerard lowered his voice, as if he thought someone might be listening in. 'Let's pretend I have a friend who holds a secret about the rich and famous, powerful people, but he's worried about going public.'

'Are we pretending about the secret, or that it's a friend?'

Gerard pursed his lips. 'Perhaps we pretend it's me.'

'Okay, if it makes it easier for you. Why would you be worried about going public?'

'Because when you threaten to bring down people of power, you expose yourself to danger. If I do this, I might not survive.'

'That's very dramatic.'

'Heed my words, Mr Steele, and make a note, because if I go missing you'll know the truth. There are dark forces at work here.'

'Dark forces?'

'Very dark.' His eyes gleamed with excitement when he said, 'These dark forces go to the very top of government.'

Charlie stifled a groan. Working in criminal law meant exposure to some of the craziest people, although Charlie wouldn't have put Gerard into that category. Unusual, but not crazy.

'Go on, which government?' Charlie said. 'And if this is another Establishment paedophile ring, remember that there's a man sitting in prison for spinning that lie.'

Gerard leaned forward and whispered, 'Our government, of course.'

'Look, Gerard, you're a shoplifter hiding away in the north of England. Who's going to take you seriously?'

'That's why I need you. You're a lawyer. People will pay attention to you.'

'But I'm not seeing the legal problem.'

'Simple. I want you to stop him, using whatever legal means are available. The courts, the power of the writ, but you must protect me, because you're my lawyer and have my best interests at heart.'

Charlie closed his eyes for a moment and rubbed his forehead. Work was drying up, but he was sure there was something better he could be doing with his time.

'Stop who?'

'Whom.'

'Sorry?'

'The correct word is whom.' Gerard waved it away. 'The benefit of a good education. But of course, your question. I'm talking about Spencer Everett.'

'The Home Secretary? *That* Spencer Everett?'

'Good. You've heard of him, then.'

'Gerard, he's the Home Secretary, in charge of law and order, and I'm a criminal lawyer. Of course I've fucking heard of him.

'Tut, tut. Mr Steele. No need for the coarseness.'

Gerard bent down to put the plastic bag he'd been carrying onto his lap and rummaged inside.

That put Charlie on edge. He'd learned from experience that the clients to avoid are the ones who bring bundles of papers in a carrier bag, usually the result of late nights spent obsessing about whatever occupied their mind. He didn't want Gerard to be like that.

'It's okay, Gerard, I know who he is.'

Gerard brought out a jumble of papers and slammed them onto the desk. 'You need to read these, his web of lies. Read what he says and know the truth, that he's fooling everyone. The man of the people? It's all lies. If he's Home Secretary now, where's next? Prime Minister, that's where. We have to stop him. You, me. It's our duty.'

'Gerard, you're not telling me what your legal problem is. I'm a lawyer, not a campaigner. Have you tried the media?'

'They don't want to know. They dismissed me like I wasn't right in my mind. Talked about libel, about proof.'

Charlie wanted to say that he wasn't surprised, but chose silence instead.

'If the press won't help me, there must be a legal mechanism,' Gerard said. 'That's why I need you, Mr Steele.'

Charlie scrutinised Gerard for any signs of a mental breakdown, but he seemed just the same as always.

'What's your beef with Spencer Everett?'

'We were at Oxford together.'

'University? I didn't know you'd gone to Oxford.'

'A law degree.' He gave a wry smile. 'You didn't know that I could have been sitting where you are. Although obviously,' and he cast his hand around the room. *Somewhere better*, he meant. 'I once had promise, Mr Steele, but I got broken.'

'By Spencer?'

Gerard narrowed his eyes. 'Too soon for that. I need to know whether we can use the law to stop him. A private prosecution, perhaps.'

'For what?'

Gerard grimaced. 'I can't tell you, not yet, not until I know you can help.'

Charlie shook his head. 'I don't prosecute people. I chose my side. I defend people.'

'But if I pay you?'

'No, I'm sorry.'

'An injunction, perhaps?'

'To stop doing what?'

'Speaking. Or travelling here, to protect me.'

'What do you need protection from?'

'Rebound. Collateral damage.'

'You're not giving me enough, Gerard. We need legal grounds, you've got to understand that. You've got to give me more. And what do you mean by collateral damage?'

Gerard slumped in his chair. 'Perhaps this was a bad idea. I'm sorry. I'll go.' He stood as if leaving, but his movement was laboured. Or hoping Charlie would stop him with a spark of inspiration.

As Charlie stayed silent, Gerard turned as he reached the door. 'Just remember this moment. One day, you'll know I'm right.'

Charlie watched him go, puzzled, wheeling his chair backwards so that he could peer through the blinds.

As Gerard emerged onto the street, he looked around and clasped his bag of papers to his chest. He scurried down the street, checking back as he went, as if expecting a pursuer, before he rounded the corner and he was gone.

Charlie laughed to himself.

If there was one thing that kept him involved in criminal law, it was the craziness of it.

His phone rang. He recognised the number. The police. One of the local custody offices. That could only mean one thing: a client needed his help.

Seven

Jessica Redmond wiped her palm on her trouser leg before she reached for her wine glass. She took a deep breath and tried to calm her nerves. After six months as an intern, she'd got to know some faces, but the Home Office in its upper echelons had an ever-changing cast list. Here were two new actors, men from a security company sitting across the room from her.

It felt like she'd come a long way since her Business and Politics degree at one of the lesser universities. For her, there was no chance yet of paid employment. The plum roles always went to the Oxbridge set. For her, employment for free was all she could offer. But few graduates got to be behind the scenes with the Home Secretary.

And especially a Home Secretary like Spencer Everett.

The only other person there was Spencer's assistant, Wendy Preston, although she behaved more like Spencer's boss.

Dougie McCloud, Spencer's strategist, had decided to be elsewhere, and she didn't blame him. Dougie was quiet and serious, intense even, the one who steered Spencer, because Spencer was prone to making gaffes. Dougie preferred to stay hidden from view, the silent puppeteer. Wendy Preston's role was to bully Spencer, not just advise. A tough northern woman, blunt accent, straight bob, harsh manner, hard stare, she barked instructions at Spencer like a headteacher.

He needed it though. Spencer was full of vision, but it made him chaotic at times, and he needed Wendy to keep his focus.

There were rumours about them. Dalliances, a romance, whatever you wanted to call it. Not that it mattered about Spencer. He was a single man, a widower, but Jessica couldn't imagine Wendy letting rip with passion. Everything was under control.

The two people from the security company were the reason she was there though, not Wendy.

Jessica hadn't caught their names, but she'd need to know them by the end of the evening. As an intern, her role was to take minutes, to be the silent note-taker. And be the tea-maker, the bag-carrier, the person to take away the plates.

Her desire to stay in the background made sense. Nothing was constant in politics, as cabinet reshuffles and by-elections and general elections and changing fortunes could make the Home Secretary popular one week, then on the backbenches the week after. The smart money was on staying neutral, not being a Home Secretary's favourite.

As an intern, she learned more from watching, listening, observing, although the conversation so far had been mundane. The two men were guarded, and Wendy wasn't known for her warmth.

Spencer came into the room, breathless, apologising for his lateness.

Everyone stood, Spencer shaking hands, his smile easy, disarming. His CPO was with him, his Close Protection Officer, a Special Branch officer assigned to him, who got to visit restaurants and pubs and go wherever the Home Secretary went, always a pace or two behind, unless Spencer wanted the conversation.

They were in Spencer's house, an imposing Victorian redbrick surrounded by Hampshire wheat fields and orchards, with high and wide bay windows that provided views over the gentle rise and fall of the countryside. There were pictures of his wife dotted around, killed in a car crash a few years earlier. Thankfully, no children, but the public had loved Spencer for the dignified way in which he managed her death. Grief-stricken, but stoic.

The living room was on the other side of the hallway to the formal dining room, where a chandelier hung over a long mahogany table, but Spencer had opted for the living room to keep it informal. He'd ordered pizzas and had already rolled his sleeves up.

Jessica knew it was an act. It conveyed a busy man, ready for work, only enough time to sneak in a take-away. The men didn't know that Spencer had spent the afternoon watching television and had gone out before they were due, just for the effect of rushing back in again.

Wendy raised her glass towards Jessica and snapped, 'Get these refilled.'

Jessica flushed and left her seat, but not before taking off her jacket and draping it over the back of her chair. The two men handed over their glasses but didn't pay her any attention.

As she went out of the room to get more, she glanced back. Wendy and Spencer were in close conversation with the two men, who until that point had hardly said anything, the delay for Spencer filled by awkward silences. The only vibe she'd got was that one of the men was wondering whether Jessica was a prize he could collect at the end of the evening, once the wine had flowed enough.

As Jessica returned with two bottles of white from Spencer's wine rack, Wendy holding hers out to be filled, everyone stopped talking.

Jessica smiled and excused herself. 'Sorry, need to go to the little girls' room.'

She tried to keep her pace slow and relaxed until she was in one of the bathrooms. She sat on the seat, closed her eyes and exhaled.

She hoped the voice recorder was working, hidden in her jacket pocket, the red light blacked out by a small piece of tape, but it would take just a brief search of her jacket to find it. She shook her head in disbelief. She was bugging the Home Secretary. How had it got to this?

It was too late to pull out now. She took her phone from her pocket and sent a text. *All in place. Might have something. Speak later.*

She flushed the toilet for effect and headed back down the stairs.

As she went back into the room, she thought no one had paid her any attention. But Wendy never dropped her stare as Jessica took her seat.

Eight

Charlie faked politeness with his client, Kyle McCarthy, as he waited for his phone to reboot, returned to him by the custody sergeant, Kyle putting on his belt and boots in the police station waiting area.

Kyle stood, his boots now laced. 'Do you think they'll charge me, Mr Steele?'

He'd been arrested at a local train station, loitering in the men's toilets for over an hour, standing at the urinal and making out like he was shaking it, enjoying the view along as other users joined him.

Charlie stared at his phone as it brought itself back to life. It was about time he invested in a newer model. 'I suspect so.'

Kyle stepped forward and whispered, 'But how can I be guilty of, what was the charge again?'

'Sexual activity in a public lavatory.'

'But what if I can't, you know, get it hard? I've got a medical problem. I can prove it, just like I said.'

'Sometimes, Kyle, in this game, you get judged on effort, not outcome.' Charlie raised an eyebrow. 'And it's the second time in three weeks.'

Kyle stepped away, his hands clasped to his head. 'And I'll have to go to court? My neighbours will know. My kids.'

Charlie groaned as the texts came in, along with a reminder on his calendar.

'Didn't you hear me?' Kyle said. 'Everyone will know.'

Charlie jammed his phone into his pocket. 'You want to keep your hobby private, you do it in your own home. You do it in the station toilets and everyone gets to know. That's just how it is. I've got to go.'

As Charlie left, cursing, Kyle shouted, 'I expected more support.'

Charlie turned to shout back, 'If you want to avoid jail, I'll see you at court. If you want someone to blow you a kiss as they lead you down the stairs, go somewhere else,' then he set off running.

Shit. Another fuck up. School Open Evening. Progress reports from Molly's teacher, coming to the end of the school year. Dreaded but compulsory. He'd forgotten.

He'd put a reminder on his phone, timed to go off an hour before, but the phone had been taken from him when he went into the police station.

Shit!

He hailed a taxi and willed the driver to go faster, until the school loomed large ahead. Small and modern, with childish paintings stuck to the windows, yellow fences all around, unsure if it was to keep the children in or the predators out. Perhaps both.

He banged his hand on his seat as he saw parents spilling out, children clutching their hands. He threw a note towards the driver, much bigger than it needed to be, and dodged through the crowd coming at him, so he looked like someone collecting a child rather than a parent who'd missed the whole event.

He slowed as he saw Isobel.

She was easy to spot. She had that fiery redhead thing going on, with long curls over pale skin and bright blue eyes, so a lot of their marriage had been loud arguments, followed by the very best making up.

Or, at least, once upon a time. After a while, there were just the separate lives, until there was the day he came home early and found someone else in his bed.

He should have seen it coming, but he hadn't been home enough, too many hours at court or locked in his study, until he and Isobel had become strangers sharing a house. He didn't blame her, they'd both let it drift, but that didn't make it hurt any less.

Her eyes flashed with anger when she saw him. She was holding Molly's hand, who grinned and jumped with excitement when he got close.

'Hey, Daddy!'

She went as if to run to him, but Isobel's grip tightened.

'Sorry, sweetheart,' he said, as he knelt down to give her a hug. 'I got held up at work.'

'Were you helping the naughty people again?'

Damn, six-years-old was so cute.

'Your Mummy called me to tell me that you are a complete superstar,' he said. 'That you're so clever, how all the teachers say you're just the best.'

Molly laughed as Isobel's nostrils flared, as Charlie dared her to contradict him. 'Not the very best,' Molly said. 'But they said if I keep on trying, I might be.'

Isobel bent down to kiss Molly's hand before saying, 'Go to the car, I'll be there in a minute.'

'Okay dokey,' she said, and set off running. 'Bye Daddy.'

'Careful near the road,' Charlie shouted. As he waved, the ache in his gut grew as she got further away. There'd been too many missed moments.

Isobel folded her arms. 'Where were you?'

He straightened. 'At the police station.' He looked after Molly. 'You didn't give her the car keys.'

'Simon's in the car.'

Charlie bristled at the name. 'Bully for Simon. Has he moved in yet?'

'Not now, Charlie.'

'When? We both know it's going to happen.'

Isobel turned away.

'Don't block me, Isobel. If he's going to move in with my daughter, we need to talk about it.'

She turned back and stepped closer. 'Would that be the daughter with the parents' evening you were meant to attend? This isn't a contest, Charlie, two stags clashing antlers. If he moves in, or I move in with him, we'll do it without consulting you. But Simon made time tonight, which is more than you did.'

'Good old Simon. He wins.'

'It's not about winning. It's about Molly.'

'Is it? Because sometimes I just think it's about us. You know how it is with my work. It's not like yours, all regular hours and patting old ladies on the hand as you draft their wills. If I get a call, I've got to go, or else I don't get the case. And criminals don't keep regular hours.'

Isobel looked around, other parents feeling the need to stare at the floor, then leaned in to whisper, 'You need to stop letting her down.'

'I need to see her.'

'Get yourself a proper home, instead of whatever you're in at the moment, and you can have her all weekend. Simon and I fancy Porto sometime, I've heard it's lovely there. The Douro Valley. The tiled buildings by the river. It would help us out.'

'Don't, Isobel.'

'Don't what?'

'Taunt me about you and him. I get it, I blew it.'

Before Isobel could respond, his phone went again.

He ignored it at first, until Isobel said, 'The down and dirty of Manchester need you. Don't let me delay you.'

'What about Molly?'

Isobel glared at him, until she said, her tone softer, 'Call me. We'll arrange something. But no overnight stays.'

'Okay, done.'

'And no clients. Even if you get the biggest case you've ever had, you ignore the call.'

'Agreed.'

She nodded and set off, and he watched her go as his phone buzzed in his hand, cursing as he thought back on how he'd spoiled everything.

He had to focus.

He answered the phone. 'Hello?'

'Mr Steele, it's Gerard.' He sounded out of breath.

Twice in one day? Charlie wasn't in the mood for Gerard's theatrics. 'How did you get this number?'

'I called the emergency line printed on your letterhead and you answered.'

Of course, Charlie realised. He had rerouted it to his own phone earlier, so he had just one phone to carry around with him, rather than the firm's phone that he used for emergencies.

'Gerard, what's wrong?'

'There's been someone in my house, I can tell. Things have been moved. Like I told you, dark forces.'

'That's a problem for the police, not your solicitor. Call them.'

Gerard scoffed. 'The police? Oh, my good man, haven't you thought that they may be the very people who have been in here?'

'Gerard, I'll call you tomorrow,' and he clicked off.

He needed a drink. And he knew where he was going.

Nine

As the taxi arrived at Spencer's home, the two men from the security firm swayed in the doorway, the aroma of consumed wine heavy around them. Jessica was there to wave them off, Spencer dozing in a chair, Wendy cleaning glasses in the kitchen.

She'd found out their names, and the one called Henry had started to pay her attention. His smile had broadened, his tie slackened, his gaze less harsh. Jessica had spotted him giving her the once over whenever she stood. As the evening wore on, he'd stopped being discreet about it.

Jessica guessed that he'd reached the point where he thought she'd be flattered, his clasped hands resting on his paunch as he leered at her.

The other man headed for the taxi, but Henry paused. He leaned in and whispered, 'Do you want some company tonight?'

Jessica tried hide her grimace. 'No, I'm fine, thank you.'

'I could treat you very nicely, and in luxury.'

'I've got plenty of luxury here, don't you think?'

Before Henry had the chance to press her further, Wendy appeared behind her and said, 'That's enough now, Henry, leave the poor girl alone.'

He gave a mock bow, then held out his hand as if to shake. When she took his hand, forced by politeness, he got down on one knee and kissed the back of her hand.

THE PHOTOGRAPH

'My dear, a treasure such as thee,' he said, and laughed as he straightened, before he stumbled backwards and landed in a flower bed by the porch. 'Fuck,' he muttered, before getting back to his feet, his shirt hanging out now, mud on his trousers.

Wendy folded her arms. 'Taxi now, Henry. You'll regret this in the morning.'

He gave a salute and clambered into the taxi, blowing kisses as it took off.

'I saved you,' Wendy said, and headed back into the house.

'I wasn't about to succumb,' Jessica said, but Wendy didn't respond.

Jessica went back inside and stood over Spencer. He was snoring gently. She eyed his office further along the hallway, but Wendy was still up. She'd have to wait for another time.

She shouted, 'I'm going to bed now, Wendy.'

There was no response.

Jessica was staying in a small room at the back of the house, a single bed in there, no pictures on the wall. Spencer hadn't wanted her to spend the night in a hotel or travel back to London, and it made sense that she slept overnight. She'd done it before, and was always in the same room.

Once inside, she rested against the door and took some deep breaths. The voice recorder had run out of memory some time before, but she might still have caught something useful.

She moved away from the door as she made a call.

He took a while to answer.

'I think I've got something,' she said, keeping her voice low.

His voice was slurred when he replied, 'Not now, it's all changed.'

She sat up, surprised. 'Nick, what's wrong?'

'Everything,' then he hung up.

As she was left with just the silence of her room, she stared at the handset before throwing it across the room and spitting out, 'Shit!'

***

The crime scene tape was still stretched across the beach, but only between two of the metal posts jammed into the sand. Elsewhere, it had snapped, making it flap and crack in the breeze.

Earlier, the dunes had buzzed with activity, uniformed officers sweeping the sand and the long grass, searching for a scrap of anything that might help with the investigation.

Amy didn't think it would provide any leads. The kids around the fire would have seen something, and the beach was a regular haunt for dog-walkers, but sometimes it was useful to show activity on the television news. It attracted local interest and could lead to a crucial tip.

Amy closed her eyes. She loved the beach at night, and she wanted to reclaim it. The stars overhead. The brilliant white tips of waves in the moonlight. The town twinkled further away, the multi-coloured strings of lights that dipped and rose between lampposts on the sea-front, the neon flickers of the arcades and pubs just beyond. A lone lamp lit the entrance to the harbour, the old stone of the harbour walls lost in the darkness.

She thought there might be some people poking around. Murder cases attract all the amateur sleuths, those people who hog the online forums, desperate to find the clue that everyone else had missed, but there was no one else there. Perhaps it would be the next day that the ghouls arrived. Even the too-curious don't want to appear over-eager.

One thing troubled her though.

Why there? Was Sarah attacked on the beach? If so, what was she doing there, and how did she get there? A car was seen to leave her house, but Sarah's own car was still on the driveway, so it must have been someone else's car.

Or was the beach a dumping ground? Did the killer know something about the strength of the tide, that it would take her away so that she'd never be found? There was no fighting the sea. Anyone who lived on the coast knew that. It claimed everything in the end.

She was over-thinking it. Perhaps she gave the killer too much credit. It was time to go home, to catch up on sleep.

She got to her feet and brushed the sand off her clothes. As she straightened, she saw someone. A man, she presumed, the sea-front lights catching the gleam of a bald head. Someone was watching her.

The man ducked from view.

'Hey?' She walked towards the man and waved her arms. 'Stop, I need to talk to you.'

The sound of someone running drifted towards her, shoes slapping on the concrete.

She ran too, knowing there was something out of kilter, a man watching but trying to stay hidden.

As she made it up the concrete slipway, there was no one there. She turned as she looked all around her, in case he'd found somewhere else to hide, sucking in air after her sprint, but the sea-front was deserted.

A car started, the deep rumble of a four-by-four, and set off quickly, heading towards the town centre, until all she was left with was the sound of her own fast breaths and the steady thump of the tide.

Ten

Charlie raised his head and groaned. The sun streamed in, made him squint and want to bury his head under the pillow.

Someone was next to him, a cup of something being placed on the floor as the alarm sounded. The room swam as he tried to get a fix on what he was supposed to be doing, why the alarm was set.

Work, that's right. It wasn't the weekend. It was eight-thirty, and he had to be in his office before nine, suited and ready.

Someone in the room coughed. He opened one eye. The view came into focus and he saw it was Eleanor, standing above him, her hands on her hips.

'Do you remember what you always said?'

He raised a hand in protest. 'Not now, too early.'

'Never when you're in court,' Eleanor said. 'You always told me that, because if a client complains about you, you can defend yourself, but if they add on that you stunk of booze, you've no defence. And here we are again. Are you looking for another complaint?'

'Yeah, yeah, I know.' His voice sounded thick with sleep. 'It was just one of those nights.'

'Isobel?'

'I was late for the parents' evening, and we had a row.'

'So, you got wasted to make yourself better?'

'We've all got a self-destruct button,' he said. 'You know that as much as anyone.'

She folded her arms at that. 'Learn from my mistake then,' before looking around the room. 'And you need to get your own place.'

He forced himself up from the mattress he slept on, in the corner of the room above his office.

At some point, he would get his own place, but he enjoyed having low overheads. City centre living had got expensive, and he didn't feel ready for a return to the suburbs. He'd found a launderette, and a bar that showed sport, and there was always a book to read if he fancied an evening in, even if the bare floorboards and grubby woodchip wallpaper made for drab surroundings.

If splitting up from Isobel had told him anything, it was that there was a sense of freedom to be had in not knowing what was coming next.

But Isobel was right. He had to do it for Molly.

'I hope the hangover is worth it,' Eleanor said. 'You're due in court in just over an hour.'

The night came back in a blur.

He'd gone to a place he used to enjoy when he was a trainee lawyer. Isobel had never been so keen, but that was why they worked. Not because they were duplicates of each other, but because their differences gave each their own space.

In the beginning, at least.

There were bands on most evenings. The early part of the week was all about the newbies, the try-outs, most of the audience from the two universities. At weekends, the crowd-pleasers entertained. The tribute bands, or those *three guitars and drums* sort of bands that played the songs that everyone loved, and the hen nights filled the dancefloors.

The night before, it had been some earnest young folk band determined to play the traditional way, with contorted wails for some long-gone girl.

His face flushed as he remembered his stumbles.

Amongst the t-shirts and the tie-dye and the piercings and the sleeve tattoos, he was the guy in a suit, his shirt undone, getting trashed at the bar, until one of the doormen decided he'd had enough when he got off his barstool and stumbled into a group of people, sending at least one to the floor.

He'd apologised, tried to make out it was an accident, but the words didn't come out right. His night was done.

He looked over to his suit, crumpled on the floor. He'd have to wear his back-up.

'Give me ten minutes and I'll see you downstairs.'

She scowled. 'Don't be long.'

He took a sip of his tea and raised his cup. 'And thanks for the drink.'

As he stumbled to the bathroom, just a toilet and a shower, he saw his phone flashing.

Piss first, and teeth, then work.

He scratched his head as he pissed. Had he given his number out to anyone the night before?

It could be Isobel, to carry on the discussion. Maybe it was the lawyer in both of them, that arguments were there to be won, not conceded?

He cleaned his teeth, then went back to where he'd been sleeping. He opened a window to let out the headiness of stale alcohol.

As he checked his phone, he saw that there were ten missed calls, all from the same number, along with a voicemail. He slumped back onto his mattress and listened.

It was Gerard again, except that he didn't sound as calm as he had done the night before.

'They're here again, Mr Steele.' His voice was a frantic whisper, and there was the sound of the wind. He was outside. There was a squeak, a creak, like an old hinge.

'Just know that they came,' he said. 'Just know that they came.' Then, he clicked off.

Eleven

Jessica tried to make like someone with a hangover, her eyes closed as she lay on a sofa. She could hear Spencer and Wendy elsewhere in the house, going through the plans for the day.

Jessica knew the schedule. A meeting with some of the Chief Constables. A *Teams* call with an American Governor to discuss a trial scheme involving prisoner rehabilitation. A debate in Parliament in response to a Private Member's Bill about protecting businesses from protest marches. The day was topped off with a discussion about the award of a new contract for the building of an immigration detention centre, the reason for the people from the security firm being there the night before.

Spencer was busy, which Jessica knew he didn't enjoy. He was an instinct-politician, trying to reflect the public mood. The fine detail bored him.

He sauntered past her. 'Tell me if you need anything,' he said. 'We'll be leaving in around thirty minutes. Sometimes, hair of the dog is the best cure.'

'Too early for that,' she said, and closed her eyes.

The problem was that she liked Spencer. He was engaging company, always ready with a quip, and he had time for her. He asked about her family and remembered her name. He knew about her.

It was a politician's trick, she knew that, because she'd read about how Bill Clinton had that knack of remembering names and details, left an impression on people that he cared about them.

Unlike Bill Clinton, Spencer Everett didn't try to fuck his interns.

Her first few months in the House of Commons had been spent dodging lecherous middle-aged men, those who saw the House of Commons bar as an extension of whatever boarding school rugby team they'd once been a part of, with the touch-ups, the flirts, all done with the promise of career advancement.

There was one who was fond of what he dismissed as *sleepy cuddles*, his way of expressing his admiration for an intern's commitment at the end of a gruelling day, but what intern had the power to object? Whatever enjoyment he got from it, and Jessica had heard how apparent his enjoyment was, the intern felt revulsion at the same level. Too old. Too gross.

Spencer was different. He treated her well, made as if he enjoyed her company, and seemed interested in advancing her career, with no expectation on her to repay her gratitude.

So why the fuck was she doing what she was doing?

No, she knew why. She just had to remind herself. Like the days she spent with her father posting leaflets, campaigning for his council election. Or stuffing envelopes, or listening to him debate, hearing his passion. He had dedicated his life to public service, to his beliefs, because he believed in them.

Think of her father, she told herself. Politics should mean something.

She listened out as he went past and headed for the front door. Wendy followed, and as Jessica opened her eyes, she saw them in close discussion outside, their backs to the window.

Spencer had a small office at the end of the hallway. It was the one place she'd never searched, even though she had been in his house often, Spencer fond of seeing people away from Westminster.

She'd be spotted as soon as they came back in, but the cigarette smoke drifting upwards told her that she had around five minutes.

She scurried along the hallway, then into the office. Inside, there was a wooden desk and a computer monitor. There were filing cabinets on one wall that were never locked, and papers piled onto shelves along the other wall.

Jessica went to the desk and opened the first drawer, glancing along the hallway to the door at the end.

There were papers in no particular order. Some were letters from constituents, presumably unanswered, and others were drafts of parliamentary documents and Home Office memoranda.

She turned on her phone and called the last number she'd dialled, cupping her hand over the receiver.

It rang out until it went to voicemail, so she rang it again, not willing to be fobbed off.

He picked up.

'I can't do this anymore,' he said. He sounded drunk still, his words all running together.

'You can do this,' she hissed. 'You promised me.'

'No, you don't understand.'

'I understand perfectly well. You said you'd see this through, Nick, whatever the cost. Don't go bailing on me.'

A pause, then, 'It's not about bailing. The stakes have changed, that's all. They're coming for me.'

'How? Who? I don't understand.'.

'You don't need to, except to know that I've finished.'

'Just tell me what to look for.'

'Follow the money, it's always the way. Grand Cayman, Caribbean, somewhere like that.' Then, he clicked off.

Shit! How could he do this?

Her gaze flitted around the room, looking for a clue amongst the bookcases and framed photographs. Some of them showed Spencer with heads of state. Others were of Pippa, his late wife, both of them smiling, hugging.

As she looked, one caught her eye.

Spencer and Pippa somewhere hot, palm trees behind, both in white t-shirts in front of low-rise buildings painted in bright colours, blues and yellows and reds.

Grand Cayman, he'd said. Caribbean. Follow the money.

She went back to the drawers and rummaged through the documents, but she couldn't find anything relevant. There wasn't enough time to be thorough.

She went to the framed photograph and examined it again, wondering if it was a clue.

Why would he have it there? Although his wife died in a holiday accident, her car found at the bottom of a ravine near Ronda in Southern Spain, she was in the process of divorcing him when it happened.

Perhaps the photograph was the clue.

She scoured the image, but nothing stood out. Perhaps it was just what it was, Spencer recalling happier times with a woman he once loved.

She was about to put the picture back when something about the frame felt strange.

She turned it over and saw what she expected to see, a hard back to a photograph frame, except that a couple of the small metal lugs keeping it in place were broken off, as if they had been bent and reshaped too many times. And the back of the frame felt spongy, as if there was something packed in behind the picture.

Jessica looked back along the hallway. The outlines of Spencer and Wendy were visible through the frosted glass in the door, about to come back in.

Her fingers picked at the metal lugs, fumbling, needing to rush, until the back of the frame popped off.

The front door opened, and Spencer and Wendy came back into the hallway.

Her chest tightened with fright. She couldn't be caught.

There were three sheets of paper inside the frame, which fell onto the desk.

She grabbed the papers and sank to her knees under the desk. Footsteps got closer, Wendy muttering, 'Where the fuck is she?'

Spencer shouted, 'Jessica, we're going, the car is here,' before saying, 'she might be in the bathroom. She looked a little green around the gills earlier.'

There were footsteps on the stairs, heading upwards.

There was no turning back.

She didn't have time to look at the papers. Instead, she spread them on the floor and pulled out her phone, snapping pictures of whatever they were, before folding them again and trying to slip them back into the frame.

Her fingers were slippery with sweat as she tried to press the metal lugs back into place.

Footsteps got closer, like sharp clicks, Wendy's heels on wood, and paused outside the office, as if she were listening out. Jessica didn't know if she'd been heard, or whether she could be seen from the other side of the desk, as she tried to think of a credible story if Wendy caught her.

Of course, there wasn't one.

The footsteps moved away. Jessica let out a breath of relief as Wendy went into one of the other rooms, swearing as she looked for her.

Jessica scrambled from under the desk and put the frame back where she thought it had been before, a rough estimation, and glanced along the hallway. Empty, thankfully, although it sounded like Spencer was moving along the upstairs landing.

Next to the office, there was a door that led to the back garden, a long sprawl of grass, hedges and flowerbeds.

Jessica nipped out of the office and tried the handle. It was unlocked.

She flung open the door and turned her body so that she was facing along the hallway, as if she were just coming in.

The noise must have attracted Wendy's attention, because she appeared from the room closest to the front door.

'Where the fuck have you been?'

'Sorry, I needed some fresh air,' she said, her nerves making her breathless.

Spencer bounded down the stairs and laughed. 'Fresh air and a good breakfast are always the cure.' He clapped his hands. 'Come on, ladies, back to the capital.'

Wendy didn't respond as she headed towards a car that was ticking over outside, Spencer behind.

As Jessica followed, she glanced back into the office, looking for signs that it seemed different, disturbed.

It looked the same. No one would know.

Twelve

It was only the second day of the investigation, but already Amy could feel the pessimism creeping into the team. No hot leads, no calls from someone the killer hadn't noticed. Mickey Higham was quiet, ensconced in his room, staring out of the glass wall of his office.

Amy knew that murder investigations were always the same. A rush of adrenaline and a flurry of activity, then they get bogged down by the routine. Following an electronic trail. Trying to retrace the victim's last steps, or working out who were their friends and who were their enemies. Waiting for forensic results and post-mortem reports. Sometimes, they got lucky, and the obvious suspect turned out to be the easy catch. The nervous husband. The distraught lover.

She'd checked the CCTV from the town centre for the vehicle that had left the seafront the night before, but nothing struck her as suspicious. The nearest camera had too many side streets in-between, so the driver only needed to duck down one of them to stay out of view.

This murder was starting to feel different to most though. An architect as a victim but dumped somewhere public, not found in her home. Her husband had an alibi, but that didn't rule out a professional hit, except that architects in Cookstown don't hire hitmen.

And one truth about people hired to kill is that they talk. If they'll end someone's life for a few thousand pounds, there's no chance they'll protect whoever hired them when they're cornered by the evidence.

She was just thinking that another coffee might be a good idea, when her email pinged. As she checked her computer, she saw it was from Sarah Marsh's phone company. She'd sent in the request the day before, and had chased it when she got in, frustrated at their lack of urgency.

As she checked the attachment, she grinned. She had them. Sarah Marsh's phone logs.

She printed them off, knowing it was easier to go through them with highlighter pens, different phone numbers in different colours, so that a pattern stood out, only ever looking at the last three digits, just to save time, as any potential duplication is a thousand-to-one chance.

Amy spread out her highlighters, green and orange and red and blue, before bending down to the paper. She saw that the last number she dialled ended in 142. There was another one earlier that morning. And three times the day before.

Amy marked them all in red and skimmed through the earlier days. There were a couple of calls six days earlier, but as she rushed through, turning the pages, her pen running down the columns, she saw there were no other calls to that number in the previous six months.

She sat back and took another drink of coffee.

The last call she made must be significant. She knew that Mickey Higham had said to focus on the husband, but that shouldn't mean there are no other lines of enquiry.

She went to the back of the report, to the cell-siting data, which would give an approximation of where Sarah had been when she made the call. It read like a map, except that it was covered in circles, those areas triangulated between phone masts, one for each day.

The most recent showed her to be in Cookstown, but the ones before that showed her route back from the conference in Leeds, her phone sending out regular pings, her husband left behind. Her final call was made when she was still twenty miles outside of Cookstown.

As she looked at the number Sarah had called, she spotted that it was held by the same phone provider. She might get lucky.

She filled out the same request as earlier and fired it off, sending an email to stress its importance. As she waited, she pulled up her own mapping software to see where Sarah had been when she made that final call. Right in the middle of the overlapping circles was a hotel, Waterstone Hall, a stately home with a hotel attached.

Her email pinged again. There was a new phone report. Perhaps yelling at some poor sap from the phone company earlier that day had worked.

She brought up the report.

The number was owned by someone called Nick Cassidy, with a London address. As she scrolled through the report, she found the same cell-siting data, and it was more recent than Sarah's.

She grinned. At the same time as Sarah was calling him, he was in the middle of the same set of overlapping circles. They were meeting up at a country hotel when Sarah's husband was still away at a conference, and she must have called him to let him know she was there.

There was something else about the phone number that troubled her though. As she stared at her desk, she realised she was looking at the same notepad she'd used the day before, when she'd scribbled the number down from the strange call she'd received, telling her that things weren't what they seemed. The call that Mickey Higham had dismissed.

Mickey had kept the note but had told her to ignore it, so she wasn't going to search for it in his office. Instead, she held the notepad to the light, and realised she could see the faintest outline of the phone number she had written down, left as a minor imprint on the page underneath the one she'd used. As she tried to work it out, she saw that the phone number ended in 142.

'Well, well, well,' Amy said, before collecting her jacket from the back of the seat to head out of the office. Like she'd thought earlier, a thousand to one chance of it belonging to someone else.

The caller had been Nick Cassidy.

Thirteen

Charlie cupped his hands on the glass as he tried to peer into Gerard's home.

The voicemail from Gerard had unnerved him. He knew he had to be in court soon, to mitigate a sentence for a woman accused of pissing into her neighbour's plant pots, the end to a dispute over parking, but the court would wait.

He'd made some effort to look respectable, shirt and tie, navy suit, although the booze hung around him like a cloud. A breakfast from a drive-thru had helped, the wonder-cure, but it still felt like someone was drumming their fingers against the inside of his forehead.

Charlie stepped back, looking for some sign of Gerard being there, but the house seemed lifeless.

Gerard lived in a stone bungalow at the very edge of Manchester, where the dreary inner-city sprawl and newly-built suburbia gave way to stone houses and tight streets, ancient old villages in the dark shadow of the Pennines, rolling moorland hills empty of trees that never brightened, even in summer.

The house needed some attention. The paint on the stone sills was flaking and a gutter hung loose at the side. There were none of the light touches present in the cottages nearby. No flowers shining colour from hanging baskets, or wooden wheels propped up as garden ornaments. It was a stone block, nothing more, with windows on either side of a black door, the glass dusty, cobwebs in each corner.

A neighbour appeared from the house next door, her arms folded, her eyes filled with the weariness of living next to someone who brought down the tone of the neighbourhood. 'You looking for him? Bailiffs? Detective? What's he done this time?'

Charlie went over. 'I'm his solicitor. Have you seen him?'

'Got any proof?'

Charlie passed her a business card.

She examined it, before tutting and saying, 'The only thing I do when I see him is clutch my purse tighter and make sure my doors are locked. Bloody thief, and if you're his solicitor you'll know that, making excuses for him all the time. They should make him move, with all that stealing. We're scared to leave our houses unlocked.'

'I just need to find him, not have an argument.'

She studied Charlie for a few seconds, before nodding to a large slab in the middle of what was meant to be a rockery, except that nothing was growing between the stones, so that it was just a spread of rocks and mud. 'He keeps a key under there. I've seen him get it when he comes home drunk.' She raised an eyebrow. 'Which he does a lot, staggering and carrying on.'

Charlie thanked her and lifted the stone. There was the brass glint of a Yale key.

He waited for the neighbour to go back into her house before he unlocked the door and pushed it open, although he could tell he was being watched, her fingers visible on the edge of the curtain.

'Gerard?'

No response. Just silence, the house gloomy and dark.

As he stepped inside, his feet echoed in the hallway. Everything was still.

A beam of light broke the gloom in the living room as it streamed in through a gap in the curtains, dust swirling. Books dominated, piles of them, many of them old hardbacks with yellowed pages and tattered spines. Shelves of first edition Penguins filled a bookcase against the wall. He backed out and went into the dining room. More books there. Some thrillers, but many were historical biographies.

There was a high-backed chair in the corner, a lamp behind, so Charlie guessed it was his reading spot.

Charlie shouted again, 'Gerard?' even though he knew there was no point.

He was looking for signs of an intruder, remembering the message, even expecting the place to be trashed. There were wine bottles on the floor and dirty plates on the table, but there were no signs of an untidy search. Just the debris from a scruffy man living alone.

They're here again, he'd said on the voicemail. Whatever they were after, they either found it straight away, or it was Gerard they were after.

Charlie crept forward, tensed for Gerard to leap out on him, every nerve tight.

As he looked through the kitchen, he noticed that the back door was ajar, swinging gently on its hinges as it was teased by the breeze.

Had it been open before? Had someone come in? Was he still alone?

'Hello?'

He waited, breathless.

Still nothing.

He opened the door to reveal the back garden, not much more than an unruly lawn with a path cutting through it, grass growing high through the gaps, dandelions providing the brightness. A stone wall bordered the garden, a small gate in the centre. Beyond, there was a copse of trees and the Pennine hills, sunlight catching the purple heather.

Why would the back door be open?

Then Charlie remembered how it sounded like Gerard had been outdoors when he'd made the call.

He set off along the path, the grass swishing on his trousers, the morning dew making his shoes gleam. A dog walker strode along on the other side of the wall, a woman in a beanie hat and fluorescent jacket. There must be a trail through the copse.

The gate squeaked as he opened it.

He stopped.

There'd been a loud squeak on the message.

He lifted his phone to his ear to replay it. There it was. A metallic grind, then the high-pitched squeal of rusted paintwork.

He gave the gate another push. The same.

Gerard had been going this way. Had it been his escape route, hiding in the trees, or running along the path that went behind the houses?

Charlie stepped into the trail, saw that it was not much more than a worn path through bracken that weaved between the trees.

As he contemplated whether to turn back, he had a court hearing to attend, the frantic barking of a dog broke the peace, followed by a scream. It was coming from the copse.

Charlie set off running.

He knew what he was going to find before he got there, dog-walkers always find them, but he pushed on regardless, the bracken scraping against his suit, the sunshine lost as he entered the shadows of the trees, the dog barking harder.

As he broke into a small clearing, the dog-walker was on her knees, tears streaming down her face, pulling hard as her dog strained on the leash, desperate to get whatever lay ahead.

Charlie stopped, breathless, then sank to his knees next to her.

It was Gerard, his legs hanging limply, his face crumpled and purple, his head sunk into the noose, the rope over one of the branches. A log stump was kicked over on its side underneath him.

He put his head back and stared up at the sky in despair. Gerard had sought his help and now he was dead.

And his secret had gone with him.

Fourteen

Waterstone Hall was a few miles outside of town. For all of its grandeur, a castellated house on a grassy island in the still water of a lake, accessible from the main hotel building by a small stone bridge, it made its money from weddings. The Hall was a photo-backdrop, the corporate glitter of the hotel hosting the ceremonies.

Amy had parked in front of the main hotel building, the shiny bricks in contrast to the dark stone of the old hall, with a high glass atrium and newly-planted ivy already creeping up the exterior. Lights twinkled inside, even though it was bright outside.

The way in was through a revolving door and into the hush of reception. The floor was gleaming tiles, marble-effect, and large chrome chandeliers hung from the ceiling. A television played to an empty bar further along, as a man in white shirt and black bowtie restocked the shelves.

A woman behind the reception desk stood almost to attention, then beamed a smile that competed with the chrome for brightness. A badge on her green uniform said she was called Patsy.

'Good morning,' she said. 'Do you have a booking?'

Amy pulled out her identification. 'I'm hoping to speak someone who might have stayed here. Nick Cassidy. Do you know if he's still in the hotel?'

Her smile faded and her confidence wavered. 'I don't know if I can give out that information. You know, data protection and all that.'

Amy sighed, feigning annoyance. 'I know he's been here, because his phone signal has been located here. It's really important that I speak to him. I won't make a scene, I promise.'

Patsy looked behind her, as if to check whether there was anyone else listening, before she tapped at a few keys. A smile of recognition lit her eyes. 'Yes, him. He was staying here. He checked out earlier.'

Amy felt a stab of disappointment. 'Do you have his address?'

'Why don't you just ask him?'

'What do you mean?'

'He hasn't left yet,' Patsy said. 'There's a marker on his bill for more car parking fees, because it's still out there, and you only have the space for thirty minutes after you check out.'

'Do you know where he is?'

'In the old Hall, just over the bridge,' and she pointed towards the large glass doors at the other end of the bar. 'He's been there all night. The staff were talking, saying how he wasn't drinking much but not moving. The staff tried to get him to go, told him that the bar couldn't stay open all night, but he started using room service instead, getting drinks brought to his table. We didn't know what to do, because he's been drinking for twenty-four hours straight and shouldn't drive, but we can't stop him either. Although you could, I suppose.'

'Which is his car?'

Patsy pointed to a red Clio, parked slanted into a marked bay, with scrapes along the door. 'That one.'

Amy thanked her and stepped away. She made a call to the control room and asked to be put through to any cop on patrol near to the hotel.

After a few silent seconds, a voice said, 'PC Braddock, how can I help?'

'DC Gray here. I'm at the Waterstone Hotel and I think someone will be leaving soon in a battered red Clio after a long boozing session. If you pull him for drink-driving, it'll buy me some time to talk to him if he doesn't feel like a chat right now.'

'Big case?'

'Murder.'

'I'm on my way.'

Amy clicked off and headed through the bar, through doors that opened onto a wide patio filled with tables and heaters, bordered by planters. It faced a lake surrounded by trees, with a grassy island close to the hotel and connected by a stone bridge. In the middle was the old house, four storeys high, manor-style.

This was the wedding shot, the sun gleaming off the still waters of the lake, the old house standing proud on its splendid green island, the stone bridge curved, so that its reflection made a lovely oval.

Amy walked over the bridge, her footsteps loud cracks in the calm of her surroundings. Geese strolled on the grass. A man fished from a small boat on the lake.

The entrance door was open, the lobby dominated by a sweeping staircase, a reception desk to one side. The style was grand and old, darker than the main building, wood-panelling replacing the white paint of the corporate side. Amy could almost see the price-rise, as if they were two separate hotels, this one the snooty older brother looking down on the younger, trashier version over the water.

Doors opened into a bar that was more like an old dining room, the ceiling high, the light clusters black iron, the tables long and formal.

There was a man sitting in a chair at the other end of the room. He nursed a glass and shifted in his seat as Amy made her way over.

She pulled out her identification and sat down opposite. His fingers gripped the chair arms.

'Mr Cassidy?'

'How did you know?'

'Guesswork.'

'Did the hotel call you?'

'No, although they want you to leave. Your car parking is overdue and you're hogging a space. But I'm here because of Sarah Marsh. You've heard what's happened to her?'

He swallowed and took another drink. 'I heard something about it on the radio.'

'How well did you know her?'

'Not that well.'

'But you met her here, at a very grand country hotel?'

He paled. 'How do you know that?'

'Her phone tracked to here, as did yours, and you were the last person she called.' Amy leaned forward. 'Do you want to tell me why you met her?'

He shook his head. 'Not a chance.'

'Why not? If you've nothing to hide, that is.'

'Why are you doing it like this? All nice and quiet, hoping I'll go with you without making a fuss?'

She was confused. 'Should I be making more of a noise?'

'Are you alone?' He put his glass down. 'Are there more of you outside? This is a set-up.'

'No, please, sit down, Mr Cassidy. I just want to find out what Sarah was doing here.'

'I'm wondering whether you already know.' He jumped to his feet and went to go past Amy, his gaze darting to the windows, looking for the ambush.

Amy reached out to grab his wrist, but he shrugged her off. 'Leave me alone, I'm not going the same way.'

Amy went for a stronger grab, but he pushed a chair towards her and set off running.

Taken by surprise, she was slow to react, reaching out at thin air as he bolted through the dining room. As she started to run after him, she stumbled over a chair, so that he was through the doors before she was able to set off.

She went after him, not knowing what to do when she caught him, whether to arrest him for Sarah's murder, or just get him to calm the hell down.

By the time she burst back into the sunshine, Cassidy was running over the bridge and back towards the main part of the hotel.

A young waitress appeared on the bridge, her arms filled with packets of napkins, as if she'd just taken a delivery. Cassidy couldn't stop, his attention behind him, looking for Amy, so he sent her crashing to the ground when they made contact, making her cry out in pain.

He stumbled but was soon back on his feet, his soles skidding on the cobbles.

The waitress was kneeling, bent over, packets of napkins strewn across the bridge, and it made Amy pause when she saw blood dripping from her nose, wide dots of red on the ground.

She waved Amy on. 'Catch him,' she said, before sitting back on her haunches, blood streaming down her chin.

Cassidy carried on through the hotel reception. He clattered into the automatic doors when they didn't open fast enough, making Patsy on reception shout out, then back off when she saw Amy in pursuit.

Cassidy made it to his car before Amy emerged onto the car park, starting the engine and reversing as she ran towards it, forcing her to leap out of the way, her shoulder jarring as she landed hard on the tarmac.

He didn't pause to see how she was. He slammed the car into first gear and raced towards the distant exit.

A blue light strobed ahead, followed by the whoop of a siren, then the unmistakable crunch of metal hitting metal.

Amy hauled herself to her feet and made her way to the same exit.

When she got there, the red Clio was jammed into the passenger side of the squad car, which had been wedged against a tree, the uniformed officer scrambling over the seats before tumbling out of the rear door and onto the ground, panting, a trickle of blood coming from a cut on his forehead.

'The little fucker ran off,' he said, between gasps of breath, pointing towards a field, where in the distance she could see a man disappearing out of view.

Amy kicked the bumper of the red Clio and hissed, 'Bastard,' before pulling a phone from her pocket.

How the fuck was she going to explain this?

Fifteen

A man approached Charlie from the back of Gerard's house. He had detective written all over him. From his grey suit, too stiff, to his lilac shirt, too pressed, to his short-cropped hair, he was a detective from Mould No. 1, confirmed by his identification swinging from a dark blue lanyard.

Charlie was sitting on a wooden bench in the corner of Gerard's garden. He guessed it was a spot for contemplation, because its elevated position gave him a view over the house and along the stone wall at the back, to where the track wound its way through the trees. In the distance, he could just make out the city centre, beyond the high-rises of the inner city, a shaft of sunlight catching the glint of polished glass.

Charlie preferred the older parts of the city. The old redbrick railway arches. The tile-fronted pubs. Streets that once teemed with so much life that cholera ripped through them, families cramped into one room to keep the cotton looms going, Manchester built on industry.

It was changing slowly. Money was creeping in, sending glass buildings skyward, plush restaurants replacing old city centre haunts, but Charlie still sought out the wet cobbles and the darkest corners. That was his Manchester.

As the detective got closer, Charlie wasn't sure if he recognised him, because after a while they all blur into one, a collage of lanyards and short hair.

Charlie gestured to the seat next to him. 'Take a seat, detective.'

'DS Broome,' he said, sighing as he joined Charlie on the bench. 'It must have been a shock.'

'I've had better mornings.'

'And you're his solicitor, so you said on the phone.' Broome frowned. 'If you don't mind me asking, why was his solicitor looking in the woods for him?'

'I needed to see him. I was worried about him, so I let myself in and had a look around. I heard a scream. I ran to it, and there he was.'

'Why were you worried?'

'Just legal stuff.'

Broome nodded to himself before saying, 'Had he given you any indication that he might kill himself?'

'Gerard was just Gerard. You know how he is.'

'Which is?'

Charlie smiled, despite himself. 'Come on, detective, you must have looked him up before you came here. Bit of a thief. Bit of a drunk.'

Broome pointed towards the house. 'Not the kind of place most shoplifters live in. Round here, done up, that place will go for half a million. Did he have any family?'

'Are you thinking it might not be suicide? That someone was after the inheritance?'

'I'm not thinking anything, Mr Steele. I just follow the crumbs.'

'And what do the crumbs tell you right now?'

Broome thought about that for a while, before saying, 'A lonely man who drinks too much kills himself in the woods behind his house. That would be a reasonable conclusion.' His eyes narrowed as he looked at Charlie. 'Unless you can tell me anything different.'

Charlie didn't respond. Instead, he thought about Gerard's visit the day before, and the phone call, and how much he should say.

'Mr Steele? Anything?'

'Not me, detective,' he said, eventually. 'He just calls me when he gets into trouble.'

'Because if it's anything different, your arrival here might look suspicious.' He pointed to the house next door. 'People haven't seen you here before, so this seems like something out of the ordinary. And out of the ordinary and a dead body in the woods raises a big red flag.'

Charlie narrowed his eyes. Broome was sharper than he looked.

'At least you're keeping an open mind,' Charlie said.

'So, you don't think it's suicide?'

'Like you said, detective, you follow the crumbs, but I've none to throw down.'

Broome tapped his foot as he looked back towards the woods, the way sealed off with yellow crime scene tape, crime scene investigators in white forensic suits just visible, moving like ghosts amongst the trees.

'You defence lawyers always see us as the enemy,' Broome said. 'That isn't how it is. But if there is anything you know that can help shed light on why he did this, it might be in your interests to tell me.' Broome smiled, although it didn't reach his eyes. 'It would be embarrassing to see you getting booked in, taking off your belt and shoes at the custody desk, just because a death looked mysterious and you were too secretive. I can bet that half the station would have a need to pass through, to see a defence lawyer in a cell.'

'I'll do you a deal, detective. As soon as you suspect it's not suicide, give me a call. Until then, I'll decide what I say. I'll even give you my phone number.'

'Stay close, Mr Steele.'

'I'd rather you stopped pretending you can make me.'

Broome flinched. 'Have it your way.'

Charlie faked a smile. 'I always do, detective.'

Sixteen

Higham stormed through the incident room as he pointed his finger at Amy, then jabbed it towards his office. No one said anything, everyone with a sudden excuse to stare at a computer screen. Once in there, he slammed the door behind her, making the papers on his corkboard flutter.

'What the fuck did you do? I'm in charge of this investigation, so I expect you to keep me updated.'

Amy took a deep breath before she answered. She knew she'd messed up, but that didn't mean she was going to be bawled out by Higham.

'Following your orders,' she said.

'Bullshit. I didn't tell you to go to a hotel and make someone crash into a cop car.'

Amy perched herself on the edge of the desk and folded her arms.

'Don't go for the angry boss throwing his weight around, it's not a good look,' she said. 'My report will say how I was doing exactly what you said, because a room full of people heard you tell me to assemble the last twenty-four hours of her life, so I did. I worked out where she was before she came back to Cookstown, and who she was with. Nick Cassidy was the last person to speak to Sarah on the phone, and it looks like they met at a country hotel. I went to speak with him, to see if he had any information about her.'

'You should have spoken to me first.'

'Would you have told me to go, or not go? After all, I gave you his number yesterday and you didn't do anything about it.'

He ground his jaw and said, 'Okay, I'd have told you to go, but why didn't you take someone else with you, to wait by the exit? We could have surrounded the place. He should have been brought here, told he had to make a statement or something, anything to get him here.'

'What, surround the place and arrest him because he spoke to her miles from where she was killed? Come on, boss, we had nothing on him.'

'That's all we have now, don't you get it? No forensics on him, with time now to work out a story. He knows we're looking for him.'

'It doesn't have to be like that.'

He paused, his hands on his hips, his jaw clenched.

After a few moments, he said, 'Go on, how is it different?'

'He's not a suspect. If you plan to kill someone, you don't spend a week calling the victim on your own phone, then meet up in a hotel with cameras everywhere.'

'Heat of the moment? Crime of passion?'

'Not going for that either, because when it's spontaneous, one of two things happen. They are either consumed by remorse and confess, or else they try to bluff it out, make out like they're helpful, do all they can to make themselves seem like the last person we'd ever suspect. Nick Cassidy bolted, petrified, thought he was being ambushed, and he knew I was a cop. No, boss, he's a witness, not a suspect, but whatever he's a witness to, it made him nervous. Yes, we need to speak to him, except before we had nothing to bring him in on. Now? You can bring him in for failing to stop after an accident, or driving whilst unfit, and grill him all day.'

He took a few deep breaths and appeared to calm down. 'Yes, maybe you're right. Okay, track his phone, alert everyone, but I want in on this. I've managed to keep the Major Crimes Unit off this case, but we can't lose control of it. It's our town, our case. If you work out where he is, I'm going to get him. Not the squad. Me. You understand?'

'I get you, boss.'

'Good. Now, fuck off and do some police work.'

Seventeen

Monica kept her gaze fixed on her computer screen as Charlie strode back into the office, even as she held out two yellow sticky notes, phone messages scribbled onto them.

'I saw a dead body, that's all,' Charlie snapped. 'It's not catching. But I don't want any clients today,' and he slammed the door into his room as he went inside.

He collapsed into his chair and put his head back, took deep breaths as he watched a cobweb flutter in the draught through his window.

He should apologise to Monica. She didn't deserve that. He held out his hand. It was steady.

He stood and began to pace, his hands on his head, pushing back his hair. He went to the window to check outside. There was no one there.

Gerard had sought his help and Charlie had dismissed him. He'd called him when he was scared and Charlie had ignored it, too busy drinking out his frustrations. By the time he'd done something, Gerard was dead. How was he supposed to deal with that?

There was a knock on his door, but before he had chance to shout *go away,* it opened and in walked Eleanor.

'I sorted out your hearing,' she said. 'It's been adjourned until next week.'

He stopped pacing. 'What did you say?'

'The truth. You'd gone to see a client and found him dead. You were shaken, and the police needed to speak to you.'

'Good, thanks.' He took another deep breath. 'It was, well, I don't know how to describe it.'

'First corpse?'

'Yes. Hopefully, my last.' He held out his hand. Still steady. 'Of course, you were a copper. Old hat for you.'

'You get used to it, but the first is the worst. Do you want to know about mine?'

'Not really, but you'll tell me anyway.'

'A woman rolled up in a carpet, killed by her husband, the carpet in the yard, waiting for him to work out what to do with it.'

'Sounds grim.'

'It was. Her sister had called it in, because he was a violent bastard, drunken bully, and her sister hadn't seen her for a while. I went round to ask him where she was, just to put the sister's mind at rest, and went in the back way because he wasn't answering my knocks at the front. It was one of those small concrete yards at the back of a terraced house, with the carpet wedged into the corner, attracting flies. And the smell, phew, even though she was outdoors. So, I had a peek inside.'

'And?'

'There she was, bloating, turning all colours of the rainbow. I went in and put handcuffs on him, no questions, nothing. Cuffed him to a radiator pipe and waited for back-up.'

'Didn't it turn your stomach?'

'Too much adrenalin, that was the problem. I mean, she did stink. Like a mix of rotting meat and vomit, the stomach gases I think, but by the time I'd calmed down I wasn't near the smell. Later on, I was like you, shaken, fidgety, but, in the moment, I was too fired up.'

He went to sit down. He wiped his forehead, perspiring. 'When I first saw him, it was disbelief, like I expected him to open his eyes and say it was all a joke, but the dog was barking and the woman was screaming and it felt like chaos. But now, it's something different.'

'How different?'

'Like I feel responsible somehow.'

Eleanor went to the window and opened it, before lighting a cigarette. As she blew smoke into the dank air of the back street, she said, 'Why responsible?'

'He came to see me yesterday. Don't you get it? He sought my help and I didn't give it. And the thing is, he always pays. I could have pretended to look into it and billed him for a few hours work, but the thought that I was there for him might have made a difference.'

'Because you're a decent man, Charlie. Even if you did take your wife for granted, and you live in a bare room like a squatter.'

Charlie gave a small laugh. 'I'd forgotten what a beacon of support you are.'

'What did he want to see you about?'

'He's got some complaint about Spencer Everett, that he knows a deep secret about him, and Gerard wanted to stop his career somehow.'

'Spencer Everett? As in, Home Secretary Spencer Everett?'

'They were at university together.'

'What's the secret?'

'He wouldn't say, except that dark forces were involved.' He raised an eyebrow. 'His words, not mine. It was delusional. Certainly not a legal problem. But, well, that call last night. He said there were people there, at his house. That's why I went there, because it bothered me. And it's why I went into his garden, because I could tell that he was outside when he called.'

'You don't think it was suicide?'

'I don't know. What I saw looked like suicide, and the detective who turned up thought so too, but that isn't what I heard yesterday when he came here, nor what I heard on the phone.'

'And did you tell the detective this?'

'Well, no.'

'Why not?'

Charlie picked up a pen to tap on his desk. 'The instinct of a defence lawyer: if in doubt, say nothing.'

'I'm not buying that,' she said. 'You think there's more to it, and you didn't trust the police to find that out.'

'I don't know, I really don't.'

'Well, I can help you with that,' and she tossed an envelope onto his desk. 'I looked for Gerard on the computer to check for any outstanding fees, and guess what, we have his last will and testament.'

Charlie looked at the envelope, then back at Eleanor. 'His will? Why would we have his will? I don't do probate work.'

'But Mr Greenhalgh did, before he retired.'

'Where was it?'

'In the safe, in the folder marked *Wills*.'

'Why haven't I seen that before?'

'Because you never go in the safe. No one does. We're a criminal firm now, so we don't keep documents for clients anymore. But the firm once did. The wills folder was at the back, and Gerard's was the only one in there.'

Charlie stood again. 'Hang on, I'm not getting this.'

'When I saw the entry against his name, I called Mr Greenhalgh to ask him.' She flicked ash out of the window. 'He says hello, by the way. Anyway, Greenhalgh retired and the practice was sold to you, as you know. He wrote to all the people who had nominated the firm as executors, told them he was retiring and that the firm would no longer be doing that type of work. He asked them to find a relative or another firm of solicitors to take up that role, and he drafted a free codicil to amend that clause in the will once they told him who was to be nominated.'

'How come we have it then?'

'Because Gerard refused. He said he liked you and trusted you, so he left it with us.'

'Great. Not only do we have his will, but we're the executors too?'

'Seems that way.'

'But why don't I know this?'

'Come on, Charlie. You were buying a law practice, taking on bank loans and responsibilities. Greenhalgh says he asked you, but most likely you weren't paying attention. What did one man's will matter in all of the turmoil? Gerard was only in his forties. You might have sold up and retired before he died.'

'I don't do probate work, that's why it matters. Isobel does probate work, and I remember the things she had to do. Register his death. Arrange the funeral. A house clearance, all sorts of things I've never done before. Jewellery valuations. Auctions. House sale. Deal with relatives who ring up and always start with *it's not about the money*, but it was always about the damn money.'

'This is your chance to learn then, because it's an easy will, everything to his three nieces. But you're missing the major point here.'

'Which is what?'

'It's all private rates, not the legal aid rates you'll get if you turn this down to help out another shoplifter. Trudging through all of Gerard's stuff and selling it, all at a couple of hundred quid an hour. Drain his estate for what you can, and at the end, his nieces will just be happy to get a six-figure sum from their weird, shoplifting uncle.'

'You really have no heart, Eleanor.'

'I do. It's your bank manager who has a heart of stone.'

Charlie sat back down again and realised that she had a very good point.

Eighteen

Jessica Redmond checked behind as she ducked into the gardens next to Parliament. Spencer was having a meeting in the House of Commons tea-room with a group of constituents, using the grandeur of his surroundings to deflect any awkward questions.

She was in a triangular park squeezed between Parliament and the Lambeth Bridge, lined by tarmac paths and plane trees. One side was busy with the sound of tourist buses, motorcycle couriers and black cabs, all streaming past black Victorian railings. The other was bordered by the Thames, which gently lapped against a concrete wall. The occasional cruiser broke that calm, but the park was an oasis of quiet against the tourist mayhem of Westminster and Whitehall.

She did her best to look natural, although she struggled not to rush. She sat on a wooden bench and pretended to take in the view.

After a couple of minutes, she pulled out her phone and pressed the last number dialled, her earphones plugged in and the microphone lead lifted to her mouth so she could whisper her conversation.

As soon as he answered, she said, 'What do you mean, you're going in?'

'Like I said in the text, I'm surrendering. Don't stop me.'

She fought the urge to scream down the phone and instead whispered, 'What the fuck are you talking about?'

He was outside, she knew that, from the sound of passing cars and the whistle of the breeze. 'Danger, that's what. I'm surrendering to the police.'

'Wait, hold on,' she said. 'For what reason?'

There was a pause, then he said, 'For what I did. I'll be safe there. Hide in plain sight, that's the best way.'

'Nick, you're pissed, and you're not making sense.'

'Do you blame me?'

'Please, Nick, help me out here. I've risked everything for your story.'

He breathed heavily into the phone, before saying, 'I'm out. I'm not doing this anymore. If you want to, have fun, but me? Nope. I'm done.'

She put her head back. How could he do this, use her, then drop her?

'Nick, what do I do?'

'Speak to a lawyer.'

'Which lawyer? What are you talking about?'

'Pippa. Sweet, darling Pippa.'

'Spencer's wife? She's dead, for Christ's sake.'

'And she was divorcing him, remember, so she must have had a lawyer, and lawyers know secrets.'

'So, I speak to Pippa's divorce lawyer. Then what?'

'You find another reporter,' he said. Then, he clicked off.

She stared at her phone in disbelief, then shouted, 'fuck!'

***

Amy was writing up her report about her visit to the Waterstone Hotel when a young constable put his head around the door and said, 'Amy, there's someone to see you. I think it's about the murder case.'

Amy looked around the room. There were only three people left in there, No one else volunteered.

The constable must have spotted her hope that someone else would step in, because he said, 'It has to be you. That's what he said.'

She sighed. 'Okay, show me.'

She followed him along the short corridor and into the public waiting area, brightly-lit. There was a man there, facing away and out of the window.

'Can I help you?'

He turned and she recognised him straight away. Nick Cassidy.

She reached behind her back and pulled the cuffs from the holder attached to her belt. He held out his hands, knowing what was coming.

The cuffs clinked as she put them on. 'Nick Cassidy, I am arresting you for driving whilst unfit through drink and failing to stop after an accident. You do not have to ..."

'Protect me,' he said, interrupting the caution, his words slurred.

'Pardon?'

'You heard me. Protect me. I'm relying on you. Speak to Tammy.'

She wanted to step back, the smell of booze too strong, his jaw slack, his eyes struggling to focus.

'Tammy?'

He tapped his nose and winked. 'You know who I mean.'

'It doesn't matter what you want me for,' she said. 'It smells like it will have to wait until later. Come on,' and she led him through the door and towards the cell complex.

Nineteen

As Charlie inserted the key into the lock at Gerard's house, Eleanor said, 'You kept it?'

'More like I forgot to put it back.'

'Did that excuse ever work when Gerard was shoplifting?'

'I wish I'd thought of it now.'

Charlie pushed open the door. 'Although it's less effective when you're running down the street, being chased by a store detective.'

Eleanor stubbed her cigarette out on the stone step and chuckled, although it turned into a wheezy cough as they went inside.

'The house seems different,' Charlie said. 'Before, it felt threatening somehow. Perhaps because of the call, that it was from a man in fear. Now, it's just an empty house.'

They went into the living room, and it was as dreary as he remembered, the windows covered in road soot and dust. There was a constant hum of traffic, and the picture frames rattled as a bus went past.

Eleanor lifted a newspaper from a chair arm, folded over at the crossword page, the puzzle half-completed. 'Where do we start?'

Charlie had called Isobel before they set off. She had been frosty at first, but when she knew it was for a legal matter, she told him what he needed to know before hanging up.

'We make an inventory of each room,' Charlie said. 'List anything of value, actual or sentimental. We can get a house clearance company to remove the furniture and auction it. The rubbish gets dumped.'

'How was Isobel about you asking for advice?'

A smile played at the side of Charlie's mouth. 'Curt, is the best way to describe it.'

'It'll change. Tensions ease, provided neither of you turn it into a war.'

'I'm not discussing my marriage, not today. I thought we were doing an inventory.'

Eleanor put on her glasses as Charlie pulled open a drawer.

'Antique watches,' he said, looking in.

He lifted one out, a gold pocket watch on a chain.

'I had a few cases where he was pinching them,' he said. 'He'd ask to examine them, then bolt out of the door. Must have been a phase. Better contact the police about these. Let's not get into selling stolen property.'

He handed the watch to Eleanor, who placed it on the top of the drawer unit. She wrote *GW1* on a sticker and took a photograph of the watch next to it. She made a descriptive note in her notebook, then did the same with the next, working her way through the drawer.

'This is like my name,' she said. 'Eleanor Rigby. About the lonely people. I was named after the song. My Dad was a Beatles fan. And this house reeks of loneliness.'

'But your surname is Lane. Why not Penelope, so you could be Penny Lane?'

'My Mum objected, said it was too obvious.'

As Eleanor documented everything in the drawers, deciding what might be worth something, Charlie explored the house more.

The books might be valuable. Many were old, but that didn't guarantee anything. There were the Penguin first editions, and he wondered whether Gerard had read them. Was it just a hobby, something to collect?

He went through to the bedroom but found just clothes, apart from some jewellery in a leather box in his top drawer, rings and necklaces, a couple of bracelets. They were old, scuffed and grimy, and women's jewellery. He suspected they would have little monetary value, but they might represent something of his family history. They should be given to the three nieces.

It was as he was leaving the bedroom that he saw it.

It was an envelope, tucked behind a chest of drawers, just one corner visible. The chest of drawers had a wooden lip at the back, so it couldn't have slipped down there. It was more as if it had been shoved there in order to hide it, but done in a hurry.

Like when someone is in your house.

He pulled it out and tipped the contents onto the bed.

There were newspaper clippings, along with some letters. As he rummaged through them, he saw they were all about Spencer Everett, charting his rise as an MP, from backbencher to front bench favourite. As he leafed through them, reading the contents, he shouted, 'Eleanor, come through here.'

When she appeared behind him, he lifted some up and said, 'This is part of it.'

She came closer. 'What are they?'

'Clippings, letters. Gerard had an obsession about Spencer Everett. And the letters he wrote must have been copied at one of those local places. You know, four pence a copy or whatever.'

'What do they say?'

'There are only three, but I've put them in order. The first one is to Spencer Everett himself,' and he handed it over.

The letter was handwritten on lined notepaper, Gerard's handwriting showing some elegance, and a forward slant.

Eleanor read.

Dear Spencer,

It pains me to write this letter, given our friendship all those years ago, but I see your efforts to be a public figure and it seems quite improper, because of what I know.

It is time to come out in the open. I appreciate the impact it will have on you, and your efforts to live a productive life, but sometimes we must do the right thing. We will all pay a price, but it is right that we do, as the cause is the right one.

As a man of honour, I will allow you to go first.

If you write to me at this address, I can help make the arrangements. I've been talking to a reporter already, as well as the others, and we are all in agreement.

If you do not agree, I will go public regardless.

Otherwise, I hope this reaches you in good health.

Yours,

Gerard Williams

She put it down. 'What on earth is this about? Is there a reply?'

'This is where it gets more formal,' and he handed over a second letter, from a London law firm.

Dear Mr Williams,

We have been instructed to write to you by Mr Spencer Everett, who is disturbed by your recent demand that he goes public with some unspecified information.

Although our client does recall that he enjoyed a brief friendship with you during his time at university, he does not have any notion as to the information referred to by you. We would remind you, however, that any attempt to defame Mr Everett with untruthful allegations will result in legal action being taken against you, the cost of which would be considerable. Further, you should be aware that the burden of proving the truthfulness of the allegations will fall to you in the event of legal action for defamation.

We would further remind you that any attempt to obtain any monies from Mr Everett in exchange for the non-publication of so far undisclosed allegations could well amount to blackmail, a criminal charge that would result in your imprisonment.

At this stage, however, Mr Everett would be content if you would agree to not make public whatever lurid claim you seek to make, as well as cease communicating with him.

Yours sincerely
Joshua Rosberg
Senior Partner

'To the point,' Eleanor said.

'But we have no idea what the allegations are. It's all very oblique, hint-hint. Why didn't Gerard just come out and say it?'

'That means Gerard had something to hide.'

'What do you mean?'

'It's obvious, isn't it?' Eleanor said. 'The only letter he sent to Spencer that he copied does not say what the secret is, nor did he tell you. That means one thing only: Gerard was scared. If not, he would have told you.'

'Or maybe it's all bullshit and bluster, hoping for a pay-off to stay silent about some ancient rumour about whatever Spencer got up to at university. Spencer Everett's star has risen quickly, so now he's someone to exploit. Remember, Gerard was a crook by occupation, even if it was small-time.'

Eleanor raised an eyebrow. 'And the man who came up with this bluster was found dead in the woods.'

Charlie handed over a final piece of paper. 'He wrote back to the law firm last week.'

Dear Mr Rosberg,
Thank you for your recent letter, the contents of which I found quite surprising.

I must stress that the information I have is known to Mr Everett and I feel obliged to pursue this. It is a matter for Mr Everett as to whether he goes public on his own terms, or whether I take control of the situation.

I look forward to hearing further from you.
Yours sincerely
Gerard Williams

Eleanor held up the letter and said, 'You're going to have to show this to the cops.'

'Yes, maybe.'

'There's no *maybe*.'

When Charlie looked unconvinced, Eleanor said, 'This is no time to salvage your conscience. Okay, I get it, you feel like you didn't do enough to stop Gerard swinging from a tree, but you are withholding evidence from a murder investigation.'

'Look around,' Charlie said. 'Where are the cops, the crime scene investigators? They looked around the woods, took away the body, and that was it. This is no murder investigation.'

He picked up the envelope to put the letters back in, when he spotted something else inside, tucked into the corner. He shook the envelope harder, to tip it out.

It was a photograph.

Creased and faded, it showed a group of young men, five in total, their arms around each other, laughing and posing. The setting was summer, obvious from the glow to their skin and the brightness of the sky.

Charlie picked it up. 'Isn't that Spencer Everett in the middle?' He pointed to a tall man, young and beaming a smile, his blonde hair long and lush.

Eleanor examined it, then said, 'That's Gerard there, the one on the far left.'

As Charlie looked closer, he saw that she was right. Gerard as a young man, full of hope for the future, a broad smile and dark hair. 'Time was tough on him,' he said. 'There, he looks carefree.'

Charlie turned over the photograph. On the reverse was the handwritten inscription, *My last moment of true happiness*.

Twenty

Amy took a long drink of coffee as the car pulled up.

She was sitting on a bench close to the harbour, needing a break from the squad. She preferred the breeze on her face and the salted air in her nostrils.

The car door flew open, and Tammy Trenton marched towards her.

Tammy Trenton was a bundle of anger in baggy jeans and a long, ragged jumper, her tangle of long hair wrapped into a knot and tied up by a silk scarf.

Amy lifted her hand in salute. 'You came.'

'You know I'll always jump when you call. Have you got news?'

'You tell me. Nick Cassidy.'

Tammy shrugged. 'What about him?'

Amy smiled. 'It is you then. He just said *speak to Tammy*, and here you are, the only Tammy I know. '

'Where is he? What has he said?'

'Me first. What has he got to say and why is he involved?' Amy held up her hand. 'No, I'll rephrase it, because I can guess why he'd mention you: Natasha. But why now, and what's the connection with Sarah Marsh?'

'Don't dismiss Natasha like that. For a moment, I thought you might be doing something for me. But no, it's never about my Natasha.'

'One case at a time, Tammy.'

'Yeah, but you overlooked mine. Somehow, mine gets lost in the queue.'

'I've no news on Natasha, but I need to know about Nick Cassidy.'

'This is a two-way thing. Just because you've got the police badge doesn't mean I tell you everything. What's the sudden interest in him?'

'He's in the station now, drunk and under arrest, and was possibly the last person to speak to a woman who turned up dead on the beach. And before he was dumped in a cell, he said I should speak to you.'

'So, it's about her, not Natasha. Like always. A rich woman gets washed up on the beach and everything stops for her. But a girl like my Natasha? She never came home, but you stopped looking pretty quickly.'

'It wasn't like that. Natasha went missing, and I'm sure they did all they could to find her.'

'Are you really sure about that?' Tammy folded her arms and glared at Amy. 'I thought you were different. When you first joined up, you were better, more interested. I realise now that you're just good at the bullshit. When I start calling, they send the new girl to keep me quiet, all sugar and spice. Look at you now. No sugar or spice anymore.'

'What do you mean?'

'You're different. You're climbing the ladder, I can tell. So, go on, what do you want? You know your job is to shut me up, nice smiley Amy, but I made a promise to Natasha that I wouldn't let you forget about her. I said I'd keep coming here and prodding you, so that one day the right copper might look again at her case. But now you're calling me, so I can't help but wonder why.'

'I told you, Nick Cassidy. He spoke to a woman who ended up dead, and he mentioned you. I want to know if there's a connection.'

'Ask him. He wouldn't tell me anything. He was drunk and was wanting to know about Natasha.'

'Did you tell him?'

'I was going to, but I got suspicious. He was rambling on and on, talking about Spencer Everett, so I knew he wasn't interested in Natasha. He was using me for some big story he wanted to write, so he was interested in himself, nothing more.'

'Spencer Everett? As in the Home Secretary?'

'Is that what he is? I don't know, I don't follow politics. I've heard of him, posh guy, but I didn't know who he was.'

'Did he say why he was interested in Spencer Everett?'

'He never got that far. I told him he was a user and he had to stop calling me.'

Amy nodded to herself. 'Okay, thanks.'

Tammy scowled. 'That's it then? I'm done?'

'What do you want me to say? Pretend we found Natasha, just to make you feel better? Because you know we haven't.'

'Just keep looking. Dig through the files. Ask your father. Do what you can do.'

'My father?'

'He must have talked about it, right? Young woman never comes home. That's front-page stuff, except for girls around here, when she was forgotten the following week.'

Amy looked up at Tammy, and saw how she wore her grief like a shroud, enveloping her.

Amy patted the bench. 'Sit down, Tammy.'

'I can't. I'm angry. I'm always angry.'

'Please, sit.'

Tammy pondered that for a few seconds, before she sat next to Amy. Tammy stared straight ahead as Amy said, 'You know I can only do so much. Natasha's disappearance was before my time.'

'But not your father's. He was the top detective around here, and it happened on his watch.'

Amy sighed. 'I'm not him.'

'But you must have heard him talk about her, even if it was just bitching?'

Amy didn't respond.

'There we have it,' Tammy said. 'Natasha never entered his head. Invisible. Didn't count. Just some dumb girl from the wrong family.'

'She wasn't that. He didn't bring his work home, that's all. We were his safe place.'

'Do something now. Find her.'

'It's not as simple as that.'

'It's exactly that simple.' Her shoulders sagged. 'Truman Buford fucked it up with that false confession, made everyone stop looking, but that was bullshit.'

'You don't know that.'

'I went to see him in prison. I looked him in the eyes, from across a small table, close enough to hit him, and I heard the sincerity in his voice, his denials, and I didn't see any guilt.'

'Tammy, I've been a cop long enough to know that people will lie about everything, and you confronted him, wanted a confession you could use to keep him in prison for life.'

'I just wanted answers.'

'He wanted freedom, and he was a junkie, and junkies are selfish liars.'

Tammy pursed her lips. 'She was my daughter, and she was going places. Me? I knew what I would be. Helping out at the scrapyard, buying and selling, just trying to get by. And I was fine with that, don't get me wrong, but Natasha? She was going to go to university.

She was clever, bright, and then?' She snapped her fingers. 'Nothing. Snuffed out, like she'd never been here. I've got to do this for her, and I'm going to keep on bothering you on the anniversary of her going missing, and whenever something like this happens, until someone admits that they know what happened to her and kept it quiet.'

'And you're doing it for you too.'

'I don't follow.'

'Whatever happens, even if you don't get the answer you want, you'll know that you did everything.'

'I've got to. I lost everything when she was taken. Just promise me that you won't forget her. Do what you can. Make me trust your word.'

Amy reached out and clasped her hand, Tammy's fingers cold and thin. 'I promise, and if I ever hear anything, I'll do something about it.'

'It'll get me out of your hair.'

'Amen to that,' Amy said.

Twenty-One

Jessica held her phone in front of her and checked the address.

She was outside a building in Essex Street, close to the Royal Courts of Justice, its pale grandeur visible at the top of the street, dead-ended by an archway at the other, with steps that led to the Victoria Embankment. Narrow and cramped, the street seemed to be permanently in shadow, most of the buildings housing barristers' chambers, the tenants identified by brass nameplates by the door. There were no identifying marks on the doorway Jessica was interested in.

She read the address on her phone again, obtained from an internet search. Bridget Temple, lawyer to the stars, operating out of Essex Street. Pippa Everett's hiring of her had made for a couple of newspaper stories, with hints of titillating details to come, but her death in Spain had brought an end to that.

She'd expected a sign or lettering in gold leaf, but it was just three storeys of latticed sash windows and a black wooden door, with books and folders on some of the sills.

There was a button below a loudspeaker. It buzzed when she pressed it.

A clipped voice crackled in reply, 'Good afternoon,' but nothing further.

'Er, hello, I'm looking for Bridget Temple.'

'And you are?'

'I don't want to tell you that straight away, but I've been told I need to speak to her. It's about Spencer Everett. Bridget acted for his late wife.'

Jessica expected the conversation to come to an abrupt end, but after a few seconds the door clicked, her signal to enter.

Inside, the reception area was set out like a parlour, with velvet chairs and modern art on the wall. A woman was waiting to greet her, her suit clean and uncreased, her hands clasped in front of her.

'Is it Bridget?'

The woman smiled, but it was frosty. 'I'm her assistant. How can I help?'

'It's Bridget I need to speak to, I think.'

The woman's smile widened. The hardness in her eyes deepened. 'And if I agree with you, that might happen, but first you need to tell me why.'

Jessica wondered whether she should carry on. She didn't know the woman, nor did she know Bridget. She thought she'd trusted Nick Cassidy, but he'd backed out of the deal.

But Nick had directed her towards Bridget. She had to keep going.

'I've been working with a reporter called Nick Cassidy,' she said. 'He's writing a story about Spencer Everett, except he's gone cold, said it was too dangerous and is handing himself in to the police. He told me to speak to Bridget.'

'Why the police?'

'He didn't say.'

The woman pursed her lips as she took in the information. 'And you are?'

'My name is Jessica Redmond. I'm Spencer Everett's intern.'

Her eyelids flickered her surprise. 'And you've been helping this Mr Cassidy?'

Jessica nodded.

'Give me your number,' the woman said. 'I'll pass it on to Miss Temple. It'll be her decision what she does about it.'

'And if she decides to do nothing?'

'Then, you'll hear nothing, obviously.'

'And that's it?'

The woman nodded.

Jessica frowned. 'And what's your name?'

'I told you. I'm Miss Temple's assistant.' Another cold smile, then, 'Good afternoon, Miss Redmond.'

Jessica nodded to herself before leaving, pausing to look back at the building once she was outside.

She wasn't sure if she'd got anywhere, but at least she was taking it as far as she could.

Twenty-Two

Amy headed for the Missing Persons Unit before it closed down for the day, Tammy Trenton's rage still fresh.

Calling it a Missing Persons Unit was disingenuous. It wasn't a unit. It was one ageing constable given a role to see him out until retirement. All the action was further along the corridor, where the murder investigation occupied two rooms.

Amy tapped on the door to attract the attention of the sole occupant. 'Hi, Kirmo.'

Dave Kirmond had once spent his time as the local copper everyone knew because of his bulk, always too slow to get out of his car if he saw something suspicious. By the time he got moving, people had run from the scene and were never caught. Now, he was ticking off his calendar, his huge frame more suited to desk work, where he spent his time tapping though social media pages of whoever was the subject of the latest alert. His shirt buttons strained on his stomach, and his cheeks wore the sheen and flush of too many hours at The Ship Ahoy, a pub overlooking the harbour that sold cheap beer, the haunt for the locals who had nothing much else to do. The boards around the room were plastered with images of faces, some printouts yellowing with age, the lost people of Cookstown forever trapped in time.

Kirmo looked up, then sat back. 'Detective Constable Gray. To what do I owe this honour?'

Amy leaned on the doorjamb. 'You're being very formal.'

'You turned up the lady on the beach, which makes you special to me.' He grinned. 'Let's not bullshit each other, we know that there were no heroics, just turning out way past your bedtime, but it saved me another job. If she hadn't been found, she'd have been swept up by the tide, and her case would have stayed with me.' He shrugged. 'You want me to be warm and fuzzy? Get me another job, because in here, in this office, I deal in misery.'

'Misery? This is where hope is found. Emotional reunions. Questions answered. Murder is where the bad news lies.'

'You believe that? We're a seaside town. People come here to disappear, because if you're wanting to run away, why not head for somewhere that'll make people think you've run into the sea? A pile of clothes on the beach and it's time for a new life. Or else people run away from here, just to go somewhere exciting. From this desk, either I find them, then persuade them to go back to whatever shitty life they had that made them want to run away in the first place. Or else they never turn up, and those left behind don't get answers. This is no place for happy reunions. It's either bad news or no news.'

'I've never thought of it that way, but what if they turn up dead? That's at least closure for the families?'

'And you think that's a happy ending?' He shook his head. 'You're too dark for me. So, what is it, Amy? You haven't come here for my patter.'

She went inside and closed the door behind her. As she took a seat opposite, she said, 'Natasha Trenton.'

He rolled his eyes.

'You know the name,' Amy said.

'I deal in missing persons. Of course I know about Natasha. Or, rather, Tammy.'

'I've just had a talk with her, because of Sarah Marsh getting all the press. She's angry that Natasha has been forgotten, but the rich woman gets front page news.'

'Yeah, she gets angry a lot when she calls here, but if shouting makes her feel better, let her shout, because I can't give her anything positive. Her daughter went missing, and we haven't found her. Like I said, there are no happy endings.'

'How well do you know the case?'

'Well enough, but look around. We've got nearly four hundred people still missing in our Force area. I look for the kids mostly, because if an adult wants to disappear, let them go. Here, in this little town, I get perhaps two cases a week, and two-thirds of my cases are kids running away from care homes or abusive households, but nearly all turn out to be short-stay runaways, where they hide out at a friend's house, often scared to go home. But I find them, and sometimes they tell me things before I hand them back, the stuff that goes on behind closed doors.' He winked. 'That's when the parents wish we'd never found them.'

'And you're saying that Natasha didn't count because she wasn't a kid?'

'If an adult doesn't want to be found, they won't be found, and I can't make them. There was one chap I heard about, right, because us missing person coppers talk to each other, in case someone turns up in a different county. This man just disappeared. Married, job, kids. Parked his car on a seafront somewhere. No one saw him leave, and everyone guessed he'd ended up in the sea, so it was all about waiting for him to turn up on a beach further along the coast, or snagged up in fishing nets, part-time fish food, broken, bloated and dead.' He laughed. 'He turned up eight years later, living in Newquay, selling burgers from a van, with a whole new family.'

'And you think that for Natasha?'

'I don't know, except that families don't often know much about what their nearest and dearest are doing. For a woman Natasha's age, I can bet those London lights shone really brightly, and back then no one left a trail they didn't want to leave. She was a pretty girl. Maybe she had promises of modelling work, or met a guy who promised a new start away from her family. It won't have been easy living in the Trenton household. If Natasha wanted to run, let her go.'

'And if it was something more sinister?'

'I wait for the body to turn up, because we don't know for sure until we get a corpse.'

'What about the confession?'

'Truman Buford?' He waved his hand in dismissal. 'I don't know if it was real or just attention-seeking. We didn't have a body, and for a rich man's boy, he was messed up. Kudos to the old man though, for trying to do the right thing.'

Amy's eyes wandered to the pictures around the room. Most were children, and most were police mugshots, their miserable lives carved into their expressions, with eyes already too old for their years.

'Can I look at the file?'

'You can take it and keep it, if Tammy wants to deal with you.' He stood and went to a filing cabinet in the corner of the room, breathless as he went, his girth swaying, his arms out wide. Sweat stained his underarms. 'I keep it close by because I know Tammy will keep calling.' He pulled out a file with tattered corners. 'Here.'

Amy flicked through the contents but didn't take anything in. She looked up. 'What do you think, Kirmo, deep down?'

He sighed. 'It was a long time ago, and if she's alive, she'd have turned up by now. She's dead, guaranteed. It was harder to trace people back then. Mobile phones didn't have GPS, so we couldn't narrow a signal down, and people didn't live their lives by a screen. Now, I can message all their friends straight away and work out their deepest thoughts, because people overshare. Back then, it was about posters and door-to-door, but no one saw anything.'

'Tammy needs to know that we did all we could.'

'No danger flags, so I can only do so much. I feel for that woman, but like I say, this isn't the room for happy endings.'

Twenty-Three

Jessica ducked as she went into the back room of a small pub across the road from the Royal Courts of Justice.

All she'd been given was a time and place by the woman she'd spoken to at the law firm earlier, her name still unknown.

The pub was dark, the windows old and dusty, the interior cramped, with low beams painted black, the walls crammed with framed pictures of the Strand in Victorian times, with trams and men in long coats and women in wide dresses.

Lawyers filled the main bar, their conversations loud, shirt necks open, their tabs and collars in leather bags that littered the floor. The back room was serene in comparison. There was a woman sitting at a table, her hair cropped short and grey, her blouse bright white, as if straight from the packet, her suit jet black. The other tables in there were empty.

'Bridget Temple? Pippa Everett's solicitor?'

'Close the door,' the woman said.

Jessica did as she was told, and the clamour from the room next door disappeared.

'Are you Jessica?'

When she nodded, the woman said, 'Show me your ID.'

Jessica rummaged in her purse and handed over her driving licence and her Parliamentary pass.

She examined them for a while, before she handed them back and said, 'Yes, I'm Bridget Temple. You better sit down.'

Jessica did as she was told as Bridget reached for a bottle of wine that was sitting in an ice-bucket. 'I know they say that it's best at ten degrees or higher, but if it's my fucking wine, I'll drink it how I like it.'

The expletive came in a rich, textured voice and surprised Jessica.

'Do you want a glass or not, my dear?'

'Er, yes, thank you.'

It was then that Jessica noticed a second glass, which Bridget filled. 'Drinking alone can be fun, but drinking with others is funnier.' She raised her glass and clinked it against Jessica's. 'Cheers.'

As Jessica took a sip, Bridget said, 'You might be wondering why we're meeting here, not at my office.'

'Well, I did wonder.'

'One, I've been in court all day, so my head is mashed and I feel like getting pissed. But two, and this is the important part, it means you're meeting me on my terms. At my office, people can hear. Here, no one else can plan any surveillance.'

'Surveillance? I don't understand.'

Bridget sat back. 'You work with the Home Secretary. You've had the Official Secrets Act drilled into you. So, you're taking a risk, which means whatever you're up to is worth the risk, so people will want to stop you. And I have to be careful what I say, because it's supposed to be confidential, that lawyer-client thing?' She waved her hand. 'The confidential stuff doesn't worry me. All lawyers talk, but if you try to use it against me, I'll deny telling you anything, then sue you for slander. I'll use every ounce of my legal being to crush you in every way. Emotionally, spiritually, financially. You understand that part, I assume. You transgress on my patch, make me seek legal recourse, I will fucking destroy you.'

'I don't want to cause trouble. But I want to do the right thing.'

Bridget softened. 'Talk to me then. You're an intern with Spencer, so I was told. Why would you want to go against him? And don't make this some kind of exploitative bullshit, whining because you work for free, or because he's looked at your tits or something. If we're talking, it's because we can help each other. If it's you moaning about your internship, get on social media and pull a fucking pouty face, because I'm not interested.'

'Have you ever heard of a reporter called Nick Cassidy?'

Bridget didn't react. 'Why do you ask?'

'He told me to speak to Pippa's lawyer, which is you.'

'How do you know Nick?'

Jessica thought about how much she should say, but realised that she'd already crossed the line. She might as well keep going.

'He approached me when I was leaving work one day, said he wanted a quote about Spencer. I'd seen him at press briefings before, so I knew he was a journalist, but I didn't know why he was asking me. Until he made his pitch, that is.'

'Pitch?'

'He asked me why I was interested in politics, what had motivated me to work for nothing.'

'And?'

Jessica pulled a face. 'It's a cliché?'

'I still want to hear it.'

'I wanted to change things. Naïve, I know, but I'd helped my dad deliver leaflets when I was younger, seen him stand for the council, because my father had a passion for politics. It rubbed off on me.'

'And where do Nick Cassidy and Spencer Everett fit into this?'

'Nick told me Spencer was on the take. He said that Spencer would take money from lobbyists, and that some of these people were dangerous. Arms dealers, people like that, and I know Spencer wants the top job, Prime Minister, so Nick reckoned he'd have to repay the debt somehow.'

'And there's only one way to please an arms company,' Bridget said. 'Start a war.'

'That's what Nick said. I could save lives.'

'And you believed everything he said?'

'Not at first, but there was always a trail of men in suits seeking out Spencer's audience. And there was the security firm.'

'Security?'

'They're about to announce a new immigration detention centre. A huge place, like a super-prison. This company is going to get the job of building it and running it, and Spencer is somehow involved with the company, except he's keeping quiet about it.'

'And it pisses you off?'

'Of course it does.'

'Politics has worked like that for centuries, my dear, and someone had to be given the contract.'

'It doesn't make it right.' Jessica took a drink of wine. 'Nick wanted help with his story, and I was willing to give it. If it cost me my internship, so what? I could always get a job that actually paid me for working.'

'What did you discover?'

She was about to take out her phone when she stopped. 'How can I trust you?'

'Because Nick trusted me.' Bridget smiled. 'He's digging into Spencer Everett. He was bound to get to me.'

'And did you help him?'

'I'm helping you, aren't I?'

'How did you help him? Dirty laundry from his divorce?'

'Sort of,' she said. 'Pippa Everett was murdered.'

Jessica's mouth dropped open. 'What?'

'You heard.' She waved her hand. 'I know I'm a lawyer, so it should all be about the evidence, yadda, yadda, but sometimes it's about your gut.'

'But she crashed into a ravine when on holiday. That's what the police said. I read all about it.'

'Too convenient,' Bridget said. 'Do you want to know what I'd do if I were staging it? I'd arrange to meet her there, with a promise that no one must know, because they're going to tell her what she needs for the divorce, but they can't be seen together. Once there, hit her head with a rock, the same type as they'll find in the ravine, and put her back in the driver's seat with no seat belt on. It was a convertible. Just roll the car off the edge. She would never survive it, and it would be written off as a tourist going too fast on a twisty road.'

'You think that's what happened?'

'It's my guess.'

'That's quite a claim. Why haven't you said it publicly?'

'Because there's no evidence, and I'm not going to get paid. My professional engagement with Pippa Everett ended when she died in that ravine. And before you say anything, I'll let you into a secret: lawyers talk about justice, but none of us give a fuck. We want to win, that's all. Some of us want to win by playing by the rules. Some of us don't care about the rules. But it's about winning, not justice. Any lawyer who cares about that is either skint, so needs a cause, or has already made their money by not giving a fuck and needs an end-of-career hobby. I do what I do for the hourly rates, and to pay for a house that is bigger than I need. I'll leave justice to the reporters.'

'You used Nick.'

'No, he was using me. It suited me to go along with him, that's all.'

'And now?'

'If he's backing out, someone else needs to tell the story, because I'm not writing it.'

'And you think I should?'

'Why not? You're all puffed up with righteousness.'

Jessica thought about it as she took another drink of wine, before she said, 'Okay, I will.'

'I knew you would. That's why you came to my office.'

'What did you tell Nick that he was able to use?'

'Follow the money,' Bridget said.

'That's what Nick said.'

'It's always the key,' Bridget said. 'Pippa was going to out him. Give her half of what he owned or she'd talk. And she meant half of everything, not just what he told Parliament and the taxman, because he had assets abroad, hidden away. If he didn't pay up, she was going to destroy him.'

'And he didn't want to pay up, I'm guessing.'

'The greedy ones never do.'

Jessica eyed her carefully. 'Pippa was more than just a client, wasn't she?'

'Why do you say that?'

'You make out that it's only about the hourly rates, but you're taking risks when you're no longer getting paid.'

'I'll tell you another time. Don't worry though, you're not my type. Too young. Too hetero.'

Jessica blushed. 'Okay, what do I need to know?'

'Nevis,' Bridget said. 'And Geneva. That's where he would take her, but he would disappear for a few hours, saying he had business to attend to.'

'Nick mentioned the Caribbean, and there was a picture of Pippa and him on a Caribbean island in his study.'

'Did you look at it? Any clues?'

'There were papers stuffed in the back of the frame.'

Bridget's eyes widened. 'Did you take them?'

'No, I put them back.' When Bridget grimaced, Jessica added, 'I took pictures though.'

'Show me.'

Jessica reached into her bag for her phone and scrolled through her pictures folder. 'There,' she said, and handed it over.

Bridget dug some glasses out of a case, platinum glinting from the arms, and peered closer, her fingers pinching the picture to make the detail larger.

A grin spread across her face. 'You are a fucking genius.'

Twenty-Four

Amy stood behind the custody sergeant as he unlocked the cell door.

'Has he slept it off?'

'He's been quiet all day,' he said. 'The clock's still ticking though.' As he opened the door, he blocked her way in and asked, 'Are you sure about this?'

'It's a welfare chat about a motoring case. He crashed into a police car.'

'We both know that's not what it's about,' he said. 'I've heard the chatter, that he's a suspect in the murder case.'

'He hasn't been arrested for murder.'

'Not yet.'

'So, it's not a problem then. Until he is, he's here for a motoring case.'

The sergeant faltered, before saying, 'You've got twenty-four hours, no more. You won't get the extra hours in a motoring case.'

'And in the morning, when he's had time to think things through, we'll have a talk. This is just to check if he's fit for interview.'

The sergeant scowled, but stood aside so she could enter.

The door closed behind her with a clang.

The cell felt cold. Nick Cassidy was sprawled on the concrete stack that doubled as a bed, a blue police blanket over him. The light was low, reliant only on a row of opaque glass bricks just under the ceiling, although they were at pavement level outside. She wrinkled her nose at the stench of vomit, with a pool on the floor and more on the blanket.

'Mr Cassidy.'

He didn't respond.

She nudged his leg with her foot. 'Mr Cassidy, wake up please.'

He groaned and shuffled onto his side, before grimacing and throwing his blanket to the floor.

Amy folded her arms. 'Take some deep breaths and sit up.'

He waved her away before swinging his legs to the floor.

'Be careful where you put your feet.'

He looked down and groaned. 'I had a bad day.'

'You wanted to see me.'

'You came looking for me,' he said. 'I wanted to know what you had to say.'

'You mentioned Tammy Trenton when you came in, so I spoke to her. She said you were chasing her about a Spencer Everett story.'

He dropped his head and groaned. 'Shit.'

'Yeah, that's how she thinks of you too. It's been twenty years since her daughter went missing, and she thought you had something to offer. That's not why I was looking for you though.'

'Oh, I can guess that, I'm not stupid. I met a woman, then she was killed a few hours later. It doesn't look good.'

'So, why did you run? It made us wonder about you.'

'Because Sarah was murdered. I was scared.'

'Bullshit. I told you I was the police.'

'And you'd already called me and told me you were coming for me.'

Amy was confused. 'No, I didn't.'

'Someone did.'

'Did you get a name?'

'Just a man, but he said he was police. Told me he would find me, but he sounded threatening, then you arrived. I panicked.'

'You've sought me out though.'

'It's complicated. But it wasn't me. I never left that hotel. You can do checks.'

'Talk to me then, Nick. What do you want to tell me?'

'About Tammy or Sarah?'

'Sarah Marsh's murder is the one I'm investigating. What's the connection between your story and Sarah Marsh?'

'I'm wondering whether it's a wise thing to do, to talk to you.'

'Wise?'

He put his head back against the cold tiles. 'Sarah is dead. When I saw her, she wasn't. How big a hint do I need?'

Amy stepped forward, despite the stench coming from him. 'You said you could trust me. Now's the time.'

He closed his eyes. 'Am I safe in here?'

'You're in a cell. They're built to stop people getting in or out without a key, and there are cameras everywhere. I reckon you'll be fine. If you've got information, talk to me.'

They were interrupted by the unlocking of the cell door. When she turned, Mickey Higham was standing there, his hands on his hips. 'What the fuck are you doing? Get out of there, now.'

Amy held her hand up to Nick to let him know that she'd be back in a moment, but when she left the cell, the custody sergeant reached behind her to pull the door closed, the key turning with a clank.

'She told me it would be okay,' the sergeant said. 'Have a go at her, not me,' and he set off walking.

Amy folded her arms. 'Cassidy wanted to talk to me. That's why he's here.'

'He's a suspect in a murder case,' he said, stepping closer.

'Not yet.'

'Just because we haven't arrested him yet for the murder doesn't mean he isn't a line of enquiry, so you going in there could fuck everything up. You'll be accused of applying pressure, or anything some defence barrister can think up.'

'It wasn't like that. I was just seeing what he wanted.'

'It was exactly like that. Go back to what you were doing before, and I don't want to see you in this cell complex again until the killer has been charged.'

She wondered whether she should protest more, but the glare in Mickey's eyes told her to leave it.

As she walked back along the corridor, to be buzzed out by the custody sergeant, she realised she needed a break.

Twenty-Five

Charlie found a table in the corner of the pub, *The City Arms*, an old Manchester stalwart, shelves crammed with bottles of spirits and beer pumps standing to attention. The place smelled of years of spilled ale, the atmosphere dark, with tables varnished black and peppered by beermats.

It was Charlie's favourite pub, where solicitors, barristers and accountants rubbed shoulders with labourers and shop-workers. What brought them there wasn't prestige or style. There was no chrome, or twinkling lights or large windows. It was a taste of how city centre pubs used to be.

Eleanor followed him, carrying two glasses filled with amber beer, foam spilling over the side.

As she set them down with a clatter, she said, 'I can't make it a late one.'

'Got other plans?'

'It's midweek, Charlie. I can't recover like I used to do. You should go to bed early too. You look like shit.'

He took a sip and raised his glass. 'As ever, my champion.'

'I mean it. You're a good-looking guy, but you look like you're not eating properly. Your shirt is too slack around the neck, and I don't think you have an iron. You've got to get a grip of your life. If you can't, your work will suffer, and that affects me. My job. My prospects. I didn't start working for the defence to babysit you.'

Charlie took a drink and the beer flowed through him like relief. 'I'm going to find somewhere to live, I promise, but there's something I'm going to do first.'

'You have to run a business, that's what.'

When Charlie didn't answer, she said, 'Go on, tell me.'

'I'm going to look into Gerard's secret.'

'You're what?'

'You heard. He sought my help and I rebuffed him. Now, he's dead, and it's troubling me. Yeah, guess what, a lawyer with a conscience.'

'You rebuffed him because you're a lawyer, and he didn't have a legal problem.'

'Ah, but that's changed. Now, I am the executor of his will, and it is my duty to find out more.'

Eleanor put her drink down. 'Hang on, cowboy. Your job is to cash in his estate, then distribute it to the beneficiaries, to share out the sweetie jar. You haven't been appointed as his personal detective.'

'I feel responsible, that's all.'

'You're not. Get over it.'

'Okay, maybe I'm doing it for me. I want to feel good about something, be engaged by it. And like you said, I can bill the estate.'

'You can't bill the estate for digging into his life.'

'Are you sure about that? Won't his family want to know about his death? He might have had life insurance, and it won't pay out if he killed himself. What's the worst that could happen? They object to my fees and ask for them to be reduced? Fine, I'll reduce them. It'll still pay better than waiting for a call from a police station.'

'Okay, where are you going to start?'

He pulled out the photograph he'd found in the envelope in Gerard's house. He slammed it on the table. 'Here.'

Eleanor stared down at the photograph, then back at Charlie. 'Why?'

'Because he kept it, and wrote on the back *My last moment of true happiness*. Why did he write that? And why on the back of that picture? The letters are recent, but the photograph isn't, yet he kept them together. There has to be a connection.'

'How are you going to look into it?'

'Tomorrow, I go to where the story began.' He raised his glass. 'Oxford University.'

Twenty-Six

Amy's sleep had been unsettled, memories of Tammy Trenton's anguish coming back to her. Morning had brought some resolve to find out more.

Amy's mother was in the kitchen when she arrived, still in her dressing gown, cradling a mug of tea, her wake-up drink.

'Hello, love,' she said. 'This is an early visit.'

'I've always preferred the mornings,' Amy said, then kissed her mother on the cheek. 'Where's Dad?'

'At the back. He's been brooding since that woman was found on the beach. Tossing and turning all night, so he got up to watch the morning grow.' She pulled a face. 'He misses the job, wants to take charge, tell everyone what they're doing wrong.'

'Cops never retire. They just stop working the shifts.' She went towards the back door, where her father was visible in the garden.

They no longer lived in the house she was brought up in, which had been a spacious newbuild on the edge of Cookstown, with neat lawns, driveways, new cars everywhere, the suburban dream. Rapid promotion had bought him a redbrick character house in a small village of honeysuckle a few miles from Cookstown, with two inns, a square-spired Norman church, and a red phone-box, missing only a village green for the complete set. In winter, it resembled something off a Christmas card, with snow on the neat red roofs and tiny wooden doorways.

She ducked under a rose-framed wooden arch and along the path at the side of the house, to a deck that was in the shade of a hazel tree, twisted branches pointing to the sky.

He was sitting in a chair, a steaming mug in his hand, gazing over the lawn that stretched towards a patio and a barbecue set. The once strong man had sunk over the years, lost some weight, and acquired spidery red lines across his cheeks. That was the way with age, she supposed. Being a detective had given him a purpose, a status even. Being retired just gave him time to think.

He glanced up as Amy came onto the deck.

'Hey, it's my little girl,' he said, and smiled as he raised his mug. The smile didn't flash as quick as it used to. 'There might be tea in the pot, if you want one.'

'I'll get myself a coffee near the harbour,' she said, and kissed him on the top of his head.

'How is it down at the station? I've seen the news.'

'You know just how it is, then.'

'No suspects? No leads?'

'You're a civilian now, I can't talk about the case. I just wanted to see how my old Dad is getting on.'

He narrowed his eyes. 'I know you well enough that you don't just call by.'

'You're too suspicious.'

'Being a detective gave me a good nose for bullshit. Come on then, spill the beans. What's going on? Got a boyfriend? Got a promotion?'

She shook her head. 'None of that. What have you been doing with yourself?'

He leaned back in his chair, closing his eyes for a moment before saying, 'Oh, the usual, you know me. Golf and a few beers, and keeping out from under your Mum's feet. I should go down to the station, see how the boys are doing. Has the Major Crime Unit taken over yet?' He waved his hand. 'They thought they were above us, but I don't think they ever got how it is in Cookstown.'

She leaned against a decking post as she listened.

She'd heard most of his stories before. That was always the way with cops, that they play on repeat all the time, but she enjoyed the spark the memories gave him. 'Never go back, that's what you said when you retired.'

'Six years, that's all it's been. Do you know what the hard part is?'

'Filling the day?'

'I can do that easily.' He took a swig of his tea. 'It's just that none of it means anything in the end.'

'I don't understand.'

'I was a senior detective, and for a while I was someone around here. Now, I'm just another old man sitting in his garden. Like it doesn't matter what I did before.'

'Don't be all melancholy. You've got too much time on your hands.'

He smiled and reached across to pat her hand.

He'd never been a man of words, so she had always recognised his love from the little things. The ruffle of her hair. The smile that beamed warmth. The pat of her hand.

She sat on a painted wicker chair opposite, which creaked as she relaxed. 'I spoke to Tammy Trenton yesterday.'

He scowled and clenched his jaw. 'What did she want?'

'Her daughter went missing, and she wants to know what happened to her.'

'What was special about yesterday? It's usually an anniversary or something, but I don't think it's one of those.'

'Another murder. Tammy is angry that it gets all the attention, because the victim was an architect, and Natasha's case doesn't.'

'She got a lot of attention.' His brow furrowed. 'Does she think that a dead architect shouldn't have attention paid to her? Her daughter wasn't found, and we can't do much about that, but there is a murderer running free. What are they saying? The husband? It's always the husband when it's a woman like that.'

'Why with a *woman like that*?'

'I don't like to generalise.'

'But you'll do it anyway.'

He held up his hand. 'Murdered women are either killed by their partners or they live dangerous lifestyles, like prostitutes, because they work in places where people have learned to look the other way. But an architect? Husband or lover every time.'

'Or jealousy, perhaps, from someone who has less money than Sarah had?'

'That inspires burglars, not killers. But hey, you don't want a retired old copper like me telling you how to do it.'

'Yeah, something like that.'

'I just like talking about the job. You won't know what it's like until you retire, but all you're doing now that gets you down, like the long hours or bad shifts or the sights you see?' He smiled. 'You'll miss them all in the end. So, come on, tell me. You got any good leads? Give me a hint.'

'No way. You and your friends like your stories, and I'm not saying anything just so you can spill it over a gin.'

'You must have something though. They all make a mistake. Any forensics or leads, like people seeing him dump the body?'

'I can't tell you that, you're retired.'

'But I've got expertise. There might be something you've missed. I can help, but you can take the credit.'

'There's nothing to tell you. As far as we know, no forensics.'

He took another drink from his mug.

'If you want to help, there is one thing,' Amy said. 'Natasha Trenton.'

'She's too long gone to be found now.'

'Yesterday, I looked Tammy in the eyes and I saw hurt and anger, a woman who pines for her child. The next time I see her, I want to know that we did enough, that it isn't one of those cases that we got wrong because her family meant that her face didn't fit.'

'Is that what you're looking into?'

'Not officially. But I might have a sniff around.'

Her father shifted in his chair, so that he was facing her. 'Don't. You're wasting your time, and if Tammy thinks you're helping, she won't leave you alone.'

'But did we do enough?'

'We did everything we could. What else does she expect us to do? You know the story.'

'Give me your version, not the official one.'

'It's the same. Natasha was working for the Bufords over the summer, helping out, maid-type of work, and one night she worked late. She finished her shift and slipped away. Her home was around five miles away, all country roads. She never made it. We spoke to everyone at the house, and no one saw anything. There were no cameras on her drive home. Her car turned up, but nothing else, and you'll get no thanks for chasing dead leads on a case that is twenty years old.'

'You haven't mentioned Truman Buford.'

'He was an idiot, the family shame. You know, with some people it doesn't matter how much you have, if you're an idiot, you're an idiot. Rather than doing something useful, he was stoned all the time. But I'll tell you what I think, and it's this. She was a pretty girl and he was fixated on her, maybe romanticised some of that *wrong side of the tracks* stuff, the way some rich kids do. Perhaps he saw her when she left the Buford house, persuaded her to give him a lift into town, so he could score drugs, or hang out with his deadbeat friends. He tried it on, she fought him off, but he couldn't take no for an answer. So, he lost it. Killed her and buried her.'

'Was he that callous?'

'Just an idiot. But he must have had some humanity, because he told his father what he'd done, and he told us.'

'Was he telling the truth?'

'There were no forensics, and Truman didn't even remember saying it. He couldn't tell us what he'd done with her or where, so all we had was a stoned confession to his father that we couldn't corroborate. Somehow, news of his confession got leaked. Before we knew it, everyone thought he did it, which sent him worse, because wherever he went people thought he'd killed her, all because his father tried to do the right thing. We used to find him in a right mess, stoned or drunk, his car crashed. Let me tell you what I always say about drugs.'

'I know it, I've heard it so much.'

'And I'll keep repeating it. Drugs send you to one of three places: the gutter, prison, or the grave. Truman Buford's family was too rich to let him go to the gutter, but drugs took him to prison in the end. Once he was there, he didn't stand a chance. Junkie or not, he was a rich kid in a jail full of bad people. I'm not saying he deserved to be killed in there, but his life was going one way. That's just how it is.'

'What alternative theories were there?'

He shuffled in his chair. 'Did she just want to get away from Cookstown, and couldn't stand one more night with the Trentons? Just as possible. Was she was working to build up an escape fund, because who'd want to be surrounded by the Trentons, drinking and stealing and whatever else they got up to? And she was a pretty girl, and they were bad people, so I don't want to even consider what they might have done to her when she was growing up. Tammy is grieving, but how much did Natasha trust her to help her?' He held out his hands. 'Either Truman put her in the ground, or she ran away. Take your pick.'

Amy considered her father, and saw what others had always seen in him: an honest man who'd once been in charge of the Cookstown Police. Trusted.

She smiled. 'Thank you.'

Twenty-Seven

Charlie parked away from the city centre in Oxford.

The drive had been long, more than three hours of motorway drudgery and speed cameras, and he'd hit a slow-moving queue, the city not built to cope with twenty-first century traffic. Just wanting out of his car, he found somewhere to park close to the river, and realised that he could have a quiet stroll before he found where he needed to be.

It was more of the Oxford he expected. The glass cubes of the university boathouses, teams of rowers gliding along the Thames, the oars moving in smooth metronomic fashion, hypnotic swishes as they broke the still water. Oak and willow trees lined the footpath, which he shared with cyclists who went too fast, rucksacks slung over their backs. Canal boats were moored as he got nearer the centre, but these weren't quaint river cruisers. They were homes for those people who'd chosen to live on the water, with paint that was faded and cracked, the windows covered in lichen, gas bottles strapped to the top, men and women in pale dreadlocks and tie-dye making idle chat.

A brief stint along the Oxford streets ended when Charlie diverted through the gardens and gothic splendour of Christ Church College.

The city retreated. In the distance, cattle grazed. Red ivy climbed the walls. Lavender bloomed around the old chapel. Groups of tourists clamoured to take photographs as students and lecturers swaggered through them.

This was the Oxford he expected. Academic splendour. History and beauty.

He stopped by an information board and felt his own education pale in comparison. Thirteen Prime Ministers had come through Christ Church College. Lewis Carroll lectured there. James the First hid there when he was on the run from Cromwell's army. Success breeds success.

This was a whole different world, certainly a different one to his own.

Charlie's education had been at his local comprehensive in a town thirty miles north of Manchester. When he chose Manchester University, it seemed the best of both worlds: far enough away so he had to leave home, but near enough to go back when he had clothes to wash, or needed a good meal.

As he stepped away, he wondered why he'd never thought of applying to a place like Oxford or Cambridge. Had his own background held him back? Or had he simply allowed it to?

He smiled to himself as his memories rushed back at him.

He'd loved university. The sense that his adult adventure was just beginning, late nights with great people, and of course it was where he'd fallen in love with Isobel.

Those early days had been so special.

She'd lit up his lecture theatre the first day he saw her, both of their eyes wide as they took in the tiered seats, so different to school, Isobel in jogging pants and trainers, her long hair pulled up into a knot on her head.

She'd been one of the first people he spoke to, both of them just looking to find an ally, and for a while it was just a friendship. At least as far as she was concerned, as she had a boyfriend from her schooldays who'd gone off to Newcastle. They'd tried to keep it together for the first year, but distant love was hard to maintain, and they drifted apart.

For Charlie, it had been different. He was single when he started university, and when he met her, he ached for her straight away. He kept it quiet though, not wanting the friendship to become awkward, but it was on a drunken night out on her birthday that everything changed, when there was a mutual spark for the first time. Just a look, the way she smiled, a flirt, followed by a kiss that was more than just friends. Then, they were a couple. Inseparable through their last year, they made it through Law School together, both qualifying as solicitors in the city where they met.

He shook away the memories. He didn't want to dwell on why it went wrong, even though he had turned it over in his mind on a continual loop. Had they been too busy chasing the dream and forgotten about each other? A house in a pretty part of town they couldn't afford, places in law firms, a beautiful child? What came next? A small place in Provence? Just one big pursuit of whatever, yet all the time they had all they needed. Each other.

He took a deep breath. Those thoughts were for another time, so he walked on, towards Christ Church Meadow, longhorn cattle grazing in the distance, plane and poplar trees the backdrop, ancient oaks too, the gables and chimneys and leaded windows of Merton College beyond the rugby pitches, lined by black railings.

He quickened his pace as he strode past walled gardens, then along cobbled streets, before turning back towards the centre, more hustle and bustle ahead.

He was heading for Brasenose College, where Spencer Everett had studied, information gleaned from a quick internet search. He needed to find someone who remembered him. Maybe Gerard too.

His route took him along the High Street, a long curve that headed towards the main shopping street, the way ahead cluttered with chain-store neon and crowds.

He was still in the part of the city that housed the university colleges, all a mix of architectural styles. The neoclassical blocks and columns of Queens College opposite the Gothic Revival style of University College, with vaulted ceilings and lancet windows, each concealing lawned quads and ornate libraries and grand chapels and narrow passages and ancient living quarters, like cramped stately homes.

As he turned into the cobbles of Radcliffe Square, the concentration of tourists increased, peering through any gaps they could find to get a view of the quads, hoping for a glimpse of college life. Students hurried past, towards the Radcliffe Camera, the domed library in the middle, Venetian in style, with pillars all the way round, closed off to visitors. Members only.

Cyclists weaved their way through, although it didn't seem an ideal place for bikes, with cobbles and narrow streets and tourists dawdling everywhere.

Charlie gazed around, and found it easy to tell the students from the visitors. He enjoyed the feel of the place. There was a certain calm that didn't seem to fit with the volume of people, as if the tourists were very much aware that they were intruding on a lifestyle, the students trying to go about their studies and having to dodge cameras and tour groups.

He followed the signs and found what he was looking for, at a gateway opposite the Radcliffe Camera, tucked away in the furthest corner of the square. Brasenose College.

He was unable to walk straight in. There was a security guard in a white shirt and peaked cap standing next to a payment kiosk.

Charlie passed forward a business card. 'I'm wanting to speak to someone who worked here twenty years ago, who'd remember the students.'

The security guard planted his feet apart and examined Charlie's card. 'A solicitor? Are you hoping to sue someone? Or is some dirty old lecturer in trouble, hashtag-me-too and all that?'

'No, it's not that.'

'Because they used to be, you know, dirty. They'd invite the young women to their rooms to go over their work, and sit there in silk dressing gowns, hinting at good grades for, well, you know what.'

'I promise you, it's not about that. The university isn't in trouble, but I need to speak to whoever knew the students, who had regular contact with them.'

He scratched his forehead as he thought about that, until he said, 'That would be the Chaplain.'

'Chaplain?'

'Each college has one. It doesn't matter if you're a Christian, he's there for everyone.'

'Where will I find him?'

'Try the Chapel first. He likes spending time in there when the tourists pass through.'

'Thank you,' Charlie said, and he headed towards the sunlit quad on the other side of the gateway, a perfect lawn surrounded by latticed windows.

The guard held out his hand to stop him.

Charlie was confused. 'What's wrong?'

'You have to pay for the tour.'

'But I'm here to visit someone, not for the tour.'

'Still got to pay.'

Charlie fumbled in his pocket for change and handed over the money to an old man in the kiosk.

The Brasenose Chapel was in the next quad, another perfect patch of lawn with a cobbled edge, overlooked by the cloistered rooms and offices of the college. Wooden benches were spaced out around the quad, occupied by students chatting, with files tucked under their arms or clutching rucksacks. That was part of the student life that he'd loved, having the time to be carefree, the real world held back.

The chapel dominated the quad, with a peaked roof and stained-glass windows, the entrance through a narrow stone arch and into the hush of an old church. Oak panels lined the walls and oak pews ran the length, facing inwards rather than forward, towards a brass eagle mounted in the centre of the black and white tiles, laid in a diamond formation.

A man was sitting in a pew, dog-collared, his arms resting on the pew in front of him. The sunlight beamed in through the windows and made his pate shine.

Charlie approached. 'Are you the Chaplain?'

He turned at the question and smiled, his eyes old and kind. There were wisps of white hair around his ears. 'Call me Jeremy. How can I help? Do you want to know about the church?'

'I wish I could ask more,' Charlie said, looking around. 'It's beautiful, restful, but no, I'm here for something else.' He pulled out the photograph. 'I want to find out more about these people,' and he passed it over.

The Chaplain took it from him and reached into his jacket pocket for some reading glasses with smudged lenses, one of the nose-guards missing, so that it made a red dent in one side of his nose. As he peered at it, his eyes lost some of their kindness.

He passed it back. 'How can I help?'

'Do you know the people in it?'

'We all know one of them. Spencer Everett. Politician on the rise.'

'Can you remember what he was like when he was here?'

'Not really. I know the ones who speak to me and seek my counsel, and the lost souls needing help. Those who think they can carve their own path don't need me. I know he was one of the rowdy ones. Never saw him at church, but I knew of his reputation.'

'What about the others?'

'People like Spencer attract followers. Seems like he still does. If it's Spencer you want to know about, you need to speak to one of his old professors. Professor Martin.'

'Why him?'

'Her. Professor Sheila Martin. She wasn't a fan of his rowdy crowd back then, and she lets us all know what she thinks of him now. She'll be able to tell you what you want to know.'

'Where will I find her?'

The Chaplain checked his watch and his smile returned. 'The Turf Tavern. She enjoys her lunches there. If you catch her now, she'll talk. If you leave it, she'll be sleeping off her lunch and you won't see her until later.'

Charlie thanked him and turned to leave, but stopped when the Chaplain said, 'What's your interest in him?'

'One of the other people in the photograph was my client, and he died unexpectedly. I'm trying to find out why.'

The Chaplain paled. 'How did he die?'

'The police think suicide. Found in the woods behind his house, hanging from a tree.'

'And you think differently?'

Charlie shrugged. 'I'm not ruling it out.'

The Chaplain hung his head for a few seconds before letting out a long breath. 'Which one?'

Charlie took out the photograph once more and held it out, pointing it at Gerard. 'On the left.'

The Chaplain put his head in his hands.

Charlie stepped closer. 'What's wrong?'

The Chaplain mumbled something to himself before sitting up and saying, 'He came to see me. About a month ago. He was troubled.'

'Did he say why?'

'I knew what it was about, because he'd confided in me all those years ago, but he told me in confidence, and that's how it remains.'

'Why now though, after all these years?'

'It would involve telling the same secrets, and I am not only a man of the cloth, but also a man of my word. I'm sorry. I wish you well in your quest, and you should carry on. It's the right thing to do.' He smiled. 'As a man of God, I can provide you with some answers, but for the ones you seek, you'll have to look elsewhere.'

Twenty-Eight

The other people around her paid no attention as Amy moved the collection of cups that had gathered on her desk, despite the loud bangs and clatters.

The kitchen was further along the corridor, but Amy's desk was the closest one to the door, so it had been used as a dumping ground.

'I'm no maid, guys,' she said, as she put them onto a tray, although no one acknowledged her. She moved them onto another desk and logged on to her computer.

Something occurred to her. She called the custody office.

When a tired-sounding sergeant answered, she asked, 'Has Nick Cassidy been charged with the driving job yet? It's getting near twenty-four hours now.'

There was the tapping of some keys. 'They took some blood and released him a few hours ago.'

'Did anyone speak to him about the murder?'

'Not that I can see.'

She thanked him and sat back. She could get Cassidy's address, but she'd been hoping to speak to him before then, to find out what he wanted to tell her, why he felt in danger.

Nick Cassidy would have to wait, because the Natasha Trenton case was still itching her.

She opened her drawer. The Natasha Trenton file was in there. She'd resolved to ignore it after speaking to her father, but ignoring things had never been one of her strengths. She didn't know if it was the emotion in Tammy's voice that still lingered, or whether it was just her innate desire to solve puzzles.

As she glanced up, everyone else seemed pre-occupied. No one would ask her what she was looking at.

She opened Natasha's file.

What she noticed first was the dryness of the paper, yellowed on some edges. It magnified the tragedy. Natasha had faded into history.

Maybe Tammy had a point.

There were witness statements and police reports. Some from names she knew, cops who had been drinking buddies of her father. Some dead, some retired. There were other statements from much younger cops but who had aged themselves, their words from twenty years earlier locked on paper, even if time had left its own mark on most of them.

The call to the police had come from Tammy the next day, when she realised that Natasha hadn't come home and wasn't just sleeping off a late night.

Amy's mind drifted to the Bufords' house, a sprawling place just outside of Cookstown.

She'd driven past it many times, and when she was a young girl she would peer along the curved driveway to the mansion at the end. Dark red brick, with two wings at each side, an archway in the centre leading to a courtyard beyond. There was a field at one side, where Amy had dreamed of riding horses, playing at being the rich man's daughter, hair streaming down her back as she galloped on some splendid Arabian stallion.

It was as close as she'd got. Whenever her father had driven past, the curve of the driveway made her view of the house nothing more than a glimpse, a snapshot of another life.

As she read the file, she saw that there'd been no answer at the Buford house when the police first arrived, but it turned out that everyone was saying goodbye to some visitors they'd had. When they were able to talk, the Bufords told detectives that Natasha had been working the night of her disappearance, later than normal, then set off home. They weren't aware of anyone following her or threatening her.

The enquiry didn't get anywhere.

Natasha's car was found on the Baptist estate, just a cluster of narrow streets with a reputation for drunken fights and not talking to the police, a dumping ground for the families who get evicted from everywhere else. Her family didn't know why she'd be near the Baptist estate, but what eighteen-year-old tells their parents what they do in their spare time?

The lead detective kept on going back to the Bufords, speaking to other staff, until they complained and he got moved.

It was a witness statement in the middle of the file that caught her attention.

It was a report from a young constable who had spoken to Clarence Buford, and been told of a confession from his eldest son, Truman. The old man was shaken, distraught, but said that telling police was the right thing to do.

Truman had told his father that he might have killed Natasha, how he was stumbling back from a party, stoned, when she pulled over to give him a lift. During the journey, he must have grabbed at her or something, maybe misread things, and after that it was all a blur. He can't remember what happened afterwards, or where she went.

The Crown Prosecution Service wouldn't touch it. The confession was made when Truman was high, and there was nothing to back it up. Truman couldn't even remember making the confession, but it got leaked somehow and he went further downhill.

When he went to jail, for drink-driving and a crash that put someone in a wheelchair, he was a man who'd got away with murdering a woman because he was a rich man's son. A knife in the dining hall ended Truman's life, on a day when everyone seemed to be looking the other way.

She closed the file and stared through the doorway, at the man prowling in the opposite room. Mickey Higham.

He must have spotted her looking, because he wandered over.

'Amy, glad you're here,' he said. 'Can you do the trawl for CCTV, see what you can find.' He glanced down at the file she was reading. His cheeks flushed. 'Why have you got that file. It's a waste of time.'

'Tammy Trenton came by yesterday, angry that the rich woman gets all the attention. I wanted to satisfy myself that we hadn't missed something.'

'Forget it. It's an old mystery and we've got something more urgent on our hands. If you start jumping every time some local …' He paused and sighed. 'Well, some noisy local speaks up, then the whole job goes to shit.'

Amy thought about telling Mickey that Nick Cassidy had been talking to Tammy, but decided not to, for now. 'Just some neighbourhood PR,' she said, instead.

'End it. There's nothing to see. Natasha ran. Tammy can't deal with it, sees herself as the victim, so she makes it someone else's fault. It's bullshit.'

As he made his way back to his room, she looked again at the statement she'd been reading, the one that had made her look up and across the room.

It wasn't the contents of the statement that had surprised her, she knew the story, but the name at the top.

The statement about Truman Buford's confession had been made to a young police constable.

Police Constable Mickey Higham.

Twenty-Nine

Charlie's mind raced as he made his way to the Turf Tavern, a mapping app open on his phone, wondering what Gerard had told the Chaplain.

He ducked down a narrow passage, one-person wide, and the sunlight disappeared, until he emerged into a dank courtyard outside a tiny white pub, the entrance like a wooden lean-to painted dark green. There were tables outside, filled with a mix of students and locals, enjoying the slivers of sunshine that found its way in there.

Inside, the pub was illuminated by dim caged bulbs and divided into a succession of tiny rooms, all with low beams and separated by doorways that required most people to duck their heads.

Charlie approached the bar. 'I'm looking for Professor Sheila Martin. Do you know her?'

The barman clutched the hand pumps as if protecting them. 'Do you want a drink or not?'

Charlie scanned the pump labels before pointing to one. 'A pint of that,' he said, just for the sake of making a selection.

A group of men talked loudly in one corner, one of them complaining that a friend didn't take his shooting seriously enough, his voice rich and booming, all the time sweeping his long fringe away from his eyes. A couple made their way through the pub in clothes with ill-matching colour schemes, the man in mustard corduroys that weren't long enough to meet his brogues, topped off by a pink shirt. The woman styled a green jumper with bright red trousers that hugged her figure.

It wasn't the clothes that Charlie noticed, but the way that the people wore them, as if they didn't care what anyone thought of them. They had a confidence that came from money, and Charlie realised how different it all was from the north. It wasn't just about geography though. It was about the people, their backgrounds. It felt like a different country.

As the barman plonked the beer in front of him, he said, 'She sits through there, by the window,' and he indicated with a nod of his head that she was through a low doorway.

Charlie thanked him and ducked as he went through, into a part of the pub that had tables pressed against bare stone walls and lit by low-hanging lights. Students craned inwards, engaged in lively conversations.

In a seat, alone, was a woman, pushing seventy he reckoned, her hair long, straight and grey, in a baggy purple jumper and long patterned skirt, leather sandals on her feet. She raised her wine glass at Charlie, almost empty, and smiled.

'Professor Martin?'

'The Chaplain told me you were on your way. My consultation fee is that you fill this. Anything dry and white will do.'

Charlie decided he liked her as he went back to the bar. When he returned with a large glass of white, she asked, 'A local, or just passing through?'

'First time.'

'And how are you finding Oxford?'

Charlie recognised traces of the north in her accent.

'A lot of rich, ruddy faces,' he said. 'No one looks like they've struggled in life.'

'And by the sound of you, we are both escapees from the north,' and she clinked her glass against his. 'You've paid your fee. What can I do for you?'

'Spencer Everett,' he said, which made her lip curl.

'The Chaplain mentioned his name.'

'I want to know more about his time here.'

'Why?'

Charlie reached into his inside pocket and produced the photograph. He slid it over to her.

As she put on glasses she'd retrieved from the coat hanging on the back of the chair, Charlie said, 'I'm a solicitor. The man on the left, Gerard, was my client. He had a beef about Spencer, said there was a dark secret that he was pressing Spencer to reveal.'

'Did he tell you the secret?'

'No, but Gerard has died, possibly murdered, found hanging from a branch. If he was killed, it was because he was going to go public with what he knew.'

'That's quite a thing to say.' She pushed the picture back across the table. 'You'll end up being sued. Or worse, by the sounds of it. These are rich and powerful people, so I'd rather stay out of it.'

'I'm after proof, not allies,' Charlie said. 'If I can prove that he was murdered, and I can find out what he knew, I'll go public with the facts, but not the source.'

She shook her head. 'I don't know his secrets, if you mean anything worth publishing, that is. He's a former student, nothing more.'

'But you remember him. I have to start somewhere. Tell me about the people in the picture. The Chaplain said you might remember them from back then.'

'Well, yes, things were different. There weren't as many students as there are now, so you got to know them, socialised with them even, although that did sometimes lead to problems.' Her eyes darkened.

'Problems?'

'Seedy, single old men surrounded by young women eager for their approval. But all they wanted was guidance, help, decent marks. The lecturers and professors wanted to give it, but expected blowjobs in return.' She raised her hands. 'Sorry for being blunt, but that's how it was. Just imagine that you're a young woman who is bright and intelligent, a good future ahead, and you realise that the only reason you're getting help is because some old tosser wants to see you naked. It ruined them, and the old guys got away with it.' She smiled. 'Not now though.'

'Is that the main way in which it's different?'

'It's the numbers. Now, it's a sea of faces, none of them standing out, just too many of them. But that's why I remember Spencer, because it was a smaller crowd. I remember Gerard too. He was one of Spencer's hangers-on. And that's what he had, hangers-on.'

'How do you mean?'

She leaned in. 'Let me tell you about Spencer Everett, and those like him. Rich and spoilt, brought up on entitlement, and acted like he thought all others were beneath him. This place is full of people like him. Private school, careers planned out. That down to earth thing he's got going on now, man of the people, holding babies at election time, shirt sleeves rolled up, man of action? It's an act, a con. When he arrived, he thought he was special, because he'd spent his whole life being told how wonderful he was, so he swanned into my lecture like he was there to be admired, with his hair flowing and his teeth gleaming.' Some light returned to her eyes. 'He got a shock.'

'Let me guess,' Charlie said. 'He went to university thinking he was the clever one, but when he got there, everyone was clever. That's how universities are, and he was no big deal.'

'Exactly,' she said. 'He dealt with it by exaggerating his background, turned himself into a character from *Brideshead Revisited*, with a long scarf and the arrogance that comes from breeding and money. And, of course, the trashing thing.'

'Trashing?'

'Taking over restaurants and making a mess of the place. Not quite up there with the Bullingdon set, because they were in a league of their own, and what a set of arrogant arseholes they were. A Bullingdon-lite, shall we say, where he and his hangers-on would treat the staff like dirt and throw food around, all in the name of wild living, and leave a tip large enough to make them forget about it. He wanted to be a hellraiser, but all I saw was someone who turned up hungover to lectures and struggled to do well.'

'He's doing okay now. Member of Parliament, Home Secretary, his star on the rise. People are already talking about Number 10.'

'People like Spencer always land on their feet. It's just how it is.' She took a sip as she thought back. 'Let me qualify this, though. He buckled down in his final year, so perhaps I'm being unfair. He was young and stupid, and we've all been that. In the end, he got serious and did okay.'

'And Gerard?'

'He was quieter, just got swept along by Spencer.' She frowned. 'Didn't he tell you what he knew?'

'No, but he was close to doing that. It troubled him, whatever it was, and he'd been in touch with Everett, letting him know that he was about to go public. And now, Gerard is dead.' He scowled. 'Not dead. Silenced.'

He passed the picture back over. 'Look at the reverse,' he said. '*My last moment of true happiness*. It must mean something, and specific to that picture. Do you know the other people in it?'

She peered closer, screwed up her eyes as she cast her mind back. 'The man in the middle. Another northern boy, farmer-type, and he was going places. Something Buxford or Bedford.' She pulled at her lip. 'No, Buford, that was it. Lewis Buford.'

'And the others?'

She tapped a person at the opposite edge of the group to Gerard. 'I'm surprised you haven't asked about him. The one on the right.'

'What about him?'

'He killed himself too. Or so the police say.'

Charlie felt a rush of blood, a tingle in his fingers as he held the picture. 'What? I mean, how, when?'

'His name was Ben Leech. One of the quieter ones, a thinker. He ended up as a lawyer, like most on the course, and lived somewhere not far from here. I don't know the full facts, but it sounded a lot like your chap, a suicide in the woods. Took some pills before slashing his wrists, just a couple of months ago. Tragic. Awful.'

'I didn't know that,' Charlie said, shocked. 'Gerard never said.'

'Does it change anything?'

'It changes everything.'

Thirty

Amy leaned into the car through the side window, to put the coffees into the central console. She was with Rob, the young copper who'd found Sarah Marsh on the beach, who was labelling an envelope before slipping a memory stick inside.

'You didn't have to,' Rob said, looking up as he noticed the coffee.

'You found her body,' Amy said. 'This is your reward. Now for the grunt work.'

'I just don't want to get it wrong,' Rob said. 'I've never been involved in a big investigation like this. Even bagging these video clips makes me nervous. What if I make the wrong note, and some defence lawyer rips me to bits?'

Amy climbed into the driver seat. 'If we catch the killer, the case won't turn on whether you have written up these labels the right way. But what if we collect the footage that identifies him? Think of the pride you'll feel. Remember, you didn't get it wrong when you called me in. Rely on that gut feeling. It'll get you far, and one day might even save your life.'

Rob smiled to himself as he put the envelope into the large plastic bag they'd brought with them.

'Anyway,' Amy said. 'This is Cookstown. If we mess up and let him walk free, the people around here have a way of getting their own justice.'

Rob's eyes widened. 'You can't want that, vigilante justice?'

Amy winked. 'Let's make sure we do things right first.'

As Rob grabbed his coffee, he asked, 'How many more cameras?'

Amy wiped at the windscreen, steamed up from the drinks, to get a view of outside.

They were outside a grocery shop with a beaten wooden exterior and flaking paint, made modern by a shiny plastic sign. It catered more for the locals than the tourists, staying open late for milk and bread, and those mid-evening chocolate runs.

'All the way from here to her house. Just wait until we sit down to watch them. That's when the fun starts. We'll need plenty of this,' and she raised her coffee cup.

'What if he detoured, took a long way round, knowing we'd do this trawl? Or the back streets?'

'This is why we started here. We'll get every car from the best three cameras in each direction from Sarah's house from the time the neighbour saw a car leave, until the time the call came in, because that must have been when he was leaving the beach. Get the dashcams from the squad cars too, because he might have passed them. Once we get the car, if we don't get a number plate, at least we can track where he went, and maybe at some point we get a face. Or an address.'

'I don't mean to sound unenthusiastic,' Rob said. 'It just sounds so daunting, you know, like we could miss something just because there'll be so much.'

'That's why I drafted you in. You care about getting it right. Now, we need to time the route.'

'Why?'

'Because there'll be a gap between the cameras. If we know the gap, we'll know when each car will reappear, so we'll know it's the same car. Remember, the footage might be grainy. If it doesn't re-appear, we can work out where it turned off between the cameras and get to know its route. This is how it works, slow and laborious. Do it once and its done, but what we find could break the case.'

'And if it doesn't?'

'Stops some slick defence lawyer claiming that we should have done it. No judge will criticise us for being thorough. Get your stopwatch going on your phone.'

Amy turned on the engine and drove back along the road towards Sarah Marsh's house, to time the drive between the first two cameras they'd collected footage from, an off-licence and a grocery shop, both with cameras trained over the front door, but with angles wide enough to catch the traffic. As they passed the off-licence, she shouted, 'Start timing,' then kept just below the speed limit until they returned to the grocery shop, when she shouted, 'Stop.'

Rob noted the time as Amy carried on, slowing to a crawl as they looked for any cameras on buildings. There were some businesses ahead, so they'd be knocking on more doors.

Rob was peering towards the passing doorways when he asked, 'Why do you like being a detective, murders and stuff?'

'As opposed to what?'

'A plod, like me. Or a drugs detective or whatever, you know, something more specialised.'

'What's wrong with being a murder detective?'

'I don't know, just thinking out loud. If you're a plod like me, you engage with the whole community. Old people who want to feel safe, or kids you can reach out to who are maybe going down the wrong path. If you work murder cases, all you can do is patch people up who are already damaged. You never bring peace. Just vengeance.'

'We're lucky, Rob, because we don't get many murders around here. The occasional sinking fishing boat kills more people in Cookstown than other humans, but there's no hurt like what you see in the eyes of the ones left behind. You can never make it fully right again, I know that, but bringing a killer to justice helps people to heal.'

'And those cases where the killer isn't put away?'

Amy sighed. 'It keeps on burning.'

That made her pause.

'I'm just going to make a detour,' Amy said. 'This one is off the books, okay.'

'I'm here to help and to learn.'

Amy turned off and into a road of pitted tarmac, the entrance to the Baptist estate. Cars were parked haphazardly, even though some houses had driveways. Overgrown privet fences lined the paths. Some youths loitered at the end, with low-slung pants and baseball caps, their pale faces gleaming over the blackness of their clothing.

As she drove, Amy asked, 'Do you ever get called to here?'

'Baptist? All the time.'

'Why?'

'Everything. Drinks, drugs, fights. Broken windows.'

'You said you make people feel safe. Why not here?'

'Because they never seem like they want us here. We've had our squad cars stoned, tyres slashed when we're in a house, all these young kids making gun gestures and shouting *Feds* and *Five-0*. Don't they realise how stupid they sound, that they're kids in a quiet seaside town, not some inner city?'

'If a car was abandoned around here, do you think the locals would call it in?'

Rob looked around. 'I don't know. Most people would say no chance, that it would be stripped and sold on, or the plates swapped, like it was finders-keepers.'

'Except someone did, once upon a time. Natasha Trenton's car. This is where it was found, and it was reported, because people around here aren't always how people think they are.'

'I heard about Natasha. Or I heard about her mother, Tammy. She doesn't let up. I see her in the paper all the time.'

'Her daughter went missing. I'd be the same.'

'Why are you thinking about Natasha's case?'

'Nick Cassidy met our victim, and was also in touch with Tammy, which suggests a link.'

'Why is this off the books then, if it's related?'

'Because Mickey Higham doesn't want me to look into it.'

'But you're here.'

'I don't like being side-lined.' She smiled, just to put him at ease. 'Don't worry, I'll make it my own mission. Just don't tell anyone we came down here.'

'I can do that.'

But as Amy turned her car around, ready to find some more CCTV, her mind was already fixated more on Natasha's case than Sarah's.

Thirty-One

Charlie took a drink of his latte and waited.

After he'd left the professor, a quick internet search for Ben Leech had led him to a website, *Justice for Ben*. It read like a one-woman pressure group, run by Ben's widow, as she tried to persuade the police to regard it as something other than a suicide.

Charlie had reached out to her, and he'd expected her to respond, because her website told him that she was looking for answers, except he thought she'd want to meet at her home, where she'd be in control. Her paranoia had sunk too deep for that. It had to be in public, in front of witnesses.

He was in Abingdon, a few miles south of Oxford, an ancient market town where centuries-old cottages curved towards a Norman church. An abbey dating back to Saxon times was hidden away by a river. In the centre of town, an open square faced a stone hall mounted on columns. Charlie was at a table outside a café that sold great coffee and cake, watching the traffic wind through.

Charlie put his cup down. He'd spotted her.

A woman was making her way across the square, walking a direct line, not idling, but checking around too, as if making sure she wasn't being followed, her hands thrust into her coat pockets. It had to be her.

As she got closer, Charlie stood. 'Mrs Leech?'

She flickered a smile, but wariness filled her eyes. 'Mr Steele?'

'Call me Charlie,' he said, and put out his hand to shake.

She shook, but it was fleeting. 'Call me Cathy,' and she took a seat opposite.

There were dark rings under her eyes and a red tinge to her cheeks. Her collar was up on her coat, so that she seemed to sink into it when she sat down. Perhaps that was the intention.

'You said you're a solicitor, like Ben?'

'Yes, but I didn't know your husband. I work in Manchester.'

'But you said you might have some information for me. How do I know you're bona fide, that you haven't been sent to warn me off?'

Charlie pulled out his wallet and passed it to her. Her hand trembled as she took it. 'All my ID is in there. Driving licence. Business cards. Bank cards.'

She stared at the wallet. 'So, I can prove who you are, but that doesn't mean I know your motives.'

Charlie reached into his inside pocket and produced the photograph. He slid it across the table. 'Your husband is in that picture,' he said, then tapped on Gerard. 'That man was found dead in the woods behind his own home, presumed to be suicide. Gerard Williams. He was my client.'

Her hand went to her mouth, her eyes wide. Tears began to run down her cheeks, her chin trembling. 'Dead in the woods?'

Charlie nodded.

She looked at the photograph again. 'Ben looks so young,' she said, before picking it up and examining it more closely. 'I just don't know who to trust anymore.'

'You've got to trust someone. Why not start with me? We both want the same things.'

'Which are?'

'Answers. You want them about your husband. I want them about Gerard.'

She nodded and clenched her jaw as tears brimmed in her eyes. 'I like it here, this cafe. It's a nice place to sit and take everything in. Ben and I would come here on Sunday mornings and walk along the river. We met at Oxford, when Ben was in his final year, and we just stayed around.'

'It's a pretty village.'

She pulled a cigarette packet from her coat. As she lit and inhaled, blowing the smoke away from Charlie, she said, 'I know, a doctor smoking. I tell people what to do, but I'm not so good at it myself. Right now though, I don't care.' She held up the cigarette, her fingers trembling. 'I need this.'

'Don't let them win,' Charlie said. 'Whoever is behind this, they took your husband. They took my client. Don't let them take you too.'

She paused for a moment, before grinding the cigarette into the ashtray.

Charlie allowed her to take a drink before asking, 'How was Ben before he died?'

She took a deep breath before answering, 'Troubled,' she said. 'And whatever was going on inside his head, he didn't share it with me. And I shouldn't say this, but I hate him for it, because he's made me feel like this, like I just want to die one minute, then make those responsible die the next, then I hate myself for making it all about me. But I'm the one left behind without any answers. He knew the answers, but he didn't share them with me.'

'Like Gerard,' Charlie said. 'He wouldn't share what he knew, but he hid this photograph, along with letters he was writing to Spencer Everett.' He turned the picture over. 'Look what he wrote. *My last moment of true happiness.*'

She examined the photograph again. 'Ben looks brighter here than when I first met him. He was always a serious person. I took it upon myself to bring his fun back. And I did. We were happy.'

'Did he ever talk to you about Spencer Everett?'

'Not really. Ben knew him, and he changed whenever Spencer came on television. I asked him once, what's your problem with him. He said he was just someone he used to know, but never went further.'

'But you can tell from the picture that they were good friends. I don't think the picture was taken abroad. It looks too English.'

She looked again at the picture. 'I don't know where it is. I'm sorry.'

'And he never told you what was bothering him?'

'No, and I tried to get it from him, but he kept telling me it was about work and not to worry. What about your client, Gerard?'

'Silent on it too,' Charlie said. 'But he was all angsty about it when I saw him, different to how he was normally.'

She took a sip of coffee before asking, 'Why do you say *different*?'

'Because he was agitated, wound up. I'd never seen him like that before.'

'That's just how Ben was.'

'And you don't think your husband killed himself?'

'No, I don't.'

'Why not?'

'He wasn't the type.'

'Is there one? Like you said, he was different before he died.'

Redness crept up her cheeks. 'Do not tell me that I didn't know my husband.'

'I'm sorry,' Charlie said. 'I'm not here to cause you hurt. But you must know that suicides are often hard to predict.'

'You've travelled all this way because you don't believe Gerard killed himself, and you can't have known him that well if he was just a client.'

He sat back. 'No, I suppose not.'

They both sat in silence for a while as Charlie allowed her to decide what she was going to do.

She broke the silence, tears starting again. 'I was a strong person before all of this. To you, I might look like a grieving widow, but I was someone before that. I'm a doctor. A GP.' She scoffed. 'We sound like the perfect power couple, doctor and lawyer, but that's how I know he didn't kill himself, because I'm a doctor, but no one will believe me.'

'Tell me why you're so sure?'

'Only if you promise me that you'll try to do the right thing. I created the website to build pressure, but no one takes any interest. There are times when I think of surrendering and going to join him, but I won't let them beat me.'

Charlie leaned forward and softened his tone. 'You have my word. I'm seeking the truth too.'

She studied Charlie, before setting her jaw and saying, 'Okay, I'll trust you. It started with a visit from a journalist three months earlier.'

Thirty-Two

Amy didn't hear his approach at first, until he opened the gate and it creaked on its hinges.

She was standing outside her car, gazing along the route back to Cookstown, wondering whether she was doing the right thing.

She'd left Rob at the station, told him to start logging cars from the CCTV they'd collected. She hadn't told Rob where she was going, but there was no point in two of them looking at the same computer screen. Now, she was on a quiet country road. On one side was an open field that sloped down to a stream that meandered its lazy way to the harbour. Behind her was the entrance to the Buford family home, wrought-iron gates that hung between two brick pillars.

As she turned, the man said, 'Excuse me, but you're blocking the driveway.'

His age was hard to pin down. Beyond sixty would be Amy's guess, his moustache flecked with grey, but she'd seen too much outdoor working do strange things to a man's complexion. He was dressed in blue overalls that were stained with oil, with worn dark patches on the knees. The checked shirt underneath was ragged on the collar.

'Mr Buford?'

His laugh creased his face. 'You think I look so grand? No, I'm Pete. I fix things around here, that's all.'

'Have you done that for long?'

His smile faded. 'Now you're a woman who's suddenly got a lot of questions, so I'm guessing that you're here on purpose.'

She pulled out her ID.

As he inspected it, he said, 'What's a young copper like you doing at a grand old house like this?'

'Just feeling around an old case.'

'I would have thought you'd be too busy to worry about the old stuff, with that woman turning up dead like she did.'

'I can't talk about that case, but what are people saying?'

'Just about the same as everyone else, that the husband probably did it. Isn't that always the way? But now you're asking my opinion on a new case when you said you were here for the old stuff, so I'm wondering whether you're being straight with me.'

'Sorry Pete, I don't want to come across like that.' She stepped closer, making him fold his arms, but she saw the curiosity in his eyes. Amy knew that people liked being in on a secret. 'But there is an old mystery, and you might have been here when it happened.'

He wiped his hands on his overalls. 'I don't know anything about any mysteries.'

'A young woman who worked here twenty years ago went missing. Natasha Trenton.'

'I don't know anything about that.'

'Sometimes, people don't realise how much they know. Did you work here then?'

'I've looked after this house since I left high school. My father did before me, served the Bufords through the generations.'

'You must remember her. Pretty, young, worked in the kitchen.'

'I remember the girl, bless her heart, but that doesn't mean I know anything about what happened to her.' He narrowed his eyes. 'And it's starting to feel like I'm being interrogated here.'

'I'm just fishing around, because people talk and people hear things. This is Cookstown, where everyone knows everyone else's business.'

'Well, I don't know any more than you do. As far as I know, she left town and never came back. And people do that around here. There isn't so much for the young ones, and the bright lights catch their wandering eyes.'

'Bright lights? London? Is that where people think she went?'

'Hell, I don't know. The ones who head to London go with a head full of dreams, but London isn't for everyone. Some of them just want the dirty big city, and there's plenty of those. Leeds, Manchester, you take your pick. Places big enough to get lost in, if that's your fancy. But you didn't know who I was, so I'm guessing you're not here to see me.'

'Mr or Mrs Buford, if possible.'

He checked his watch. 'Mrs Buford is probably indisposed right now, but I can ring ahead for you.'

'I'd like that.'

'Don't expect a yes, though. The old man isn't so keen on visitors these days.'

He went to a chrome plate embedded into the brick pillar and pressed a button. When it was answered with a curt, 'yes,' he said, 'There's a detective here to see you, Mr Buford, about that young Natasha who went missing all those years ago.'

A pause, then, 'Detective? Which one?'

Pete turned. 'Sorry, remind me of your name.'

'Detective Constable Gray.'

Pete repeated it into the speaker, and the reply came back, 'Jimmy Gray's daughter?'

Amy nodded her agreement.

'Seems that way, Mr Buford.'

Pete and Amy stared at the small speaker as it remained silent, until eventually the same voice said, 'Send her up.'

Pete let go of the button. 'Looks like you've got an audience.'

Amy thanked him and climbed back into her car.

As she crawled along the driveway, she was aware of Pete watching her as he closed the gates behind her.

Thirty-Three

'Who was the reporter?' Charlie asked.

Cathy Leech took out her cigarette packet again. She went to remove one, but thought better of it and put the packet on the table. 'Nick Cassidy, but I didn't know he was a journalist at first, and he frightened me. He just called at the house one day when Ben was out. I don't work Wednesdays, all of my patients know that, so I was home alone.' She flashed a brief smile. 'It was good to have a break in the middle of the week, because it kept me fresh, which made me a better doctor, except it made me easy to track. Nick Cassidy knocked on my door, and it changed everything.'

'How?'

'By giving me a message to pass on. I didn't know what it was about, but I thought it might be dangerous.'

'Dangerous, how?'

'Ben was a lawyer, commercial litigation, and when he sued a company, it can destroy it, and people stand to lose a lot of money. And people don't like losing money. Ben told me some things, how directors would ring up making all sorts of threats, but he brushed them off. There were rules, he said. People knew he was just doing his job, and whatever problem people had with him, it stayed in the office. This was different though.'

'Why?'

'Because it came to our house. And it was the way Cassidy was. Polite, but there was a threat behind the message, and a threat delivered politely is the most frightening of all.'

'Threat?'

'He gave me his name and said *tell your husband that I called and he ought to rethink my offer.*' She held out her hands. 'That was it, but it was like he was saying *I know where you live,* knowing it would put pressure on Ben.'

'Did Ben tell you who he was, or what it was about?'

'No, which made it worse. He got defensive, angry, and we argued, which was rare for us. We were two busy professional people who didn't mind working long hours. What we had was company in our down-time, someone to relax with, but I'd never seen him like that before. All sorts of things went through my head. Criminals. Paedophile hunters. A lover's husband.'

Charlie raised his eyebrows. 'Paedophile hunters?'

She waved it away. 'It was an irrational thought, I know, but what other kind of person doorsteps someone to frighten them, because we've all seen it on the news?'

'How do you know he's a reporter then?'

'I found his business card in Ben's things. I called him, wondering whether he might have something to do with his death, but he hung up on me.'

'How did Ben die?'

Cathy's lip trembled, and she took a moment to compose herself before saying, 'Pills and a slash of his wrists, except that he couldn't have done it.'

'Why?'

'Because the medicals don't add up. They said he'd taken more than twenty coproxamol and cut his radial artery.' She shook her head. 'Bullshit. They said twenty because they found empty blister packs, but they weren't prescribed to him, and he would have needed more than twenty coproxamol to do it, if he was going for an overdose. And when he was found the next morning, there wasn't much blood around him, which isn't consistent with a slashed radial artery of a living person.'

'How did the police interpret that?'

'Fobbed me off. Said that it might have soaked into the ground, but why didn't they dig it up to check that? And it had been cold too, a late winter blast at the start of spring, so they said it could have restricted the blood loss. But he either died from blood loss or he didn't.'

Charlie checked around him, worried someone might be listening, before he leaned forward and lowered his voice. 'Was there any sign that he might do this, or any hint as to why he might?'

'Only that he seemed distracted and irritable, but that doesn't mean he was about to kill himself. If you want my opinion, and I know you do, because that's why you're here, it was staged to look like suicide. He was killed somehow, poison perhaps, and his wrist was slashed to make it look like he did it himself.'

'Wouldn't the poison show up though, when they did the toxicology?'

'The co-proxamol showed up, or at least what they thought was co-proxamol. I'm going to go all medical here, but you've got to understand. Co-proxamol is the generic name for the tablets, but it shows up in blood as dextropropoxyphene. In overdose cases, you'd need at least three micrograms for every millilitre of blood. I looked into it, desperate for answers, so I know this. Do you know how much there was in Ben's blood?' She held out her hands to Charlie. 'One microgram.' Her eyes were filled with anger. 'One fucking microgram. A third of what you'd expect to kill him. It's bullshit.'

'But what did the pathologist say about that?'

'That it could be enough if there were other depressants involved, like alcohol, but there was no booze in his system. In the end, he said it could have been due to an undetected heart problem, so not as much was needed to kill him.'

'But you're not convinced?'

'Course not, because there were too many improbables. Not enough blood at the scene, so improbable. Not enough dextropropoxyphene to kill, so improbable. And you know what you get if you multiply improbables? A conclusion you can disregard, that's what.'

Charlie sat back and rubbed his eyes. Life a couple of days earlier suddenly seemed a lot less complicated. 'Who would kill him, if it wasn't suicide?'

'I was hoping you'd be able to tell me that, but it was someone who wanted to silence him, and what started it all was the visit of Nick Cassidy. Start there. I've tried, but he won't speak to me. Here,' and she dug into her pocket and pulled out a piece of tattered card. 'It's what he gave me, his business card.'

She pushed it across the table. As Charlie examined it, she said, 'One condition though. If you find out, tell me, because I want justice for Ben.'

Charlie put his hand over hers and squeezed. 'I promise.'

She stared at his hand for a few seconds, then, 'There's one more thing that makes me certain he didn't kill himself.'

'Which is what?'

'Ben's left wrist was slashed. But he was left-handed. Who would slash their dominant hand with their weak one, the one with the least control?' Her jaw was set as she said, 'No one, that's who. He was murdered. And I want to know by whom, and why?'

Thirty-Four

Clarence Buford was waiting for Amy as she drove up to the house, his hands in his chino pockets, his hair thinned to a few golden strands over a tanned dome, dotted by liver spots.

The house was just as she remembered. Wide redbrick, with four thick white columns propping up a balcony that ran the whole width of the upper floor, and four high sash windows on either side of the double front doors. In the centre, an archway led to a courtyard beyond, cobbled, with stables on the other side.

Buford stepped forward as Amy climbed out of her car, by a fountain that trickled water from a bronze vase.

'Detective Constable Gray,' he said, his voice coming with an old man's croak. 'I'm delighted to make your acquaintance. Your father was a great servant to our town. I can be sure that you're the same.'

'Thank you, Mr Buford. I didn't realise that you knew him.'

'Call me Clarence. Formalities are for those occasions that are a little more, well, formal. And your father was the most senior officer in Cookstown. People in my position come across the likes of him all the time. He's a good man. Will you say hello for me? Tell him to give me a call. We can go golfing and talk about the old days. He'd like that.' He waved his hand. 'Enough of my nostalgia. What about you? Can I get you a drink?'

'No, but thank you, sir. I'm just chasing something up, so I don't think I'll be long.'

'Those who rush by miss all the best views. Come on in anyway,' and he led the way into the house.

The interior shone with opulence, with marble floors in the hallway that ran into the rooms on either side, and a wide staircase that swept to the upper floor. A glass chandelier dominated the entrance, teardrop crystals in ever-widening layers, sparkling in the light that streamed through stained glass panels above the doors.

It was vulgar, Amy thought, meant to display his wealth more than his taste.

'You've got a lovely house, Clarence,' she said.

'Thank you, my dear. Now, take a seat and tell me what's on your mind.'

He showed her to a sofa that was a mounted on gilded legs, gold leaf along the top, so that she felt she ought to be hand-fed grapes as she sat down.

'Natasha Trenton,' Amy said. 'She worked for you twenty years ago, but went missing after her shift.'

He nodded, and there was an emotion in his eyes that she couldn't quite place. Sadness, perhaps.

'I remember her,' he said. 'But I confess not as well as I ought to, given what her family has been put through. She helped out in the kitchen, you see,' and he winked. 'I'm sure you'll appreciate that isn't my domain.'

Amy faked a smile. 'What do you remember about her?'

He sat back and steepled his fingers against his chin. 'Before I answer, young lady, can I ask why this sudden flurry of interest? That poor girl went missing twenty years ago and I've heard hardly a peep, and here you are, looking as keen as mustard.'

'I spoke to Natasha's mother yesterday. I promised her I would chase things up.'

'I'd like to think that my taxes were being better spent, because I would have thought you'd be too busy right now, with that woman turning up dead.'

'The world still turns, Clarence, and we don't ignore other cases.'

He didn't respond, so she sat back and let the silence grow.

Clarence let it grow with her, the only sound being the creak of his chair springs when he crossed one leg over the other, but he broke it first.

'We couldn't tell her family much,' he said. 'Children run off all the time, especially from around here. Cookstown is heaven for most of us, but some feel that it holds them back. Have you seen her family?'

'I've met them.'

'It wasn't a good environment, that's all I'll say. I can bet she'd been planning to go for a while, and that they didn't take so kindly to her leaving. If giving her job helped her to get away, I can be proud of that.'

He raised a finger, crooked at the tip.

'How do you think they'd react if she'd gone and made a good life for herself, coming back here and flaunting her newfound success? Badly, that's how, so perhaps she stayed away and built something new. Pretty girls like her always turn out fine, because there's always someone willing to help them out.'

'You do remember her then, because I haven't shown you a picture or anything, but right away you know about her family and how she looked?'

He cocked his head. 'Just be careful what you're insinuating. Remember who I am in this town. I did the right thing back then, telling the police what Truman had said, how he came over all upset and filled his mind with all sorts of untruths. Don't you try to throw it all back on my family. We cleared that up years ago.'

'Clarence, I'm just making an observation, and I'm pleased to have jogged your memory. I don't mean any disrespect.'

'Have you got any designs on promotion, following in your father's footsteps? You won't get far as a detective if you intend to go around upsetting people who've done so much for this town.'

'I'm just asking questions.'

'You're fly-fishing, skimming across the surface, seeing what comes up, but sometimes you pick the wrong river. Whatever happened to that girl, or wherever she went, it's got nothing to do with me or this family, and I don't take kindly to your tone. A pretty girl once worked for me, then she ran away. That's all I know.'

'What about your wife, if the kitchen is more her domain for hiring and firing? She might have known more about her. The things she said, girl-to-girl confidences.'

'Mrs Buford didn't speak to the housemaids. We didn't hire them to be our friends.'

'She might still have something to contribute though.'

'Mrs Buford isn't for speaking to any visitors. She's indisposed.'

'That's what Pete said. Do you know when she'll be well enough to speak to me?'

'She's not a well woman. I'd rather she wasn't bothered.' He stood. 'I think this meeting is done, detective.'

She wondered whether to push him any further, but she realised that it wasn't going to do any good.

'I apologise for disturbing you, Mr Buford.'

'Apology not needed, and I hope you catch your killer.' As he showed her to the door, he said, 'You make sure you remember me to your father.'

'I will.'

As she went back to her car, she could feel Clarence Buford watching her, making her glance back to the house as she turned the key. Clarence stood with his hands thrust into his pockets once more, but he stood a little straighter this time, and she thought she saw the twitch of a curtain in one of the windows.

Thirty-Five

As Charlie sat in his car, pondering his journey home, he tried to work out what he should do next.

Gerard had got himself wrapped up in something that might have cost him his life. He might have been prepared to overlook that, clients die all the time, drugs and booze the two main reasons, but there was something different about Gerard's death. And the hollowness in Cathy Leech's eyes had woken something inside him.

He'd become jaded by his job, but the story she'd told had brought back an emotion he thought he'd left behind a long time ago: a desire to right a wrong.

Becoming his own boss had turned justice into a pound sign, not a cause, with clients abandoned if they couldn't get legal aid and couldn't afford his bill.

That was the nature of business, he wasn't so naive, but he'd gone into criminal law as an idealist, wanting to fight injustice. Somewhere along the way, he'd forgotten about that. Until Cathy Leech, that is. Gerard had stirred it. Cathy had brought it alive, a loud clamour in his head.

He called Eleanor.

The phone rang out a few times before she answered, and when she did, she sounded breathless. 'You could have texted, Charlie, just to let me know what was going on.'

'I've only been out for a day.'

'Yeah, but what do we tell your clients when they ring up?'

'Tell them whatever the hell you want, because I'm onto something here. Spencer Everett is the key to it all. Gerard had been making waves, and I can bet Spencer didn't like it.'

'Charlie, have you been drinking? You sound excited.'

'Just alive, that's all.'

'And you think Spencer Everett had something to do with Gerard's death?'

'That's what I'm here to find out.'

'He's the Home fucking Secretary, Charlie.'

'Yep, and that's a powerful position. Next stop Number 10, a rich future ahead. The power to award contracts, vested interests, the speakers' circuit. He's got a lot to lose. And you've seen how people love him, lap it up, all that country-house elegance. Gerard must have known something that would make Spencer lose everything, which made Gerard a threat.'

'What are you going to do?'

'The safest place is out in the open. If we expose him, he'll be scared to act. Gerard stayed in the shadows and he was killed. There's something else too.' He dug out the photograph and put it on his dashboard. 'The guy on the right of the picture. He's called Ben Leech, and he killed himself too, so they say, a few months ago. I spoke to his widow, and she's convinced it was a murder.' He tapped on the photograph. 'You've got Gerard on the left, and between Gerard and Spencer is a man called Lewis Buford. I'm looking at him next.'

'Wasn't there a fifth guy?'

'Yeah, behind Spencer and Ben Leech, his arms around their shoulders. I don't know him. He's the mystery man.'

'What do you do now?'

'I haven't decided.'

'You'll want to know where the picture was taken, surely?'

'That would help.'

She chuckled as she said, 'You're not the only one who's done some research. The sooner this is over, the sooner the firm goes back to normal.'

'What have you found?'

'There's a sign in the picture, the one behind them on the wall,' she said.

He peered closer at the picture. 'Old-fashioned neon, fixed to a whitewashed building. *Banham's Ice Cream.*'

'That's the one. I searched the internet for those words. Guess what: it's still there.'

'Good work. Where though?'

'Cookstown, on the Yorkshire coast,' she said. 'The ice-cream parlour is long gone, but the sign is a local icon, and there have been campaigns to stop it being taken down. They still light it up, even though the shop isn't there anymore.'

Charlie tapped his phone on his chin as he thought about what to do next.

He could hear the soft mumble of her voice, so he put the phone to his ear. 'I've got an idea.'

'Uh-oh, what are you thinking now?'

'Tomorrow, can you get a barrister for any trials I have booked in?'

'Charlie, don't do this. Come back to Manchester.'

'And if there are any routine hearings, get another firm to cover them.'

'What the hell, Charlie?'

'It looks like I've just got myself a trip to the seaside.'

Thirty-Six

Once back at the station, Amy wanted to see how Rob was getting on with the CCTV trawl, but she was still distracted by Natasha's case.

She went back to her desk, the file of papers relating to Natasha's disappearance shoved into her drawer. She lifted it out, then scoured it until she found what she wanted: the exhibit list.

It was a list of all the pieces of evidence that were sent to the CPS when they were asked to look at Truman Buford's case, following his confession. There were some paper exhibits, like call logs, but it was the schedule attached to the inside of the file cover that interested her. As she skimmed through it, she saw there was no CCTV listed.

They hadn't looked.

It was only twenty years earlier. They had CCTV then as well, and the internet was taking off, full of home webcams, people spewing out streams of the road outside their houses just for the novelty of being able to do so. There would have been something.

She slammed the file back into the box and headed for the Missing Persons Unit. She glanced into the room across the corridor, checking for Mickey Higham. He was in his glass office at the end of the room, visible through vertical office blinds, and she fought the urge to confront him. He'd been involved in the case but had done little about it.

But now wasn't the time. He was the boss, however much she wished it were different.

The door was open to Kirmo's room. She tapped on the doorframe to attract his attention. 'It's me again.'

Kirmo sat back and clasped his fingers together, before resting them on his stomach. 'You bored of Natasha's file already? Don't you be dumping it back on me. You wanted it, you have it.'

'I'm not giving up on her yet. Do you know whether anyone looked for CCTV?'

'Why would they?'

'To see where her car went.'

'We know where it went. Dumped on the Baptist estate.'

'Okay, to see who was driving it.'

He leaned back further, making his chair creak and his stomach push harder against his shirt buttons, revealing the white vest underneath. 'It wasn't a murder investigation. Like I told you, an adult didn't go home. We can think the worst, but it doesn't mean the worst happened. We don't get the resources for that kind of work, to assume every missing person case is a murder.'

'But it could turn out to be one. Did she have any markers?'

'High risk? Vulnerable?' He shook his head. 'Just a normal young woman at the start of the rest of her life.'

'But she was about to go to university. She didn't have to run away to leave Cookstown. She was going anyway.'

'What can I say? We looked and couldn't find her. Truman couldn't tell us where he put her, even if he had anything to do with it. Until there was something cold and dead to poke at, it was just a missing person case about someone who was allowed to go missing.'

She frowned as she thought back to the exhibit list. Something occurred to her. 'I was looking on the exhibit list and her car is on it. Where is it now?'

'I don't know.'

'What do you mean, you don't know? You've lost an exhibit?'

'Not lost. Given back. We had no reason to keep it, and we've only got so much space.' He raised his hands in apology. 'I know what you're going to say, but I was just a plod back then, nothing to do with me. And that's why I don't know where it is, because I don't know what Tammy did with it. She might have sold it. For all I know, she might have filled the boot with soil and grown weed in it.'

'I'll start there then, with Tammy.'

'Amy, are you really doing this?'

'I looked in her eyes and I saw anger. I want to replace it with hope.'

'Too long now. All the hope is gone. False hope is still no hope, and it's harder to recover from.'

'Let's make it a certainty then, because the not-knowing is killing that woman.'

'Just be careful.'

She was about to turn to walk away, but that made her stop. 'What do you mean, be careful?'

'Just that. You can lift rocks if you want, but sometimes there's a crab with large claws waiting to jump out at you.'

'Kirmo, if there's a dirty secret around Natasha's case, I'm going to find it.'

'Don't say I didn't warn you.'

Before she could ask anything else, Rob appeared behind her.

'I think I've got something,' he said.

'Show me,' Amy said, then followed him back to his desk.

Rob's monitor had a few video clips open, the toolbar filled with small icons. The desk was littered with post-it notes covered in scribbles. He clicked on one of the icons to make an image fill the screen.

'This is from the corner shop on Hill Road,' Rob said, and a still image of a familiar two-lane strip filled the screen, along with the edge of a building and some parked cars.

'I paused it at the right spot,' he said, and pressed play. 'See there, a dark saloon.'

The screen showed a car approaching the camera, although most of the detail was lost in the bright beam of the headlights. 'It might be the lights from the shops playing tricks with the colours, but I reckon it could be blue.'

Amy sat down next to him, leaning forward to get a better look. 'I can't see the driver. The headlights make it too hard.'

'I know, but watch,' and he scrolled the footage back. 'I've got to get this just right,' and he concentrated as he made it play frame-by-frame, his finger poised over the mouse button like a gamer. 'There,' he said, smiling in triumph as he made the image freeze. 'Just in that one frame, the glare from the headlights isn't as bad, like it hit a dip in the road or something, and there must be a streetlight at the side of the shop, because it catches the badge on the car.'

Amy brought her chair closer. She screwed up her face as she tried to decipher the tiny metallic glint in the footage.

She turned to Rob. 'A Mercedes?'

'That's what I thought.'

Amy sat back. 'Okay, what makes you think this car might be of interest?'

'Watch,' he said, and ran the footage backwards on half-speed before pointing at the monitor. 'See how it joins Hill Road further back, way in the distance, because you see the beam sweep into the road, then the indicator switches off.'

Rob played the footage backwards and forwards a few times, until Amy said, 'That's the road that goes past Sarah's house.'

'That's why I watched this camera,' he said. 'I could see where Sarah's road joins Hill Road, because if a car has taken her body to the beach, it's got to come from there and drive past this camera, right? In the hour before we got the report and right up until then, only nine cars turn out of there. Six head towards town, and three head in the direction of where Sarah was found.'

'But why does this one excite you, because you haven't shown me the other two?'

'Look,' and he took the footage forward another thirty minutes before pressing play.

Amy watched as Rob once again had his finger poised over the mouse button, watching the timer carefully.

'There,' Rob said, and pressed pause.

The footage stopped on the image of a car.

'Is it the same one?' Amy said.

'Maybe. I can't make out the number plate, but if I take it forward,' and he made the footage go frame-by-frame once more. 'The same logo, this time on the boot. Mercedes. Five minutes to the beach. Twenty minutes to dump the body, then five minutes back. The timings fit, and watch,' and she let it play once more.

Amy watched as the car drove along Hill Road, until the turn signal started to flash and the brake lights went on. 'It goes back towards Sarah's house,' she said. 'Why would the killer do that? He didn't clean up the scene, so why would he go back?'

'Because that's where the car is from,' Rob said. 'I did a vehicle search for a blue Mercedes in Cookstown. One comes back as registered to Roland Marsh.'

'Sarah's husband?'

'That's him, and when I checked him out, both cars are in his name, so I don't know if it was her car or his, but,' and Rob smiled. 'It's not for me to say, but is everyone sure Roland Marsh was at the conference?' He pointed towards the screen. 'Did Roland Marsh take his wife's body to the beach?'

'The car will still be there,' Amy said. 'Someone needs to get that car secure, there could be forensic traces.' She grinned. 'I hope this is the breakthrough, because I want it to be you who finds it.'

They were distracted by a shout.

Amy went to the room next door, where Higham was rushing for the exit.

'What's going on?'

'It's Nick Cassidy,' he said, his breathing fast. 'He's jumped in front of a train.'

Thirty-Seven

Jessica Redmond had called in sick, told Wendy that it must have been something she ate the night before. Wendy sounded like she didn't really believe her, but sacking an intern would mean finding another one, and who turns away a free worker? Instead of being in Parliament, Jessica was in her flat in Highbury, shared with overseas students, five of them in total, her room the smallest.

The price of living in London, she told herself, but she had started to think that the price was too high. Her father paid the bills. It was his final contribution to her career, he'd said, so she felt some guilt for working against her boss when her father thought she was carving out a future.

There were papers spread around on the floor, some of them sent from an anonymous email address that Bridget said she used sometimes, which she'd printed off so that she could make sense of them.

They were receipts in the main, from hotels in Nevis and Geneva. They didn't mean much in themselves, but they supported the story. Spencer couldn't say he'd never been to either place if they had the paper trail.

And the trail was an obvious one. Jessica felt a tug of disappointment that Spencer was such a cliché.

Nevis was a favoured country for offshore companies, secrecy being the key. She'd done some research on the Nevis link, and as far as she could tell, it was an easy place to hide your assets. Appoint an agent, open a company, and no one outside of Nevis would ever know your involvement. Many of the former tax havens, like the British Virgin Islands, had been bullied into revealing their information by the governments that held some sway over them.

Nevis had stuck up its middle finger, and all the dirty money headed there instead.

Bridget had clarified what the documents were that she'd photographed from the back of the picture frame in Spencer's office. Bank account numbers and transactions, showing payments made from a company based in Nevis, Willow LLC, to a bank account in a small Swiss bank, Credit Monbijou.

The circle was almost complete. They could prove payments between a Nevis company and a Swiss bank account. They could even prove a link between Spencer and Willow LLC. She lifted the print-out from the Land Registry for the opulent apartment Spencer lived in whenever he was in London. Overlooking Hyde Park, it was owned by Willow LLC and rented to him, with Spencer claiming the rent back from the taxpayer.

He was making the public pay for his own property.

As she sat back against the bed, surrounded by paperwork, she pondered on how greed brought most people down. Jessica remembered the photograph of Pippa and Spencer. They must have travelled together when he registered the company, and she would have enjoyed the money when it came in, but Pippa wanted her piece of Willow LLC when the marriage went sour. She knew the real ownership details, and there'd been no mention of Willow LLC in his list of assets in the divorce papers.

Pippa's death had silenced her, but it seemed that Nick Cassidy wanted to prove a link between the companies who lobbied Spencer and payments made to Willow LLC.

The final piece of the jigsaw was proving Spencer's ownership of Willow LLC. It would prove that he was a fraudster.

Bridget had told her that it might also prove that he was a murderer.

Thirty-Eight

Amy was the first out of the car as they arrived at the level-crossing, Mickey Higham skidding to a halt in front of the gates. A train was static, the gates closed, the warning lights flashing red. There were lines of traffic on either side. Some cars were doing U-turns further up. A uniformed officer was trying to direct people away, giving hints as to alternative routes.

The trains out of Cookstown did a long curve onto the headland, taking in the nearby villages, before heading back up the coast. It was a single track for ten miles, so Amy knew there wouldn't be a train coming the other way, as the southbound train wouldn't be allowed to leave its station until the northbound one had passed through.

A group of people were speaking to a couple of officers, who were taking details. The passengers, Amy presumed. An ashen-faced man in a train company uniform was sitting on the pavement, his head hanging down. Mickey Higham went round the side of the safety barriers and headed along the track.

Amy approached the man in the company uniform, who looked up as she held out her identification.

'He was just lying there,' he said, his chin trembling, tears in his eyes. 'I couldn't stop.'

'Was he awake?'

'I don't know. He was across the line though. I had no chance. Neither did he.' He wiped his eyes. 'My first one. Do you know what it felt like?'

'I can't imagine.'

'Nothing, that's what. I saw it and I heard it, the thump, but the train hardly felt it. Just his life wiped out like that,' and he clicked his fingers.

Amy put his hand on his shoulder. 'It wasn't your fault, just remember that.'

He nodded his thanks, but looked just as miserable as when she'd first walked over.

She headed to where Mickey had gone, and took a deep breath as she steeled herself for whatever sights lay ahead.

Trees lined the track on both sides, which was on a slow bend, so that the driver would have had limited vision as he approached. There were fences, but it wasn't an electrified line, so someone determined to lie in front of a train would find it easy.

Mickey Higham was ahead, one hand on the fence as if for support. Further along, meat and bone glistened in the sun that filtered through the trees.

He turned as she got closer. His face was grey as he held out a wallet. 'They found this at the side of the tracks. It must have been thrown out as he was dragged along. It's how they knew it was him.'

As she looked along the tracks, she felt sadness rip through her. There was a siren in the distance, an ambulance, she presumed, but it was a wasted trip. They'd be scraping him up with shovels.

Higham turned to Amy. 'What did you say to him?'

'I was just trying to find out what he knew.'

'Until you spoke to him, he was just a drunk sleeping off the booze. You have your little chat, then suddenly he's jumping in front of a train like it all got too much.'

'Hey, that's bullshit, boss. You released him, not me. Why didn't you spot the suicide risk?'

He ground his jaw. 'Let's see what the complaints board has to say about that.'

'What?'

'Go home.'

'Home? Why?'

'Find a different squad. You're off mine. Go.'

And with that, Higham folded his arms and stared straight ahead.

She started to protest, but he held out his hand. The conversation was over.

She trudged back along the track, towards the stopped train, and realised that she had a long walk back into town.

'Fuck!'

Thirty-Nine

It was the brightness of the sky that struck Charlie at first.

The drive had been longer than he expected, the motorway not serving the eastern side of the country as well as the west, as he meandered through what felt like endless countryside. Flat farmland and patchwork fields. Livestock in some, replaced by wheat and barley as he got nearer the coast. Or sometimes the vivid yellow of rapeseed, interrupted by villages of rose-lined cottages. Traffic was light, different to the constant queue and snarl of Manchester, with just the occasional car or the slow-down of a tractor, clumps of mud thrown into the carriageway.

The colours seemed brighter than at home, where Manchester often seemed shrouded in grey, rain never far away. As he drove, the greens seemed greener, the brickwork redder, the lawns more lush.

Cookstown appeared as a slow spread on the horizon, no towns or villages to shield it from view, the presence of the sea becoming more obvious by the brighter gleam of the sky, like up-lighting, turning it a lighter blue, dotted by the pinpricks of distant gulls.

As he drove in, he realised how far this place was from anywhere. The pace seemed slow. No rush hour or throngs of people. As he got closer to the sea, along a narrow curving road of shops and houses painted white, his usual soundtrack of cars and people was replaced by the screech of seagulls.

His phone rang, paired up to the Bluetooth.

It was Eleanor, the gravel in her voice filling the car. 'How's it going, traveller?'

He laughed. 'I made it. This place is a long way from anywhere, like it lives in its own bubble. Pretty though. Looking forward to getting parked and having a drink.'

'Get in your hotel first,' she said. 'It might be one of those places where a stranger in town soon gets noticed. I don't want you getting locked up for brawling with suspicious locals.'

'You ever been over this way before?'

Eleanor chuckled and wheezed. 'I don't like to venture far. I'm scared of flying and I get bored of driving. Give me the Manchester drizzle any day.'

'You're a strange one. Any problems at work?'

'Just the usual. I've sorted out barristers for all your work. What are you going to do? And for how long?'

'I want to find out what I can about the photograph.'

'And if you don't find anything?'

'I'll have a couple of days by the seaside and think about my future.'

'Okay. Stay safe,' she said, then clicked off.

As he stepped out of his car, the air felt clean, the long-forgotten tang of salt on his lips rushing him back to childhood holidays in North Wales. The steady roll of the sea was audible, just the gentle rhythm of the tide, and he wandered towards silent fairground rides along a stretch of tarmac that ran high above the beach. There was a headland to the north, a grass-topped chalk finger that put the town in a bay, a haven for the trawlers as they chugged and bobbed the final few miles.

Charlie guessed that it wasn't always calm. Even on a still day, the sea rolled, and he imagined that on wilder days the silver-topped waves would crash hard.

He smiled. It was all of his childhood holidays wrapped up in a few winding streets. Like the way the amusement arcades further along beeped the promise of fun, even though there was no one in them.

He did a circuit of the town centre, and he reckoned Molly would like it here. There was a certain simplicity about the town that attracted him. No heavy industry, or glass office blocks, or a rich man's weekend getaway, but filled with traces of old times that he found comforting. Butchers, greengrocers, bakeries, with none of the chains that cluttered high streets in most towns. But these weren't artisan places aiming for a nostalgia kick. These were family businesses, passed down and kept going.

Then, something caught his eye, and he broke into a grin. 'I don't believe it.'

Fixed to a white-washed building, in bright neon, were the words Eleanor had spotted on Gerard's photograph. *Banham's Ice-Cream.*

His grin broke into a laugh. He'd found it.

Forty

Amy threw her bag onto the sofa and sat down with a slump.

She lived in an old fisherman's cottage in a narrow street close to the harbour. Small windows and uneven walls and a stone floor, with just one room at the front and a kitchen at the back. It was cosy in winter, and she loved its history, feeling lucky to afford it. A house like hers in a Cornish fishing village would be the price of a lottery win, but the second-home boom hadn't really hit Cookstown, with most of the visitors coming from the old mining towns of West Yorkshire. The big money headed south.

She groaned and put her head back. She closed her eyes and wanted to let the day just fade into memory.

She hadn't told Mickey Higham about Sarah's husband's car being used to transport the body. They needed to preserve the car. She'd text someone soon. Right then, she needed a drink. Then another one.

A knock on the door interrupted her thoughts. She was about to get up when her father opened the door himself and stepped inside.

She gave a tired wave. 'Hey, Dad, hi.'

'I've just been to the supermarket, right out of the good stuff at home, so I thought I'd say hello to my favourite daughter.'

It brought a laugh. 'I'm your only daughter.'

'It still counts.'

She sat up. 'Come on, you never just call round.'

'I spoke to Mickey Higham,' he said. 'He told me what happened. He's pretty angry, but don't let it bother you. People kill themselves. It happens.'

'It wasn't bothering me,' she said. 'I didn't do anything wrong. It was Higham who released him.'

'Just let him cool down. He might not want you on the investigation, but it won't cost you your job.' He frowned. 'Perhaps that's a good thing.'

'Why?'

'I heard from Clarence Buford today.'

Amy narrowed her eyes. 'You make it sound like you're old buddies, but I've never heard you use his name before.'

'I was a senior police officer. I met people like him.'

'Why are you telling me?'

'He told me you spoke to him earlier.'

'I don't want to talk about it.'

'That doesn't mean you can't listen. I don't care what you think about Clarence, because he's rich and reclusive, which makes him a mean old bastard, but he buried his son, and he blames himself for that. He turned everyone against Truman when he'd just tried to do the right thing. It goes quiet, finally, then you turn up and make out like Natasha's disappearance was all about the Bufords.'

'Come on, Dad. His son confessed to her murder, and their house was the last place she was seen. It *is* all about the Bufords.'

'But Truman is dead now, so there's nothing to be done. And if he didn't kill her, then it's nothing to do with them. All they did was give the girl a job.'

'And if Truman did kill her?'

'Her whereabouts died with him.'

'And we should stop looking, because Natasha Trenton doesn't count? What I see is a mother hurting, so I want to do right by her.'

'Think how it looks for me.'

'For you? I don't get it.'

'I was the officer in charge of the Cookstown station at the time. If you start making out like we didn't do enough, then it looks bad on me.' He raised his hand. 'And before you say anything, I know Tammy is hurting, and I feel for her, I really do, but it only works if you find that poor girl's body. In the meantime, all you do is make out like I didn't care about her, and that isn't right. That isn't my legacy.'

'That's unfair, Dad. You know I wouldn't do anything to hurt you, but there's a missing woman, and it sounds like all that matters is the rich man.'

'It isn't that, but we know that one of two things happened: she ran away, or Truman Buford was telling the truth. If he killed her, his secret died with him, and we'll never find the body. If she ran, shouldn't we leave her alone, because she must have had a good reason?'

'But why would she run?'

'Because Natasha was a smart girl, growing up surrounded by crooks and idlers, her mum included. Perhaps she saw her future as not being so bright, and all her friends were going places. Jobs, college, because she was hanging out with the good kids, not those like her family. I don't know who her father is, and maybe Tammy doesn't either, because we all heard the stories about her, like how any man who wanted a good time only ever had to go to Tammy's, but Natasha got some good brains from somewhere, and it didn't come from the Trentons.'

'What has Tammy's past got to do with Natasha's disappearance?'

'The reason she ran. Just think about it. Surrounded by trash and she wants away. Tammy knows nothing about that girl's life, because that's just how it is. Did I know everything about your life when you were eighteen?'

Amy allowed herself a smile as she remembered the parties she'd lied about, or the sleepovers she said she was having when she was staying over at a boy's house.

'Okay, no,' she said.

'And I don't want to know, but maybe Natasha had a secret life too, so one day she went. Left her car behind and ran. Possibly with a man, or perhaps she tracked down her father and he could offer her a new start. If that's where it ended, she might have called Tammy one day and told her where she was. But guess what happens? Truman Buford starts sounding off about how he killed her, so everyone thinks she's dead.' He held out his hands. 'She's struck gold. She can be whoever she wants to be, because no one is looking for her anymore. We're not, that's for sure. Maybe one day she'll call Tammy, but if she doesn't do that, she's got a good reason. So, leave her be. If you go looking, it isn't what Natasha wants, and it'll make me look really bad, for no good reason.'

Amy sighed. 'Okay Dad, thanks.'

He went to her and gave her a hug. 'You're a good detective, but sometimes, you can't please everyone.'

Forty-One

'Hang on, Eleanor, I'm going to send you something.' Charlie clicked off the call and dug out the photograph from his pocket.

He'd had a freshen up before he left the hotel he'd found. It called itself a hotel, but it looked more like a storage space by the harbour that had been fitted out with a row of rooms, so that the doors opened straight onto a cobbled slipway. He wanted to explore the town, but he headed first for the neon sign. *Banham's Ice Cream*.

Charlie held out the photograph so that the background matched up with it, the building edges and sign perfectly in line with the picture from many years earlier. In his other hand, he had his phone on the camera setting. He moved a little, crouched, then pressed to take the photo.

He examined it and grinned, before sending it to Eleanor. There was a spinning arrow, then it cleared, so he knew it had been sent. He typed *now for beer. I'll call you tomorrow*, and put his phone away.

The neon sign showing *Banham's Ice Cream* was lit, red and blue against a sky that was bright and clear and acquiring a mauve hue. The shops had closed, but still the empty arcades beeped and blinged. The only other lights were from the pubs that occupied the street corners, with swinging signs and small windows in old buildings. No glass and chrome in Cookstown. Thankfully.

Charlie could see why Gerard would be happy here, but why was it his last moment of happiness? What happened here?

He decided that he'd begin his search properly the next day. He was more interested in the bar opposite, *The Ship Ahoy*. A wooden sign showing a painted galleon hung outside, the building painted white, like all the rest.

The interior was dark, the lights set low, the bright spot being the pool table in the furthest corner and more signs behind the bar. *Budweiser, Coors*, an American affectation to attract a younger crowd. There was a juke box against one wall, and high brown tables filled the room, so you'd stand and lean against them rather than sit.

There weren't many people in. Two young men in faded baseball caps were playing pool, so that the quiet was shattered by the occasional crack of the balls. An older man sat at the end of the bar, a bunch of keys fastened to a belt-loop, and their weight had pulled his trousers below his waist. He was nursing a pint glass of something frothy. A young woman in a long denim skirt sat further along, long blonde hair cascading over a suede waistcoat.

The barman approached him. A thickset man in a black t-shirt and a greying goatee, biker-style. 'What are you having?'

Charlie gestured towards one of the pumps and said, 'One of those, please.' All it had to be was beer.

The barman grabbed a glass and said, 'New to Cookstown? Not seen you in here before.'

He thought back to Eleanor's comment about strangers getting noticed. 'I'm from Manchester,' he said. 'Just here on business.'

As the beer started to fill the glass, held on a practised tilt, the barman cocked his head. 'That's a first. No one ever comes here on business.'

'It must happen sometimes.'

'We get tourists and day-trippers, and those who've got a caravan somewhere, but business-types?' He shook his head. 'Not ever.'

'What does the town live on then?'

'We get by doing our own thing. Summer trade, mostly. Bed and breakfasts and old-school hotels, food stalls and gift shops. During the school holidays, it gets bustling, but sometimes it feels like all we've got left is pubs and charity shops.' He smacked the glass onto the bar in front of Charlie. 'I sound like I'm complaining, but I like it this way. No one bothers us. We need the summer money, but then you can't get parked and have to queue in the pubs. But we've got Goldie.'

'Goldie?'

He gestured towards the woman sitting further along the bar. 'She comes here to belt out a few country hits. Cookstown's sweetheart.'

Charlie looked past her, to where there was a small stage set up, with speakers and a microphone, a guitar case leaning against the back wall.

'Sounds interesting. I don't mind a bit of country. My dad used to like it. Drove my mother mad, but he was always blasting it out, dreaming of going to Nashville one day.'

'Did he ever get to go?'

Charlie shook his head. 'He was always more of a dreamer than a man of action.'

The barman shouted along to Goldie, 'Looks like you've got a fan for the night, Goldie.'

She raised her bottle to say hi, her smile bringing out her dimples, freckles scattered across her nose. 'I play here twice a week. If you stay, you'll double the crowd.'

Charlie smiled. 'Nice to meet you, Goldie.'

The barman leaned in and whispered, 'They come here hoping she'll take a shine to them.'

She tutted. 'And if you get a better class of clientele, I just might.'

The barman stretched his hand across to shake. 'I'm Scott. How are you finding Cookstown?'

Charlie shook. 'Hi, I'm Charlie, and I'm liking it so far.'

'Nothing moves very quickly around here, but when you get used to it, it's the perfect pace.' He straightened to shout down the bar. 'Hey Bobby, do you think this Mancunian is going to find it too slow.'

The man further down the bar looked away from the television and grinned. Most of his teeth were missing at the front. 'That's why we need these places,' he said, chuckling. 'If you're going to move slow, do it with a beer in your hand. It's like a public service.'

Scott laughed. 'A public service? I like that. I'll get myself listed on the Cookstown website.' He began to wipe the bar with a cloth that had been draped over his shoulder. 'What business brings you here.'

Charlie weighed up the barman. He seemed friendly enough, but he was keen on asking questions. But Charlie reckoned that in places like Cookstown, a barman will know most of what goes on.

'A friend came here twenty years ago or so,' Charlie said, making up a story. 'He always told me it was a great place to come, maybe buy a cottage and let it out. He's passed on now, too young, so I don't know exactly when it was, but the *Banham's* sign was there, because I've got a picture of him in front of it.'

'That sign has been there for years. Hey, Bobby, how long has the Banham's sign been there?'

'More than fifty years now. Even there when I was a kid.'

'There you go,' Scott said. 'Historic, so they say, but I just think they forgot to take it down until it became a fixture. The ice cream shop is long gone, but everyone likes the sign, so it stays there.'

'I like it too,' Charlie said. 'Has a bit of old seaside charm.'

'Did your friend stay here for long? I might know him. A lot of people know everyone else, or so it seems.'

'Just one summer, I think.' Charlie took a drink, good and creamy. 'Have you lived in Cookstown all your life?'

'Here and hereabouts. I've been running this place for a few years now.'

Charlie dug into his pocket and produced the photograph. 'Would you be able to date this picture? I know it was around twenty years ago, but not exactly when.'

Scott looked closer, then smiled. 'Easy.' He passed the photograph to Goldie. 'The fair?'

She squinted as she looked at it, before she nodded her agreement. 'Looks like it.' She passed it back to Charlie. 'Whichever year it was, it was the last Saturday in August.'

'How can you be so sure?'

Scott leaned over the bar and his finger pointed to the background in the picture, behind the group of smiling young men. 'See the bunting coming down from the place next to the shoe shop, and the guys further back, drinking.'

'Yeah, I see.'

'Next to them, there's the back wheel of a hog bike. And one of the guys is wearing a black waistcoat. I can bet you that's leather, one of the crew.'

'Yeah, but why the end of August.'

'Cookstown Fair,' he said. 'Takes place over the last weekend in August. Starts on a Wednesday. Ends on Saturday night with a folk night, with a stage by the harbour. Has done for forty years, and makes this place as busy as it gets. We get a lot of bikers, because they get to skip the queues on the roads. The fair is the reason for the bunting, and if you look closely, the guy with his back to the camera has a fiddle in his hand. He'll be one of those who belt out sea shanties. The tourists love it, with the fishing boats in the background.'

Charlie smiled. 'You're good.'

'Not good. I just know my town.' He glanced down at the picture again. 'Is your friend called Buford?'

'No. He was called Gerard Williams. I know there's a Lewis Buford on there.'

'They're a big deal around here. Lewis is a judge or something now. The local paper crows about it all the time, as if we're just desperate to have someone in this town make it big, but he was already big. His family owns half the town.'

'That's just the way,' Bobby shouted. 'Old Clarence Buford owns the town, but I've never seen him do much for it.'

Goldie spoke up. 'The old man owns a lot of the arcades, bought up half of the seafront when the town was making money. Now, if anyone wants to start a business anywhere near the harbour, you can bet they're paying rent to Clarence Buford.'

'Lewis is one of the sons,' Scott said. 'Clarence, his old man, owns a lot of the land around here, just about everywhere.'

'His other boy didn't do so well though,' Bobby shouted.

Scott put his towel over the end pump and said, 'You're right there. Just shows that you need more than DNA to get on.'

'Who was the other boy?' Charlie asked.

'Truman Buford. Thought he was something special because of what his family had, but it turned out that he was just an arsehole who couldn't take his beer. There were even rumours that he killed one of the maids.'

'Really?'

'It didn't come to anything. Last I heard, he went to prison and was killed in there. I can bet he wouldn't have been popular. I didn't own this place back then, just drank here, part of the hog crew that comes here sometimes, but I saw him get kicked out more than once. I've even done it myself.'

'What had he done to deserve it?'

'Touched up my girlfriend.' He held up his hands. 'Not that I was getting territorial or anything. She was as tough as they come, but it was the way he did it that got to her.'

'I don't understand.'

'If a bloke comes on to her because he's drunk, well, that's the way of the world. But Truman? He looked her up and down like she was beneath him. He didn't come onto her because he thought he had a chance. He did it because he thought money and status meant that he could.'

Scott shrugged an apology, although there were traces of a smile at the memory. 'The next time he came in here, I grabbed him by his shirt collar and took him down the side. I kicked him until he was groaning. I'm not proud of this, but I pissed on him too.'

Bobby started to laugh, slapping the bar in delight. Goldie groaned her displeasure.

'That's right,' Scott said. 'I stood over him, my hog crew behind me, and pissed all over him. It sent a message: whoever he thought he was, just because his old man had money, it counted for fuck all in this pub.' He grinned. 'Welcome to Cookstown.'

Forty-Two

Amy sat up in bed, suddenly alert.

One of the security lights had come on over the yard. Amy's bedroom was at the back of the house. She checked her watch. Close to three in the morning.

She listened out, her body still. There was wooden decking in the yard, so footsteps would echo. She could sit and wait, and hope that any burglars would be too unsettled by the light to make a bold move. Or she could confront them, shout and holler to attract witnesses.

Her mouth was dry as she got out of bed, her head still fuzzy from the booze. She swayed, and had to hold out her arms to steady herself.

Jeez, it came back to her now. The first bottle had gone down quickly, but she had decided against the second bottle. She was drinking because she was angry, and she didn't want to do anything she couldn't remember the following day. Being thrown off the squad deserved a drink, but she knew she had to work out what to do next. Recovering from a hangover wasn't in her plan.

She peered out from the side of the curtains. There was nothing there, as far as she could tell, then jolted back when something clattered, like a garden chair being knocked over.

'Shit!'

The door.

She'd stomped her way to bed and couldn't remember whether she'd locked the back door. It was one of those things that she did on autopilot, then couldn't remember whether she'd done it, so she had to keep going back to check on the lock before she could settle.

She hadn't done the second check the night before.

Amy tried to keep her footsteps quiet as she went down the stairs, the passage tight and narrow, with a door at the bottom that opened into the living room.

She inched the door open, so that it wouldn't creak. She was primed for an attack, her muscles tensed.

As she looked, everything appeared as it had the night before. A glass and an empty wine bottle on the floor. The kitchen door was closed.

Had she closed it? Why would she?

She crept towards it, trying to keep her breaths quiet, so that anyone on the other side wouldn't hear her. Sweat prickled her forehead. She picked up a poker from a set by the fire.

She flung open the kitchen door, the poker raised, hoping to surprise the intruder.

The security light clicked off outside, leaving her in darkness.

Perhaps it had been a cat.

But she'd had cats in her yard before, and they'd never set off the lights. They were designed to be less sensitive than that.

There was a small glass pane in the centre of the door, a decorative touch. She knew the brightness of her skin would be revealed as she got close to peer through, but she had to know who was outside.

She pressed her face against the glass. The view outside was blurred and distorted, but everything looked normal.

Amy grabbed the door handle, about to open it, when she paused. Perhaps she ought to call the police.

But would they come out? To a disgraced detective, who was scared because a security light had come on, and she'd been too drunk to lock up properly?

She opened the door and stepped out.

The night air chilled her, the wooden decking cold under her feet, distant noises drifting towards her. The tide. Traffic in the distance. She tried to see into the darkness of the yard.

It all looked the same. Silent.

She stood still, a pale glimmer in the dark, her heart pumping hard, waiting for someone to jump out at her.

There was no movement, no sound.

She stepped backwards into the house and turned the lock.

There'd been nothing there, she told herself. An animal crossing the beam, most likely. Go back to bed. Be strong.

In the distance, an engine started, followed by the crunch of tyres as a car slowly pulled away.

Forty-Three

Charlie opened his eyes slowly, thick with sleep. His head felt like he'd been hit with a hammer. He moved his legs. They were leaden.

Hangovers are a bitch. He was waking too often like this.

He checked his watch, expecting it to be late in the morning, especially from the ferocity of the light outside, but it was just past nine. He groaned and wiped his eyes. He needed more sleep, but his body had decided that enough was enough.

The hotel room looked especially drab in the pale glow of the morning. Brown counterpane. Brown wallpaper. Brown carpet. Sunlight streaked through the too-thin curtains. Brown, of course.

He willed his body to wake as he went through the events of the night before.

One drink had led to another, then there was music, the night turning into a party he hadn't expected. He remembered lots of laughing, and singing along to Goldie.

Ah yes, Goldie.

The memory brought a smile.

She'd sung like an angel, perched on a chair, lost in her music. He'd known some of the songs, along with a few of her own thrown in, which were softer, more soulful. She'd announced it as Appalachian folk, but he didn't care about the label. It was the perfect start.

He swung his legs out of bed. He wasn't in Cookstown to watch a beautiful singer sing beautiful songs.

He closed his eyes as he waited for the room to stop moving. He thought about calling Eleanor, reminded himself that technically he was working, finding out what had happened in Gerard's past, but he knew he was enjoying it for a different reason: he was away from everything. From the weekly battles with Isobel. From the feeling that he was always letting Molly down. From the relentless plough through the tall tales from his clients, his tired mind trying to find another excuse to spin before the court. Instead, he was in a pretty seaside town that felt a long way from everywhere, rubbing away the hangover from an evening of good company.

But he needed a plan.

He remembered something.

He reached across for his wallet, and rummaged through his receipts until he found it. One of Goldie's business cards, her website and email listed. On the reverse, she'd scribbled her number. He'd done the same on the back of one of his own, although he couldn't recall who'd asked first.

As he looked, her name was in blue ink, next to a small drawing of a flower.

Sweet.

He keyed her number into his contacts, and was about to send a message, but stopped himself. He'd been drunk, so had he come across too strong? Was she merely being polite? Her number might not even be a real one. Being a pretty singer in a seaside bar meant that she'll be used to dealing with drunks who come on to her, and even better at finding a way to get rid of them. Give them a fake number.

On the other hand, some local help would be useful. What did he have to lose?

He sent her a message. *Hi. It's Charlie from last night (the drunk Mancunian). Enjoyed the night, enjoyed the chat, loved the music. What about a coffee? I could do with some local info.*

Perhaps that was too forward. Suggesting a coffee didn't really mean that he wanted a coffee. She'd know what he meant.

He typed another message. *Hi. Sorry, Charlie again. Sorry for being forward. If you don't want a coffee, it's fine. Sorry for bothering you. PS. Your music was great.*

All he had to do now was wait.

He was about to head for the shower when his phone pinged. When he picked it up, Goldie had replied.

Hi cute early bird Manc guy. I'll do better than coffee. How about a good breakfast?

He smiled to himself.

The day was brightening up.

***

Goldie was sitting in a dusty blue camper van when he arrived, her legs swinging from a side door. There were stickers in the back window. CND. Rainbows. A guitar.

The breakfast place, Crabbies, wasn't far from Cookstown, but it was a whole different scene. No sandy beaches, but a coastline of high chalk cliffs and crystal water lapping onto pebbles. If Cookstown was seaside, this was coastal, with crab-pots hanging from the side of the café, next to a steep concrete ramp that ran down to the beach.

Crabbies was all about the view into the cove, with floor-to-ceiling windows along one side, and a veranda with metal bistro tables.

Goldie jumped down when he parked, her pumps kicking up dust, and smiled a warm good morning. 'Do you want to dine outside?'

He couldn't stop the smile from being returned. She'd looked pretty the night before, in the dim lighting of the pub, but the morning gave her more of a glow, her blonde hair now the colour of straw and her skin make-up free. She was less of the folk singer too. The night before, the style had been about pleasing the audience, the denim skirt and suede waistcoat just how she was expected to be. In the morning, it was tight jeans and pumps, a faded purple t-shirt and her hair pulled back into a ponytail.

He thought of the clogged city centre he was used to, and preferred the cool breeze in his hair. 'I can't think of anywhere better to be.'

'I knew you'd like it,' she said. 'It's a bit wilder out here. Coves and caves, rocks and crabs. See that concrete ramp there? It's where the lifeboat gets launched. There's even an old Cold War radar station along the cliffs there, hidden underground. I've been in it. Very creepy. Built to monitor the Russians, but it's as if they just abandoned it one day.' She waved at someone inside before asking Charlie, 'Full breakfast with all the trimmings?'

'Perfect.'

She put her two fingers in the air at whoever was inside, to indicate the order, before settling down at a table closest to the barrier, a sheer drop on the other side. The interior kept up the fishing theme, with more crab-pots in one corner and nets along one wall, but the tables were full of people who didn't look like fishermen. Pensioners with pale legs in shorts that rode high up their thighs, some with mobility scooters parked outside.

'There's a caravan park just up the road,' she said, spotting his gaze. 'But the way you were chugging them down last night, it seemed like hangover food was needed.'

Charlie winced. 'Was I that bad?'

She waved him away. 'I play in dive bars, I've seen worse. And you didn't get all sleazy. Just drank until you looked sleepy.'

He laughed. 'But if I was just the pub drunk, why did you agree to meet me?'

'Why the hell not? You're a guy on a quest. Singing is my job, but it's a night-time thing. Sometimes, the days are too long to fill.' She leaned back and narrowed her eyes. 'Come on, why are you really here?'

'What do you mean?'

'I might be some hick singer, but I didn't come down on the last cloud. You're a lawyer, and you're hanging around a small seaside town, asking about an old photograph. You want to know when it was taken? Go on the internet, hit the forums, someone will know. There's more to this.'

'So, that's why you agreed to meet. You're suspicious.'

'And you're a lawyer, which makes people nervous. Until they need one, that is, but you'll get why I'm curious about a lawyer from the other side of the Pennines turning up and asking questions.'

Charlie didn't answer straight away as their food arrived.

They both ate in silence for a couple of minutes, the food bringing Charlie back to life, until he said, 'How do I know I can trust you?'

'Damn, I knew there was something going on,' she said, laughing. 'I should give up playing the guitar and become a detective.'

'Can I though?'

'Use your lawyerly instincts. But I'm just a local with a lot of time to kill. You could make my day more interesting. For that, you've got my attention.'

Charlie thought about that, and realised he'd have to take the bait.

He took the photograph from his pocket. It was becoming more creased. He needed a better way of carrying it.

'The friend I told you about, the man in the picture who'd died? He was my client, and this picture struck me as strange. So, I'm here, wanting to know more.'

She picked up the photograph and examined it with more scrutiny than the night before, as if the answer was written in there somewhere. She frowned. 'I know him.'

'Everyone knows him. It's Spencer Everett.'

'As in Home Secretary Spencer Everett?'

'One and the same. And look at the message on the back. What is that all about?'

Her eyes widened. 'You think this photograph might be connected to his death? Does it involve the Home Secretary?'

'I'm not saying anything. I'm just trying to discover the truth, nothing more.'

She sat back, patting her mouth with a napkin. 'Okay, let's start. What do you want to know?'

'About what happened back then. We've already worked out which weekend it was, but who'll know what happened that night?'

'It depends on what it is. If it's something personal, you'd need to know who to ask. If it's big news though, try The Buford Library.'

'Buford?' Charlie laughed. 'What, as in Lewis Buford, one of the other guys in the picture?'

'Weren't you listening last night? The Bufords are powerful people. They've got money and status and they make donations, because it stops anyone caring where their money comes from. They donated a building to be used as a library, so they got their name on it. And others too. They call it Cookstown, but it won't be long before it becomes Bufordsville or something. But in the library, they'll have all the old newspapers.' She drained her coffee. 'Let's finish this and do some detective work.'

'Only on one condition,' he said.

'Which is what?'

'You don't give up on singing.'

She leaned across to kiss him on the cheek. 'I think I can promise that, cowboy. C'mon, let's go.'

Forty-Four

Amy looked up at Tammy's house from her car seat.

She'd woken with a sense of purpose. Her night had been disturbed, and she'd spent the rest of the night on the sofa in fitful sleep, a hammer within reach, but it had given her fresh resolve. She wasn't going to be pushed aside by Mickey Higham. Tammy had sought her help because she was angry, and she was angry because she felt powerless.

Tammy must have seen her arrive, because the door opened and she appeared in the doorway, her arms folded.

As she stepped out of her car, Tammy pushed open the door and said, 'Have you been sent to hush me?'

'Tammy, I'm not your enemy here. I'm looking at Natasha's case, but …,' and she wondered whether she should tell her that she was off the Sarah Marsh case, but decided against it. 'But my boss is mad about it.'

'For wasting time on people like me?'

'Natasha's case is twenty years old, and there are always other things to do, but I want to help, I really do.'

Tammy paused, her hand on the door edge, before relenting and stepping aside. 'You'd better come in.'

As Amy went inside, her eyes went straight to a photograph of Natasha.

'She's pretty,' she said, careful to use the present tense.

Tammy let out a long breath. 'Inside and out. I miss her every single day. When I wake up, there's a moment when I feel okay, but then the thought of being without her crushes me again. People tell me that time heals, but that's just bullshit. Healing means going back to how you were before, but nothing is ever the same. You just get used to the pain.'

'Does not knowing make it worse? Or does the hope keep you going?'

'Not knowing is the torment. I watch stuff on TV and people talk about closure, but I don't want that. Who wants to know that their baby is dead? I brought her into the world myself and I brought her up alone.' She waved her hand in dismissal. 'You'll have heard the gossip, that I don't know who her father is. What can I say? I was going through a wild time, and I got reckless with two or three blokes. I could have got them tested, I suppose, but they were all losers, so I thought, fuck it, I'll be all she needs. People don't see the effort though. They see just a crazy woman who lives in the woods, and reckon that Natasha wanted to run away from me. It wasn't like that. I wanted a better life for her. Better than my life. Leave here if she wanted, I said, I won't hold her back. I told her to look up, not down. If she thinks people regard her as less, prove that she's more, and wipe the sneers from their faces.'

'I'm not judging you,' Amy said. 'And I don't think the police were back then, because I know cops, and I know how hard they try.'

'Maybe you see what you want to see.'

'Her car was found on the Baptist estate. Did she know anyone from there?'

Tammy shook her head. 'I knocked on every door on that estate. No one had seen her before.'

'Why was her car there?'

'Come on, you're a copper. If you wanted to ger rid of a car so that it's never seen again, most people would dump it there, expecting it to be stolen and stripped before the sun comes up.'

'If I wanted to get rid of forensic traces, I'd burn it out.'

'And attract every copper in Cookstown, thinking that they've got city behaviour coming to their patch of seaside bliss? That's you not thinking it through. No, you'd dump it there, expecting it to disappear.'

'Except that someone called it in.'

Tammy allowed herself half a smile. 'Maybe not everyone on the Baptist estate is as bad as people think they are.'

'You got the car back,' Amy said. 'What did you do with it?'

'Still got it.'

'After all these years?'

'It's my baby's car. I'm not selling it. And you coppers might not realise the forensic value of it, but I do. That car is staying right here until I find her.'

'Can I see it?'

'Follow me.'

Tammy took Amy to the back of the house. It was the same as at the front, a patch of mud surrounded by trees, more chickens in a pen.

Tammy must have noticed her looking, because she said, 'I made those pens, the tops too, to keep the foxes out. I sell the eggs. Got a small delivery round. Even got my own boxes printed up, though I make sure my name isn't on them. *Cookstown Fresh*, that's what I call them. It keeps me calm, gives me something to do. I love them chucks. Come on, the car's this way.'

They walked to a wooden out-building, the doors joined by a thick chain, held in place by a hefty padlock. Tammy unlocked it and pulled on one of the doors. It didn't swing freely, as it scraped on the grit trapped underneath.

Tarpaulin covered the car. Tammy pulled on it to reveal a model that would just about grace a classics rally, except that rust was eating its way through the metal around the headlights, and the white paintwork was scuffed and dull.

'A Ford Escort Mark III,' Tammy said. 'Nat was so proud of this car. It makes a grinding noise when it starts and it's missing two trims, but it was her first car. It gave her freedom.'

'It doesn't matter what you get later,' Amy said. 'You never stop loving your first car.'

'You cops didn't love it so much though. Wanted it out of the compound. But there is some of Nat in there. The CD's she'd made. Some old sweet wrappers. A lipstick. Something else too. See if you can spot it.'

Amy walked around the car.

It was in poor condition. There were some bumps at the back, and the rear seats had tears in them, but nothing that drew her attention.

Amy shook her head. 'Help me out here.'

'They took it to the compound on a recovery truck, and brought it here the same way. It's just as it was left.'

'Nope. I can't see what you mean.'

Tammy reached for a plastic sack that was in the corner of the building, then opened the driver door. She draped the sack over the seat and said, 'Get in.'

'You sure?'

'I'm sure. Get in.'

Amy did as she was told, fighting the urge to sneeze as she settled into the driver seat, the dust disturbed. A musty smell filled her nostrils. Mould grew on the window seals.

Tammy leaned in. 'Anything?'

Amy looked into the centre console, the door pockets, leaned across to peer into the glovebox. 'No, nothing.'

'How tall are you?'

'Five-seven.'

'Three inches taller than Nat. Stretch your legs.'

Amy saw straight away what she meant. 'I couldn't drive it like this. I can just about get my foot on the accelerator.'

Tammy slapped the roof. 'There you go, detective. If you can't reach, Nat had no chance. And if Nat couldn't reach the pedals, that means someone else was driving. Whoever dumped her car, you can be damn sure it wasn't Nat.'

Forty-Five

Charlie turned in his seat. 'Goldie, I'm intrigued. What's your story?'

They were in her camper van, Charlie's car back at the hotel, heading towards the library.

'Why do you want to know?'

'You're a folk singer spending time with a lawyer. Something brought you to this point, so I'm interested.'

She kept her focus on the view ahead. 'There isn't a whole lot to say.'

'Oh, come on, now you're being coy. You're pretty. I'm guessing you're single, or else you wouldn't be with me now. There's always a story there.'

A smile curled her lips. 'You think I'm pretty?'

'You only need a mirror to work that out.'

She laughed. 'That's sweet, thank you. My story? Failed dreams, I suppose. I played my guitar, sang my songs, even joined a band, and we got a few spots in London. We got close to a break, supported some of the stars and got good crowds, almost signed a record deal once, but in the end it wasn't going to happen.'

'How do you know that?'

'Time tells you. You think you've made it when your band gets a support slot for someone big, but then someone new comes along, and you realise that they're shooting past, someone else's new star.'

She gripped the wheel and let out a sigh. 'For every star who makes it, there are a hundred times as many who get left behind, like me, with a battered old guitar and a tale of broken dreams.'

'Sounds like a country song in its own right.'

'It's been written before,' she said. 'Don't get me wrong, this isn't self-pity. If I'm going to live out a simple life, there is no better place than Cookstown to do that.' She pointed. 'And here we are. The library.'

He looked out of the window to a high redbrick building at the end of the main street, the awnings of small shops and whitewashed buildings further along. A concrete plinth over the entrance had the legend *Buford Library* chiselled into it.

As they went inside, the sounds of the town outside were replaced by the hush of a library, no other silence quite like it. Calming, peaceful.

Goldie led the way. She marched up to the counter and said hello to the woman working there, a middle-aged woman with hair sprayed so stiff that nothing moved, even when she got close to the fan that was rotating further along, making a small pile of paper flutter, trapped under a paperweight.

'Hi Goldie, lovely to see you. How's the music coming on?'

'I get to make people happy.'

'That sounds a good way to be. What can I do for you?'

'Where do you keep the old newspapers?'

She turned to point behind her, her hair staying rigid. 'They're all in this cabinet here, held on microfiche. When are you looking for?'

'Twenty years ago. August and September. *County Press*.'

She went to the cabinet and flicked through folders, going from one drawer to another, until she picked out two envelopes. 'Here we are. August and September.' She reached into the envelope and pulled out what looked like an X-ray image. 'See here, the sticker at the top. That's the date of the newspaper, sometimes more than one sheet. Just put it under that scanner, over there by the genealogy section, and zoom in and move it around using the wheels. You'll soon get the hang of it.'

Goldie thanked her and set off, clutching the envelopes. Charlie followed. 'Do you know her?'

'This is Cookstown. Everyone knows everyone. Sometimes I like it. Other times, it drives me mad.'

They took a few minutes to work out the machine, both staring at a screen that was like a battered old computer monitor with a tray underneath, grey plastic wheels jutting out at the front.

Once they were ready, Goldie lifted out one of the slides. 'Let's start with the day before. If it's to do with the Cookstown Fair, let's get a feel of it.' She loaded the sheet and began to skim through. 'What are we looking for?'

'I don't think we'll know until we find it. I'm surprised that Cookstown has a daily paper.'

'It doesn't really. It's a local version of a paper produced for the whole area, but with some articles replaced with local stuff. Now, we don't even have that anymore. It's all gone online.'

They each pored over every story, looking for a hint, but it was routine news and reports from the fair, the machine crashing and whirring as they moved between articles and pages, zooming in and out, but there was nothing that gave them any clues. A few car crashes, talk of a drunk driver, and tales from all the small towns nearby where nothing much happens. The paper from Saturday was just the same.

As Goldie loaded in the Sunday paper, which consisted of three sheets of microfiche, Charlie said, 'We need to see whether the vibe changes. If a dramatic event occurred, the tone of the paper will be different.'

The Sunday paper took longer to wade through. There were opinion pieces and more reports from the Fair, along with summaries of the church services and a rundown of the people who'd appeared in the local courts.

Eventually, Goldie put them back in the envelope. 'Nothing there.'

'One more day,' Charlie said.

'You sure?'

'A few more minutes won't matter.'

Goldie skimmed through again, the cogs on the control wheels clanking as she turned them, headlines rushing past, pausing just long enough to glance at the contents.

'Go back,' Charlie said, his tone more urgent.

'Where?'

'Two pages. I saw something.'

Goldie went back.

'There,' he said, pointing at a story. 'Zoom in.'

'I remember this,' Goldie said, as she read.

Concern Grows For Missing Cookstown Woman

Concern grows amongst the Cookstown Police for missing woman, Natasha Trenton.

Natasha, 18, did not return home from work on Saturday night and her whereabouts are not known.

In a press conference, Detective Chief Superintendent Jimmy Gray said, 'Natasha Trenton left her place of work Saturday night, as a housekeeper at the home of Clarence Buford, and did not return home. It is too early at this stage to speculate where Natasha may have gone, but if she is watching this, she should contact her family to let them know she is safe.

Police appealed for anyone who might have seen her car, a white Ford Escort.

Clarence Buford said, 'Natasha was a valued member of our staff and we remember her leaving Saturday night. We hope she's safe and well and she shouldn't worry about missing work. She should contact her family, so they know that she's unharmed. In the meantime, we're praying for her.'

Goldie sat back and whistled. 'It's the one Scott talked about last night. You remember, the barman. He mentioned that there were rumours Truman Buford had killed a maid, and here it is. Buford, a missing woman, and the night the photo was taken.'

Charlie took out the photograph again. 'And my client's last moment of true happiness.'

Forty-Six

Isobel growled in frustration when her phone rang.

There were papers everywhere as she tried to balance a set of estate accounts, the numbers not matching by the mighty sum of five pounds. She felt like throwing in the fiver herself, but that wasn't how it was done. The beneficiaries had to sign off the estate accounts as being accurate before she could distribute the estate, and she could hardly send them a bundle of documents with a five-pound note stapled to the front.

She ought to ignore the call, but her secretary knew she was busy, so it must be important for her to be interrupted. It could be about Molly.

She snatched at the receiver. 'Yes?'

'Isobel, there's someone on the phone for you. He mentioned new business.' She lowered her voice. 'Sounded quite posh, so there might be some money in him.'

Isobel looked at the paperwork spread around her, and wanted to scream that she had too much other stuff to do, but her target had been raised and she was struggling to reach it. That was the downside to doing well. If she made her target, they don't give her a pat on the back and ask her to repeat it. Instead, they raise the target, and expect her to go even harder next time.

'Okay, put him through,' she said, as she wiped the fatigue from her eyes. When her phone clicked, to tell her the connection had been made, she said, 'Hello, Isobel Atkins speaking.'

She'd changed her name when she'd married Charlie, just to have the same name as any children that came along, so she was still Isobel Steele at home, but she had kept her own name for her professional life.

'Hello, my name is Thomas Riley,' the man said. 'My father needs a will drafting most urgently.'

The words *most urgently* grabbed her attention. Usually, that meant that there was someone who was gravely ill, and the final outcome was when the real money came in.

'If you don't mind me asking,' she said, 'but is your father proposing to appoint this firm as executor?'

She wouldn't normally be so blunt, but the thought of administering an estate for a man about to die gave her renewed hope of meeting her target.

'He is, if you have the time,' he said. 'It's a complicated estate, but worth many millions.'

She gave a silent punch in the air. 'When is a good time to meet?'

'In around an hour?'

'Yes, fine,' she said, checking her watch. 'Although it's your father I need to speak to. I mean no discourtesy, but I have to be satisfied that he can give me clear instructions. Do you know where my office is?'

'My father will be in attendance, but I was thinking of somewhere much more informal. My father won't like attending an office, you see. He's wanting to spend whatever time he has left in fine restaurants, so please join us.'

She eyed the outstanding paperwork, and compared it to an hour or so in a fine restaurant.

It was an easy problem to solve.

'Yes, I'd love to, thank you. Who am I to disappoint your father?'

'The Palace Restaurant in an hour. Just ask for Mr Riley. We'll be waiting. And don't worry, I'll keep him off the whisky.'

As Isobel ended the call, she smiled. Her day was perking up.

Forty-Seven

Goldie parked at the locked gates to what looked like a large country house, wrought iron hanging between two brick gateposts.

It hadn't taken long to get there, along a twisting rural road that went past small houses set far back from the road, until the view opened up, with a field and a stream to one side.

She leaned forward over the steering wheel. 'This is the Buford house. What do we do now?'

Charlie peered forward, straining to see what was on the other side, but there were only glimpses. Some red brick, grass. A horse grazed in the distance, sleek and brown. 'Say hello seems the best way.'

Goldie frowned. 'Now, are you sure you know what you're doing? These people are powerful. You don't want to be upsetting them.'

'If you're worried about what happens after I've gone home, you wait here. I'll say you gave me a lift, that's all.'

'I didn't say I was scared,' she said. 'I was wondering whether you were, but if we're doing it, we're doing it together.'

He looked across to her and said, 'I need you for the local knowledge.'

'You make it sound like you're planning on staying around.'

'I like the company,' he said, and jumped out of the campervan to go to a steel plate set into the gatepost. He pressed the buzzer and waited.

A voice crackled, 'Can I help you?'

'Good morning. My name is Charlie Steele and I'm a solicitor. I've come from Manchester to see Mr Buford.'

'What is the purpose of your visit?'

'I'm hoping Mr Buford might be able to help me with the distribution of an estate I'm administering.' It was a loose truth, but he didn't want to give away the real reason for his visit. Not yet, anyway.

To his surprise, the gates clicked and began to swing open.

He turned to Goldie. 'We're in.'

He got back into the camper. As they rumbled along the driveway to the house, the grandeur slowly revealed itself.

'Wow,' Goldie said. 'This is all a bit posh, and I'm in my battered old campervan.'

There was a large archway in the centre of the house leading to a courtyard. Goldie whistled. 'They've got stables.'

They both stepped out as a door opened. An old man walked towards them.

His pace was slow. He waved. 'Mr Steele, you say? It's a fine morning to meet a solicitor from the other side of the Pennines.' He shook Charlie's hand as he reached him, his grip surprisingly firm.

'Mr Buford?'

'That's me.'

There was a croak to his voice, and he moved like the old man he was, slow and full of effort, but there was a shrewdness in his eyes Charlie had seen before in old men who'd fared well in life. They knew their best days were gone, but it was a reminder of what had made them succeed.

He held his hand out towards Goldie but addressed Charlie. 'And your pretty friend?'

Before Goldie could answer, Charlie intervened. 'Goldie gave me a lift here, that's all, saw a stranger in trouble. She doesn't know anything about my case. That would be a breach of client confidentiality.'

'Well, I don't want to keep your lift waiting. Why don't you go, my dear, and I'll make sure Mr Steele makes it back into town?'

'So kind, Mr Buford,' she said, her tone one of sweet insincerity. 'I wouldn't want you put to any trouble. Can I take a look at your horses?'

'Call me Clarence, and of course you can. Some of the finest beasts around here.' He turned to shout at a man on his knees, tending some flowerbeds. 'Pete, come here.'

The man struggled to his feet, taking his time to straighten as he made his way over.

'This is Pete,' Clarence said. 'He does work for me around here. You are?'

'Goldie Brown.'

'Goldie, delightful to meet you. Pete will show you the horses. Mr Steele, follow me.'

Charlie did as instructed as Pete wandered off with Goldie, through large wooden doors into an ornate hallway. Light bounced around, from the large window at the top of the stairs to the mirrors, making a huge chandelier sparkle so much that it made him squint. Clarence took him through the house, past rooms that were filled with furniture that reminded him of a French Renaissance house, with gilded arms, paintings dominating the walls. Rolling landscapes but dark in tone, in the style of an old European Manor House.

They wandered along a corridor lined by wooden panels, Elizabethan-era now, until a door took them to a stone patio overlooking green fields broken up by hedgerows. More horses grazed there.

'Is this all your land, Clarence?'

'As far as you can see. I love this county. My family has owned some of this land for centuries, but I've bought more and expanded my estate. Not for greed, you understand, but to stop developers coming here. I'm not having my view spoiled by trashy new housing schemes.' Clarence turned to him, his hands in chino pockets. 'Tell me about this estate you've got to administer, and why it's got anything to do with me.'

Charlie spotted the change in tone. His croak had acquired a little more bite, and he realised that Clarence wasn't showing off his fields. He was pointing out to Charlie how much power he had.

What Clarence didn't realise is that being a lawyer involved upsetting people by asking awkward questions.

'My client was murdered, so it's my duty to find out by whom and why, so I can sue those responsible.' Again, it was stretching the truth, but it suited his needs.

'I can assure you, Mr Steele, that I haven't murdered anyone, so I know I can relax a little.'

'My client knew your son, Lewis, even spent time here, about twenty years ago, when Lewis was studying at Oxford. You might remember him. Here, I've got a picture,' and Charlie handed over the photograph.

Clarence took it from him, and Charlie could see him working out how to respond.

'I think I remember those friends,' Clarence said. 'But it was a long time ago, and you'll understand that I'm a very busy man,' and he handed it back. 'Why does your client's death bring you to Cookstown?'

'He seemed to place a lot of importance on his visit here. I can prompt you, if you prefer. He was here when your staff member went missing, Natasha. In fact, the night this picture was taken, I think. I saw your quote in the local paper, about praying for her safe return.'

Clarence pursed his lips and stepped closer. His voice was low when he said, 'You need to be careful what you insinuate, Mr Steele.

You're a guest around here, and we have a certain way of doing things. Making trouble for me isn't a way to make friends.'

Charlie stood his ground. 'I appreciate the friendly advice, Clarence, but why do you think it would make trouble for you?'

'It's in your tone, your manner, and from your presence on my property. I'm thinking that this meeting is done. Ordinarily, I'd invite you here for lunch, show the generosity of the Buford family name, but I'm suspicious of your motives.'

'I'm sorry you feel that way.'

Clarence pressed a button on a small device attached to his belt. It must have called Pete back, because when he emerged, with Goldie alongside, he was holding a black walkie-talkie.

As Charlie was joined by Goldie, Clarence said, 'Good day, Mr Steele. Miss Brown.'

Charlie realised that he'd need to find another way out, with no sign that Clarence was going to let him back through the house. As he scanned the garden, he saw a woman making her way across the lawn.

Her gait was unsteady, her walk just a shuffle, holding what looked like a bottle of something alcoholic. As she passed a weeping willow, she let the leaves run through her hands, her eyes never leaving Charlie.

She was elderly, around Clarence's age, skinny, so that Charlie could see the ridges of her collarbones through her dress, her hair grey and wiry, no real style, as if she'd just got out of bed.

Charlie and Goldie exchanged curious glances as the woman sat on a wooden bench by the willow tree. She raised the bottle as if in salute, before taking a drink from it and leaning back on the bench, her eyes closed and skyward.

Forty-Eight

Parliament in session was always busy. Journalists, lobbyists, MP's, aides and visitors, either going somewhere with a purpose, or else finding an excuse to just hang around. Manoeuvring, dealing, reporting, observing. Tea-rooms, bars, libraries, corridors, offices, all bustling under high vaulted ceilings, alongside statues and grand paintings, although most of it was a Victorian reinvention. The terraced streets that had once served the mills in Jessica's northern hometown were older than the Houses of Parliament, but that didn't prevent her from being awestruck whenever she went in there, even though it had become just a workplace that had taken over her life. Always tired, always skint. Sometimes, she'd walk home rather than take the Tube. When her wage was zero, every penny counted.

Today, it felt as if everyone was watching her, following her. Even the police seemed more interested in her, their fingers tight on their triggers.

Spencer's office was a tight space along a narrow corridor just behind the main Commons chamber. His name was on a plate on the door, slid into a brass holder. It reminded him that it would take a moment to replace him. The paint was old, but it was modern inside. A desk. Carpeted floor. A computer. Filing cabinet. A bland space in a beautiful building, designed to be functional, nothing more.

Jessica checked along the corridor before she ducked inside. No one there. The sound of debate drifted in, jeers and shouts and *hear, hear*, but they were distant, a familiar pattern. Jessica knew Spencer's routine for the day, and he would be in the Commons for most of it, then in one of the divisions casting his vote. It was all a charade. Everyone knew how the vote would go, but the formalities of democracy had to be carried out.

As she looked around the room, she didn't know where to start.

She was looking for paperwork relating to the Swiss bank account, and hopefully transaction details.

She paused for a moment. Was she really doing the right thing? Spencer was on the take, but so what? Weren't they all? And what had Nick Cassidy said? Some doubt about whether dodgy finances would lead to all of *this*? Lead to what? Too cryptic.

It was just nerves, she told herself. Stick with it.

The Willow documents had been in a photograph frame at Spencer's house, the picture a clue, a taunt almost. Was there something similar here?

There were photographs around the room, but nothing showing anything Swiss. Mainly Spencer with other politicians, his ego covering plain magnolia walls.

She knew the shelves and the cabinets, and Spencer never went in them. Her role was to pass things to him. Coffee. Papers. Letters.

She went to his desk instead and pressed a button on his keyboard. His screen lit up. For a moment, she was hopeful, but a password was required.

She went to the drawers instead, but the contents yielded no surprises. Jumbles of paper. Pens. A half-finished whisky bottle. Letters from his constituents. As she rummaged, her focus was on the contents only, her eyes flitting across letterheads and documents and discarded scraps of paper, her hand shuffling through them, feeling out for a hidden compartment.

She didn't hear the door open. Took no notice of the footsteps that got closer.

Until she heard her voice.

Jessica jumped, startled, then sat back in the chair, unsure what to say, as Wendy stood in front of her, her arms folded.

Wendy's eyes were blazing when she said, 'What the fuck do you think you are doing?'

Forty-Nine

Goldie drove for a hundred yards, her gaze flitting to the rear-view mirror, before she said, 'What do you think?'

Charlie turned in his seat and looked back through the rear window, Clarence Buford's home retreating into the distance. 'He was irritated. Behind all that fake politeness, he wanted to know why I was there, and he wasn't happy when I asked him about Natasha.'

'His house was the last place she was seen, and there's what happened to Truman too. The whole suspicion must hang there like a cloud.'

'I'm a defence lawyer. I've seen lives ruined on the back of suspicion, when the truth was different. People have their own reasons for staying quiet.'

'Which is why I'm going this way.'

Charlie turned to face forward again. 'I thought we were heading the wrong way back into town, but I thought, well, you're the local.'

'Well spotted, but I've got my reasons.'

Goldie yanked on the wheel and skidded into a clearing, dust spewing, gravel rattling against the underneath of her campervan, before she turned it around so that she was facing back towards Clarence Buford's house.

As they waited for the dust to clear, Charlie asked, 'What are you doing?'

'Why did we come here today?'

'To see what Clarence had to say.'

'No, wrong. What did you expect? A confession? No, we came here to see how he'd react. So, we'll sit here and see what happens, now that he's all shaken up.'

Charlie smiled. 'Have you done this before? You sure you're not a retired detective?'

'I watch a lot of television.'

They didn't have to wait long. Two songs on the country station Goldie was tuned into, her fingers drumming on the wheel.

A four-by-four pulled out of the Buford house. Even from that distance, it was obviously an expensive one. The paintwork gleamed a deep black and the chrome wheels beamed back the sunshine. The windows were tinted, so it was impossible to see who might be driving, but the cost of the vehicle made it worth following.

It turned towards Cookstown.

Goldie grinned. 'Showtime.'

She kept a respectable distance, not wanting to give herself away.

'What did you think about the woman crossing the lawn?' he said. 'Mrs Buford, you think? She looked out of place though. Shabby looking, drunk maybe.'

'It doesn't matter how rich you get, life can still deal you a bad hand,' she said. 'She had to bury a son, remember.'

The spread of Cookstown started to appear in the distance, but the four-by-four indicated to turn down one of the roads that headed back into the countryside. Goldie slowed and appeared uncertain.

'What's wrong?'

'It's a quiet road. If we turn to follow, he might suspect us.'

'My guess is that he suspects us anyway, but if we don't follow we'll never know where he went.'

'You sure?'

'Dead sure.'

Goldie turned to follow.

The road ran straight between lush green fields, sometimes through narrow tunnels of trees, and houses started to appear. At least the gates did, the houses hidden away between the undulations of the countryside, or else concealed behind clumps of thick woodland. There was a small village ahead, brick cottages around a green, a church at one end.

'I always promised myself I'd live around here,' Goldie said. 'Sell some records, have a couple of kids, maybe some pigs.' She held up her hand and said, 'He's pulling over.'

She slowed down as they got close. As the driver door opened on the four-by-four, Goldie slowed to a crawl.

'There he is,' Charlie said, as Clarence stepped out.

He approached a cottage with a rose-lined porch.

Goldie spoke in a low voice. 'Who's the old coot going to see?'

The front door opened. A man stepped forward, his hands on his hips.

Goldie said, 'Shit,' and sped up.

'What is it?'

Goldie shook her head and kept on driving.

'Goldie, tell me.'

'If you were hoping that old Clarence might be hiding away his dusty old secret, you might have it wrong,' she said.

'How do you mean?'

'That house? It belongs to an ex-copper. Everyone knows Jimmy Gray. Used to speak in the papers like he was the local hard-hitting sheriff, but he forgot that we all knew he was just stuck in some outpost. And he was also the copper mentioned in the newspaper report about Natasha Trenton.' She frowned. 'If old Clarence is hiding a secret, he's going a funny way about it.'

Fifty

'It's not what you think,' Jessica stammered, as Wendy came round the desk towards her.

Wendy slammed one of the drawers closed. 'You better start talking.'

Jessica swallowed, unsure what to say. Wendy stood over her.

Tears welled up in Jessica's eyes. 'I'm sorry, really sorry. Don't tell anyone.'

Wendy sat on the edge of the desk, so that Jessica was hemmed in against the window. 'You either tell me, or you tell the police, because it looks to me like you're stealing something. What is it? Secrets?'

'No, it's not that.'

'Do you want me to get Special Branch involved? Are you vetted properly?' She banged the desk. 'Spencer is the fucking Home Secretary. Do you realise how much shit you are in right now?'

'It's nothing serious. I'm just looking for something.'

'Who are you working for?'

'No, no, I can't tell you, but it was nothing bad, I promise.'

Wendy picked up the internal phone. 'I'm calling security, then the police.'

'No, don't, I'll tell you.' Jessica hung her head as she wiped her eyes with the back of her hand. 'I was trying to find out if Spencer is a crook, that's all. Dishonest expense claims, backhanders from lobbyists, that kind of thing.'

Wendy muttered, 'Jesus.'

'I'm sorry, I know it's wrong, but it's important to me. He's supposed to be a man of honour, but the more I learn, the worse he seems.'

Wendy laughed, but it was laced with sarcasm. 'Do you think he's any different to the rest? You came here with your ideals, and your good intentions, and now it hurts because you think Spencer is only in it for the prestige and the money. Spare me the fucking violins.'

'But we should have ideals. My Dad has given his life to politics, because he believes in things. Knocking on doors, leafleting, campaigning, because he wants a better world.'

'And you end up with people like Spencer Everett? That's life, sweetheart. I'm sorry the real world has let you down.'

'So, is he crooked?'

'Do you think so?'

Jessica shrugged and scowled. 'I'm starting to think that way.'

'Tell me what you know.'

'Why should I?'

'Because I can be on the phone to MI5 in ten seconds, and you'll spend a week in a police cell as they turn your life upside down. Everything you thought was a deep secret will be exposed. Everything you've looked at online. The messages you've sent. The boyfriends you've had. There won't be a private space left in your life if you don't talk to me right now.'

Jessica knew it was all over. Her internship. Her career in politics. All she could do was go home to her father and tell him how she'd failed.

'It started with a reporter called Nick Cassidy,' she said.

Wendy nodded. 'I know him.'

'He was doing a story about an expenses fiddle, and he said that the more he looked, the dodgier it seemed. Offshore companies. Nevis. Geneva.'

Wendy kneaded her eyebrows. 'When is he going to print?'

'That's it, I don't know. He said the story was much bigger now, and he sounded scared.'

Wendy went to the window, her arms folded, her jaw clenched.

Jessica stood. She took her Parliamentary pass from her purse and wiped her eyes. She put the pass on the desk. 'I'm sorry,' she said, and went as if to leave the room.

Wendy put out her hand. 'Wait.'

'No, I'm going. I'm guessing you're not my boss anymore.'

Wendy turned. 'You don't understand. I'm not your enemy.'

'You seem like it.'

'Do you know the secret to surviving in politics, and to being an aide? You'll think it's all about cosying up to the right people, but it's the opposite. It's knowing when the time has come to ditch someone, sensing that the shit is going to start flying. Politicians rise and fall. If you're an aide, you want to ride the risers and ditch the fallers.'

'That's mercenary.'

'It's life.'

'Is Dougie McCloud the same?'

Wendy shook her head. 'Dougie has been Spencer's sidekick ever since he entered politics. He's charting his rise, thinks he has all the answers. I don't have the history.'

'Where is Dougie?'

'Somewhere north, getting ready for the Detention Centre announcement. If the shit is going to start flying towards Spencer before then, I want out.'

'I thought you were his confidante, his friend.'

'His lover?'

'Well, yes, that too, I suppose.'

Wendy sighed. 'Don't think I don't know the rumours, but Spencer wasn't going to cross that line. Too soon after Pippa, even if they were getting divorced. So, tell me what you know.'

And she did. Willow LLC. Bridget's suspicions. The documents in the photo frame.

Wendy was silent for a few seconds, until she said, 'And you think Spencer might have been involved in her death?'

'That's what Bridget thinks, and she's spoken to Nick Cassidy.'

'You're going back,' Wendy said, more urgent now. 'If Spencer thinks you're onto him, he'll move the proof. Go back to his house, have a proper look. He won't keep things here. Too many sharp eyes. At home, that's his haven. I'll call his housekeeper and tell her to expect you. I'll stall him today, keep him busy.'

'Do I report to you?'

'Only to me.'

'How can I be sure I can trust you.'

'You can't, but I'm the only option you've got.'

Fifty-One

Amy was pacing as she waited for the manager of the vehicle compound to emerge from the back office.

She'd left Tammy's house wondering why Nick Cassidy was digging around Natasha's disappearance. There was no other reason why he would be in contact with Tammy, but Tammy wasn't clear why.

Amy knew she wouldn't be able to go through whatever property Nick Cassidy had on him when he jumped in front of the train, as that will be in the hands of the pathologist, but there might be something in his car.

When the manager came out of the office, he was tucking in his shirt and wiping crumbs from his mouth.

'Sorry, lunch break,' he said. 'Who are you again?'

Any cars seized by the police were sent to a vehicle compound run by a private company. The police got somewhere to store them, and the company made money from the release fees.

She produced her identification. Mickey hadn't demanded that she return it. 'You've got a car in here that was involved in a crash the other day. A red Clio.'

'The one that hit the police car? I think it's still here.'

'No one will come for it. The owner died.'

'What, in the crash?'

'Killed himself. We're hoping to find clues as to why.'

'Well, that's sad. Was he insured? I'll get them to collect. Looks like a write-off anyway.'

'I just need to search it.'

'If you take anything from the car, you've got to sign for it. This job, it's all about not being accused of pinching something.' He rummaged in some drawers, checking paper tags for a registration number, until he went, 'Here we are. Follow me.'

The warehouse was behind the office, a cavernous space lined with cars and vans. Some were bashed up and dirty. Others pristine, like a car showroom.

'Why doesn't anyone come to collect them?'

'No one can take the cars out unless they've got proof of insurance, and sometimes the cars just aren't worth it.' He pointed to a small Peugeot, more than twelve years old. 'Came in last night, because a seventeen-year-old had no insurance. Maybe his parents will put it on their own insurance and they'll be in for it later, but that'll cost them a few hundred quid. Is that car worth the hassle? Probably not. But the high-end ones always get collected.' He pressed a button on the fob and orange lights flashed. 'Here we are.'

Amy winced at the damage to Cassidy's car. The bonnet was crushed, the front wheels splayed, the engine exposed. It had dripped oil onto the concrete floor.

She went to the back and opened the boot. There was just an umbrella and some muddy boots, along with carrier bags. She lifted the carpet to reveal a spare tyre, but nothing else.

She opened the passenger door and looked into the back. Some discarded drink bottles and a take-away burger bag.

The centre console was filled with sweet wrappers, as were the door pockets.

She opened the glove compartment and peered inside. All she could see were petrol station receipts and a car manual. She rummaged through, but couldn't find anything else.

Amy glanced towards the manager, who was peering into a Mercedes in the line of cars opposite. She was disappointed, but it had been a long shot anyway.

'No, nothing.'

He stepped away from the Mercedes. 'I'm not surprised though.'

'Why's that?'

'Well, you guys did a good job yesterday, went through everything.'

'Why didn't you tell me this?'

'It's not my job to tell the police how to do their job. All I know is that a detective came here, found what he wanted, and left.'

She tried to keep her voice calm, so he wouldn't suspect anything. 'You know, that's the hardest part of the job sometimes, that you're told to do something, then someone else beats you to it. What did they get?'

'The log is in the office. Follow me.'

Amy went with him, her mind racing, wondering who had been sent. Once they were back in the office, he picked through a pile of clipboards until he found the one he wanted.

'It all goes on the computer at the end of every day,' he said. 'But nothing gives better proof than a signature in blue ink. Now, it says here that he found a USB stick.'

'Anything else?'

'No. Just that. A silver USB stick from the glove compartment.'

'Who found it?'

He squinted at the list and shook his head. 'My writing is getting bad. Too much computer use, that's the problem. You forget how to write. Hickam or Highat.'

'Higham?'

He clicked his fingers. 'That's him. Stocky guy. Nice suit, bad attitude.'

She rubbed her forehead, wanting to stamp the ground in frustration.

'Everything all right?'

Amy looked up. 'Yes, fine, thank you. He's just wasted my time, that's all.'

As she ran back to her car, she knew she had to confront Mickey Higham. What she didn't know was how it would turn out when she did.

Fifty-Two

Charlie held up his hand. 'Stop, wait there.'

They were back at the hotel, just so Charlie could freshen up before they decided where to go next.

Goldie stayed where she was. 'What is it?'

He pointed. 'My room is open. I know I locked it.'

'It might be the cleaner,' she said.

He gestured along the row of rooms to see whether any of the others were open. 'Mine's the only one with an open door, and where's the trolley? You know, with the fresh towels and sheets?'

He went to his door and pushed at it.

No one jumped out or ran off.

As he went in, he saw that his clothes were scattered over the bed, his suitcase emptied out, discarded on the floor. 'What the fuck?'

He went through his clothes, sifting through to see if anything was missing. His car keys were still there. He lifted them to show Goldie. 'They weren't after anything valuable.'

Goldie frowned as she looked around. 'If it wasn't a thief, who can it be?'

'I'm guessing someone who wants to know more about why I'm here. We've put Clarence Buford on notice, remember.'

'This could be a message to scare you off. To let you know that they know where you are.'

'More importantly, they're bothered by my presence. Is that a good thing, that we're on the right track? But how did they get into the room?'

They were interrupted by a cough behind them. It was the owner, a small woman with grey curls tight to her head, and sweater and trousers that were designed to give nothing away. 'I let them in, Mr Steele.'

'Why the hell would you do that, let them go through my things?'

'I run a certain sort of establishment here.' She pursed her lips. 'A respectable hotel.'

'I don't remember you asking about my lifestyle when you took my money.'

'Just because it doesn't say it on the sign doesn't mean that it isn't a rule. Everyone around here knows it. I ask for proof of identity, and if they have a Cookstown address, I tell them to go there, to their own bed. No one is using my rooms for,' and she blushed. 'For unrespectable activities.'

'What does that mean?'

She clenched her jaw, working out what to say, until she couldn't contain it any longer and blurted, 'You can't come to my town to pick up underage girls, and especially in my hotel.'

Charlie stepped towards her. 'I have no idea what you're talking about.'

'They said you'd deny it.'

'Who is *they*?'

'The police,' she said. 'They told me why you're here, that they'd received complaints about your intentions, how people know what you get up to when you go travelling. Young man, I thought you seemed a good sort. Perhaps I shouldn't have let them in, because I didn't know they'd leave it so messy, but I've got a duty to my town. If you're going to go creeping around a high school, just because you think we're all simple small-town people, you're not doing it from my establishment.'

Charlie's voice trembled with anger. 'I am not here for any purpose like that. I'm here to...'

He stopped when he felt Goldie's hand on his arm. 'Leave it, Charlie.'

'But she's accusing me of being a sex tourist.'

'No, she isn't. The police are. This good lady is doing what she thinks is right, because of what she's been told.'

'Listen to her, Mr Steele. Here,' and she pulled a bundle of cash from her pocket. 'Here's what you gave me. Please leave. And you'd be well-advised to leave town. Word like this has a habit of getting around, and the local boys don't like that kind of thing.'

He looked at the bundle of notes and said, 'Who was the copper?'

'Does it matter?'

'Did they tell you I was a solicitor? Well, this,' and he flung the money onto his clothes. 'It's an invasion of my privacy and I might want to sue. At the moment, the only person I'm suing is you.'

'You wouldn't do that.'

'Try me.'

She took a deep breath. Her voice softened. 'If I give you the name, will you leave me out of it?'

'You have my word.'

'Okay. It was Chief Inspector Higham. It means it came from high up, not a constable or anything, so I've got to do what I'm told. I was brought up to do what the police tell me.'

'I'm a criminal solicitor, so I spend my life doing the opposite,' he said. 'I'll be ten minutes,' and he slammed the door in her face.

He turned to Goldie. 'What the hell is this all about?'

'Easy,' Goldie said. 'You've rattled someone, so they've struck out with the worst accusation possible. They're trying to make you leave town.'

'But here is where the secrets are.'

'Oh, I get that. Your clothes all over the bed tells me that much. Some people want to know your business.'

'I won't leave. I'm seeing this through.'

'It's dangerous to stay.'

He sat on the bed. 'They called me a child molester. I'm not leaving for that to be my legacy around here.'

'So, what are you going to do?'

'Confront them.'

'How?'

'I'm going to the police station.'

'Are you sure about this?'

'Dead sure.'

'I better come with you then.'

'You don't have to.'

She laughed. 'I need to go with you, just to make sure you stay out of trouble.'

'Well, there is that,' he said.

He collected the rest of his belongings and headed back to Goldie's campervan.

Fifty-Three

Isobel thanked the waiter as he took her coat and hung it in a closet near the entrance.

She'd driven home first. Her clothes for work had been a suit, but she hadn't planned to see any clients that day, She had been kneeling on the floor at times, shuffling papers around. She went home to get a better suit, more professional, with shoes that were still not fully worn-in but glamorous enough for a good restaurant.

It wasn't what she'd choose to wear in the office, but she knew she'd dressed to impress. She'd kick off the heels later.

The waiter directed her to a table in the furthest corner of the restaurant, where there was a man waiting.

The mood lighting was low, the atmosphere sumptuous and dark, even in the daytime, with high ceilings and long curtains, the wallpaper gold and burgundy stripes beneath deep cornices, each alcove lit by a low-hung copper shade.

The restaurant was part of a hotel and a former bank. It used the old-money grandeur to good effect, with marbled pillars at intervals and bright tiled floors.

The man at the table stood when she got there and held out his hand. 'Thomas Riley,' he said, and smiled. 'I recognise you from your profile picture on your firm's website.'.

His tone was deep and assured, although his gaze was intense, almost piercing. He wore a blue open-necked shirt under a mauve linen jacket that looked crumpled, but in a way that showed its price-tag. The ease of his smile matched the velvet of his voice, his head shaved to a gleam.

He raised the bottle of white that was already open. 'I know you're working, but surely you're allowed at least one?'

She had to keep a clear head, with the work she had left at the office, but as he held out the bottle she saw that it had hardly been touched, and that familiar tap came to the back of her head. She should say no, but she wanted the wine.

'It won't do any harm, thank you.'

As he poured her the drink, she noticed there were only two glasses. 'Isn't your father joining us?'

'Unfortunately, he's not quite feeling up to it,' Thomas said. 'It came over him very quickly, but he asked me to speak with you, just to get an idea of how you are.'

'This isn't how we do things,' she said, as she sat down.

Dealing with peoples' estates could be delicate. Sometimes, those who feel like they deserve the money aren't always the ones who are going to get it, and she had learned to be wary of greedy relatives trying to steer elderly people into leaving them everything.

'I can't discuss much at all without your father being here,' she said. 'He would be my client and, if he's not here, I can't take his instructions. I don't mean to be impertinent, but those are the rules.'

His eyes sparkled with delight. 'A lawyer with integrity is to be cherished. And if you can't take instructions, you can't bill me for this time.'

She softened. 'Well, yes, there is that too.'

'I'm sure you'll find a way, so please, at least stay for one drink and let me find out what I can, so he can contact you and make an informed decision.'

She swallowed. He was holding out the glass to her, swirling the wine as he did. It looked cold, just how she liked it.

She should go back to the office, do some work she could bill, not engage in whatever this was, but one wouldn't matter. And the work might be lucrative.

And, she had to admit, he was a sexy guy. What was wrong with a pleasant lunch with a good-looking man?

'Thank you,' she said, and took the glass from him.

The first sip was like an avalanche of relief. Dry and crisp, a reunion with an old friend. Or was it an enemy? She'd never been sure.

For a moment, this was a world away from her files and her targets and the plough through estate accounts. Why shouldn't she enjoy it? A couple of hours away from the office would do her good.

And the second sip tasted better than the first.

Fifty-Four

Goldie pulled Charlie back as he stormed towards the police station door.

'You need to calm down,' she said.

'Don't I have good reason to be angry?'

'Maybe, but what do you think they'll do? Say sorry, and that they won't do it again.'

'I'm not after trouble,' he said. 'And I don't want to make you a target either, but is seems as if it's come looking for me. If I go in there and confront them, it makes it harder for them to do anything, because then I'm out in the open. It's harder to be attacked if you're where everyone is looking.'

'Why do you think you're going to be attacked?'

'Gerard Williams was found hanging from a tree. Ben Leech was discovered dead in the woods. A woman went missing twenty years ago, and as soon as I start asking awkward questions, rumours are spread about me.'

'Just remember, you're in a small seaside town. They can make you disappear like that,' and she clicked her fingers. 'You think the big city is dangerous? What, the place with a million cameras and witnesses, your every move tracked by whatever systems there are that you don't even know about? No, this place is much worse. The town is surrounded by miles and miles of nothing, fields where no one ever goes, and the North Sea is just there. It wouldn't take much to tip you over the side of a boat.'

'I should let it slide, because it's a small town?'

'No, but just think how you're going about it.'

He paused. 'Okay, I hear you. But it's not just what they said about me. I don't care what a hotel owner thinks, but there's something wrong here, and they're trying to stop me from finding it out. Doesn't that make you more curious?'

'I'm just a small-town folk singer, not a lawyer. But remember that if people are mad enough at you to get you thrown out of your hotel, God knows what comes next.'

He stepped closer. 'You don't have to hang around, you know. When I go, you'll still be here, and it won't be fair on you if I've made enemies.'

Goldie looked towards the police station. 'People around here have their own way of settling disputes, and it isn't pretty, that's all I'm saying. Don't end up as fish food.'

'I can't ignore it.'

'You're going in?'

'I am.'

'I'm coming in with you then. Just keep it polite,' and she set off for the station entrance.

He had to re-adjust his eyes when he got inside, the interior gloomy. Goldie was already at the counter, tapping on the counter loud enough for anyone to hear.

A man appeared from a door, sergeant stripes on his shoulders. He raised his eyebrows in surprise. 'Goldie, what are you doing in here?'

'Hi Rich, I was hoping we'd catch you on duty. How's your mum?'

'Bearing up. Got one of those motorised wheelchairs now, so she gets around. But I'm betting you didn't come in here to hear about my family.'

'We need to speak to Chief Inspector Higham.'

'Is it about the Sarah Marsh killing, because he's tied up in that right now?'

'It won't take long. I'm just trying to clear up a misunderstanding over this guy here,' and she turned to gesture towards Charlie, who stepped forward.

'I'm Charlie Steele, a solicitor here on business.'

The sergeant looked at Charlie, then back to Goldie. 'Like I say, he's pretty busy right now.'

Goldie leaned forward and spoke in a low whisper. 'Rich, this guy is talking about suing the police, but I'm trying to steer him away. Your bosses might thank you if you can make him think again.'

The sergeant rolled his eyes. 'Wait there.'

As the sergeant went back through the door, Charlie said, 'He seemed to know you.'

'I told you, it's that kind of town.'

Before Charlie could say anything further, the door opened again, but it wasn't the sergeant this time. Instead, it was a shorter man, his hair thinning, a stomach protruding over his belt.

'Chief Inspector Higham. What can I do for you?'

'I think you know who I am, because I was staying at a hotel in town,' Charlie said. 'Not anymore though, because you got me thrown out on the back of false accusations.'

Higham flushed. 'Did you see me there?'

'I was given your name.'

'Maybe you were told wrong.'

'Was I? Because if I can prove otherwise, and you're lying to me, who are they going to believe in the lawsuit? Do you think the respectable lady who owns the hotel will hold the bible and lie on oath for you?'

Higham straightened. 'There isn't going to be any lawsuit, you know that. Ease my concerns and tell me what you're doing here.'

Charlie and Goldie exchanged glances before he said, 'You already know. I spoke to Clarence Buford about Natasha Trenton. What I said made him rush off to speak to your retired boss.' He looked to Goldie. 'What was he called again?'

'Jimmy Gray,' Goldie said.

'That's the name, Jimmy Gray. The next thing I know is that I'm no longer welcome in Cookstown.'

There was a voice behind them. 'Why are you talking about my father?'

Charlie and Goldie turned. There was a woman standing there. Early thirties, short hair, dyed blonde, her arms folded across her chest.

'You said Jimmy Gray was your father?'

Higham interrupted and barked, 'Amy, my office now.'

'I want to know what's going on here.'

'My office. That's an order.'

Amy glared at Higham, then back to Charlie, before brushing past him and through the door into the private part of the station.

Higham stepped towards Charlie. 'State your business here.'

Charlie straightened. 'I've come here to find out why my client was murdered. The trail so far has led us to the Buford family, and a young woman who went missing twenty years ago. Natasha Trenton.'

Higham put his hands on his hips. 'And that makes it police business, so if you'll excuse me, I've got an investigation to conduct.'

'I'm just trying to find out what I can. But if you're not willing to help, that's fine. It doesn't mean I'll stop looking.' He slid his business card across the desk. 'In case you want to talk to me. Better coming direct than through whoever is renting me a room.'

He headed for the doors, Goldie following. He glanced back. Higham's gaze never shifted from Charlie.

As they got back onto the street, Goldie said, 'Why do I get the feeling that you just poked a stick into a wasp nest?'

***

As Amy waited outside Higham's office, the rest of the squad found a sudden need to concentrate hard on their computer screens.

Higham rushed past her, so Amy followed, slamming the door as she went in.

'What's going on, boss?'

'What are you talking about? And what are you doing here? You're not on this squad anymore.'

'I want to come back.'

'A man threw himself under a train after you spoke to him, and we only have your word what you spoke to him about, because it was all off the record, a quiet word in his ear. You messed up, Amy.'

'His death had nothing to do with me.'

'Let's see how the disciplinary proceedings work out..'

'But what about you? That man in reception. I heard what he said, about Natasha Trenton, and that you were trying to run him out of town.'

'I'll tell you about me, detective constable,' Higham said, simmering now. 'I'm your superior, so mind your tone. Being Jimmy Gray's daughter cuts you some slack, but not as much as you think.'

'But why's he in here, complaining?'

'Making trouble. He's a lawyer, it's what they do.'

'But why did he mention my father? And why now?'

'How do you mean?'

'Natasha Trenton was ancient history as far as this department was concerned. We heard from Tammy once a year. Now, there's a link between Sarah Marsh and Tammy, because Nick Cassidy had been talking to both of them, and now an out-of-town lawyer seems interested in Natasha.'

'How do you know he's from out-of-town?'

'I haven't seen him before, and I heard him say he was staying in a hotel. But why are we sending him away when there's a link?'

'There's nothing to see.'

'Aren't you struck by the coincidence?'

'I'm struck by the fact that he was wasting my time.'

'But what did he mean about Clarence Buford visiting my father? Why has my father got anything to do with this?'

'Well, there are two people you should be asking that question, and one of them isn't me.' He raised his finger. 'And before you go shooting your mouth off, and say something you regret, remember that being a retired copper's daughter counts for shit now that he's, you know, retired. People in this department know what's good for them, and that's following orders and not playing at being some maverick cop.' He banged his desk with his fist. 'I know about you going to see Clarence. Maybe Clarence was just trying to have a diplomatic word in your daddy's ear, rather than making it somehow official, because he's been through enough, with all the rumours about Truman. Quit trying to be super-cop.'

Amy folder her arms and glowered. 'Okay, but answer me one question.'

'You can ask it. It doesn't mean I'm going to answer it.'

'Why didn't anyone speak to those people staying at the Buford house on the night Natasha went missing? Lewis's university friends. The file says that Clarence wasn't immediately available as he had visitors, and they were heading home.'

'There's your answer then, right there in the file. They were going home. By the time that we got to Clarence, they'd gone.'

'It didn't strike you as suspicious that the night after Natasha goes missing, some students bolted out of town?'

'How do you know they were rushing, and not going home as planned?'

'Well, were they?'

'Seemed that way.'

'How do you know?'

'Because I asked.'

'It isn't in the file.'

'Not everything goes in the file. It wasn't important. They weren't suspects. They were just some students paying a visit.'

'Okay, I understand that, but what are their names?'

Mickey's eyes narrowed. 'Why do you want their names?'

'So I can speak to them, ask them what they know. They might not be suspects, because you're telling me that they had nothing to do with it, that they were just going home, but they might know something.'

'They had nothing to do with what?'

'Natasha's disappearance.'

'Look here, Amy, I've got a lot of respect for you, but you do as you're damn well ordered. You hear me?'

Amy stepped forward so that she was almost nose-to-nose with him. 'I hear you, boss, but I'm a police officer, and what I've learned over the years is that whenever someone gets all heated up when they tell me that there's nothing to see, it makes me think that there is actually something to see. Now, you can do what the hell you like to strike back at me, but that just makes me wonder why, that somehow we're missing a trick. If you're saying that an open case involving a missing Cookstown woman is suddenly closed, I'll go tell her mother that, and I'll leave her to raise whatever hell she wants. But if it's still open, it's my duty as a police officer to investigate.'

'And to hell with following orders?'

'Nope. It's just not to hell with a missing woman.'

As Amy turned to storm away, her hand swiped at the desk, her glare never leaving Higham's.

It was the lawyer's business card, which Higham had put on the edge of his desk when he walked in.

Now, she had a phone call to make.

Fifty-Five

It was a short walk from the railway station to Spencer's house, past a pub with tables outside, along a short country lane bordered by hedgerows, but that didn't stop Jessica from checking behind every few steps. Just an hour from the noise of Waterloo and she was in the silence of Hampshire countryside, with fields that rolled into the distance and midges that danced around her head as she walked.

The serenity didn't calm her nerves. The tranquillity just meant fewer witnesses.

She was over-thinking it, she told herself, but could she trust Wendy? She talked a lot of sense, but people like her can think their way out of problems, and Jessica knew that she was about to become a big problem for Spencer.

She had no choice though, she knew that. She had to either trust Wendy or stop what she was doing, and she didn't feel like quitting.

She texted Wendy. *Did you tell the housekeeper I was coming?*

The reply came back straight away. *Yes. But she will be loyal to Spencer so be careful. If Spencer gets into trouble, she's out of work.*

Jessica was reassured by the answer, because what she said made sense, so why warn her if it was a trap? She steeled herself for the search.

As she turned the corner towards Spencer's house, it felt quieter than when she'd been there a couple of days earlier. Horses grazed in the field next door as the sun reflected off the budding apples in the small orchard. Rabbits bounded ahead. The wheat was starting to brown in places.

The housekeeper opened the door before Jessica reached it.

'Wendy said that you were coming,' she said. 'I'm supposed to finish soon, so please hurry. I need to lock up.'

'Sorry, I won't be long,' Jessica said, and scurried along the hallway.

The room was just as it had been the day before. The shelves looked as if they'd been dusted, but that was the only change.

She examined the photographs again, but this time with fresh eyes. The photograph of Spencer and Pippa in Nevis was on a shelf, not a wall, presumably because it was easier to go into the back if all he had to do was lift it up. She should look for something similar.

Most of the photographs were like the ones in his Commons office, pictures of Spencer beaming with dignitaries and sports stars. She picked up each one and examined it, looking for the same marks as the one from Nevis, with the padded back and the broken lugs, but they all seemed like normal photograph frames.

Then she spotted it.

On the top shelf in the furthest corner, there was a picture of Pippa holding skis. There was no landscape visible, just Pippa posing with skis with a chairlift in the background, but skis might mean Switzerland.

She grabbed the frame and felt the back and grinned. It had the same padded feel as the other picture.

Jessica almost dropped the frame when there was a knock on the study door. The housekeeper looked in and said, 'Have you found what you're looking for?'

'Sorry, almost. I was just admiring this picture.'

The housekeeper softened. 'Ah yes, Pippa. Spencer was really affected when she died, and it surprised me. I don't want to talk ill of the dead, but she was a hard woman to like. Very cold with me, but perhaps Spencer saw a different side.'

'What did you think about how she died?'

'She crashed. Accidents happen. What can I say?' She held up her wrist and tapped her watch.

'Okay, sorry, I won't be much longer.'

'I'll wait at the door.'

As soon as she was alone again, Jessica pulled at the back of the frame and out spilled a small collection of papers.

Bingo.

She picked them up from the floor and looked at them, before whistling to herself.

There were details for a Credit Monbijou bank account in Geneva, the named holder being Willow LLC. One of the signatories was Spencer Everett. The other name made her gasp though. It was Dougie McCloud, Spencer's adviser.

They were in it together. Spencer as the asset, Dougie as the facilitator.

She laid the papers out on the desk and took photographs, before folding them to put them back in the frame.

As she returned the photograph to its former position, she allowed herself a smile.

She had him.

Fifty-Six

Amy tapped Charlie's business card against her steering wheel as she waited on the sea-front, close to where Sarah had been found. She'd called him after leaving the station and suggested a meeting. He'd sounded interested, but she'd made one condition: he had to be alone.

She'd been waiting for half an hour, and had been wondering whether he'd changed his mind, but then he was there, his hands in his pockets, looking around, checking his watch.

She raised her hand and went towards him, doing the same as him, checking around.

'Strange place to meet,' he said, and leaned back against the iron railings that lined the seafront.

'I can see someone coming from here,' she said.

'Are you expecting trouble?'

'I don't know, you tell me.' She softened her tone. 'I'm not your enemy here. I think we might have information to share.'

'It didn't sound like I was that welcome at the station.'

'This visit is unofficial.'

Charlie held out his hands. 'If I like what I hear, I'll share.'

'Natasha Trenton went missing twenty years ago,' Amy said. 'She was last seen at the home of Clarence Buford, where she was working. Every year, Natasha's mother, Tammy, has a blast at whichever copper gets to deal with her for not doing enough.'

'Did you?' Charlie said. 'Do enough, that is?'

'Mostly, but it was before my time, and it seems as if an adult goes missing, it doesn't get too much attention without evidence of foul play, like a pool of blood or something. Grown-ups are allowed to run away. Now, Tammy sees it as us not caring because she isn't a rich woman.'

'Is that how it is?'

'No, it isn't. We look after each around here, and my boss tells me they made all the right checks.'

'But why would my visit get Clarence all twitchy? He headed for your father straight afterwards.'

Amy shut away the image that flashed in her mind, of her father sitting in his garden, the proud retired senior police officer.

'The way my boss tells it, that was Clarence's way of getting my Dad to have a quiet word with people rather than making it all official. Clarence's son, Truman, confessed that he'd murdered Natasha, but it was written off as a garbled dream from when he was stoned. He couldn't provide any information about what he'd done to her, or where he'd disposed of the body.'

'Have you spoken to your father about Clarence's visit?'

That twisted feeling in her gut tightened. 'Not yet.'

'And I'm guessing that you're worried about what you might discover if you do.'

'Maybe. I don't question my father, he's a good man. But you're right, there's something here I'm not seeing.'

Charlie turned round to gaze at the sea. 'What do you think happened to Natasha?'

'I don't think she ran away.'

'If she didn't run away, there must be foul play.'

'That's the obvious conclusion.'

'Okay, answer me this,' Charlie said. 'Why does me asking questions of Clarence Buford make your boss try to run me out of town.'

'You weren't the only one who spoke to Clarence about Natasha. I did too.'

'You? Why?'

'Tammy made me curious,' Amy said, as she wondered how much more she should say.

Then, she reckoned she was already far enough in that there was no point in staying silent.

'Weirdly, there's a link between Natasha and a murder case we've got,' she said. 'There was a reporter who was speaking to Tammy about Natasha. He was also the last person to speak to the murder victim, a woman called Sarah Marsh. She was found on the beach, just down there,' and she pointed. 'Now, you turn up and ask about Natasha, twenty years after she went missing, and my antennae has gone a bit crazy.'

'What was the reporter's name?'

'Nick Cassidy.'

Charlie exhaled. 'Fuck.'

'What is it?'

He went into his pocket and dug out the photograph. He handed it over. 'I'm here because of the people who were at the Buford house when Natasha went missing.'

Amy examined it, and frowned when she saw the neon sign. 'That's Cookstown.'

'Twenty years ago,' Charlie said. 'The last night of the Cookstown Fair.'

Amy looked up. 'The night Natasha went missing?'

Charlie nodded. 'And turn it over to the inscription on the back.'

Amy did as she was instructed. 'My last moment of true happiness,' she read out.

'That was written by the person on the left, Gerard Williams. Lewis Buford is in the middle.'

She squinted harder at the picture. 'I don't know Lewis, but if you say it's him, I believe you.'

'Gerard was found dead a couple of days ago, and I think he was murdered.'

Amy looked up, shock in her eyes. 'And the police think otherwise?'

'They say likely suicide, but I knew Gerard. He was scared, because he'd been threatening to expose a secret about the man next to him.'

'The blond guy? Is that Spencer Everett?'

'One and the same. The Home Secretary, no less. Nick Cassidy got in touch with the man on the right, Ben Leech. He was found dead too. Again, presumed suicide, but his widow thinks differently.'

'Hang on,' Amy said, her hand out. 'Let me get this straight. Spencer Everett has a secret that your client wanted to expose, and now your client is dead, and you think that it's connected somehow to Cookstown? And the other guy? Same secret, and he's dead?'

'The inscription makes me wonder. The photograph was hidden with copies of letters sent to Spencer's lawyers, telling them what he was going to do. I didn't know about Natasha though. I didn't even know the date of the picture, until the Cookstown Fair link was discovered.'

Amy stared at the picture. 'The visitors went home the next day. This must be them, but I didn't know the Home Secretary was one of them. Now, it's looking more suspicious.'

'And there are two dead people who have had their murders made to look like suicide.'

Amy took out her phone to take pictures of the photograph and the inscription. 'What do we do?'

Charlie smiled. 'We? You're the detective, but if there's anything in this, don't we have to discount Truman Buford? If he killed

Natasha in a drugged-up haze, why does Spencer have such a big secret?'

'That can be tricky,' Amy said. 'Truman is dead.'

'So I heard,' Charlie said. 'But it makes it even more interesting.'

'Why's that?'

'Because if the scapegoat is dead, it means that Spencer's secret must be really bad. So bad that someone is prepared to kill to keep it quiet. We need to speak to Nick Cassidy.'

'We can't.'

'Why? Come on, we're sharing information.'

'I can't believe I'm saying this,' she said, and let out a long breath. 'He was in the cells, until we let him go.'

Charlie's eyes widened in surprise. 'But if you let him go, that means he's free, so I can speak to him.'

'No, you can't,' she said, and she knew how it sounded as soon as she said it, that it was another limb to the conspiracy. 'He threw himself under a train not long after his release.'

Fifty-Seven

Isobel woke with a start, before groaning and holding her head. The street outside hummed with the dregs of rush hour. The room blurred as she tried to make sense of her surroundings.

Where the hell was she?

She was lying down. As she stirred, she felt the coolness of good cotton brush her legs.

She looked down. She was in bed, naked.

But not her own bed.

She scanned the room in panic. The high ceilings. The deep cornices. The hum of traffic outside. It was the hotel attached to the restaurant, she knew it.

But why was she there, in bed, naked?

Her mind flashed back to earlier in the day. The meal. The man. The wine.

She buried her face into the pillow and groaned. No, not this. Not again.

The wine had gone down easily. Too easily, maybe. The first was followed by a second, welcomed like an old friend, then she'd been the one reaching for the bottle.

She listened out for voices, expecting a male boom from the bathroom, but there was nothing. She looked for her watch. It wasn't there. As she looked over the side of the bed, she saw it, on the small pile of her clothes, her knickers and bra on top, the last ones to be removed. She checked the time. Past seven o'clock.

She gathered the sheets around herself, worried now. Oh fuck, what had she done?

She sank back as she tried to make sense of the afternoon. When had she crossed the line?

She knew how her demon worked. She could avoid the booze, but once she had the first taste it was something she couldn't stop. It was like a switch, and it didn't take long for it to click. She might be able to walk away after the first, and maybe even the second, but a point comes when the party takes over and she's in for the long haul, where she's always the last to leave.

Perhaps she'd become too loud, shown herself up in front of her potential new client, so he'd allowed her to sleep it off without embarrassing herself at the office. He'd been a gentleman, she was sure of it.

Then she saw it, and her stomach rolled.

It was a note next to a lamp. *Isobel. Enchanting downstairs. Amazing upstairs. We must do this again. Thomas. X*

Great. A fucking scorecard.

Her eyes welled up with tears. How could she do it again?

She'd blamed Charlie last time. For the neglect. For the indifference. For just not being right for each other. Now, she had Simon, but here she was again. Perhaps it was just her. Narcissistic, self-destructive. Selfish, deceitful Isobel.

No, she had to pull herself together. Act normal. It was a one-off mistake. No one need know. Resolve to be different.

She swayed as she stood, her arms over her breasts, ashamed of her nudity in a strange bedroom.

Had it really been so easy for him? Or for her?

She had to go home. Kiss her daughter. Kiss Simon. Make him feel special. Remind herself of everything.

Never again. It must never happen again.

She got dressed quickly, then panicked.

She was missing an earring.

They were special ones, small solitaire diamonds on a platinum curl, a present from Simon. It wasn't under the bed, or next to the lamp, or caught in her clothes.

She checked her watch again. She couldn't stay any longer. He'd wonder where she was.

She found her phone. The green light was flashing. Missed calls. Unanswered texts. She didn't need to read them to know what they said. Where are you? What's going on?

She took a deep breath and smoothed down her clothes. He'd see her walk in and recognise it as her best suit, know that it was different to how she'd looked earlier.

God, she needed to get through this.

She glared at herself in the mirror and despised what she saw.

As she left the room, she wiped away a tear. At her age, the walk of shame. It was too much.

Fifty-Eight

Charlie was astounded.

'Cassidy did what?' He held out his hand. 'No, I heard you, but why would he throw himself under a train?'

'There are many reasons why men kill themselves,' Amy said.

'But you think it's connected to this case.'

She leaned back against the seafront railing and put her hands in her pockets. 'I just don't know anymore. He seemed pretty fucked up. Just sat in a hotel bar all night, drinking, then surrendered himself after crashing into a police car, still drunk. That isn't someone in control.'

'Or the actions of someone who is scared to death, because he's pursuing a story and people keep dying.'

'He seemed hunted. That's the best way I can describe it.'

'Was he charged with drink driving? You said he'd crashed into a police car.'

'No. Released under investigation.'

'Come on, that's bullshit,' Charlie said. 'He's a person of interest in a murder case. He crashed into a police car when pissed and ran off. He's let out of his cell and found dead a few hours later. That's too convenient. What was he getting close to? You must know. What had he found out? What was his story?'

'I don't know, because a USB stick had already been seized from his car before I got to it.' She raised her hand. 'And before you say anything, he was the last person known to have spoken to a woman found dead on the beach. I'd be more suspicious if it hadn't been seized.'

'Do you really think that?'

'What else do you expect me to think? That he was bumped off by another copper?'

'What's on the USB stick?'

'I don't know. I'm not on the squad anymore.'

'We need to be methodical,' Charlie said. 'What do we know about Nick Cassidy?' He held out his fingers and proceeded to turn them down one by one as he spoke. 'One, he's a reporter and had been in touch with Ben Leech, who is now dead. Two, he was the last person known to have spoken to Sarah Marsh before she was found dead on the beach. Three, he was sniffing around Cookstown and he's a long way from home. And four, he was speaking to Tammy Trenton.'

'There's a link, obviously.'

'And how did you know he was the last person to speak to Sarah Marsh?'

'We got her phone records.'

'And how did you know where he was?'

'Once we knew his phone number, we got his records, and got his GPS location.'

Charlie beamed. 'There you have it. You have Cassidy's phone records.'

Amy rolled her eyes. 'For Christ's sake, Charlie, it's actual evidence. Start copying that and I'm in deep shit. No, we both are, because if I get dragged down, you're coming with me.'

As they both stared out to sea, Charlie said, 'why here?'

'What do you mean?'

'Just that. It's a question I always ask myself when I look at a case. Everything happens because of a choice or a decision. A stranger is attacked and robbed. Why did the robber choose that spot? Does that lead to another suspect? A burglar steals the diamond rings, but how did he know they were there? Is it just an insurance fraud gone wrong? Why did the family go out? Was the burglar watching, or was it opportunist? Facts create opportunities, even if it's accidental, and exploring those facts might lead to a reason why my client is innocent.'

'And in this case?'

He gestured towards the beach. 'Why was Sarah Marsh found here?'

'It's quiet. Look, not many houses.'

'I can bet there are quieter places to dump a body. Was she caught on CCTV anywhere?'

'Her car was.' Amy grimaced. 'And driving back.'

Charlie raised an eyebrow. 'She didn't drive herself back, so you can bet she didn't drive herself there too.'

'Do you think we haven't thought of that?'

'Hey, I'm just talking it through, but Cookstown is surrounded by miles of fields. Look at us here, gazing out to sea. People are drawn to it. People walk their dogs on the beach. If you are dumping the body, you are visible from a long way off.'

Amy stared towards the steady roll of the sea, white tips in the distance, and realised he was right. They'd wondered whether Sarah was meant to be washed away, but bodies in the sea always turn up eventually.

But what was the point of this? She was off the tram. What could she do?

She put her head back and groaned. She should leave them to it. They wanted her off the investigation, so fuck them. Let them mess it up.

Then she remembered Roland Marsh, and the empty look in his eyes, and her memories of Sarah's body on the beach.

But as she looked more closely at the sea, at the relentless roll of it, back and forth, in and out, twice a day, as predictable as the sun setting, she got some clarity.

She'd thought that the solitude of the beach was chosen because it was deserted, but Charlie was right, there were easier ways to dispose of a body. And the discovery was a fluke, because a neighbour spotted something. If Rob hadn't got there in time, or if he'd ignored it, thinking it was a fly-tipper, not a police case, Sarah would have been washed away.

It was so obvious.

'Shit,' Amy said.

Charlie turned towards her. 'What is it?'

'I know why she was on the beach,' she said. 'We presumed it was to let the sea take her, except we thought it was a way of hiding the body. It wasn't. It was about the forensics.'

'What are you thinking?'

'If whoever had killed her had just buried her, those bodies turn up sometimes. Try digging in a field and someone will see you, or it becomes the site of unexpected building work, or people wonder why there is a person-sized patch of disturbed ground on their land. Dig a hole in the woods and you can't go more than a foot down because of the roots, and all that loose soil attracts dogs. When a body turns up, there might be forensics. Here, she was either going to be taken away by the tide, or the waves would wash away the forensics, just as if she'd been through a washing machine. It would play havoc with the time of death, which would make it hard for Roland to prove an alibi, with her blood in the boot of his car. But the discovery of the body gave us a window to check CCTV.'

'Perhaps it's more than that.'

'What do you mean?'

'Maybe she was a message. If Sarah's murder is connected to everything else, was it a signal to anyone who is thinking of talking?

It does both things. It serves as a warning, but washes away the forensic evidence at the same time.'

'But what if it didn't do its job?' she said. 'We found her more quickly than expected, so the tide never got to her. There might be some traces left. It's the first rule of forensic evidence, that every contact leaves a trace. So, what traces are still there?' She stepped away from the rail. 'I need to go to the station.'

'What do you want of me?'

'Wait for my call,' Amy said, then ran back to her car.

Fifty-Nine

Jessica waited for Wendy in Trafalgar Square. She was edgy, her eyes always on the faces in the crowd, looking out for the threat, the person hanging around more than sightseeing.

She'd picked it because it was close enough to Parliament to be convenient, and busy enough to allow them to mix in with the tourists and buskers, but now she wondered whether it was too open.

She spotted Wendy making her way through the crowd, past the busker and the street entertainer shouting out an elaborate set-up to his stunt.

As she got close, Wendy had no time for niceties. 'What did you find?'

Jessica showed her the pictures on her phone of the Swiss bank account. 'Hidden in a photo frame, just like the Nevis one, Pippa with skis. So obvious, but easy to overlook.'

'And you think this proves it?'

'We've got the documents in his possession.'

'But if he hears about this, he might move them.'

'I can tell people where they were,' Jessica said. 'I'm the witness.'

Wendy didn't respond to that.

'What now?' Jessica asked.

Wendy pursed her lips and frowned as she thought. 'We work out how to play it,' she said, eventually.

'Why not just pass the material to the reporter?' Jessica said. 'Does it matter how the information was found? Once it's in the public domain, that'll be the least of his problems.'

Wendy leaned on the wall and looked along Whitehall. 'We can't do it now. He's got the announcement this weekend about the new detention centre.'

'Can't we stop that? This is all part of it. The backhanders, the favours.'

Wendy scoffed. 'Can you think of the money involved? No, he has to make the announcement as planned. We're heading north in a couple of days. There's a press gig in the afternoon, in the Town Hall, all about investing in the north. We can't derail that. There are jobs and investment, so it's about more than your political conscience.'

'But they've obtained that contract through fraud.'

'Have they? Can you prove that? Can you say what input Spencer actually had? Do you really think Spencer considered all the bids in private and then gave the contract to those who paid him the most? That's bullshit. It goes through a process of vetting and weighing up and costing. Spencer is just the signature at the end. No, what they were buying was an ally, nothing more, someone who might speak up for them, but the same decision might have been made. Spencer was exploiting his position, and he will fall for that, but let's not spoil the party too much. We'll never work again if we do that.'

Jessica sighed. 'Yes, I guess. What about after the weekend, when it all comes out?'

'We make ourselves out to be the honest ones and hope that someone else will give us a job.' Wendy gripped her hand. 'It'll be all right, I promise. This is politics. It's a dirty game.'

***

It didn't take Amy long to get to the station, as she raced through the back streets to avoid the lights. She kept her gaze downwards as she rushed through the corridors, until the Incident Room loomed ahead.

This was it, she thought. She was about to cross a line that she might not come back from.

As she went in, to her relief, the blinds were down on Mickey Higham's room. Everyone looked up, but no one said hello.

She stopped at the first desk and asked if any forensic results had come in, but the detective checked around him before leaning in to whisper, 'We can't share it with you.'

She leaned in closer to hiss, 'Take a tip from a concerned member of the public. Chase the forensics.'

'Why the importance?'

'Because the body was supposed to be washed away, the forensics stripped clean by the North Sea, but we got there too quickly.'

'Roland?'

She shook her head. 'I don't know who, but I think he's the one taking the fall if we don't do our job properly.'

He nodded and made a note. 'I'll do it when you've gone, so it doesn't look like I'm collaborating with you. And I take the credit if it comes back good.'

'I'm that much persona non grata?'

'We've got strict orders.'

'From Higham?'

He shrugged and went back to his screen.

Amy left him to it. He was a good guy simply trying to follow orders.

When she got to her own desk, she saw that the papers were spread around. Someone had gone through her notes. She was looking for Nick Cassidy's phone logs, her back to the Incident Room.

She shuffled through, not wanting to be there too long or attract any attention. She found them, off to one side, a coffee cup resting on them.

Amy rolled them up and shoved them into her jacket, pausing only to straighten herself so her clothes looked natural.

There was a noise behind her, someone breathing heavily.

As she turned, it was Higham, his eyes furious, his cheeks tinged red.

'What the hell are you doing here?'

Amy reached for her mug on the far corner of her desk, thinking fast. 'If you think you're having my personal property, you can think again. This is mine, and I've got a coat somewhere.'

Higham breathed deeply through his nose, his jaw clenched. When he spoke next, his voice was low and quiet, but packed with menace. 'You need to do what you've been ordered to do. Do not interfere. Your time on this team is done.'

Amy stepped closer. 'I will do what I need to do to make this right.'

Higham paused for a moment, before saying, 'Think of your father.'

She stalled, taken aback. 'What do you mean?'

'Just that.'

'Explain, please. Why is this to do with my father?'

'It's all to do with him,' Higham said, his voice now a snarl. 'Don't you get it? Everybody's hero, Jimmy Gray. It's all to do with him.'

Amy stepped back, her mind racing. 'Please, Mickey, tell me.'

He slammed his hand on the desk, making papers flutter, and some fly off. 'You dig anymore, you say goodbye to him.'

She looked at Higham, hoping to see him smiling, that it was just a joke, but he wasn't, and it was no joke. His hands were on his hips and his glare was fixed hard on her.

She turned away from Mickey and set off walking, through the desks of the Incident Room, not seeing anyone, just the exit ahead.

She didn't look back at the station as she left, the air cool on her face. There was no point. Whatever happened next, she knew she'd never be setting foot in there again.

Sixty

Charlie paced as he waited for Amy to answer. Goldie was sitting in the open door of her campervan, feet swinging.

He was about to hang up when Amy answered.

'Don't,' she said.

He stared at his phone, confused. 'Don't what?'

'I can't do this, not anymore. Just leave me alone.'

There was a slur to her voice that told him she was drinking, and the anger in her tone let him know that she was intending to get drunk. Very drunk.

'Where are you?'

There was a few seconds' pause, then she said, 'Smugglers,' and hung up.

Goldie asked, 'What was that about?'

'No idea. Have you heard of Smugglers?'

'A pub a couple of miles out of town. Are we going?'

'Seems that way. My car or yours?'

'We'll take the van. If it ends up as a boozy night, we can sleep in it.'

The Smugglers Arms was a village pub further along the headland that catered for the Sunday lunch crowd and walking tourists. Charlie could see the attraction of the place if Amy wanted to simmer alone, the beer garden facing along the long grass strip that ran along the cliff edges.

Amy wasn't in the main bar, so they kept on walking through, scanning the corners, but it was filled by elderly couples making half-pint glasses last a long time. Then he caught a glimpse of her silver-blonde hair through one of the external doors, her arms folded, facing away from the bar. He glanced through to see what she was drinking, white wine, so by the time he went out to her he was holding a metal ice bucket in one hand, with a bottle of nondescript Sauvignon jammed into some ice, Goldie carrying three glasses.

As he went through the door, she whirled round in her chair, her eyes wild, like a cornered animal.

He raised the bucket. 'We need to talk. And I'm guessing we'll need plenty of this.'

She drained her own glass and put it to one side, taking one of the fresh glasses and filling it from the bottle.

He poured his own drink and said, 'Okay, I'm not interested in guessing games. We can all get trashed together, but that's the only game I'm playing. If you've got something to say, come out with it, but you've got to be honest with me.'

Amy studied him, then jabbed her thumb towards Goldie. 'You can get rid of Patsy Cline if we're having this conversation.'

Charlie felt Goldie's hand on his shoulder. 'It's alright, Charlie, we'll talk later,' she said. 'This is getting ugly.'

Amy flashed a sarcastic smile and raised her glass. 'Go find a different Kenny, because this one is bad news.'

'No, stay, please,' Charlie said, then turned back to Amy. 'I don't know what's happened, but you need to talk. If you didn't want to, you wouldn't have told me you were here.'

Goldie paused as she decided what to do, before settling back in her chair.

Amy put her head back. 'I'm scared, that's all.'

'Of what? The last time we spoke, you were getting Nick Cassidy's phone records.'

'I don't want them, not anymore. Here,' and she took them out of an inside pocket of her jacket, rolled up, and tossed them across the table. 'You followed Clarence, and he went to my father's house. What if my father was involved?'

Charlie was confused. 'Do you think he was?'

'I don't know,' Amy said, her voice louder. 'I do not fucking know, and that's the problem.

They were interrupted by the barman, who had appeared in the doorway. 'We don't have any trouble here, do we?'

'No, it's fine,' Charlie said. 'It's been a difficult week.'

'You want to argue, go scream on the clifftop, let the wind take it away. But it's drifting into here, and this is no town centre pub, if you get my meaning.'

'Yeah, no worries, pal.'

When the barman retreated, Charlie asked, 'What's been said?'

Amy folded her arms and glowered. 'Mickey Higham told me that Natasha Trenton was all about my father, told me to back off or else it will hurt him, but how can I do that? How can I look at my father in the same way if he had anything to do with it, or look Tammy in the eyes and be honest? I don't know what to think.'

Amy closed her eyes and her chin trembled. A tear escaped. Her voice cracked as she said, 'He's my hero. How about that for a cliché? It's true though. I became a copper because he was a damn good one, and I wanted people to look up to me like they looked up to him.'

'But this came from your boss, the one who doesn't want you to look at Natasha's case. It might be bullshit.' He turned to Goldie. 'It could be bullshit, right?'

'Classic deflection,' Goldie said.

Charlie reached across for Amy's hand and squeezed it. 'Wait for the morning and a clear head. For now, don't listen to what he said.'

Amy pulled her hand away and reached for the bottle. 'Only one thing for it, then. Oblivion.'

***

They weaved along the clifftop together, another bottle of wine finished after the first, each holding a beer bottle, just something for the walk. Cookstown shimmered in the distance, a mirage of grey stone and twinkling fairground lights as the lighthouse at the tip of the headland swept the bay.

'Why are you so interested in this case?' Amy said, her voice slurring, bumping into him as he walked. 'And you too,' gesturing to Goldie with the bottle. 'I'm a cop, I'm supposed to be interested. You? You're a pub singer. And you? You're a lawyer, and they always tell me they don't get involved, or have an opinion. A neutral voice, they say.'

'That's just lawyer bullshit, a way to make ourselves feel better for doing something we don't enjoy. Like grilling a victim of crime, trying to pass the blame their way.'

'It's too late, and I'm too pissed to get this deep.'

'You asked so I'm telling you, because it's all bullshit, lawyers and what they say. All of it. Rule of law, we say, that we believe in a person's right to fight a case, be found not guilty even when they did it, if the evidence isn't there. But the law is what we make it, and when it's tweaked to stop lawyers playing games, we moan. It's just about not losing.' He shook his head. 'Jeez, I hate lawyers.'

'That's why you're doing this,' she said. 'You're lost. You need a calling, to do something righteous, and this is your cause.'

Charlie looked towards the sea, just a dark sheet beyond the fringes of grass at the cliff edge, as he thought about his life. Where he was living. His divorce. Molly. It wasn't the right time, not with drink involved.

'It'll also wait until the morning,' he said.

'Why, are you planning on staying that long? Because you don't have to walk me home. I've been in tougher spots than this.'

'We can't drive anywhere, we're pissed, and we all seem to be going the same way,' he said. 'People are dying too. For all of our sakes, let's stick together.'

'Deal.'

They made small talk as they went, Amy and Goldie pointing out buildings that meant something to them. The café Amy worked in when she was sixteen. A wall outside an amusement arcade where Goldie used to hang out as a teenager. The now-demolished nightclub they both used to go to, one of only two in the town, so that every night-out was filled with people they knew. As they talked, Charlie enjoying the reminiscences, Amy and Goldie realised they'd known each other years ago, part of different crowds whose paths sometimes crossed.

They skirted the harbour, none of the boats in, so it was mostly in darkness, apart from the lights that lined the harbour wall and the blinking white light at the end. The tarmac was cold and grey, the night silent, not much happening in Cookstown this late.

As the beach to the south of the harbour came into view, a long stretch into the far distance, Amy pointed and said, 'We were lucky to find her so quickly.'

The tide was still out, leaving the flat sand gleaming wet and reflecting the moonlight, broken by the long, jagged fingers of the breakwaters.

'It would have been easy to miss her,' Charlie said.

'And if we hadn't, the tide would have taken her, I reckon.' Amy pecked him on the cheek and gave Goldie a hug. 'I'm leaving you two lovebirds.'

'Do you want us to walk you home?'

'It's my town. I'll be fine.'

As they watched her go, weaving along, Goldie said, 'You didn't say where you were sleeping tonight.'

'I haven't thought that far ahead.'

'You better get thinking. I live just along there,' and she pointed towards a static caravan site, a field dotted by white rectangles, all with their large windows facing the sea. There were lights on in some, moving silhouettes visible through thin curtains.

'A caravan?'

'The only place I could afford with a sea-view.'

'Do you want some company?'

'I'm okay on my own.' She smiled. 'But I reckon you'd be fun for a while.'

They did their own weave along the seafront, laughing as they exchanged stories, her falling into him whenever she found something funny.

By the time they got to Goldie's caravan, Charlie's head had cleared.

Goldie stumbled as she put her foot on the step, her key dropping to the floor. As she rummaged for it, giggling, Charlie used the light from his phone to help her.

She went inside and headed straight for the bedroom. She flopped down onto the bed, her coat still on. 'The room is spinning.'

He went to the kitchen to fetch her a glass of water. When he took it into the bedroom, she said, 'I don't want you here.'

Charlie passed her the glass. 'That's okay. I'm hard to offend.'

She took it and gasped when she drank it. 'I mean, I do want you here, because I've got needs, if you know what I mean, but I hardly know you.' She waved her hand and started to wrestle her coat off. 'Ignore me.'

He leant against the doorjamb.

She stopped. 'Are you going to join me or not?'

He smiled and shook his head. 'Not when you're this drunk.'

'But booze makes me horny.' She sat up and grabbed his waistband and yanked him closer. 'Leave your manners at the door.'

Before he could decide whether it was a good idea, he was startled by the loud shatter of a window, and a thud as a rock hit the opposite wall. Glass showered over them.

Goldie screamed. Charlie shouted.

Goldie rolled off the bed and crawled to the wall by the window, wincing and shouting as she shuffled across broken shards. 'Who is it?' There was blood on her hands.

Charlie went to the floor and crept to the window to join her, so that he could rest against the wall. His breaths were coming fast. Goldie moved the curtain to have another look, then jumped back when there was another smash, glass exploding, this time in the other room.

'What do we do?' she said, her chest rising and falling. 'We can't go outside.'

'Get our phones out. Take pictures through the window.'

Another loud smash came from the window above them, both shouting out as shards of glass peppered their backs.

'We need to get out,' she yelled, a mix of panic and anger in her eyes.

Just then, there was a bright flash as something came through the window, followed by a whoosh as it smashed and bright flames spread across the room.

'Go, go,' Charlie said, and they bolted out of the bedroom.

Goldie grappled with a fire extinguisher on the wall, then ran back towards the flames and sprayed the bedroom with water.

The flames battled against it, and she thought she was winning, when there was another smash in the living area and a whoosh of flames.

'Get out,' Charlie said. 'We can't fight it.'

He ran for the door and pressed down on the handle. It wouldn't open.

'It's jammed. Is it bolted?'

'No, it's a Yale lock,' she shrieked. 'Twist and push.'

'I am but it won't open.'

Goldie joined him, looking into the living area. The flames had spread across the floor, and were starting to pick at the wallpaper.

She pushed against the door, but it was stuck solid. 'There's something behind it. They've trapped us.' She turned to look around, desperate for a way out.

There were big windows at the front, facing the sea, flames getting higher in-between.

They looked at each other, and both thought the same thing: they had no choice. They shielded their faces from the heat. There was shouting outside, other residents perhaps, but no other window was big enough.

'I'll go first,' he said.

Goldie didn't wait for his gallantry. Instead, she grabbed her coat and put it over her face, before sprinting towards the flames, screeching as she ran through.

As she jumped onto the bench seating, Goldie launched herself at the window, shoulder first, her head tucked into her jacket.

It smashed on impact, the crackle of flames broken only by her shouts of pain as she landed on the ground with a thud.

Charlie turned, looking for a different route. He kicked at the door, but it didn't budge.

Shit, there was no choice.

He grabbed the phone records Amy had given them earlier, then ran for the window.

The flames were sharp on his skin as he rushed through, his foot planting hard on the bench as he hurled himself through the hole made by Goldie.

For a moment, he was airborne, and the air felt like cold relief.

He grunted as he landed, pain shooting through his body, his shoulder jarring. He lay on his back and tried to get his breath, wincing as he moved. There was glass on the floor around him that jabbed against his skin.

He opened his eyes. The sky was vivid orange as flames leapt out of the window, drawn to the air outside. A car sped away. There were shouts from the nearby caravans. Sirens howled in the distance, getting louder.

He yelped in pain as someone pulled on his arm.

It was Goldie.

'We've got to go,' she said.

He took deep breaths before he was able to say, 'Help will be on its way.'

'No, we're going,' she said, her voice firmer this time. 'They've burnt down my fucking home. They're not getting away with this.'

And with that, Charlie scrambled to his feet and followed her as she ran, heading for the beach, the glow of the flames getting smaller, the roll of the tide getting louder, as he ran towards a future that seemed full of danger.

He shook his head. 'This place is fucking crazy.'

Sixty-One

Isobel could tell it wasn't a normal hangover. She didn't know if it was because it was tinged by panic, or because something had been slipped into her drink, but she felt dreadful, like the first shriek of a migraine.

Her phone pinged.

She winced as she moved. Pain flashed across her forehead as she stretched for her phone, lying on the floor next to her side of the bed. Simon was downstairs, playing with Molly, her giggles drifting upwards. He hadn't moved in officially, but he never stayed in the bachelor pad he was trying to sell.

She checked her watch. Just before eight. She was late. Why hadn't Simon woken her?

As she checked her phone, her stomach lurched.

It's Thomas, from yesterday. We need to talk. Call me.

Fuck, fuck, fuck.

She tapped her reply, her hand shaking.

We can never talk again. Don't call me or message me.

Her stomach rolled with nausea as she waited for a reply.

I'm at the small park at the end of your street. If you're not here in ten minutes, I'll knock on your door.

She thought she was about to throw up.

She lay back and thought about what she could do. Confess all to Simon? That would take away Thomas Riley's power, but confess to what? That she'd been drugged? Raped? Would he believe her?

And did she believe it? Was this just guilt and regret, knowing that the wine had made her reckless?

She stumbled out of bed and put on some clothes, leggings and a jumper, quick and easy.

As she went down the stairs, she shouted out, 'Just nipping to the shop.'

A quick, 'Okay,' told her that he'd heard her, then she was outside, her forehead glistening with sweat.

The park was a small field of grass with swings at one end, overlooked by the houses nearby. She took Molly there sometimes, just to get her away from the television.

Thomas Riley was sitting on a bench closest to the swings, recognisable from the gleam of his bald head.

He didn't turn around as she approached and sat on the same bench, but as far from him as she could. Instead, he crossed his legs and said, 'Isobel, good morning. So lovely to see you again.'

'What do you want?'

He turned towards her and feigned hurt, his hand against his chest. 'My dear Isobel, please don't be so confrontational. We had such a wonderful time yesterday.'

'Yes, about that.'

He held up his hand. 'No, please, no more need be said. A gentleman never tells, Miss Atkins.' A slow smile. 'Except that it isn't Miss Atkins. It's Mrs Steele, now divorced.'

Isobel opened her mouth to speak, but she was stunned, unsure what to say.

He waved her concern away. 'Don't worry, I'm not here to stalk you, desperate to relive our delightful few hours. You have your own life, as lovely as it looks.'

Tears jumped into her eyes. She tried to blink them away, her chin quivering. 'What do you mean?'

Thomas tutted. 'Come, come, Isobel. Yesterday, you were so much more hospitable. So much more, what's the word? Revealing, that's it.'

He pulled out an iPad from the briefcase he was carrying. He navigated to the pictures folder, then held it out to her.

Isobel's hand went to her mouth and she emitted a small moan.

The image was blurred through her tears, but she could see enough. She was on the hotel bed. As he scrolled, watching her all the time, she saw how the cloth of her suit was replaced by the gleam of her skin, as she was pictured on the bed, naked, splayed.

She closed her eyes.

'I won't play you the video,' he said. 'It's a little too racy for this time of day.'

She thought she was going to be sick. 'That's a crime, you bastard.'

'What's a crime? Taking a picture of you wanton and lustful?' He tilted his head. 'Yes, now that I think about it, you're probably right. So, report me, do your worst. Call the police. And don't forget to tell your new man how easily you ended up in my hotel room, writhing on the bed, naked. Simon, is it?'

She fingernails dug into her knees as she tensed. 'You spiked my drink.'

'Did I? Are you sure you can prove that? Or did you just guzzle at the bottle like a hungry baby?'

'Bullshit. I don't get drunk that quickly. I don't end up in bed with people like you after a couple of glasses.'

He faked a gasp. 'Your words hurt me, Mrs Steele.'

'And if you drugged me, and did whatever you did, that's rape. Do you hear, you sick bastard? You fucking raped me.' She bent over and put her head in her hands. 'I can't believe I'm saying those words. You dirty sick bastard.'

His smile didn't shift. 'You know you're not going to report me. You won't even tell Simon, because I've got the pictures from a great afternoon, and these things have a habit of getting leaked.'

She sat back and wiped away a tear. 'What do you want?'

'Why do you think I want something?'

'You haven't come here for a second date, so there must be a reason. And don't think about blackmail.'

'Or else? Because we both know you won't be calling the police.'

Her shoulders sagged. 'Just tell me what you want?'

'Your husband.'

She was confused. 'Simon? We're not married.'

'No, not Simon. Charlie. You've got to tell him to stop what he's doing.'

Tears ran down her face. 'Are you saying that you did all this just so you could get at my ex-husband? You drugged me, debased me, took embarrassing pictures of me, just to make him give up a case?' She shook her head in disbelief. 'What the fuck is all this?'

His smile broadened. 'What do you want me to say? You want me to apologise? Okay, that's fine. *I'm sorry.* There, I've said it.'

He held up the iPad again. 'Do you think your boss would like this? I bet he would. Most bosses want to fuck the women who work for them. I'm sure that's what he thinks every time he looks at you. How you look under your suit. How you are when you're fucking. Well, I've got all the answers he needs. He'll schedule a few minutes every day in the staff toilets to go through these.'

She bent over, her arm over her stomach, trying to stop herself from vomiting. 'Okay, stop, I get the point. I'll talk to Charlie.'

'You won't just talk to him,' he said, his tone acquiring more bite. 'He'll stop, because if he doesn't, these pictures and videos will be on every porn site you can think of, and every lawyer in Manchester will be sent a link.'

He patted his stomach.

'Some of them will like that little bit of mummy-fat you've got, see you in a whole new light.' He held out his hands. 'You have no choice, you know that.'

'But what if he doesn't? Why should he stick up for me?'

'Because you're Molly's mother. He wouldn't want his daughter to be damaged in any way, would he?'

She felt the blood drain from her face. 'Molly? What do you mean, damaged?'

'Emotionally, or otherwise?' He shrugged. 'Who knows? I've got quite an imagination. Just sort it.'

He stood and walked over to her. He held the iPad in front of her and hit the play button.

She recognised her voice even though it was slurred, and through her tears she could see that she was naked on the screen.

'Please stop.'

He paused the footage, then shot out his hand and gripped her jaw, making her grunt in pain as he applied pressure.

'You've got until this time tomorrow to make him stop.' He spoke through gritted teeth, his polished demeanour gone. 'We'll go as far as it takes, trust me. You don't want that.'

He brought her face to his, maintaining eye-contact all the time, until he was close enough to kiss her on her lips.

'It was very special,' he whispered. 'We must do it again.'

And then he pushed her back against the hard slats of the bench, so that she gasped in pain, his fingers leaving red marks on her cheek.

She didn't watch him go. Instead, she stared at the ground in shock, scarcely able to believe what had just happened.

When she looked up, he had gone.

Snatches of memory from the day before seemed to rush at her, but they were just that, snatches, flashes of images.

She ran for some bushes, needing to vomit.

She didn't make it.

As a young mother wheeled a pram into the park, Isobel was on her knees, vomiting into a litter bin.

It was over. Everything she had worked for was finished.

Sixty-Two

The sun rose through the window in Amy's spare room.

Charlie was stretched out on the floor next to the bed, curled up, his head rested on his jacket. Goldie dozed in the bed, her covers up to her neck.

Amy came in with a tray and three mugs of tea. She sat on the end of the bed and passed one to Charlie, who thanked her before tapping Goldie's leg with his toe.

Goldie groaned and rolled onto her back, squinting as she tried to open her eyes.

Amy passed a mug towards her. 'Dolly and Kenny don't look too healthy this morning.'

Goldie grimaced. 'Shit. I was hoping it had been a drunken dream.' She lifted her arm and saw the small nicks and grazes on her forearms. 'I'm guessing not.'

'So, what now?' Charlie asked.

Amy shook her head, a smile of regret on her lips. 'I'm out.'

'What do you mean, out?'

'Mickey Higham reckoned my Dad is involved with Natasha somehow, but I just can't face that. It's too much to take in.'

'What about doing the right thing?'

'That's something I'm going to have to work out.' She sighed. 'I'm sorry, guys. Let yourself out. I've things to do.'

'And if we find anything out about your Dad?'

'Do what you need to do, but leave me out of it.' She gestured with her mug towards Goldie. 'And perhaps you should do the same. You've been burned out of your home. And you, Charlie, you're upsetting half the town. It's time to stop.'

Amy left the room.

Charlie listened out as she went down the stairs, then turned to Goldie.

'Perhaps she's right,' he said. 'This is my cause. Too many people are getting hurt. I don't want it to include you.'

'Fuck you, Charlie. They burnt down my home. It might be just a static caravan, but it was all I had. They're not getting away with that.'

He raised an eyebrow. 'If you're sure.'

'Never been more sure.'

He smiled and picked up Nick Cassidy's phone records. 'I was hoping you'd say that. We've got these to go through. And there is one person from Cookstown who keeps popping up, and I've made no contact with him. Lewis Buford.'

'The judge?'

'That's him. It's about time I paid him a visit.'

'I'll start on the phone records,' Goldie said. 'There is one other person who might be useful though. Nancy Buford. She must know something, and Pete and Clarence don't seem keen on us speaking to her. Forever *indisposed*.'

'I agree,' Charlie said. 'Always go where the opposition don't want you to go.'

'And right now?'

'What, this minute?'

She shrugged, a playful glint in her eye. 'Last night, were we going to, you know, get it on?'

'You were drunk?'

'I think I offered.'

'I wouldn't have accepted.'

'Because you didn't find me attractive?'

'Because I didn't want to accept just a drunken offer.'

'You're a gentleman.'

'You said that last night. And drunk words are true words, but,' and he smiled. 'I was succumbing.'

She threw back the covers and shrugged off the t-shirt she'd been sleeping in. 'I'm not drunk now, if it makes you feel better, I need some comfort.'

As he slipped into bed with her, she added, 'Just call it unfinished business.'

Sixty-Three

Amy drummed her fingers on the steering wheel, not looking forward to what lay ahead.

Tammy wasn't alone this time. One of her brothers, Wayne, was unloading car parts from the back of a scuffed and battered Transit. He wore the standard issue of oil-stained blue overalls, sweat glistening under the peak of a faded maroon baseball cap. He was carrying damaged bumpers and headlights to a workshop at the side of Tammy's property.

Amy wasn't ready to ask Wayne where they came from. There were two engine blocks underneath a plastic sheet, ready to be stripped down and the parts sold on.

The Trenton brothers ran a scrapyard on the edge of Cookstown, half-way along a street that ended where a factory once stood, long since closed down but left to rot rather than redeveloped.

There were rumours that stolen cars were stripped and broken down there, all the identifying marks scrubbed from them. It looked as if they used Tammy's place as storage.

Amy stepped out of her car. There was no point in putting it off.

Wayne looked over, then concealed the engine blocks under the plastic sheet.

'I'm not here for that, Wayne, so keep it calm,' she said, and carried on to Tammy's door.

There was no response from Wayne, although he watched her all the way, wiping his hand on his overalls as if removing the oil would remove the suspicion.

Tammy opened the door before Amy reached it. She folded her arms. 'Have you got any news for me?'

'Let me come inside.'

As Tammy paled and gripped the door handle for support, Amy grimaced and wished she'd chosen her words better.

'I've no news,' Amy said. 'I'm sorry.'

Tammy took a few deep breaths before she straightened herself. 'I thought you were going to tell me you'd found my baby's body.'

'I know you did, but a talk might do us good.'

Tammy's nostrils flared. For a moment, Amy thought Tammy was about to run at her and scream and bawl until she left, but instead she stepped aside to let Amy through.

Tammy turned to Wayne. 'It's okay, I've got this.'

He didn't respond. Amy was glad to get away from his stare.

As Tammy followed her in, she said, 'I've seen that look before.'

Amy turned to her. 'Which look?'

'The one that tells me that there's nothing you can do, that I should just learn to accept it.'

'It isn't like that, Tammy.'

'Isn't it? You here to tell me anything different, how you've found her, or you've got some new taskforce all ready to go, cadaver dogs on standby?'

'I tried, I really did.'

'Even after I showed you her car, you still come out with this bullshit.'

'I can press it again later, but now isn't a good time.'

Tammy started to pace. 'You're just like your father. I should've known better.' She stopped to glare at Amy, her hands on her hips. 'I know what they say about me and my family, but that's all on me, not Natasha. She didn't deserve to be ignored because of what people think of me.'

'I'm not ignoring her.'

'Are you carrying on?'

Amy hung her head. 'Well, no, not for now.'

'Get out of here then.'

'Tammy, please, I just want to explain why.'

'I've heard it all before.' She stepped closer. 'All of it. Every excuse you could hear. But I want you to do something, Amy Gray, and that's to look right inside yourself, then tell me, straight in the eyes, that this sudden lack of interest isn't to do with who we are, that Natasha was a Trenton.'

Amy met her gaze and was about to explain, but then realised that what Tammy was saying was correct. The police thought she'd run off to get away from her family. If she owed Tammy anything, it was to stop feeding her more evasion.

'I'm sorry,' she said, instead.

'Get out. Right now.' Tammy held her arm out towards the door. 'Leave, and don't come back.'

Amy went to the door. The only sound was the click of her footsteps on the concrete of the yard as Wayne stared, leaning against his van, watching her as she went back to her car.

She felt his eyes on her as she started her engine and made the slow crawl back into Cookstown.

***

Isobel rushed through the city streets with her coat collar up, weaving through the crowds, past the homeless asking for money and the smugly wealthy sauntering past the designer boutiques. She was in a daze. The day before had been bad. This was harder to take in.

The hotel was ahead, with its faux-marble columns and brass-trimmed menu boards.

As she reached the doorway, she paused. Did she really want to do this? She could call Charlie and ask him what it was all about.

She wasn't ready for that. He'd love it too much, after what she did to him.

And something else struck her: perhaps nothing had happened? If it had been done just to get Charlie to stop whatever he was doing, all Thomas Riley had to do was dope her and take some nude pictures. It didn't mean that she'd slept with him. After all, he'd stopped the video before it showed anything happening.

As the thought came into her head, she was filled with fresh resolve. She was finding excuses for a man who might have fucking raped her. She was trying to find some comfort when a man had taken naked photographs of her, just so that he could blackmail her.

There were no get-outs. She wasn't giving in.

The carpet-deadened hush of the lobby beat out the noise of the city once she got inside, emerging from the revolving door. The desk was mahogany, the lighting low. A couple of chairs were in front of a fire, although it was ornamental, with logs crammed into it. Her memory of it came in flashes. She'd walked through the lobby to get to the restaurant but hadn't lingered. She had no memories of it from after the meal. Just the hazy stumble as she left, half in shock, now wondering what else was behind it.

She approached the reception desk, where a man with slicked grey hair said, 'Can I help you, madam?' His eyes bore the look of someone who was paid to be subservient, but hated every moment of it.

'Hello, yes, I was here yesterday, with a client, and I think he might have taken my file by accident. I'm a solicitor. I need to be able to contact him. It's really urgent.'

'But if he's your client, madam, you'll know his number, surely?'

'It's all in the file.' She leaned in, the man following her lead. 'Please, you've got to help me. I'll be sacked if that file has gone missing.'

The man gave a brief smile that told her he was enjoying her discomfort. 'I'm sorry, I can't give out customer details.' His tone was firmer, as he ignored the pleading look in her eyes.

'At least can you look to see whether you have any of his details,' she said. 'The man was called Thomas Riley.'

The man thought about it for a few seconds, before typing in his name.

He shook his head. 'No one stayed here of that name. Do you have a room number?'

She thought back and tried to piece together the events of the day. The drink. The light-headedness. An image came back to her, of her head against a door, laughing. At the end of a long corridor. Numbers in black against pale oak doors.

'217,' she blurted out. 'I remember it now.'

The man suppressed a smirk, realising that she had gone to the room. He went back to his screen and shook his head. 'The room was not registered in that name, I'm sorry.'

She was about to turn away when he said, 'What is your name, madam, in case Mr Riley contacts the hotel? Do you have a contact number?'

'Er, yes, it's Isobel Steele.' She paused and took a breath. 'No, sorry, Isobel Atkins,' and she slid across a business card. 'I don't use my married name at work. Call me if you hear anything.'

He frowned. 'Do you have any photo ID, madam?'

'What do you mean?'

'So I can verify who you are, if I'm to be passing on messages.'

She reached into her bag for her purse before handing over her driving licence.

He looked at the licence, then the business card. 'Are you all right, madam?' before turning the screen round so that she could see it.

'I'm sorry, I don't understand.'

'You've no memory problems?'

'No, I'm fine. Why?'

He pointed to an entry against the room number 217. 'Look, there.'

'What is it?'

'I'm showing you who booked the room,' he said. 'It was you.'

She looked closer. 'I don't understand.'

'What I've just said. A late booking, yesterday lunchtime. Isobel Atkins, on behalf of Patterson solicitors. A room for two, paid in cash.'

She leaned against the desk and closed her eyes.

What the hell was going on?

Sixty-Four

The Crown Court looked grand and proud in the centre of the city, with wide steps that climbed towards oak doors, the name of the courthouse on a brass plaque by the doorway. White-shirted security guards gathered on the other side of the alarm-arch, ready for bag searches and a scan with a hand-held device, waved like a cattle-prod.

Charlie and Goldie had a plan. She would go through Nick Cassidy's call logs, calling everyone he had spoken to, just to see what she could find out. Charlie was going to see a judge.

Once inside, Charlie saw that it was just like the Crown Courts all over the country. Corridors made to look grand, hushed by carpets and populated by barristers in long, black gowns and grubby horsehair wigs. Defendants sat on airport-style seats and chewed their nails in ill-fitting suits, or prowled near to the courtroom doors as they barked complaints at representatives from law firms, paralegals who clutched files to their chests and watched the slow turn of the clock.

Charlie had checked where Judge Buford would be sitting, in courtroom number four, dealing with the steady churn of sentencing cases.

The routine was familiar. Some would emerge with relief on their faces, prison dodged one more time, whereas others would go down the steps in the dock, shackled to a security guard, ready for the trip on the van to the nearest prison, their final view of the outside world through tiny, darkened windows.

For some of the loved ones, it was a time to celebrate, as life returned to some semblance of normality, until the next scrape arose. For others, weekly visits were ahead, queuing outside the prison, the walk of shame through the security gates, their relationships watched over by suspicious guards always on the lookout for the passing of contraband by a stolen kiss, or a quick reach between their legs.

Charlie slipped into courtroom four, the public gallery right by the doorway. The only person there was a jaded-looking court reporter, scribbling shorthand on a notepad.

Charlie took a seat in the corner and watched the action, such as it was.

For more than two hours, barristers and defendants operated like a turnstile, as His Honour Judge Buford read pre-sentence reports and heard brief outlines of cases from the prosecutor, a harried-looking advocate who had every file before the court. The judge was enjoying the sport of asking questions the prosecutor hadn't anticipated, a glint in his eye as the prosecutor scrolled through a laptop to find the information he needed, the silences as he scoured feeling more heated every time he delayed.

Charlie tried to gauge Lewis Buford.

He was like so many other judges, relishing the combat of the courtroom.

Out of court, the harshest judges can be the most pleasant of people, so Charlie couldn't work him out just yet, but he seemed to take some pleasure from the discomfort of the prosecutor.

As the court hearings progressed, Judge Buford started to pay attention to the public gallery, and he noticed Charlie. There'd been a narrowing of his eyes, a more distracted tone to his voice. He started to tap his pen against his knuckles, sitting forwards and backwards.

At one point, he leaned forward to attract the attention of the court assistant, a woman in a black gown and white tabs on her shirt, who in turn attracted the attention of the usher, who came over to speak to Charlie.

'Hello, sir. Is there a case you're interested in?'

'I'm just a member of the public,' Charlie said.

The usher shrugged. 'It's a public court. Enjoy the show.'

Charlie watched as he walked back to the court assistant to relay the message, who in turn passed it back to the judge.

Another hour passed, with Judge Buford becoming increasingly irritable, until eventually he ended the session.

Normally, the judge would be the first to leave, the mutual bowing all part of the court rituals. This time, he stayed, waiting for the barristers to clear the courtroom, leaving just the usher and the court assistant.

Charlie sat and waited, knowing that this was connected to his presence, until the judge leaned forward and said, 'You, in the public gallery. What is your interest in this court today?'

Charlie rose. 'Your Honour, it's you. You are my interest. My name is Charlie Steele, and my client was murdered. You might have some relevant information.'

'What's your client's name?'

'Gerard Williams.'

Buford paled. 'And how is this connected to me?'

Charlie dug into his pocket and pulled out the photograph. 'I have a picture of you two together, at the Cookstown Fair twenty years ago.' He held it high. 'I'm happy to tell you all that I know right now, or even discuss it with the reporter outside. But if Your Honour would prefer to discuss it in chambers, I'm happy to oblige.'

Buford stood and barked at his assistant, 'Show him through.'

'But, Your Honour ...'

'Just do it,' and Buford stomped away, through a door to one side of him, the usher just about scrambling to his feet in time.

The usher exchanged glances with the court assistant, before he gestured to Charlie that he should follow.

'It looks like he wants a man-to-man,' Charlie said to the usher, before he followed the court assistant to the door that would take him into the private areas of the courthouse.

Sixty-Five

Goldie had parked her van further along the lane from the Buford house. She knew she'd never get onto the Buford land via the front gate, but there was a track that ran through nearby woods and alongside a galloping track for the horses.

She would wade through the Nick Cassidy's call logs later. She'd had another idea.

It had been a long time since she'd walked the path, one of those summer excursions she'd had as a child, because it led to a lake by an old slate quarry. As she walked, the path weaved just as she remembered it, ferns clogging the ground amongst the trees, the way ahead just a beaten-down line of dried mud and occasional glimpses of the Buford house.

She stopped at a point where the track started to curve away from the Buford land, so that it was the closest point. When she raised the binoculars she'd borrowed from a friend before she set off, she saw the woman she'd seen on the visit with Charlie, sitting at a bistro table by one of the doorways. Clarence was opposite, drinking something from a cup. The woman was drinking from a glass.

Whatever they were talking about, it became heated, because Clarence started to gesture and point, and the woman folded her arms and looked away. After a few minutes, Clarence snatched his coat from the back of the chair and stormed off. Goldie listened out, ears straining, until she heard it: the unmistakable crunch of tyres on gravel, then a flash of the black Range Rover as it headed towards the gate.

Goldie checked for signs of anyone else being there. It looked deserted, so she clambered over the fence that bordered the galloping track and skipped across to the soft undulations of the adjoining field, where sleek black horses grazed.

She was ready to run if the woman seemed alarmed in any way, but it was as if the woman was waiting for her, watching Goldie as she got closer.

When she got within earshot, Goldie shouted, 'Hi. Mr Buford said I could come back to look at the horses anytime.'

The woman didn't respond. Instead, she took a drink from her glass and folded one leg over the other.

Goldie kept going, through a small gate that led to the manicured lawn, and along a gravel path that ran between raised brick flowerbeds, the petals a bright spread of reds and yellows.

As Goldie got close, the woman said, 'I thought you'd come back. Take a seat.'

Goldie did as she was instructed. 'Why did you think I'd be back?'

She took another drink. It was a dark liquid. Ice cubes clinked against the glass.

As the woman looked back to speak, Goldie detected a slowness to her movement, the tell-tale exaggeration of drunken motion. Her eyes were vacant.

'Because you made Clarence nervous.'

'Clarence said I could look at the horses.'

'He didn't mean that.'

'You sound as if you don't like him much.'

'I've been married to him for nearly fifty years.' She raised her glass. 'Life's all about a habit. Some you like. Some you don't.'

'I don't want to see the horses, though. I want to speak to you.'

'Me? Why am I so damn interesting?'

'Because you're the only person living here who we haven't spoken to about Natasha Trenton.'

She took a deep breath, almost like a sigh, before her eyes narrowed. 'Yes, her.'

'What do you mean by that?'

'Have you got any children?'

'No, not yet.'

'I can tell that. It's not in your eyes.'

'My eyes?'

'That mix of tiredness and panic, because you worry about them all the time. You can't help it. There's love too, so much it's hard to deal with sometimes, so imagine how it must be to lose a child.' She waved her hand dismissively. 'Don't bother, because however much you try to imagine it, you'll still be nowhere near how hard it is.'

'Are you talking about Truman?'

'They're supposed to bury us, not the other way around,' she said. 'That girl going missing killed him as good as if they'd hanged him from the nearest tree,' and she wagged her finger towards the nearby willow tree.

Goldie lowered her voice when she said, 'Do you think Truman killed her?'

'I know he didn't. I knew my son.'

'But why did Truman say he'd killed her, if he hadn't?'

She wiped a tear from her cheek. 'Did he say that? I never heard him say it. On my side of the family, we cradle our wayward sons, bring them back into the fold.'

'And on Clarence's side?'

She drained the glass, then reached under the chair for a bottle that Goldie hadn't spotted. As she poured, she said, 'Like racehorses. Once they can no longer win the race, they get put down.'

'Do you remember Natasha, Mrs Buford.'

'Call me Nancy.'

'Okay, Nancy, do you remember her?'

'I remember them all.' She gave a half-smile when she said, 'They brought me my drinks, and made my life just about bearable.'

'And what was Natasha like?'

'Nice. Too nice. Like, she couldn't see how nice she was. A bit like you, I reckon.'

'I don't understand.'

'Some girls know what they have, recognise their power, and use it to get what or who they want.' A wistful smile. 'I had some of that. I know you can't see it now, but there was a time when I knew I had something men wanted. Good figure, good bones, and my eyes twinkled promise. And the trick was to let them think that they had to fight for it, that it wouldn't come easy, but it would come, eventually. And when it did, it would be better than they imagined.'

'And women like Natasha?'

'She had everything. The smile, the figure, the looks, but it was as if she didn't know the power she had. Men desired her, but it didn't register, so there was no chase. It was one-sided desire, a goal they'll never achieve. Some men don't like that.'

'I don't understand'

'If there's a nice car in a showroom window, some men will work hard and save their money, until one day they can buy it. Others? They'll steal it, just because they want it.'

Goldie leaned in. 'Are you saying that something happened to Natasha here?'

Nancy put her head back and closed her eyes.

Goldie waited it out, wondered what would come next, but nothing did.

Instead, Nancy opened her eyes and put her glass down. 'I've had enough for one day. For now, anyway.'

'You were going to tell me something important.'

'Only important to you. Not to me, perhaps.'

'But if something happened to Natasha here, it set off a chain of events that led to Truman's death.' Goldie tried to catch Nancy's gaze. 'Please, if there's something I should know, you should tell me now, because this is all going to come out.'

'Like a tree,' she said.

'I'm sorry, I don't understand.'

'It starts under the ground as nothing, but eventually it sprouts and gets taller and wider and takes over everything. Take this willow tree. Once fresh green lawn, now it's all in shadow.'

'That's very cryptic.'

'My dear, it's goodbye. I'm glad you've called by, but I really do think I need a long sleep. Please, go the way you came.'

Goldie realised that she wasn't going to get any more from Nancy, so she bid her farewell and headed back through the garden, towards the open field and the galloping track.

As she got further away, she turned to see if Nancy was there.

The only person she could see was the gardener, Pete, staring from the archway in the middle of the house, his hands in his pockets, before he turned away and out of sight.

Sixty-Six

Lewis Buford closed the door to his chambers and invited Charlie to sit down, although there was little cordiality. He placed his wig on a wooden dome on top of his desk and started to tug at the red silk sash that was draped over his shoulder.

A desk dominated the room, with a green leather inlay set into polished mahogany, bookshelves behind. Some contained legal textbooks, whereas others were dominated by family photographs. A woman in jodhpurs and a shirt, hair tied loosely into a ponytail. Two young girls in prep school uniforms of blazers and straw hats.

Buford tapped the desk with his fingernail to get Charlie's attention back. 'What are you after, Mr Steele?'

'Something simple,' he said. 'The truth about my client. But I need to know something first. Am I in here as a solicitor, an officer of the court, paying you the due respect? Or simply a man asking another man some questions? Because if you start pulling any *I'm a judge* bullshit, I'm out of here.'

'You're being incredibly disrespectful if you don't know the answer.'

'I haven't got a case listed before you, so I don't think it can be contempt of court. No, this feels a little more man-to-man.'

Buford sat down and leaned back in his chair, putting the desk between them. He considered Charlie in silence, his gaze fixed, before he said, 'Let's see how we get on.'

'Let's start with Natasha Trenton,' Charlie said.

Buford steepled his fingers under his nose. 'It sounds to me like you already know something about her. If you want a frank discussion, you need to disclose what you have. This is not an inquisition.'

'That makes it feel very one way. But, then again, it's been that way ever since I arrived in Cookstown. I've been forced out of my hotel. I've been nearly burned alive. That just makes me more suspicious, more enquiring, because I had a client who was scared, until he ended up dead.'

Buford's eyes hardened when he said, 'That should make you fearful, not enquiring. Curiosity and cats, Mr Steele.'

Charlie cocked his finger, pistol-style. 'I spot the threat, judge, but I've been threatened before. I'm a defence lawyer, so it goes with the territory. I'm more curious about the lack of concern about an old friend of yours. I expected a little more sadness.'

'Gerard?' He waved his hand. 'It was a long time ago. People move on, that's life. Some of us move up. Some go down. When that happens, lives diverge. How many of your old college friends do you still see? Not many, I'd wager. If his life didn't really go anywhere, that explains why he's obsessed about what happened twenty years ago, to Natasha.'

Charlie narrowed his eyes. 'How do you know his life didn't go anywhere? How do you know he's obsessed?'

'Just because we weren't in touch doesn't mean that I didn't take an interest. We were friends once, that counts for something, but it doesn't mean I want to invite him for cocktails. And I don't mean to be impolite, but you are his solicitor,' and he made a show of looking Charlie up and down. 'That tells me that he can't really afford the best.'

Charlie ignored the insult. 'Aren't you interested in what happened to him?'

Buford curled his lip. 'You said he was murdered. Go on, Mr Steele, unburden yourself.'

'Found dead in the woods behind his house, hanging from a tree.'

Buford's eyes filled with sadness, almost catching Charlie by surprise, but he knew that a lawyer could fake most emotions if it helped to win the argument.

'It sounds a lot like suicide,' Buford said. 'A great tragedy, but Gerard seemed troubled quite often. He had all the advantages of a good education, and the right university, but it was as if the burden was too great. Liberal guilt, I think. *Omnes ab omnibus discamus*, as my old school motto used to say. Let us learn all things from everybody. That isn't how he saw it.'

'The old school motto? Well done for reminding me of your breeding, but that just brings me back to Natasha. Is that what she was to you, someone beneath you? Because there are a few threads all being pulled together, and the closer they get, the more Natasha and your friends become entwined.'

'Threads?'

'Ben Leech? You'll remember Ben. He spent some time at your home too, in the summer after your second year at Oxford, along with Gerard, and Spencer Everett. Both Ben and Gerard were found dead within a few months of each other. You have to agree that it looks suspicious.'

'I don't have to agree anything, Mr Steele, as you well know, and coincidences happen.'

'How's this one, judge? The last night they spent at your house was the night Natasha Trenton went missing.'

'She was just an employee. I'm not to know of her movements.'

'An employee that your brother admitted killing. Or, at least, that's what the police say.'

'You have your answer there then. My poor misguided brother must have killed her. The police think that. Truman agreed.'

'What do you think?'

Buford leaned forward. His wooden chair creaked.

'Mr Steele, sometimes bad things happen in a cluster. You're a lawyer, so you say, but you appear to be entertaining yourself with plots and conspiracies, rather than evidence. How many actually come true? It turned out that Kennedy was killed by Oswald after all. And that Diana died because of a speeding, drunken driver. There isn't always a bigger picture.'

'What was Natasha like?'

Buford faltered, before saying, 'I can't remember.'

'She worked at your house.'

'I neither hired nor paid her, and she served us, not befriended us.'

'Very below stairs, Mr Buford.'

'It's the employer and employee relationship.'

'How old were you? Twenty? And she was eighteen and pretty, and a little below you in her social standing. Was that the attraction? You must have seen her, desired her, even if it was simply as a bit of summer fun. No one expected you to marry her, she wasn't from the right set, but men that age just have heads full of mush.'

'How beautifully put, Mr Steele,' he said, his voice filled with disdain. 'But I had a fiancée, so I had little interest in risking what we had for some dalliance with a local girl from one of the estates.'

'What was her name, your fiancée? She might be able to fill in some of the gaps.'

Buford's lips twitched. 'I've had enough of this charade.'

'Why are you closing me down?'

'Because I've had enough. I've a busy court to run.'

'What did your fiancée think about an attractive young woman being in the house where you lived?'

'It didn't concern her.'

'You're saying that, but I'd rather ask her.'

Buford suppressed a smile, although it had little warmth. 'Good luck with your quest. This meeting has ended.'

'Judge, we're talking. Why stop?'

'Because I don't take kindly to your tone. Goodbye, Mr Steele. Leave now, or I call security.'

Charlie knew that staying was futile. 'As you wish, but this is not the end.'

Buford said, 'We'll see about that.'

Charlie left, not pausing to say goodbye to the assistant or the usher. Instead, he needed to be outside, to make a call.

Once on the street, Charlie scrolled through the most recent numbers he'd dialled, until he came to the one he was looking for: Ben Leech's widow.

She answered straight away.

'Hi, it's Charlie Steele. I'm getting somewhere, but I need some information.'

'What is it?'

'Who was Lewis Buford's fiancée in his second year at Oxford? I don't think it was his wife, just from how he reacted.'

'Do you think she might be relevant?'

'I don't know, but it was the one thing that made him nervous.'

'Let me get back to you,' and she clicked off.

He paced as he waited.

Twenty minutes passed before she called back.

She was breathless when she said, 'She was murdered.'

'What?'

'I spoke to an old university friend, who said she was surprised I didn't know, because it was all over their Facebook groups. She was murdered, around a week ago.'

'What was she called?'

Charlie guessed the answer before she said it, but it didn't diminish the shock.

'Sarah Stewart, as she was,' she said. 'Sarah Marsh when she died. She was murdered, left on the beach in Cookstown.'

Charlie stared back at the courthouse, and he wondered if the judge was watching him, before he muttered to himself, 'Fucking hell.'

Sixty-Seven

Jessica struggled to focus as she sifted through Spencer's constituency letters in his Parliamentary office, sorting them into piles that were urgent, that he needed to look at, and the less urgent ones that would become a job for her later on.

Spencer had spent most of the day in meetings, only ever passing through to check if any messages had been left, startling her every time, wondering whether she had been found out.

She jumped again when the door opened, making some of the letters flutter to the floor.

It was Wendy.

'You're jittery,' she said, bending to help her scoop up the correspondence.

'Don't you blame me, because of what we're doing?'

Wendy closed the door and said, in a low voice, 'You need to hold it together. We'll get to the bottom of this. Calm down. Would you rather we weren't doing this, that we were dragged down with Spencer when he's found out?'

'No. It's just that, well, I'm not used to this. I wanted to be loyal to Spencer. I didn't know he'd be like this.'

Wendy smiled, a rare event, and put her hand over Jessica's. 'Come on, let's go for a drink. I think we both need one.'

Jessica agreed, needing to be away from Parliament.

They headed along Whitehall, both of them silent as they worked their way through the crowds, not wanting anyone to overhear them, until Wendy turned off into a side-street. There was a pub further along, wood and stained glass, people drinking outside, men in shirts and ties downing lukewarm pints of golden beer.

Jessica couldn't see any of the politics crowd though, none she recognised anyway, so it seemed like a good idea.

As Wendy went to the bar, Jessica took a seat outside and wondered whether she'd misjudged Wendy.

Her phone rang.

'Hello?'

It was a woman on the other end. 'Hi, I'm sorry for calling, but I'm calling about Nick Cassidy.'

Jessica flushed and got up from her table. She moved away from the pub and turned, so that she had her back to the drinkers. She hissed into her phone, 'How did you get my number?'

'I'm calling all the numbers Nick had called in the last week or so. This is one of them.'

'What's your name?'

'Goldie Brown.'

Jessica tried to work her through a mental contacts book, but the name wasn't familiar. 'Why are you calling?'

'I'm in Cookstown. Nick was here, and I'm trying to find someone who is interested in why. I might have some information they want. Nick can't use it now, obviously.'

Jessica knew Cookstown, memories of childhood seaside trips coming back to her.

'Cookstown? Why there? What are you talking about?'

'I think we're looking into the same thing. I'm sorry I can't tell you more, but we really need to speak to whoever Nick was working with. It might be for our mutual benefit.'

Jessica glanced into the pub. Wendy was being served, fishing in her bag for her purse.

'Who's we?'

'Here, I'll give you a number,' the woman said, and Jessica went back to her table so she could jot it down on a beermat. 'That number is for Charlie Steele. He's a solicitor.'

'You said that Nick can't use the information anymore,' Jessica said. 'Why not?'

Jessica listened as the woman on the other end of the phone took a deep breath and said, 'He's dead.'

'Dead?'

'Yes, and I'm sorry if you didn't know.'

'How?'

'Jumped in front of a train just outside of Cookstown.'

Jessica almost dropped her phone as the blood drained from her face. She looked back towards the bar, Wendy putting her purse away, the drinks in front of her.

Her mind raced through the events of the previous few days. Wendy had caught her looking through Spencer's things and has been acting like her friend, but she'd told Wendy about Nick Cassidy, Now, he's dead.

Wendy headed over with the drinks, so Jessica held up her phone.

'I'm really sorry,' she said. 'Just had some news from home. My uncle is very ill. I need to speak to my parents, they're really upset. I'm sorry.'

Wendy frowned. 'But I've just got these.'

'I can't stay.'

Wendy sat down, her mood cooled. 'Okay, you go. Euston tomorrow for seven-thirty. We've got a train to catch.'

'Yes, thanks, no problem.'

Jessica rushed out of the pub. As she got back onto the street, she wondered where to go. She needed to get some clothes and find somewhere to sleep before tomorrow, and work out what the hell she was going to do.

All she knew was that she couldn't stay anywhere that Wendy would know.

Sixty-Eight

Charlie had been waiting for a couple of hours in a car park across from the court building, so that he could pull out and follow Judge Buford when he emerged. He'd worked out which was his car by peering through the security gate, because there was a Jaguar with a private plate beginning with BFD.

The surveillance technique was all new to him though. Taking it steady was the presumption, putting a car between himself and the judge, using the city centre traffic as cover. He wasn't sure what to do if the judge turned off somewhere quiet, but he guessed he'd have to get creative when it happened.

Charlie jolted, sat upright, before he leaned forward to peer through the windscreen. 'Shit.'

Buford was on foot, heading out of a small, cobbled street that ran alongside the courthouse. He checked around himself as he emerged onto the main street, his hands in his pockets.

Charlie was there to follow him, but he'd been blindsided by the fact that he wasn't driving. But if he pursued him on foot, Buford would recognise him.

Charlie remembered something.

He went to the boot of his car and produced a high-vis jacket, something he kept for whenever he went walking on the moors, along with a faded Red Sox baseball cap. It was the opposite of inconspicuous, but perhaps that was the key. The judge won't be looking out for a high-vis jacket, so he might ignore him if he sees it.

Buford was rushing, looking around as he went across the road, towards a nearby park. Charlie went after him, his head down but his eyes forward, pretending to check his phone. Buford was fifty yards ahead.

Charlie wondered where he was going at first, but the more he followed, the more he realised that he must be meeting someone, and it had to be connected to his presence.

Buford bolted into the park, a long rectangle with a central avenue of trees, black iron seats lining the path that headed towards a circular fountain, surrounded by flower beds. His pace quickened, his nerves more apparent.

As Buford approached the fountain, he slowed.

Charlie veered towards a bench and sat down, made as if he were sending a text, but he never took his eyes from the judge, who was pacing, looking around, checking his watch.

The judge stopped and turned, then raised his hand as if in greeting. There was someone walking towards him.

Charlie looked over too, trying to see who it was, but there were bushes and trees in the way. He sat upright, his phone by his ear. He was using his hand to block his face, but his thumb was taking photographs in the judge's direction, jabbing at where he hoped the red shutter button was on the screen.

Charlie took some more pictures as the person came into view. It was a man, but he had his back to Charlie. As they met, their conversation turned animated, the man finger-pointing, the judge looking angry, his hand clasped to his forehead. The man was tall but stooped, older than Buford, and there was something familiar about him.

The man turned and Charlie got a half-profile. Realisation dawned on him. It was a half-profile he'd seen before.

Charlie gasped. 'Shit, no.'

He checked his screen and zoomed in on the last picture he'd taken. 'I don't believe it.'

Charlie headed back to his car, his pace quickened to almost a jog, trying to remain inconspicuous, but to get the hell away too.

He called Amy once he was back in his car.

When she answered, he said, 'You're not going to believe this. I've been following Lewis Buford and …'

Amy interrupted him. 'I'm not interested.'

'Hang on, you don't know what I'm going to say.'

'Listen to me, Charlie,' she said. 'I told you, I can't do this anymore. I'm out. You do what you like, but I'm not taking part.'

'But Amy ….'

'Goodbye, Charlie.' Then, she clicked off.

He stared at his phone in disbelief.

But, as he thought about what he'd just seen, he wondered whether Amy knew more than she let on, because the man meeting Judge Buford had been the retired detective in charge of the Natasha Trenton case, Jimmy Gray.

Amy's father.

He didn't have time to think anything more about it, as his phone rang. It was Isobel.

When he answered, he asked, 'Everything okay?'

'Charlie, I need you to come back now.' There was a tremble in her voice.

'Isobel, what is it? Is Molly all right?'

'It's not her. It's you. Come back, please. We need to talk.'

Sixty-Nine

The small room Jessica had found near Kings Cross wouldn't be in her list of recommendations. It had fake wood panelling, and the bed was squeezed in between the window and the bathroom, with only enough room for some hooks on the wall.

She guessed that no one ever planned to spend more than one night, just somewhere to flop down near two of the main railway stations.

Or even for other purposes, because she'd passed the sex workers patrolling the nearby streets, men in doorways watching, either waiting to collect the money or mug the punters, knowing they wouldn't report it. There were hairs under the sheets and drink stains on the wall. The shower leaked, so that water ran close to the bed. Upstairs, there was music playing, along with the steady creaks of two people having sex.

It suited her needs though, because it wouldn't take her long to walk to Euston in the morning. Most importantly, it was cheap and anonymous, paid for in cash. Unless she'd been followed, she wouldn't show up on any database. No credit card trail or hotel customer list.

As she sat on the edge of the bed, the call from earlier kept replaying in her head. Nick Cassidy is dead, and something is going on in Cookstown, with Spencer Everett at the heart of it.

She'd only met Nick a few times.

He'd seemed like a decent person. Not as serious as some reporters she'd met, perhaps operating on the fringes, the conspiracy theory type, but he'd been sincere and polite. That was why she'd gone along with him, because he seemed genuine.

Jessica sighed when she realised that she was criticising him for coming up with conspiracy theories. The man had died when looking into a high-ranking politician. She didn't know whether it proved that the forces at work were as dark as he'd imagined, or whether it was just the supreme irony.

But he'd been right about the backhanders. She needed to know more.

She went to the last call she'd received and pressed the call button. When the woman answered, Jessica said, 'I'm sorry for clicking off before. You shocked me. You said your name was Goldie.'

There was pub noise in the background, chatter and music. 'We need to know why Nick was calling you,' Goldie said. 'It might be why he died.'

'Hang on, that makes it sound like it might be my fault. It can't be my fault if he jumped in front of a train.'

'We don't know if he did.'

'He might have been murdered?'

'We don't know. He was arrested, then released, and went under a train not long afterwards.'

'Arrested? Why? Are they going to come for me because I spoke to him?'

Goldie fell silent for a moment, before asking, 'Who are you?'

'My name is Jessica Redmond. I'm an intern for Spencer Everett.'

'Oh shit. You work for Spencer? I can't, I'm sorry, I shouldn't really be, look, forget I called.'

'No, you don't understand. Don't hang up. Don't block me. I was the one helping Nick.'

A pause on the other end, then, 'You were? Why?'

'Because Spencer Everett is a crook. Nick was writing an exposé on him. He'd heard about backhanders and favours, and wanted to dig into his past. He thought Spencer was just some spoilt public schoolboy who'd conned his way to the top.'

'There are plenty who've done that. But why did you choose to work for someone like him? How do I know I can trust you?'

'You don't, I suppose, but I'm all you've got. What's your interest?'

Jessica wondered whether Goldie was going to hang up, as she went silent again.

'Goldie?'

More silence, until Goldie said, 'Someone went missing here a long time ago, and it seems connected to Spencer. We think that's why Nick was here in Cookstown. He'd dug into Spencer's past and discovered a secret he hadn't expected to find, something much bigger than a politician's dodgy money.'

'How big?'

'Murder, maybe.'

'Hang on, you think Spencer might be tied up with a murder?'

'Yes. No point in sugar-coating it. If you want to get justice for Nick Cassidy, and others, you need to help us find out what happened in Cookstown twenty years ago.'

'How do I do that?'

Goldie laughed. 'Do you know what? I haven't got a clue. Look, I'm sorry, I've got to go. You've got Charlie's number. I gave it to you earlier. Speak to him.'

Jessica closed her eyes as she thought about her next move.

'I'll call you tomorrow,' she said. 'I'm going north with Spencer. He's got a public announcement, to do with a new immigration detention centre. We might be able to meet. I'll pretend I want to see family and get away for a couple of hours.'

'Good idea. Call me tomorrow when you know the schedule.'

When her phone went silent, Jessica slumped back onto the bed. Murder? What the hell was she getting herself into?

As she put her coat onto the pillows, not wanting to rest her head on them, she knew she had a long, restless night ahead.

And still the bed creaked overhead, in its regular, banging rhythm.

Seventy

Goldie felt distracted as she performed. Not that it mattered. There weren't many in, and the faint ripple of applause was more polite than appreciative.

Some nights, she could lose herself in the music, so that she couldn't see the crowd, searching for the emotion that had driven her when she wrote one of her own songs, but they were becoming rarer events. She'd become a fixture, the singer who did the local pubs, with the same set, often the same people.

There were some good nights though, but she knew that it was the cover songs that brought the crowds to life, not her own. But she was paid to entertain, so she let the audience determine her direction. If the crowd was lively, she'd go with the singalongs. *American Pie*, *Brown-eyed Girl*, some Oasis. If the crowd was quiet, she'd go for the gentler stuff. *Fields of Gold*, some Ed Sheeran.

There were worse ways to earn a living, she supposed. There were middle-aged couples having a quiet drink, along with some of the after-work crowd. Two men played pool in the corner, as always, the clack of the balls audible even as she played. Three builders spilled cement dust onto the carpet, and a man in a suit strained his shirt-buttons with his stomach.

She was about to launch into another song when she saw him by the bar.

It was Pete, the handyman from the Buford house, leaning against the bar, nursing a pint of beer.

She faltered, surprised. He raised his glass when he realised she'd spotted him, but he was smiling. She flickered a nervous smile back, then started her final few songs.

Her performance was below par after that, the self-critical voice in her head tapping away at her, the bane of every performer.

She ended her set without any enthusiasm. Once the polite smattering of applause had died down and she'd packed her kit, she made her way over to the bar. Scott, the barman, handed over some notes and said, 'Not as many in tonight.'

'It's okay. I just keep plugging away. I need a beer though.' She looked along the bar to Pete. There was no point in avoiding him, so she asked, 'Do you want another?'

Pete looked at his glass, almost empty, and said, 'No, but thank you. I'll be driving soon.'

Scott slid a bottle to Goldie and said, 'I'll leave you guys to it.'

Goldie took the stool next to Pete. 'Have you come to talk to me, or just hear the set? I can send you a disc, if you're interested.'

'A bit of both,' he said, and chuckled. 'I was curious about you.'

'Me? Why?'

'Because you're from Cookstown, and suddenly you've got yourself worked up about an old disappearance.'

'Shouldn't I be getting worked up about it? A woman went missing from my hometown. That should be bigger news.'

'I agree, because I remember the girl. I remember the impact on the Buford family, with Truman getting blamed. But why now?'

She took a drink and stretched. 'It's not me, really. It's Charlie. It's his doing.'

'The lawyer? Yes, I remember. But he wasn't there today. Why did you come up?'

She leaned in to ask, 'How do I know I can trust you?'

He gestured towards his clothes. Beaten-up corduroy trousers and a shirt that had once been bright red tartan, but had been faded by years of washing. 'Because I'm just an old fool who has bent his back for that family for years, and I wonder whether I missed something back then. Funny old folk, those with money. What did Nancy say?'

'It was all a drunken blur, I think. She talked about how a tree can overshadow a lawn, and how she remembered Natasha.'

He drained his glass. 'Why did you think she'd help?'

'Just a feeling. When we went up the first time, it was as if she was floating around, trying to be seen, wanting to attract attention.'

'She's a dotty old bird, I know that much. What does this Charlie want from all this?'

'Find out the truth.'

'And you?'

'Just along for the ride, to be honest. And if something good comes out of it for that poor girl, then I'm all for it.' She put her drink down and considered Pete. 'I wouldn't have thought I was important enough to warrant a special visit.'

'It's where I've worked for years. I feel like I'm part of the story, so I wanted to hear your side.'

'Anything I can pass on to Charlie? He seems determined to solve this thing.'

'I just don't want him to make it worse for anyone. If that poor boy Truman did kill her, he can't answer for it now, but he got all the punishment he deserved.'

'Nancy doesn't think he did it.'

'Mothers never do.'

'But the police must have spoken to him, and he wasn't charged, so they can't have believed it was him either. And if it wasn't him, it was someone else.'

'Assuming she's dead.'

'No sign she's alive.'

'And you're determined to find out who it was?'

'Doesn't Natasha deserve that? I didn't know her, but that doesn't mean I don't empathise with her. Young. Female. Gone missing. It works on repeat, always has, and we've got to do something about it.'

'Leave it to the police,' he said. 'If it wasn't Truman, whoever did something to her has got away with it for twenty years. That can make it dangerous. This is no *Famous Five* mystery.'

'I know. My caravan was attacked last night, so for once in my life I want to stand up for something.' She drained her beer and said, 'And it's time for me to go.'

Pete got off his stool. 'At least let me carry your equipment to your van.'

'No, there's no need. I'm used to doing this.'

He sighed and looked around the bar. He got closer and whispered, 'There is something you might find useful. I just don't want to say it in here, because I don't know who's listening. Let me pretend to carry your things and we can talk outside. It might be nothing but, well, you never know.'

She smiled. 'Okay, we'll do that.'

'But you've got to promise not to say where you got the information.'

'I promise.'

Goldie carried her guitar and her mixing kit, as Pete carried her speaker and microphone stand out of the side door.

As she opened the door to the van, she turned and said, 'What is it?'

He was bending down as she spoke, moving a rock that was behind her front wheel. She didn't remember it being there when she arrived.

Before she could work out what was happening, he raised it and hit her hard. It crashed into her temple before she had the chance to protect herself.

She couldn't remember falling.

It was as if it was happening to someone else. The chatter drifting out of the pub seemed distant. There was liquid on her head, warm and sticky, but cooled by the sea-breeze. She was lifted into the van. She knew she should fight, but her limbs wouldn't follow her orders. She tried to say something, but it came out as a moan.

She lay back as the campervan was started and stared at the roof. She lifted a hand and moaned.

His hand reached back again in a long arc. She couldn't avoid the rock. It struck her in her forehead, making her gasp as it crashed into the bone.

After that, it was all dark.

Seventy-One

Charlie saw Isobel ahead, pacing on the spot, her arms folded, a cigarette in her fingers, smoke trailing upwards.

They'd agreed to meet in a park on the eastern edge of Manchester, away from her home, where no one would know her. His back was aching from the drive from Cookstown, the whole journey spent wondering what was so urgent, but he knew he had to be there. It was the worry in her voice.

The metal gate creaked as he entered, making her look up. There were swings behind her, and a climbing frame, but there was no one using them. She stubbed out her cigarette and sat on a bench. He joined her. The daylight had gone, so the Pennines brooded behind them as a dark shadow.

It was Charlie who spoke first.

'What's troubling you?'

She wiped away a tear, before saying, 'You are.'

'I don't understand.'

'I'm being blackmailed because of you. Because of whatever you're up to.'

'What? How?'

She thrust her hands into her jacket pockets and scrunched her chin into her silk scarf. 'There was a man.'

'What, a man other than Simon?'

She swallowed when she said, 'Yes.'

Charlie looked at her and laughed. 'You're kidding me?' He sat back and shook his head. 'You don't change. At least it makes me feel better, that perhaps it was just about you, not me.'

'It wasn't like that. For Christ's sake Charlie, this was not some dumb affair. I was, I don't know, drugged or something.'

'You were raped?'

She hung her head.

'Isobel, talk to me.'

Her voice broke when she said, 'I don't know, because I don't know if I had sex. It's all so fucking sordid. And all because of you. I should hate you for this, but well...'

'It wasn't my fault?'

'Something like that.'

'Tell me what happened.'

She raised her eyes to the sky and blinked back tears. 'Some guy called my office, said he wanted to discuss a will for his wealthy father, with the firm possibly appointed as executors. He wanted to meet in a restaurant though,, but you know how it is, that we're all fighting our corner, fee-earner against fee-earner. So, I agreed. Worst-case scenario, I get a free lunch, that's how I saw it. That was it, just a business meeting. But it gets a bit, well, fuzzy after that.'

'Fuzzy? What, through booze?'

'Yes, there was wine, but it went blurry too quickly. Just a couple of glasses is all I remember. After that, it's just snapshots. Stumbling down a corridor. A door. I'm sure he drugged me, because it was a set-up from the start.'

'How do you know?'

'Because he booked the room in my name. He left no trace.'

'Shit.' Charlie turned to face her. 'Who was he? What did he look like? What did he talk about?'

'He gave me the name Thomas Riley, but it'll be a fake name. Tall man, skinny, bald head. Quite a good-looking guy, in that steely, hard way. Like Jason Statham, but taller. I can't remember what he talked about, just chit-chat, then he started pouring the wine. I can't remember much after that.'

'Was he drinking?'

Isobel shook her head. 'Now I've thought back, he wasn't.'

'How is he blackmailing you?'

'He took photographs,' she said, and reddened. 'He knows my home address. He knows about Simon, and Molly. He knows where I work. He said he will send them to everyone, work included, if you don't stop what you're doing. He even sent me copies, just to remind me.'

Charlie felt a chill. They'd got to Isobel too.

'Show me,' he said.

'No chance.'

'Isobel, we were married. If there is anyone you can show, it's me.'

She stared straight ahead as she thought about it, before reaching into her pocket and unlocking her phone.

'Ignore the email address he used, just a random Gmail address, but he sent it to my work email. What if the IT people saw them?' She opened the picture gallery and passed the phone over. 'I haven't deleted them yet, because they might be evidence.' Her voice broke when she said, 'If he drugged me and had sex with me, he raped me.'

Charlie's eyes widened when he looked at the first image.

It was Isobel, lying on a bed, topless, unmistakeably her.

'I can't tell if your eyes are open,' Charlie said.

'Keep going.'

Charlie flicked to the next picture and muttered, 'Fuck.'

Isobel was on her back, fully naked this time, with a man's hand gripping her leg.

He zoomed in.

'Don't,' she said.

'No, it's not what you think,' and he held up her phone. 'Look, there on his wrist, his watch. It's distinctive, a blue face, I'm trying to make out the brand. And there, on the top of his hand. He's got a birthmark, just by his knuckle.'

'Oh yes, I see.' Her eyes widened. 'That means he's identifiable, provided we can catch him.'

'It's a *we* then?'

'I can't ask Simon. He won't believe me, knowing how we started, and it's connected to you. You've got me into this mess. You owe it to me to sort out this mess.'

Charlie didn't reply, so she said, 'Don't make this about revenge. Yeah, you're right, I can't keep my legs closed. If that's what you want to think, feel free. But I did not do this.'

Charlie flicked to the next picture and gasped.

She shook her head. 'The partners at Pattersons will just love that one. The bastard even got the clock in, so they'll know it was in work time.'

The picture showed her posing, her legs open, her hand placed between her legs. Her eyes were either closed in rapturous anticipation, or else she was out of it, but it looked just like what everyone would assume it to be.

He passed her the phone back. 'They look bad, but are there any pictures of him penetrating you?'

'Raping me, you mean?' A tear ran down her face as she shook her head. 'No.'

'It's a set up, like you said, but I'm guessing he didn't have sex with you. He just wants you to think that you'd slept with him, so he can blackmail you properly. Or me, I suppose.'

'I don't know what case you're working on, but you've got to stop.'

Charlie hung his head. 'I can't.'

'Why not?' She stood, pacing again. 'Is this your revenge? Well, fucking enjoy it, because I don't deserve this, whatever you think.'

'The man you met kills people, I'm sure of it.'

Isobel paled and sat down. 'What?'

'He might have killed my client, Gerard, and another old friend of his, Ben Leech. They were at university with Spencer Everett, and there's some big secret he's trying to stop from getting out.'

'How do you know this?'

'Deduction, assumption. Gut feeling. Following the evidence.'

'What evidence?'

Charlie thought it through. What was there, in reality? More suspicion than hard fact. A hard belief, but backed up by vague ideas.

'There you have it,' she said. 'You don't have any evidence. But I'm the mother of your daughter. He knows who I am, and he knows about Molly, and where we live. I'm begging you, please. If not for my sake, for Molly's sake. Walk away from it. Let it go. Don't use it as something to get back at me.'

'A man died. And what about what he did to you?'

'I'll tell you what's right. Looking after our daughter. Making her safe. Keeping her in a stable home. Not some mission you've set yourself to save the world, or whatever the fuck it is you're doing. Go on, tell me, what's the secret?'

Charlie sighed. 'I don't know exactly. A woman went missing twenty years ago. It might be connected to her, but the truth is that we don't know exactly.'

'So, you don't know what you're chasing. Great. What started it?'

'A photograph.'

'Of what?'

He took the picture from his pocket and held it up. 'This one. I found it in Gerard's house, my client. This is the key to it all.'

'Pass it to me.'

'How do I know you won't rip it up, to make me stop?'

'You don't, so you'll have to trust me.' She clicked her fingers. 'Pass it here.'

He handed it to her. 'Spencer Everett is in the middle. My client is on the left. The guy next to him is a judge now, but comes from Cookstown, where I've been for the past few days.'

Isobel lifted the photograph closer. She gasped and her eyes flashed with tears.

'What is it?'

'That's him,' she said. She thrust the picture back at Charlie. 'That's the man who drugged me and took pictures of me.'

Charlie took it back and looked at the photograph. 'Which one?'

'Just behind Everett. The only one not smiling.'

'Are you sure?'

'Of course, I'm sure. I'll never forget his face. And his eyes. Deep, penetrating.'

Charlie stared at the photograph again. The only one not smiling. That summed him up. He's glaring at the person taking the picture, one arm around Everett, but his focus is more intense than the others.

Her gaze hardened. 'I don't need you to rescue me. But I can see that you're not listening, so I'll make it simple for you. You either stop, or you don't see Molly again, because your obsession is putting me in danger, which puts her in danger.'

'That's what they want, can't you see?'

'I don't care what they want. You're making a choice now. Molly, or justice for your client. You decide.'

Charlie glared at her, but he knew he would only give one answer.

'I'll stop,' he said. 'Go home, speak to Simon. But I'll stop.'

Tears rolled down her cheeks as her shoulders sagged. 'Thank you.'

As Charlie watched her go, he knew that he'd just lied to her, because if someone was threatening Isobel and Molly, there wasn't a chance that he'd let them get away with it.

Seventy-Two

The rumble of her campervan made it through the mist in her head, as Goldie bounced around on its floor. She groaned as pain flashed through her temples, and winced as she tried to move.

She sucked in some air and took deep breaths, and the world seemed to come in more clearly. She tried to move to put her hand to her head, the stickiness now cold against her skin, but she couldn't move her hands. She tried to raise herself, but her body didn't want to respond, with the view ahead tilted.

Goldie closed her eyes and willed herself to focus, her clarity of thought coming back to her in waves. The sound of the van seemed distant and tinny. She remembered now. Leaving the pub, Pete behind her, helping her.

She thought of her parents and her family, and decided that she wasn't going to let herself get beaten by this. By him.

She tried again to move, but this time she realised her wrists were bound behind her. A thick rope rubbed against her skin, like a towrope, the knots strong.

Her head sank back to the floor. For a moment, she weakened, felt a sob well in her throat, but she shook it away. This wasn't how it was going to end. She had to focus on where she was, and where she was going.

She strained to get a view out of the side windows. There was no light outside, apart from the regular flicker of streetlights as the campervan passed them. She was able to tilt her head, so she could see the back of Pete's.

Her voice came out as a croak as she coughed and asked, 'What are you doing?'

He didn't respond. Just faced forward, his hands tight on the steering wheel.

'Whatever it is, you don't have to do it,' she said. 'I won't say anything. Just let me go. I'll say I banged my head.'

Still, he stayed silent.

She cursed herself for trying that. He'd never believe her. She would be reporting it to the police the moment she was free, she knew that.

But what did he want? Was it sexual?

No, she didn't think it was that. It was connected to Natasha Trenton, it had to be. Unless that was a kidnapping just like this one, taken away in her own car. Had it been Pete all along? The quiet caretaker, watching the staff, wanting them?

The streetlights disappeared and the road beneath them turned uneven, the camper rolling as it went, Pete fighting with the wheel.

'Where are we going?'

Still no response.

'They saw us together in the pub,' she said. 'You'll be the first person they speak to when they look for me. Think about it. You won't get away with it like you did with Natasha.'

Pete seemed to raise his hand to his face, as if wiping away tears.

'Please, let me go.'

Silence.

Fury welled up inside her. It wasn't going to happen like this. She kicked out at the side door, her foot thudding hard.

'Stop the fucking van!'

Pete didn't react.

She kicked again. Harder this time, her foot jarring, which just made her more angry, so she kicked it again, and again, her teeth bared in a snarl. 'Open this door and let me out, now!'

Pete wiped his eyes again, then he swung the vehicle in a tight curve and stamped on the brakes to bring it to a stop, gravel spewing under the van.

She realised she was breathing hard when the engine was turned off.

Pete stepped out of the driver's door and slid open the side door. He grabbed her by her collar and yanked her across the floor of the van. She was helpless to stop it, her hands bound. She landed on the ground outside with a thud, her shoulder jarring.

He was wearing brown boots spotted by paint, the toecaps scuffed. As her eyes tracked upwards, he was looking down at her, and there was an expression in his eyes that she couldn't quite fathom. Pity? Sorrow? Remorse?

He reached down to grab her under her arms and hoisted her to her feet.

She looked around to get her bearings.

Everywhere was dark, although it looked like they were on a car park, the ground covered by gravel. The lighthouse swept a beam over them, closer than before, Cookstown visible only as light pollution in the distance.

'Walk,' he said.

She resisted at first, but he prodded her in the back with his knuckle, making her wince. She didn't want to die there, in the dark, she realised. If they were walking, they might be heading to somewhere that would give her a better chance of escape.

He made her walk ahead, out of the car park and onto a track of grit and dirt that ran alongside a field. There were silhouettes of cows, close to a low building that stood out on a small ridge.

She realised where she was. Not far from where she'd had breakfast with Charlie, Brampton Cliffs nearby, a bird sanctuary on the other side of the headland to Cookstown. Sheer and high cliffs that were home to thousands of guillemots and puffins and gannets, all competing for space in every crack of the cliff-face. Four hundred feet of cries and squawks and a drop to the sea a long way below. The low building on the ridge was the entrance to the old radar station she'd told Charlie about.

That breakfast had been the start of all this. All she'd had to do was ignore a text from a guy she didn't really know.

As they walked, her eyes adjusted to the darkness, and she started to see birds in the air, swooping and darting, visible as dark dots where the patch of land seemed to give way to the silvery gleam of the sea.

Goldie pulled against him.

The cliff edge was fifty yards away, but she didn't want to get any nearer. A path ran along the top, at times close to the edge, protection from the drop provided by wooden fences, used as viewing points for the many visitors.

But, at night, it was deserted.

'Where are we going?'

'Don't stop.'

'No closer. I'm scared of heights.'

'You'd better stay by me then, because you might go the wrong way if you try to run. And don't try to sit down, because I'll drag you if I need to.'

He nudged her in the back again, which propelled her forward.

She surveyed the landscape around her, to see whether there was any prospect of making a run for it. Pete was an old man and was wearing big boots. She was young and in good shape. But she had her hands tied behind her back, which made it hard to stay on her feet and the ground might be uneven. She'd go to the floor. Right then, he didn't seem angry. She didn't want that to change.

They made their way along the footpath, Pete always behind. The wheeling birds got louder. The air was cold on her face, her hair stuck to the dried blood on her temple.

A lookout got closer, a square patch of raised decking and a wooden fence protecting people from the drop. Heavy horizontal rails, chest-height.

She tried to push against him again. 'No, don't,' she begged, until something cold and sharp rested on her neck.

He cast spittle into her ear as he hissed, 'I don't want to do this, but I'll end it here and now if you carry on. I'll let you bleed out into the soil, then throw you over the edge for the gulls to pick at.'

She swallowed and closed her eyes before moving forward, the blade nicking her skin with every step.

Goldie lost track of where she was, of how many steps she was taking, or even of how close she was to the edge, her entire focus on the blade pressed against her skin, until the sound of her footfall changed from the gentle crunch of the path to the wooden decking of the lookout.

'Wait here.'

She closed her eyes, not wanting to look down into the dark chasm below the cliff edge, brightened only by the foam of crashing waves against the rocks and cliff face.

She became aware of other noises. People walking, talking amongst themselves.

As she opened her eyes, she saw them step onto the lookout. She gasped and closed her eyes.

She knew what was coming.

Seventy-Three

Charlie banged on the door and stood back. There were no lights on in Eleanor's house. She'd left her curtains open, and he expected to see her passed out on the sofa, clutching a gin bottle, but the room looked empty.

He went back to the door and banged again, rewarded this time with a light switching on inside and the sound of feet on stairs.

When she opened the door, she said, 'Fucking hell, Charlie, it's past ten. You're going to wake up the neighbours.'

'I thought you'd want to hear the news.'

'Will it get me time off, because right now you're eating into my beauty sleep?' She must have spotted something in Charlie's expression, because she stepped aside and said, 'You'd better come in.'

As he went into the living room, he slumped onto the sofa, the middle cushion sagging.

Eleanor sat in the chair opposite. 'So, what happened?'

He filled her in on the events of the day.

Eleanor leaned forward, her stare direct. 'Are you sure you want to do this?'

'I've got to do this,' he said. 'Spencer Everett is the Home Secretary, and that's a powerful position. Next stop Number 10. It's not just about Gerard Williams. There are powerful forces at work here. I can't ignore it, not now he's gone after Isobel.'

'And Molly.'

'That's why I'm doing it,' he said, his gaze darkening. 'The safest place is out in the open. If we expose Everett and Lewis Buford, they'll be scared to act. Gerard stayed in the shadows, and he was killed.'

Eleanor lit a cigarette from the packet next her, clouding herself in smoke and inducing a deep cough, before taking the photograph from him. 'So, what now?'

'Can you speak to the detective who was at Gerard's house, DS Broome. Tell him what's been happening with me, and about the other deaths. If he knows to look for foul play, he might find it.'

'Why can't you?'

'Because you're an ex-cop, so he'll listen to you. And in case I turn up dead somewhere. You're not my messenger. You're my witness.'

***

It was Clarence who Goldie recognised first, as he stepped onto the lookout, a large walking cane in one hand, a shotgun in the other. The others were behind the bright light of the torch, just moving shadows. His footsteps were loud, echoes in the darkness, but it was the way that he held himself that she recognised. That slight stoop, his rounded shoulders, his legs bowed with age. Despite that, he walked with purpose.

He stopped in front of her. She pressed herself against the wooden rail, her hands still bound behind her, as he raised the shotgun and pressed it to her lips. 'Give me one good reason why I shouldn't.'

Goldie's eyes widened and she shook her head. Her knees weakened. When the pressure of the gun relaxed, she blurted, 'You've got your message across, I get it now. I won't say anything to anyone.'

'Won't say anything about what?'

'About Natasha.'

'But what do you know?'

She closed her eyes and realised that he was right. What did she actually know?

'I don't know anything,' she said, her head hung low. 'I'm no danger to you. You could just let me go.'

He rested his hand on the rail and leaned over her. 'It feels too late for that now, young lady. All you had to do was leave it alone.'

'I can stop,' she said, trying to appeal to him with her eyes. 'Just take me home and I'll pretend the last few days never happened.'

'Do you think I believe you?' He tapped her on the side of the head with the shotgun barrel, where she'd been hit by Pete. 'You'll mean it tonight, because you're here with us, frightened, but in a couple of days, when you start to get angry, you'll be telling anyone who wants to listen.'

She winced and asked, 'Who's *us*?'

Clarence turned round and said, 'Come out of the shadows, chaps.'

Goldie tried to look past him. For a moment, no one stepped forward, until there was the sound of another pair of shoes on the concrete floor. Then, one more.

As they came forward, more nervous than Clarence, she gasped.

It wasn't a surprise, but it was still a shock to see them.

Jimmy Gray and Mickey Higham.

'You're police,' she said, shrieking. 'Why won't you help me?'

'Grab her legs,' Clarence said.

Jimmy and Mickey paused for a moment, before Clarence barked, 'You know we have no choice.'

Mickey rushed forward. Goldie tried to back away, but all she could do was press herself against the rails.

'No, please, no,' she sobbed.

Mickey gripped her legs together, rugby-style, as Jimmy went for her torso. They grunted and heaved with effort as they lifted, and Goldie struggled and wriggled, until she was over the rail, facing forward, her feet swinging in the air, a long drop below.

She screamed.

Jimmy kept his arms under hers and pulled her back against the railings. His panting breaths were hot against the back of her neck. Her feet found the edge of the balustrade and she was able to hook her bound arms over the top rail, so that she was leaning forward like a ship figurehead.

She swallowed and closed her eyes, desperate sobs lost in the waves far below. If she slipped, she'd fall, and have no way of saving herself. She tried not to look down, her back rigid and straight.

Clarence stepped up to the railing. 'One more word, one more scream, and I'll push you. They might never find you. The sea will bash you up and drag you away. It's all rocks and coves this side of the headland, no sandy beaches to wash up on.'

She nodded but didn't say anything, breathing heavily through her nose.

Jimmy ran his hand down her body, patting her clothes, until he reached her jeans and he found what he was looking for in her front pocket. Her phone.

He passed it to Clarence, who tried to turn it on, but it was passcode-locked. He turned to Mickey and Jimmy and said, 'What do I do?'

Mickey said, 'It needs her thumb on it.'

Clarence reached for a hand, which had found a rail and clamped hard, and prised her thumb and fingers away.

She yelped and swayed, unbalanced, but he was holding her hand as he pressed her thumb against the sensor.

The screen came to life.

Clarence passed the phone to Mickey. 'You do it.'

He took the phone from Clarence and went to her contacts app. He navigated through them until he found the number he was looking for.

'Am I doing this?'

'It's why we're here.'

He shook his head as he typed.

I've worked it out. I'm watching them now, covering it all up. Brampton Cliffs, as quickly as you can. I'm parked on the car park. Don't ring. I've switched it to silent but they'll see the screen.

He pressed send, but something occurred to him. He sent a second message. *Come alone though. They'll spot you if you come mob-handed.*

'That should work,' Mickey said. He turned to the others. 'Now, we just wait.'

Seventy-Four

Charlie's phone pinged.

There were two messages, both from Goldie.

I've worked it out. I'm watching them now, covering it all up. Brampton Cliffs, as quickly as you can. I'm parked on the car park. Don't ring. I've switched it to silent but they'll see the screen. Then, *Come alone though. They'll spot you if you come mob-handed.*

He held up his phone to Eleanor. 'It sounds like Goldie is making progress.'

'You can't do much from here.'

'Hang on,' he said, and went through his contacts. When he found Amy's number, he pressed dial.

He wasn't sure she'd answer, and he was about to hang up, when he heard her say, 'Hi Charlie.'

Her tone was flat.

'Don't hang up,' he said.

'Why should I stay on?'

'Because I've found something out you didn't know about the victim in your murder case, Sarah Marsh.'

A pause, then, 'Okay.'

'She was Lewis Buford's fiancée at the time Natasha went missing.'

'What?'

'You heard. I spoke to Cathy Leech and she told me. It all ties in. She must have known something, which is why she was talking to Nick Cassidy.'

Amy went quiet on the other end.

'Amy?'

'Okay,' she said. 'What are we doing? Where are you?'

'I'm back in Manchester. But Goldie has found something. She's at somewhere called Brampton Cliffs, but she told me not to call her, to keep her screen unlit. There's something happening and she's watching.'

'Okay, I'm going.'

'Amy, we're doing the right thing.'

'I know,' she said, then hung up.

As he looked at his phone, he wondered whether he should have told her about her father meeting Judge Buford.

Seventy-Five

Goldie closed her eyes and repeated a mantra of, 'Stay strong, stay strong.' It was said through tears, her head raised in the air, breathless, scared to look down to the waves crashing four hundred feet below her. Her arms ached from keeping her body pinned against the fence. The grit on her pumps made it slippery underfoot, just the heels on the wood.

Clarence paced behind her. 'Where is he?'.

A calm and assured voice said, 'He'll come.'

It was the voice of Jimmy Gray. The tone of someone used to being in charge.

Clarence stopped. 'How do you know?'

'Because he's a luckless sap who thinks he's in love,' Jimmy said. 'I've made some calls. He plays the part of the fancy lawyer, but he's wayward, always one more bad move from being struck off. And he was a failure as a husband. This is redemption for him, trotting after the pretty folk singer. This,' and she knew he was talking about her. '*This* is his damsel in distress, and he gets to play hero.'

Mickey spoke up. 'What do we do when he gets here? If we do anything to her, he'll witness it.'

'So,' Jimmy said. 'He goes next.'

Goldie's knees almost gave way.

She tried to turn, but her sudden movement made her feet slip. She jammed her calves against the rails, her breaths coming fast. She'd almost gone.

Mickey shouted out, 'But then it's a double murder.'

Clarence whirled around. 'You getting squeamish now, Mickey? Well, it's a bit late for that. You weren't so scared when you were ....'

'Enough, Clarence,' Jimmy said, traces of anger in his voice.

'Why? Are you worried about her? Little folk girl going to hear everything, that she'll talk?'

She heard Jimmy step closer and hiss at Clarence, 'That you're giving us no choice, that's my worry.'

Goldie thought she could hear the glee in Clarence's voice when he said, 'We never had a choice, you know that. I burned her out of her caravan, but still she keeps going. That's why we did what we did back then, to stop the bitch from talking. Well, here we are again, so don't give me the moral compass bullshit. You're in it as deep as the rest of us.'

Mickey shouted out, 'He's here.'

Clarence and Jimmy made their way from the lookout and onto the dirt crunch of the cliff path.

Goldie turned her head and saw the wide sweep of headlights in the distance, the steady approach through the pitch-black.

She closed her eyes and prayed.

Goldie didn't know if it was her rescue, or whether it made whatever was about to happen more certain.

She looked along the rail, her mind racing, events changing, and saw that the edge of the lookout went close to a small scrap of grass on the clifftop to her left. It was in front of a protective fence, and she'd have to make a small leap, but it was still a piece of solid land.

She took a few deep breaths and shuffled along, careful as she went, praying they wouldn't notice her inching along, knowing that one slip would send her plummeting downwards.

She glanced towards the patch of grass she was aiming for. She was closer, and had a burst of hope that she could shuffle along whilst they were distracted.

The beam of the approaching car was a glow in her peripheral vision, the engine a distant rumble, until it went dark and silent once more.

She looked again towards the small clump of soil and grass. Not far now.

There were footsteps behind her. A ring of cold metal against her temple, the threat of the shotgun barrel.

'No further,' Clarence said. 'Or I'll push you off.'

She stifled a sob and raised her eyes to the stars. A tear ran down her cheek.

'He's coming over,' Mickey said.

Goldie turned to look.

A torch bobbed in the next field, sweeping the ground. Mickey and Jimmy stood and waited. Clarence stayed by her, the shotgun pointed at her. No one said anything.

As the beam got closer, Jimmy shielded his eyes, Mickey too.

The beam wavered and dropped, pointing to the ground, but as the torch beam moved, they all saw.

Jimmy moaned, 'No, no, no.'

Seventy-Six

Amy peered ahead, her torch beam catching more people than she'd expected. As her beam lit them up, her mind couldn't process what she was seeing in front of her. Her father was there, along with Mickey Higham. Had there been a development, the mystery solved?

She moved her beam along, then her brain whirred.

Clarence Buford was holding a shotgun, trained on someone on the wrong side of a wooden fence, her arms jammed against the rails. Amy knew that all there was below the person was a long drop into the sea, to water that barely covered the rocks.

What the hell was going on?

Then the person by the rails turned, just enough so that Amy could see her face.

Goldie.

Her eyes flitted from each person, trying to make sense of what she could see. Mickey. Clarence. Her father. Goldie about to jump off.

Clarence holding a shotgun to Goldie's head.

Reality rushed at her.

This was an execution, and it was supposed to be for Charlie too.

But, her father?

A moan escaped her lips. It grew to a wail as she sank to her knees.

She couldn't see or hear, her mind filled with images of her father, hero cop, sitting her on his knee. *Her* hero. It was all wrong, all she understood about her world turned around and twisted. Mickey had hinted at it, but this was her witnessing it, solid gold proof of his involvement.

She stayed on her knees, her head hanging down, trying to get clarity through the fog. Sarah Marsh. Natasha. Now Goldie. It all linked together.

She got to her feet and trudged over to her father, who stayed rooted to the spot, his mouth open in shock. She stared at him in the eyes and said, 'Let her go.'

He didn't respond.

'You heard me. Let her go. I don't know if you've killed before, but you don't kill anyone in front of me.'

Still, he stayed silent, staring at her.

She pushed him in the chest, knocking him back a few feet. Then pushed him again, before thumping his chest, and again. She was crying when she screeched, 'What have you done?'

Mickey Higham stepped in front of her and used his hand to propel her backwards.

'Stop it,' Jimmy said.

Mickey turned around. 'We're not going down for any of this. Prison will kill us.'

Jimmy grabbed Mickey by his collar, his voice low and mean when he said, 'And you don't threaten my daughter.'

Mickey knocked his hand away. 'Don't give me the happy family bullshit.'

Her father let go of Mickey and went towards Amy. 'I did it for you.'

'Fuck off. Did what for me?'

'This. Natasha. I did it for you.' He gripped her shoulders, stared into her eyes.

'Jimmy, stay quiet,' Mickey said.

'I did it to give you a good life,' he said.

'I had a good life, Dad.'

'I gave you a better one.'

'A better house? Is that what you mean? All of this for an extra bedroom and a garden?' She jabbed her finger towards Clarence. 'How much did he give you?'

'Enough to make a difference. Private school. A good path.'

'And yet I became a cop. Is that why you tried to talk me out of it? Because you'd wasted the bribe?'

She pushed her father away and jabbed her finger at Mickey. 'What did you have on him? Who killed Natasha?' Tears ran down her face as she looked back to her father. 'Don't tell me you did it.'

'It wasn't me.'

'You were just the cover-up then.' She reached out to him and put her hand on his cheek. 'Come on, Daddy, we can make this right. Find Natasha. Tell everyone what happened. You'll go to jail for a few years, but you'll come out with a clear conscience.'

Mickey lurched forward and grabbed her by the throat, making her gasp. 'It won't be a few years, don't you get it? We're coppers. We won't survive. You sell out your father and you'll watch him die in jail.'

She tried to compute what she was being told as she threw off Mickey's grasp.

Mickey's sneer grew. 'You can catch us all, top marks, but you wave goodbye to your father. How will your mother cope with that? All you've got to do is stay quiet and your father stays free. Walk away, Amy. That's all you need to do right now.'

She was distracted by movement behind her father, then shouts.

Clarence had pulled out a knife and was cutting through Goldie's bindings.

'That's right, let her back,' Amy shouted, and started to walk over.

Goldie was sobbing, a mix of fear and relief. 'You can lift me back now. Please. Oh my God, please.' She started to turn round to haul herself over the fence.

Clarence raised the shotgun and pointed it in her face.

Goldie yelped.

Amy shouted, 'Stop!'

Clarence kept his eyes on Goldie when he said, 'Do you know why we've no phones here, Amy? Go on, you're the detective. That's right, masts. As far as our phones say, we're all at home. Goldie's phone is here though. Charlie's isn't, but he's forensically-aware, so he would leave his behind.'

'What the fuck are talking about, Clarence?'

'That loser of a lawyer did this.'

'Did what?'

He turned his shotgun around and struck Goldie hard in the face with the butt.

Her nose exploded in blood. She slumped, one arm hooked over the rail, her feet slipping off the lip of the lookout, her legs flailing beneath her.

Amy yelled, 'No!' and ran towards her. She threw herself at the rail, leaning over as she grabbed Goldie under the arm and tried to haul her back over.

For a sickening second, Amy felt like Goldie's weight would be too much and she'd be pulled over with her, but she leant back and hauled, shouting, 'I've got you,' until Goldie's armpit was on the rail, hooking her back in place.

As Amy reached for her other arm, Goldie mumbled, 'It's the tree,' as if barely conscious.

'What are you saying?'

'The old woman talked about the tree.'

Clarence raised his shotgun again, this time smashing it against Goldie's skull, throwing her backwards.

Amy kept hold of her arm and slid forward as Goldie swung in the air, slamming Amy into the railings. They creaked. Amy felt them lean outwards.

Amy pulled, but her grip now was only on Goldie's jumper, and it started to stretch, Goldie slipping downwards.

Amy leaned over the railing and tried to get a better grip, flailing for Goldie's other hand. The sea crashed a long way below, the white tips catching the moonlight, the jagged grey of rocks showing.

Goldie swung, and Amy could feel herself tipping forward. She was on tiptoes. The rail creaked some more.

There were footsteps behind her. Someone grabbed her waist, tried to pull her back. 'Please, let go.'

It was her father.

Amy looked down to Goldie and saw acceptance in her eyes.

Amy shook her head. 'No, no, no.'

Goldie let her body relax and she smiled, tears in the blood, as her weight took her out of Amy's grasp. Then she was falling, her body rolling and turning, disappearing into the darkness.

Amy slumped to the floor and sobbed. The waves hid the sound of Goldie hitting the rocks. Whatever injuries Goldie had would be concealed by the damage caused by the fall, forensic traces washed away by the tumult of the North Sea.

Hands tried to lift her. 'Come on, let's go.'

She shook off her father. 'Leave me alone.'

'I can't leave you here.'

Clarence interrupted. 'You can. Come on.'

Amy was aware of the men looking at her, but she didn't pay them any attention. She waited until their footsteps receded into the distance and she was alone.

Seventy-Seven

Euston was its usual bustle, even so early in the morning. People gathered in the central concourse, staring at the departure board as they waited for the announcement that they could board their train, which would make them move in a swarm to the platforms.

Jessica had her headphones in, her phone trying to connect to Goldie. She'd been trying since she'd got up, but she wasn't answering.

Her eyes felt heavy, her sleep interrupted by the noises from upstairs and shouts from further along the corridor, her eyes always on the door, waiting for someone to burst in. In her head, she'd replayed the conversation with Goldie constantly, wondering if there was something she'd missed, or whether she'd sent Nick Cassidy down the wrong path and it had led to his death.

She chided herself. A man had died, and all she was interested in was whether she could absolve herself of any blame.

As she clicked the off-button on yet another failed attempt, she spotted Spencer and Wendy by a pharmacy in one corner of the concourse. They were in a close huddle, talking, the protection officer hovering close by. As she made her way over, Wendy looked up and nodded, an affirmation that they had a shared secret.

Jessica tried to disguise her doubts about Wendy as she said, 'Hi, I'm not late, am I?'

'No, it's fine,' Wendy said. 'Everything all right with your family?'

Jessica didn't know what she was talking about at first, wondered if it was some implied threat, but then she remembered her lie from the night before.

'My uncle isn't very well at all. I might take the chance to see my parents when we're in the north.'

'Yes, fine. It'll do you good.' Wendy was distracted by a rush of people heading out of the concourse and glanced at the departure board. Their train was ready. She turned to Spencer. 'Time for us to go. We can go through some of the detail on the train.'

'Yes, fine,' he said, and set off for the platform, Wendy and the CPO close by.

Jessica fell in behind them. As she went, she checked around, looking out for someone following. There was no one who stood out.

***

Amy shivered against the wooden railing.

She'd been there all night, not ready to face whatever awaited her. Tears streaked her cheeks as the sun rose over the sea, but it did little to ease the cold. She'd hoped that the onset of a new day would bring fresh resolve, but all she had was confusion and despair.

She wiped her eyes and got to her feet, wincing as she stretched her legs. Her arms were covered in scrapes and grazes from the battle to keep hold of Goldie.

She glanced over the rail, not wanting to see what was below, but as she looked there was no sign. She knew that the sea had taken Goldie away, and would maul and batter her body before serving it up for an early morning dog-walker many miles down the coast.

Just like Tammy Trenton, what Amy needed was answers. Tammy had been waiting for twenty years and she hadn't got much closer.

For Amy, it felt like the answers weren't as far away. What she was unsure about was whether she wanted to go hunting for them anymore.

***

Charlie gasped and squinted as the sunlight streamed through the window. Eleanor was in front of him.

He'd fallen asleep on her sofa. She must have covered him with a blanket.

She tapped him with her foot as her hand dug into the packet for her first cigarette of the day. 'Come on, man of action,' she said. 'This is no time for sleep-ins.'

He grimaced before hoisting himself to his feet. He grabbed his phone and went to his call log. There was a missed call from Amy.

He dialled.

When she answered, she said just three words, and he went cold. 'They killed Goldie.'

He was instantly alert. 'Killed Goldie? I don't understand.'

'How simple do you want me to make it? It was a trap. You were supposed to be there, not me. They were holding Goldie captive, to lure you there. They threw her over the cliff like they were tossing rubbish out of a car window.'

He sat down. 'What are you doing now?'

'I don't know,' she said, then hung up.

He slumped back onto the sofa and put his head back.

Eleanor asked, 'What is it?'

He didn't answer. Instead, he thought about Goldie. How she'd helped him. How they'd become close so quickly. How she'd still be alive if he'd gone into a different pub on that first night in Cookstown.

His sadness turned quickly into rage. He had to phone Isobel. 'This isn't over,' he said. 'Not by a long way.'

Seventy-Eight

Spencer had seemed quiet ever since they'd left Euston, as the train snaked its way through fields and past small villages that still smacked of southern England. Churches. Painted houses. Barns. None of the dark, stone strips of terraced housing that filled Jessica's home town.

Wendy had tried to engage him, to talk about the agenda for the following day, but Spencer had barely acknowledged her, cutting her off with, 'Just tell me where to be when we get there,' before putting his head back and pretending to doze.

Jessica couldn't relax, her mind unable to get past what Goldie had told her, and the fact that she was no longer answering her phone. She had to try Charlie Steele.

The protection officer was in the aisle seat next to her, so she summonsed a smile and asked if he'd let her past. When he stood, she looked both ways along the aisles before asking, 'Toilet?'

He pointed along the aisle and muttered, 'At the end.'

She didn't look behind as she went, knowing it would attract suspicion, but every part of her wanted to check whether anyone was watching.

Once in the toilet, she dug into her pocket for her phone, then reached into her back pocket for the beermat from the night before. The numbers were smudged but legible, the name Charlie Steele scrawled underneath.

As she dialled the number, she ran the tap. She plugged in the microphone lead and held it close to her mouth. A male voice answered. 'Hello?'

Jessica whispered, 'My name is Jessica Redmond and I'm Spencer Everett's intern. We're heading north and Goldie told me to call her, but she's not answering.'

'When did you speak to her?'

'Yesterday. She gave me your number.'

'What's your interest?'

'I was working with Nick Cassidy, feeding information to him, but Goldie told me he was dead.'

'You must really hate Spencer if you're the leak.'

'I just don't like what he does, how he makes his money.'

'That doesn't interest me.'

'Nick Cassidy was interested. That was why he was looking into Spencer.'

Charlie went silent. Jessica thought he was going to hang up, until he said, 'Tell me.'

Jessica rushed through the brief history and said, 'He puts the money into a company based in Nevis, called Willow.'

'Willow?'

'Yeah. Willow LLC is the official title. I was going to tell Goldie more, but she's not answering her phone.'

'Goldie is dead.'

Jessica thought she'd heard it wrong. She slumped onto the toilet seat. 'I don't understand.'

'She was killed because she was helping me.'

Someone banged on the toilet door. 'Will you be long?'

'Sorry, not much longer,' Jessica shouted back, then whispered again to Charlie, 'What do I do?'

'Where are you heading?'

'We'll be at Manchester Piccadilly in just over an hour.'

'I need access to Spencer.'

'To hurt him?'

'No, to get answers. I want the truth.'

'Can I trust you?'

'I'm a lawyer. Look me up, if you don't believe me. My wife, sorry, ex-wife, has got questions too. She's also a lawyer.'

She closed her eyes as she thought about what she could do. Something occurred to her. 'I might be able to get you access, but you're over in Cookstown.'

'No, I'm back in Manchester. I'll be at Piccadilly, waiting. Work out how to slip away. What do you look like?'

'Tall, gangly. Dark hair. Walking with Spencer.'

'I'll call you when I see you,' and he clicked off.

Jessica's hands trembled as she wrapped the microphone lead around her phone. There was another knock on the door, so she flushed to make it sound authentic.

She didn't acknowledge the impatient tut when she passed whoever was waiting outside. Instead, she rushed back to her seat, shuffling in past the security detail.

Wendy stared at her as she settled back into her seat, but Jessica turned away and watched the countryside rush past the window.

As they travelled, all four of them sat in stony silence.

***

Amy sat on a bench close to the harbour, just for the need to feel the breeze on her face. Her mind drifted back to her father, as it had throughout the morning, and tears jumped into her eyes.

As she watched the fishing boats resting on the sheltered water, she wondered whether she was done with the police. How could she uphold the law when she was ignoring the evil she'd witnessed?

Her phone buzzed. She saw it was Charlie, and wondered whether she should answer it.

The story was incomplete though, and none of this was Charlie's fault.

She pressed the answer button. 'If you're calling just to say hi, it's not a good time.'

'I'm going after Spencer Everett. We've got someone on the inside. I know what Nick Cassidy was doing, but his story grew.'

Charlie told her what he'd learned from Jessica, about the influence-for-hire, with Dougie McCloud selling access to the Home Secretary, as Spencer pretends he knows nothing about the arrangement.

'Goldie said something about a tree,' Amy said. 'That the old woman talked about a tree.'

Charlie thought about that, then something occurred to him. 'The company name,' he said. 'Willow LLC, based in Nevis. There's a willow tree in the garden, in the middle of the lawn. When I went there with Goldie, Nancy Buford walked by it, staring at me all the time, running the leaves through her hands.'

'Like a signal?'

'I don't know. The old woman is batshit, but maybe.'

'Christ,' Amy said. 'It's a marker. A totem. And the company name is a sick joke.'

'Search there,' he said. 'What better place to bury a body than under the roots of a tree?'

'With the help of your gardener.'

'Put the body in and plant a tree on top. The roots will spread around the corpse, sealing it shut. It will never show up on ground-penetrating radar.'

'And a dog won't dig it up.' Amy stood, enthused again. 'But for Nancy, it symbolises something else.'

'The beginning of the end for Truman, and how she's a slave to Clarence's money and status, so she drinks herself to oblivion, gazing at the tree, knowing what's underneath.'

'Shit, shit, shit. Tammy. Poor Tammy. She might get her answer. I'm seeing this through. You?'

'I'm going after Spencer. I just need to work out how.'

Seventy-Nine

Spencer had given up on pretending to sleep, and was instead staring at his phone.

Wendy frowned. 'Everything all right?'

'Yes, fine,' he said, although he sounded distracted. 'I'm just going to the buffet car.'

'You can have food here, at your table. It's First Class.'

'I want to stretch my legs. And I'm a politician. It's good to meet the people.'

'Okay, as you want.'

She moved to let Spencer out. Once he'd gone, the security detail with him, Wendy sat back down and said to Jessica, 'You seem jittery.'

Jessica leaned forward and whispered, 'What do you expect?'

Wendy gave a small laugh. 'I'm guessing undercover work isn't for you.'

'I didn't choose this, but things are getting out of hand. Tell me, Wendy, whose side are you on, really? I don't know if I can trust you. People have been killed.'

'Killed?'

'Yes, killed. Nick Cassidy, the reporter who was looking into Spencer. He's dead. And now a woman in Cookstown who I spoke to just last night. And someone twenty years ago. This isn't about lobbyists. This is way, way bigger. So, tell me, whose side are you on, because this is about to blow up?'

Wendy slammed her hand on the table and spoke in a low hiss. 'Don't threaten me. You're an intern, free labour, an overblown work experience girl. You need to remember that. But I'll tell you whose side I'm on. Wendy Preston. Now and forever. Not Spencer Everett's. Not your side. Not even on the side of good and bad. Just my side.'

'Prove it.'

'I don't have to prove anything, not to you. Since when did I hand over control to a fucking intern?'

'What about when the police come knocking?'

Wendy stared out of the window for a few seconds, before asking, 'How do I prove it?'

'I don't know, but I've just spoken to a Manchester lawyer. He says he's going after Spencer, wants to get to the truth. He's going to be waiting at Piccadilly for me.'

'How do you know he is who he says he is? If people are dying, what if Spencer is next? It does happen to politicians sometimes, you know.'

'I don't, but this is the time we have to choose. I've made my choice. Now, it's yours.'

Wendy tapped her fingernails on the table before saying, 'Okay, speak to him.'

Jessica nodded in satisfaction. 'You're doing the right thing.'

***

Charlie paced outside Isobel's workplace.

He'd called her a few minutes earlier, unsure if she'd be available, but he wanted her with him. She was now part of the plan.

He'd got lucky. She was in the office and had no clients to see.

'What do you want?' she said, as she got closer. 'You know I've got to account for every minute in this place.'

'The joys of private client work,' he said. 'You need to take Molly somewhere safe.'

'What the hell do you mean, safe?'

'Just that. I'm seeing this through.'

Isobel stepped closer, her rage making her eyes brim with tears. 'What did I say, Charlie? You had to stop. Not for me. Or for you. But for her.'

'It's got bigger than just you and a hotel room, and it isn't going to stop. We have to finish it.'

'How has it got bigger? Who have you told about what happened to me?'

'No one,' he said. 'People have died though. No, not died. Murdered. There's no guarantee they won't come after you again, because the stakes are high. Remember, you can identify the person who drugged you and took those pictures. Going after you might have been delayed, not laid to rest.'

'No, Charlie, I can't do this.'

'We've no choice. The only way this goes away is by us finishing it and exposing everyone.'

Isobel wiped her eyes as she stared at the floor. Eventually, she said, 'What next?'

'Tell Simon to take Molly somewhere,' he said. 'I have a plan.'

Eighty

As they stepped off the train at Manchester Piccadilly, Jessica hung back, anxious to see who might be watching.

Normally, arriving there was like coming home, a relief from the mayhem of her working life, the sounds and accents familiar. This time, it seemed threatening, unsure what would be waiting for her once she entered the area beyond the guards at the ticket barrier, where there were shops and cafes in a concourse surrounded by glass, people loitering on the other side.

Spencer and Wendy walked ahead, the protection officer with them. Other passengers strolled past and glanced at him, faint recognition in their eyes, but none dared to say hello.

Her phone vibrated. As she checked the text, she saw it was Charlie.

I can see you. Go to the ladies' toilet. End cubicle. Someone is in there waiting.

She looked towards the glass wall that separated the concourse from the tracks and tried to see where he was, but all she saw was the usual bustle of commuters. Then she spotted someone else: Dougie McCloud, noticeable from the polished gleam of his bald head.

Her throat tightened with nerves.

Dougie had been somewhere else all week, and she'd been pleased about that. He unnerved her, his gaze piercing, always unsmiling. Now that she knew about his involvement with Willow LLC, it made her more nervous. She remembered what she'd been told by Charlie, about the murders. In that moment, she wanted to back out. All she had to was resign and leave politics, and the threat would disappear.

As Spencer was showing his ticket to a ticket inspector, Jessica said, 'I just need the loo again.'

Wendy glanced at her. Jessica gave a slight nod.

'We'll wait here,' Wendy said, as they got past the ticket inspector and joined Dougie.

Dougie glared at Jessica. 'When did we start waiting for interns?'

'She wants the toilet, Dougie,' Wendy said.

'She's had two hours on the train for that.'

Spencer interjected. 'I don't think she's feeling good. I don't want to dwell on it, I don't need to know, but it's okay.'

'Two minutes,' Jessica said, and rushed to the toilets. She was aware of Dougie watching her go.

The toilets were quiet, most of the cubicle doors open. The cleaner's trolley was there, but there was no cleaner in sight. The door to the cubicle at the end was closed, and she could see a pair of feet under the gap. The person was standing and clearly not using the toilet, legs crossed at the ankles.

She checked around herself, worried she'd be stopped if anyone saw her, but there was no one watching.

She pushed at the door.

It swung open. Inside was a woman with a shock of ginger curls who jolted in shock, before pulling her into the cubicle.

'Jessica?'

Jessica nodded. 'Yes, that's me.'

The woman put her finger to her lips and whispered, 'I'm Isobel. You need to meet us, to tell us about what you know.'

Jessica leant against the cold tiles and tried to calm her nerves. 'Spencer's advisor knows what you're doing.'

'You've given us up?' Isobel's eyes moistened. 'Charlie said we could trust you. Why have you done that?'

'I had to tell her so I could get away. I can't just drop everything and do what I want. I do Spencer's errands.'

'She'll rat us out.'

Jessica shook her head. 'No, no, it'll be fine. People in politics are selfish and ruthless. Her loyalty to Spencer lasts for as long as it's in her interests, and she can sense that it's about to go badly for Spencer. When it all comes out, she'll sink Spencer if it helps her career, and she knows she has to be on the side of the good guys.'

'Can you get away for longer?'

'I can say I'm going to see my father. He doesn't live far away, and Spencer won't begrudge me that.'

Isobel scrambled in her bag and scribbled an address on a piece of paper. 'Be there in a couple of hours.'

Jessica looked at the scrap of paper before saying, 'This had better work. My career is screwed if it isn't.'

'There's more at stake than that,' Isobel said. 'But thank you. We'll get him.'

Eighty-One

Amy drove the long way to her parent's home, keeping the pace slow, wanting to put off the moment she saw her father. She wasn't sure if she ever wanted to see him again.

But something had niggled all her day, and the thought chilled her. Did her mother know?

As she pulled onto the drive, her father's car was there.

She faltered, overwhelmed by sadness as she looked at the house. Before, it had been her home, an idyll, a beautiful piece of quaintness, with roses around the porch and small lattice windows brightened by flower boxes.

If her mother didn't know, the knowledge would change her forever too, her home bought with blood money.

Her car door clunked as she closed it. Before she got to the door, her father opened it.

There were dark rings under his eyes, and he didn't have his usual warmth.

She fought the urge to run to him and hug him, her need to hear him tell her that everything will be all right.

Instead, she brushed past him.

He grabbed her arm, but she pulled away. 'Don't speak to me,' she said, before storming through to the kitchen, where she could hear her mother clattering pans, getting ready to cook dinner.

As she went in, her mother said, 'Hello sweetheart.' She must have spotted something in her mood, because her brow furrowed and she said, 'Everything all right?'

'I need to talk to you, Mum.'

Her mother rinsed her hands and said, 'What's on your mind?'

'Dad.'

Her hands paused as she dried them. 'What is it?'

Amy looked around the kitchen, saw how it looked the same as always. The gingham curtains. The sprigs of lavender in a small stone block. Eggs in a chicken-shaped wire basket. *Home is where the heart is* on a wooden plaque. All the things collected by her mother over the years. Country cottage as imagined by a suburban couple.

But it was no longer the same as always. Now, it was shrouded in darkness. A façade. A house she never wanted to see again.

'How could you afford this place?'

Her mother went back to drying her hands before putting the cloth on the side. 'Houses were cheaper back then.'

'Come on, Mum. House prices are relative, and this place is way above Dad's salary. He was a cop. I'm a cop. I know what the pay is like.'

She reddened. 'What are you saying?'

'That all isn't what it seems.'

She went to sit at the table, a natural wooden one, unvarnished, meant to tone in with the country cottage vibe. There was a coffee cup, steam curling from its brim. She cupped it as she sat down.

She narrowed her eyes as she said, 'Why is this important?'

'Isn't it important where a police officer gets his money from?'

Her mother looked down at the table. 'That's between me and your father.'

'Not anymore.' Amy reached out for her mother's hands. 'People are going to be looking back into his life. I don't want you caught up in it.'

'There's nothing to be caught up in.' She patted Amy's hand and said, 'I don't have to worry myself about little things like that. I let your dad worry about the money, and I make us a nice home.'

Amy pulled her hand away. 'Christ, Mum, it isn't the Fifties. I need to know where the money came from. You must have wondered.'

'He had generous friends.'

'I don't understand.'

'You don't need to understand.'

'I do, trust me. I need to know that my father isn't the man I think he might be. I need him to be the man I always thought he was.'

'Life is complicated. Being a parent is a huge responsibility. All we wanted was for you to have a better chance than we did. A better education. A better upbringing.'

'Mum, where did the money come from?'

'A little favour here, a little favour there. None of it mattered.'

'It did matter. He was a cop. Now, you're telling me he took backhanders?'

'It wasn't for anything important. He'd help people with their pub licensing applications, tell them what to say. Sometimes, he'd find a way to make a speeding case go away.'

'Or something more important?'

'No, hush, don't be silly. All small stuff. That's how it was done back then. Still is today, I bet, in towns like this. Everyone is connected somehow, and we have our own way of doing things.'

'How do you know it was minor stuff? You don't buy a house like this on speeding cases.'

She smiled, although there were tears in her eyes. 'I didn't ask the details. That was for your father. He said it was best I didn't know.'

'He was corrupt, Mum.'

'No, no, no. Nothing like that.'

'What he did was corrupt, and you turned a blind eye.' She folded her arms. 'What about the windfall?'

'Windfall?'

'Come on, you know what I'm talking about. I know you had a mortgage, because I saw the paperwork sometimes, but you can't apply for a mortgage using backhanders as income. So, there must have been a deposit. Tell me, where did the money come from?'

Her mother reddened. 'He never said.'

'Why didn't you ask?'

'It wasn't my place.'

'That isn't good enough, Mum.'

Amy raised her gaze to the ceiling. Whatever her mother knew, Amy was about to drag her into it.

But she had no choice. If she stayed silent, it meant that Goldie had died for nothing.

Amy reached out for her mother's hand again and said, 'He got it for covering up a murder.'

Her mother swallowed. For a moment, Amy thought she was going to pass out. Instead, she took a couple of deep breaths and asked, 'When? Who?'

'Natasha Trenton. Twenty years ago. Not long before you bought this place.'

Her mother pushed back her chair and went to the window. She stared out, but didn't say anything.

'Mum, talk to me.'

She leant against the sink and hung her head, before wiping her eyes and saying, 'No one was supposed to know.'

Amy stifled a sob. 'What, you knew?'

'What was done was done.'

'But you knew all the time, and you went along with it?'

Her mother's voice acquired more steel when she said, 'Look around you. See how beautiful it is. Think of your life, how charmed it has been. We couldn't bring that poor girl back. That wasn't your father's doing.'

'But what about her mother? All those years of not knowing. And what about justice for Natasha? All sacrificed, just so you can have this?' She gestured towards the walls. 'One woman's life for a cottage down a lane.'

'Us. Not just me. Us. Our family.'

'Right now, our family doesn't feel like much worth fighting for.'

'Amy, love, don't say that.'

Amy rose and leaned forward, her face inches from her mother's. 'It's a long way from fucking done. Someone else has died, another young woman, and I saw it happen. And my father was complicit.'

The colour drained from her mother's face.

'Yes, that's right. You look shocked, but maybe you're just counting the windfall.'

'Who died?'

'I can't speak to you anymore. I know what I witnessed, and I'm doing something about it. As for you, people will start asking questions, and you better have the answers. And this place? I hope it collapses to the ground.'

And with that, Amy stormed out of the cottage. At that moment, she didn't know if she would ever return.

Eighty-Two

Pizza boxes sat on the table in the centre of Eleanor's living room. Charlie passed beer bottles around. Isobel was the first one to take a drink, long and hard, her face etched with emotion. Jessica had arrived, quiet and nervous, the only one not eating.

Charlie held out his hands. 'So, what's the plan?'

Isobel took a breath to steel herself and pointed her bottle towards Jessica. 'She's closest to Spencer.'

'I don't know what to say,' Jessica said. 'This isn't what I planned. It was all about backhanders, political favours, feeding some secrets to a reporter. I thought I was doing the right thing. This is way different.'

'No, not different,' Charlie said. 'Just more serious, because it's still lies and cover-ups, except about a murder rather than money.'

'The lawyer for Spencer's wife thinks she was killed,' Jessica said. 'Murdered, then faked to look like an accident.'

'There you go, a pattern,' Charlie said. 'If people are a threat to Spencer Everett, they die. First it was Natasha. Then, Spencer's wife. There's the woman found on the beach, Sarah Marsh, who just turned out to be the fiancée of Lewis Buford at the time Natasha went missing. My client, Gerard Williams, hanged from a tree, and what about Nick Cassidy? Just a hapless reporter, until he started to get a story he hadn't bargained for. And now there's Goldie, thrown off a fucking cliff.'

'But what about proof?' Isobel said. 'We've got suspicion and rumours, nothing more. This Natasha, no one can find her. Spencer's wife has gone down in history as a car crash victim. There's the woman on the beach, but there's a whole squad looking into that, and there's no one in a cell yet. Everyone will think Nick Cassidy killed himself.'

'What about what happened to you?'

Isobel glared at him. 'Not yet, Charlie.'

Eleanor stepped forward. 'Come on, stop it. Eat, drink, plan. That's why we're all here. Charlie, what do you want?'

'For me, too many things. Justice for Goldie, and for Natasha. For Gerard, my client, and Nick too. And do you know what ties them all together? They were all going to talk. Jessica, what did you say about Spencer's wife?'

'They were getting a divorce,' Jessica said. 'It was getting messy. She knew where his money really was, and how he'd acquired it, and she wasn't going to let him walk away with it all.'

'So, before the divorce goes through,' Charlie said, 'she ends up in the bottom of a Spanish ravine. Then, Nick Cassidy comes along, digging into Spencer's story, and he speaks to Ben Leech, who ends up in a faked suicide. Nick follows the trail of Spencer's old friends and ends up with Gerard, and perhaps it was Gerard who started everything, the truth about what happened to Natasha, except that Gerard ends up swinging from a branch. Nick speaks to Sarah Marsh, and she ends up dead on a beach. In the end, Nick tries to deal with it himself and walks into a police station.'

'Dead on the tracks,' Eleanor said, before sitting down and taking a long pull on her beer.

'What are you going to do?' Jessica said. 'That's why I'm here, I presume. Like Isobel said, I'm closest to him.'

'I want all of them,' Charlie said.

'Ger Spencer and the whole pack will fold,' Jessica said. 'He's the one with the profile. If you get the judge or his father, it's a news story, but not much of one. Just two successful men getting what was coming to them. But get Spencer Everett, the Home Secretary? The press will never let it go. The Prime Minister will dump him, because he'll come with a stench, and Spencer's star will fall. So, you go for Spencer.'

Charlie frowned. 'But how?'

'You question Spencer directly about everything, in public. Could you do that, if I got you access?'

'Don't you mean, will he? He's a politician. They never answer questions.'

Jessica smiled. 'You know nothing about politics.'

'What do you mean?'

'Silence is death in politics. No, they have to give an answer, except they are artists at not really answering, giving the answer they want to give, whatever the question might be. It's how they are trained. But you, you're a lawyer. You'll ask the questions better, and he won't dare stay silent. It's checkmate. Screwed if he talks, and screwed if he refuses to answer, because who could trust a Home Secretary who is scared to deny an allegation of murder? And you don't know Spencer like I do.'

'In what way?'

'He thinks he can charm his way out of everything. It is all is an act, every part of him. His messy hair? I've seen him scruff it up just before he goes on camera. Wendy once told me that it was all about being anti-spin, that there was no polished bullshit, but just an honest man telling you how it is.' She shook her head. 'I've seen him in action, remember. When I first started with him, he was due to give a talk to some business leaders, give out some awards, and he rushed in at the last minute and made out like he didn't know he was speaking, but gave a talk anyway. He got the anecdotes wrong, forgot a punchline, even forgot the name of the organisation behind the event, but everyone loved it, guffawing and banging on the tables. Good old Spencer, because the English love an eccentric.'

'Yep, that's the Spencer we know,' Charlie said. 'Loveable buffoon, almost too clever for his own good.'

'It was bullshit. A few months later, the same thing. A business dinner, some awards. He came in late, pretended he didn't know he was speaking, so it looked like he'd made it up on the spot. And he told the same anecdotes as before, but with all the same mistakes, the same missed punchlines, and that's when I got it. It was carefully crafted, every nuance just right.'

'Why do you think that makes a difference in this situation?'

'Because he thinks he's smarter than everyone else. He won't be caught out by you. He's Oxbridge. What are we? Northerners who've done okay for ourselves, but still below him. He'll think he can bumble his way out of anything, outsmart you all. His arrogance will be his downfall. All you have to do is stay one step ahead.'

'Okay,' Charlie said. 'I like it. But we need to bring everyone down, not just Spencer Everett.'

'Spencer won't go down alone,' Jessica said. 'Get him, and the rest follow.'

Isobel spoke up. 'Will this mean my part in it will stay a secret?'

'Hopefully,' Charlie said.

'Is that the best you can do?'

Jessica frowned. 'Your part?'

Charlie dug into his pocket and pulled out the photograph. He slid it across the table to Jessica and said, 'The man behind Spencer. Ever seen him with Spencer?'

Jessica picked it up and frowned as she studied it, until recognition kicked in. 'It's Dougie McCloud,' she said, handing it back.

'Who's he?

'They were friends at university. Now, he's Spencer's special advisor. Why do you want to know?'

Charlie exchanged glances and raised eyebrows with Isobel, before she said, 'He's blackmailing me, saying that he'll release nude photographs of me, unless Charlie will drop what he's doing.'

'Hang on,' Jessica said. 'How did Dougie McCloud get hold of naked pictures of you?'

'He took them. Fooled me into a business meeting and drugged me. Took me to a hotel room to do a photoshoot that he could use against me.'

'Shit. When did this happen?'

'Day before yesterday.'

'He's been in the north all week. He met us at Piccadilly.'

'Is this the kind of thing Dougie McCloud does?'

'If you mean whether I'm surprised,' Jessica said. 'Well, no, I'm not. In Westminster, they call him The Master, because he's all about the dark arts, about manoeuvring. He scares me.'

'Why?'

'There's no warm side to him. He treats everyone as if they're a threat to Spencer, me included, which now, ironically, he's turned out to be right. But I'm not sure he's got any boundaries.'

'Explain.'

There've been rumours about him bringing down anyone who is in Spencer's way. You remember how Spencer got the job? The previous Home Secretary was caught with an escort, because he was into kinky stuff. The woman he hired planted a camera and left drugs lying around. No one said he'd used drugs, but when you're the Home Secretary, and a picture comes out where you're tied to a bed with a ball-gag in your mouth, with lines of white powder on a black tile on the bed, you're screwed. The woman sold a few media stories and made some cash, even got on some reality TV, some rubbish about single people locked up in a castle for a month with cameras everywhere, but I'd heard that she was coached. She knew who to contact, how to get an agent, when to go public. It had Dougie McCloud all over it.'

'But it nearly brought down the government,' Charlie said. 'Sleaze and lies don't sell well in the Shires.'

'These things pass when someone new and exciting comes along. And that was Spencer.'

'How do you know all this?'

'Because I listen to what they talk about, even when they think I'm just playing on my phone. I'm an intern. I work for free, a long work experience, so I take my pay in nuggets of information, because I'm there to learn.'

'Was it worth the effort?' Charlie said. 'Spencer could have just waited for the next reshuffle, had a quiet word in someone's ear that the Home Secretary was an accident waiting to happen.'

'That's my point. Politics is about winning, but for some there are no limits on how to win.'

Charlie looked around the room, then to Jessica. 'When can I get to Spencer?'

'Tomorrow morning. There's a press conference at the Town Hall about the new immigration detention centre. I could try to get you on the press list. Have identification and make it look like you're both reporters.'

'How?'

'Get a dictation machine, something like that, or have your phone open on a recording app. A notebook perhaps. Make some squiggles, because the security won't know shorthand. If you're questioned, say you run a blogsite. Make up a name. They won't check, I promise. This is not a glamorous announcement, with just the press allowed.'

'I need to do something first though.'

'What?'

'I want to spook him,' he said.

'Tip him off? Why?'

'Because witnesses perform worst when they know something bad is coming,' Charlie said. 'If you throw an unexpected question, they'll just deny it. If they know it's coming though, they try to give an answer they like, but it doesn't always fit with the other evidence. They think they're avoiding a trap they've seen, because that's all they can think about, but in fact they're ignoring the traps they haven't seen, and they're the ones that trip them up.'

Charlie and Isobel exchanged smiles. 'Let's bring the house down.'

Eighty-Three

The Close Protection Officer perked up in his chair as Charlie got closer to Spencer Everett.

Charlie had watched the restaurant for thirty minutes following Jessica's tip-off, just to assess the mood of those inside. They were in a steakhouse, one of those where they charge three times as much by installing a few copper lampshades and making sure the flames grow high on the grill every few minutes. Spencer seemed in good spirits, as far as Charlie could tell, although they were at the back of the restaurant, presumably for reasons of privacy.

'Good evening, Home Secretary,' Charlie said. 'I'm so sorry for troubling you.'

The CPO got to his feet, but Spencer waved him back down before wiping his mouth with a napkin. The waiters stopped and watched, unsure how to react.

Charlie tried to ignore Dougie McCloud, although every part of him wanted to launch himself across the table. Dougie had carried on eating, but his nonchalance was a game. His gaze was fixed on Charlie.

Dougie had lost his hair since the photograph, his head now a gleam, but the sharpness in his eyes was undiminished, his body lean and wiry.

Spencer exchanged glances with the woman sitting next to him. Wendy, Charlie presumed. Jessica found a sudden interest with the contents of her phone.

'How can I help you?' Spencer said, when Wendy seemed to give him a shrug that everything seemed fine. 'Although you can see I'm with company.'

'Yes, I can see, but this is urgent. I'm a local solicitor, and I used to represent Gerard Williams. I understand he was a friend of yours from university.'

Spencer stole a glance at Dougie, then faked a refresh of his memory before saying, 'Ah yes, Gerard. Fine fellow. But you say you used to represent him. That doesn't sound so good.'

'No, it isn't. He died a few days ago. Suicide, they say. Me? I'm not so sure. But a few of your friends have had bad luck. Ben Leech, another old friend. And Sarah Marsh. Or Sarah Stewart, as she was at university. Found on the beach at Cookstown, murdered. I understand you knew her too.'

Spencer sat forward now, his eyes wide in shock. If Charlie hadn't known, he'd have been sure it was a genuine reaction. 'Sarah Stewart is dead? Murdered? My goodness. That is such shocking news.'

'I'm sure, and I'm sorry to break it to you, but Gerard believed that these deaths were connected.'

'What had Gerard said?'

'It's supposed to be privileged, but Gerard wanted to go public, and he's dead anyway. I was wondering whether you'd assessed your security.'

'That sounds like a threat.'

'No, just concern. After all, if Ben Leech was murdered, and Gerard too, and now Sarah, well, you can see how it's going. I thought it was my duty to alert you, so you can stay safe. I don't want you to be next, Home Secretary. If it turns out I could have prevented you from coming to harm, my conscience would be troubled.'

Spencer shook his head, although his cheeks had flushed. 'I'm sure I'll be looked after.'

'Thank you, Home Secretary. And I'm sorry for interrupting your supper, but I felt I had to say something while I have the chance.'

'Your concern is noted. Good night.'

Charlie tried not to look back as he made his way back outside. Once there, he called Isobel.

When she answered, he said, 'Keep Molly safe. We're on.'

***

Jessica stood with Wendy as she smoked by a tree outside the restaurant. Wendy was pensive, her arm folded, smoke drifting upwards, staring straight ahead.

Jessica glanced back inside. Spencer and Dougie were talking, Dougie more animated than Spencer, his finger jabbing at the table as he made his point, hissing sharp words into Spencer's ear.

Spencer looked like his tone was more measured, his hand out sometimes, as if to calm Dougie.

Wendy stubbed out her cigarette. 'What's your plan?'

'I want Charlie and Isobelle Steele on the press list for the morning.'

'And what happens then?'

'Charlie and Isobel ask a few awkward questions,' Jessica said. 'And I was thinking how it might help whichever way it went.'

'How do you work that out?'

'If Spencer is dragged down, you drop him and move on. That's what you said. Stay with them until their star fades. Here, everyone will know you had no choice. If it doesn't work, he'll remain as Home Secretary, and you'll stay with him. Seems like a win both ways.'

'And what do you want, Jessica?'

Jessica thought about that for a moment, before responding, 'For him to be accountable for what he's done.'

'And if he isn't?'

'That's when I'll decide if politics is for me.'

'If the truth is important to you,' Wendy said, 'it sounds like you're already in the wrong fucking game.'

Eighty-Four

For Amy, the new day brought fresh resolve.

She'd spent the night unable to sleep. Her mother's complicity stuck with her. Every time she thought she could move beyond it, the memory of Tammy's anguish flooded back to her.

Her mother had no part in whatever happened to Natasha, but she had stayed quiet in its aftermath and let herself profit. If Amy stayed as silent, she'd be no better.

It was time to do something about it.

Amy rushed into the station and headed straight for Mickey Higham's office, brushing past people she'd once called colleagues. She collected an evidence bag from a desk she passed, then threw the door open into Mickey Higham's room. She didn't bother to close it.

Higham jumped back, startled. He glanced towards the Incident Room on the other side of the glass and asked, 'What do you want?'

'Looking twitchy, Mickey.'

'Shut the door.'

Amy turned to close it, then leaned forward over the desk. 'I'm coming back to the squad. No disciplinary proceedings. No complaint. I'm a proper copper again.'

'Why should I let you?'

'Don't you think you should be sucking up to me, with me seeing what I did?'

'You can't blackmail me.'

'It's a negotiation.'

'You drag me down, you drag your father down with me.'

Amy's cheeks flared and she fought the urge to punch him.

But that wasn't why she was there.

Mickey considered Amy for a few seconds, before putting his face in his hands. He stayed like that for a few seconds, like a child hoping the monster under the bed will leave them alone, before dropping them to plead, 'None of that was planned the other night. You've got to believe me. We were just trying to scare Charlie into staying quiet. We didn't know Clarence was going to do that.'

'Promise me that any complaint is gone and I'll listen, but my memory is that you didn't do anything to help.'

'Your father neither.'

'No, him neither. But if I can't bring Goldie back, and we're going to go on with this big secret in the air, the least you can do is let me do the serious stuff again.'

'And that's the price of your silence?'

'We've all got a price. So, I'm back? Clean slate? Untarnished?'

'Yes. But don't think you can use this again.'

Amy reached for the handcuffs attached to her belt. and thanked him. Before he could respond, she went behind him and grabbed his wrists. He tried to resist, but she got a cuff around one wrist and forced his head down to the desk. As she secured the other cuff, she growled in his ear, 'Good point, Mickey. I am arresting you for conspiring to murder Goldie Brown. You do not have to say anything...'

'Are you crazy?' His voice was muffled against the desk.

'...But it may harm your defence if you do not mention when questioned something which you later rely on in court...'

He struggled. 'Release me, you stupid bitch.'

'Anything you do say may be given in evidence.'

She put her whole body weight on him so that he couldn't move, before grabbing the mug he'd been drinking from and throwing the tea onto the carpet. She dropped the mug into the evidence bag she'd grabbed earlier, then hoisted him to his feet. She shoved him towards the door, then gripped his upper arm so that her fingernails dug into his flesh, the bag with the mug inside swinging from her other hand.

As they emerged into the Incident Room, people looked up, curious, before their expressions turned to shock.

'The cuffs are too tight,' he said, trying to shake her off, but without success.

People started to stand behind their desks.

'Here's your killer,' she said.

A detective shouted, 'Amy, what are you doing? Are you all right?'

'Never better,' she said. 'We'll need an outside Force to deal with this, because this man killed Sarah Marsh. And probably Nick Cassidy, along with a young woman called Goldie Brown. Get on the phone to headquarters.'

Someone else stepped forward. 'Don't be stupid, Amy. Let him go.'

Amy pushed Mickey towards him and put the evidence bag on his desk. 'Get that to the lab. Test his DNA against any swabs taken from Sarah Marsh.'

Mickey stopped fighting. His shoulders slumped, defeated.

The detective looked at the mug, then back at Amy. 'Are you sure?'

'One hundred per cent.'

The room was in stunned silence as Amy led Higham out of the Incident Room, towards the steps that would take them to cells.

She knew people were wondering what the hell she was up to, whether they'd just witnessed a detective write the suicide note for her career.

Right then, Amy didn't care.

Eighty-Five

Jessica and Wendy had stayed silent during breakfast, as Spencer ate his at a table by his window. The room was spacious, with a large bed at one end and a sofa and table at the other, all in subtle greys, with ceiling-to-floor curtains and views towards the rotunda of the Central Library.

Spencer had opted for room service, and what he called a breakfast conference, but nothing had been said. Jessica and Wendy had eaten croissants from small plates balanced on their knees as Dougie and Spencer tucked into a high-class version of the full English.

The atmosphere had been tense, even though no one had spoken, the only sounds being the scrapes of cutlery on plates and the occasional clink of a cup on a saucer.

Wendy broke the silence, leaning back into the corner of the sofa as if it were a chaise longue. 'We need to be on the train for lunchtime. Get the press conference done and get out.'

Dougie put down his cutlery. 'Do you still think he should?'

'What do you mean?'

'There's a lawyer making trouble.'

'Are you worried about anything he had to say?'

Dougie scowled. 'I just know that lawyers can't be trusted.'

'I'll do you a favour, Dougie. You stick to the big ideas, and I'll stick to the day-to-day stuff, because if there's a lawyer making trouble, the worst thing you can do is fall silent. Just keep that in mind.'

She stood. 'And with that, us ladies will leave you chaps to make yourself pretty. Just remember, Spencer, you're a people-person. The public love you. Just ruffle your hair and use your charm.'

As Wendy and Jessica went onto the hotel corridor and closed the door behind them, their rooms at opposite ends, Wendy said, 'I've prepared a press release.'

'Already?'

'The art of politics is to have an answer for every occasion. I've drafted three. There is one for when nothing happens, and Charlie Steele has got it wrong. Another one for when Spencer is revealed to be a freeloading politician on the take, where we act dumb.'

'And the third?'

'Where he is found to be complicit in a historic murder. In that version, we're the fucking heroes.'

Eighty-Six

'Are you sure you know what you're doing?' the custody sergeant asked, leaning on the custody desk. 'Mickey Higham is in a cell, and he's not going to be happy.'

'I was there,' Amy said. 'I saw what he did.'

'Yeah, but, well, we heard he booted you from the squad, so people might say you've got a grudge.'

'And I invented a dead woman at the bottom of a cliff?'

'Is there a body?'

'Look, I arrested him. It's all on me, not you. The big boys are on the way to interview him. If you don't think he should be in a cell, release him. You're the sergeant, it's your call, but if anything goes wrong, like evidence being destroyed, you'll end up explaining yourself, not me.'

'Don't push it, Amy. Your old man was a good copper, but it doesn't give you as much credit as you think.'

'I just need to speak to him. Give me five minutes.'

'To gloat?'

'To find out where else we should be looking, because Mickey Higham is a bit part in this.'

'So, leave it for the big boys. It sounds like an interview.'

'This is personal. My father's involved.'

That made the sergeant's eyes widen.

'Yeah, exactly,' Amy said. 'Not quite so admired now, I'll bet.' She softened her tone. 'Just five minutes, sarge.'

'You're not seeing him alone, but I need to do a welfare check. If you follow me, you might get to say hello.'

He stood to grab a set of keys from his desk and shuffled down the corridor, Amy behind him.

As he opened the door, he said, 'How are you doing, Mickey?'

Higham didn't answer.

As Amy looked in, Mickey Higham was sitting on the plastic mattress with his head in his hands, not looking up.

Amy brushed past the sergeant and sat next to him. 'What's going on, Mickey?'

He dropped his hands and sat back, so that his head was against the wall. Amy could tell that he'd been crying.

'I want immunity.'

'For murder?'

'I'll talk if they give me immunity. Tell them that when they arrive, but only if they let me out of it.'

The sergeant stepped inside. 'Do you need anything, Mickey?'

'For this to end, for the truth to come out.'

'Talk to me,' Amy said.

'If you're expecting the big reveal, forget it, not until I have immunity.'

'Mickey, you know how it works,' she said. 'You can't just demand it. I know what I saw. Even if it isn't conspiracy to murder, it's conspiracy to kidnap. You're screwed. They won't give you immunity for that, not when the victim of the kidnap ended up dead.'

'Fuck,' he said, and slumped. His chin trembled and a tear ran down his cheek. 'What you saw wasn't my doing. It was supposed to be a frightener, nothing more.'

'Mickey, you don't have to talk,' the sergeant said. 'This is a welfare check, not an interview.'

Amy glared at the sergeant as she said, 'But you need people on your side too, because it'll only be worse for you if you stay quiet. I saw what happened.'

'You're the only witness, remember that,' Mickey said.

'You say that like a threat.'

'Not a threat. Just advice, as your boss. As someone who wants you to be a better copper than your father, but there are more powerful people than me to worry about. And there's your old man, of course. He'll get dragged into this.'

'I know that.'

'You'll shop your own father?' He shook his head. 'You're something special.'

'No, I'm a cop. It's what I signed up for, and he took part in a murder. I can't ever forget that, however much it breaks my heart. And what about Sarah Marsh? Did he take part in her murder? Did you?'

Mickey ground his jaw. 'Prove it.'

'They're looking for traces of you all over Sarah Marsh's body.'

'I was at the scene, remember. The autopsy too. Cross-contamination.'

'Oh, very clever. Was it just you, Mickey?'

'Your old man will fall.'

'Do you think I didn't know that when I arrested you?'

'Don't let him manipulate you, Amy,' Mickey said. 'Despite all of this, and what you saw, I'm a good man. I was a good copper who made one stupid mistake many years ago, and it's bound me up in this so tight I can't get out of it.'

'Truman Buford's confession?' she queried, then she guessed the answer. 'You lied. Truman never confessed.'

He shrugged. 'It sounds like you have it all worked out.'

'Why did you say that he did?'

'I was told to, by your old man. And before you get all righteous about it, I was a young copper, and your old man ran this town like his own fiefdom. It was a different time. Us young coppers loved him. Now, the young cops are different. Back then, you did what you were told by your boss, because you worked for him, and you drank with him, and you followed orders. So, I made something up, but I didn't think I was doing a bad thing.'

'How much did they pay you?'

'Pay me?' He looked confused. 'They didn't pay me.'

'They paid my father.'

His brow furrowed and went as if to say something, then stood up and paced. 'They paid him?'

Amy nodded. 'Seems that way.'

'The bastard. I don't believe it. He told me to make up the confession because it was a good thing, because Truman was behind it, not for money.' He stopped pacing. 'Who paid him? Clarence?'

She nodded again. 'Whose idea was it?'

'Your father told me to do it, but Clarence was driving it.'

'Truman's own father? Why would he want that false rumour made public?'

'Your father told me Clarence felt bad about Natasha, and he wondered deep down whether Truman had done it, because he was out of control. Drugs, drink. He knew there wasn't enough evidence to charge Truman, not from some drunken confession, but it would give Tammy some closure, perhaps even get Truman back on the right track.'

'You were lied to,' Amy said. 'People close to Lewis Buford have been dying recently. Two men who were with Lewis on the night Natasha went missing, then Lewis's former fiancée was found dead on the beach. Lewis is the key, not Truman, and people were starting to talk. That's why you released Nick Cassidy. You didn't want him to say anything.'

Something occurred to her.

'Was there anyone waiting for him when he was released?'

Mickey's voice was a hoarse whisper when he replied, 'Your old man.'

Amy felt a jolt, but she tried to push it aside, didn't want to feel the emotion she knew would come later. 'Clarence sacrificed Truman,' she said.

'Why would he do that?'

'To save Lewis, the one who was going places. Clarence discarded his wayward son so that Lewis could have the career he went on to have. Everyone thinks Truman did it and stopped looking at Lewis.' Amy stood. 'You need to tell them everything.'

'Whatever the cost?'

She thought about Tammy and her twenty years of torment. 'Yes, however bad it gets.'

***

Isobel was staring into her lap as Charlie approached her.

She was on sitting on the granite edging around the grass at Piccadilly Gardens. People were streaming past her, towards shops and workplaces, everyone with a purpose. A street-cleaner drove his cart along the pavement further along, painting a wet stripe, the warning beeps too loud that early. Later on, it would become busy with the loiterers, the dealers and crooks, muggers and users, but for now it was a city getting ready for another day ahead.

She looked up as Charlie got closer and faked a smile. 'Hi Charlie.'

'A tough night?'

'Yeah, something like that.'

'What have you told your office? Or Simon?'

'I've told work that I'm under the weather. They won't enquire. You know how it is. I'm a fee-earner. I could go cycling around the moon for all they care, provided I make my fees. And if I didn't, it wouldn't matter if I was the best lawyer in the building. They'd still move me on.'

'And Simon?'

She reached into her bag for a cigarette. As she lit it, she said, 'I haven't told him anything. I've nothing to confess, but why make it hard for myself?'

'Don't worry, I'll keep you out of it. Whatever has happened in the past, you're still a woman I fell in love with, and you're the mother of my daughter. But you deserve to see their downfall.'

'Bullshit. You want me to see you being the hero.'

Charlie laughed. 'Yeah, maybe. A little bit. This is no romantic gesture though. You and Simon seem happy, keep it that way, but you and me on good terms is better for Molly.'

She reached up to take his hand, gave it a squeeze, and got to her feet.

Isobel hugged him, drew him close, and for a moment he could smell her perfume, the one she always wore, heady and flowery. It reminded him of their life. Of nights in. Of nights out. Of those kisses before they each left the house for work.

He pulled away.

'Come on,' he said. 'Let's do this.'

Eighty-Seven

Amy parked in front of the closed gates of the Buford estate, to block any vehicles trying to get out.

As she stepped out, the house looked quiet ahead, no handyman to greet her. Clarence was nowhere in sight, although that didn't surprise her. She thought about pressing the button on the intercom, but decided that she wasn't waiting for a welcome.

The gates were grand and ornamental, so easy to scale. She wedged her foot into a crossbar and clambered over the top. The gates clanged as her feet smacked onto the ground on the other side, but she didn't wait to see if there was a reaction. Instead, she dusted herself down and marched towards the house.

The courtyard beyond the central archway came into view, but there was no one there. The house seemed as if it was empty, and she wondered whether Clarence had gone on the run, but when she tried the front door it swung open.

She went inside and shouted, 'Clarence Buford? You need to come out now. This is the police.'

Her voice echoed. She checked in the living room, where she'd been invited on her last visit, but it was empty.

Just as she was about to go to the back of the house, Clarence appeared at the top of the grand stairway.

When he saw that she was alone, he barked, 'What do you want? Daddy's not here.'

Amy ran up the stairs, anxious to get to him, unsure if his shotgun was propped up nearby. As she got close, she pulled the handcuffs from the back of her belt and clipped them onto his wrists.

He pulled against her, shocked, but she propelled him to the banister rail and pushed his head back, so that he was leaning over the drop below.

'These high ceilings make for a long fall,' she said, her voice a growl, 'Remember how it felt for Goldie.'

He tried to resist, but she was too angry, wanting to see the terror in his eyes as he realised he could topple over.

'Do it,' he said, his eyes ablaze, his ground-down old teeth gritted, browned by cigars. 'See your life disappear, killing an old man.'

A figure appeared along the landing. Nancy Buford.

Amy relaxed her grip when she saw her, allowing Clarence to push himself away from the drop. But Amy still had hold of the handcuffs as she swept his ankles with her foot.

He went down hard, his face smacking on the floor, despite the carpet. Blood seeped from a nostril as she pressed down onto the back of his neck and hissed, 'You're under arrest for the murder of Goldie...'

'You crazy bitch.'

She kneed him in his thigh, making him cry out. 'Stop resisting.'

Nancy stumbled as she came forward and slurred, 'This is the time then?'

He lifted his head. 'Stay quiet.'

Amy punched him on the back of his head, forcing him down again. She looked up to Nancy. 'Tell me about the willow tree.'

Nancy stared forward, her arms by her side. The glass in her hand tilted, so that the remains of her drink spilled onto the carpet.

'Dig that thing out,' Nancy said, her mouth set in a grimace. 'I want to see it as firewood.'

'Is she there?' Amy asked, kneeling on Clarence's back. 'Natasha? Is she under the tree?'

Nancy slumped against the wall and slid down. She put her head back. 'Lovely girl.' Her voice broke when she added, 'Let me tell you, young lady, my life ended that day.'

'Spare me the sad story,' Amy snapped. 'You could have said something, eased her mother's pain. But you stayed quiet to keep all of this. The house. The prestige.'

Nancy turned her head and smiled, but it was filled with sadness. 'Some make sacrifices to keep it. Some make sacrifices to acquire it. But your daddy knows all about that.'

'Don't justify it.'

Clarence tried to rear his head. 'Stop talking, you stupid, drunken bitch.'

'I drink so I don't have to see you with a clear head,' Nancy said. 'Don't think I stayed quiet to protect you. I'd sell you out in a heartbeat.' She looked to Amy. 'I had to protect my son, you've got to believe it.'

'That isn't a good enough reason,' Amy said. 'It's crashing down now. Help yourself. Tell us the story.'

Nancy put her head back and said, 'Dig, and you will find her.'

Amy got to her feet and pulled on Clarence's handcuffs, yanking him to his feet, his progress slow. As she pulled him to the stairs, she said, 'Save it for the judge, Nancy.'

As she descended the stairs, Amy went purposely too quick for Clarence, taking some pleasure from his curses and yells as he stumbled, Amy not caring whether he made it down the stairs standing or was dragged behind her, his frail, old body jarring with every step.

The hallway was filled with demonic, drunken laughter from Nancy.

'Save it for the judge?' Nancy shrieked. 'Isn't that just the greatest irony?'

***

'Suspect number two,' Amy said, as she pushed Clarence into the custody desk, propelling him forwards so that his head struck the computer monitor used by the sergeant. 'Clarence Buford. I witnessed him murder a woman. The same case as Mickey's.'

The custody sergeant leaned forward and spoke in a low whisper. 'Amy, there are people looking for you. From MCU. You're getting yourself in trouble.'

'Not as much as this guy.'

The door into the custody suite buzzed, and Lewis Buford entered. His eyes flitted between Clarence and Amy, red-ringed, stubble on his cheeks. 'I'm here to represent this man, my father.' Amy was about to interject but he held up his hand to silence her. 'I might be a judge, but I am still a barrister, and my father will want me to represent him.'

Amy allowed herself a grin. 'So glad you could make it, Lewis. I suspect we'll get to you eventually. Who told you he was here?'

Perspiration speckled his lip as he said, 'That is none of your concern, but, as you can imagine, news of your rather rash actions spread quickly. My father is a powerful man, as you know.'

'Drop the threats, Lewis.'

'A statement of fact, officer. How you take it is a matter for you.'

Amy stepped closer to him. 'I'll tell you something else, Judge Buford. The police diggers will be at your house soon, taking up that willow tree. What will you make of that?'

Lewis opened his mouth to speak, but nothing came out. He looked to Clarence, who clenched his jaw and nodded.

Amy raised an eyebrow as Lewis stared at the floor, trying to compute that fact. 'Anything to say about that, judge?'

He looked up. 'I'm not the suspect here, I don't have to answer your questions.'

'For now, perhaps,' Amy said. 'When you do, you can tell us how your brother's death turned out to be a waste of a life, even if you and your father were prepared to burn him on the fire of local opinion.'

She got so close that their foreheads were almost touching.

'The net is closing, Lewis. Whatever is under that tree will be dug up and examined, and years of secrets are going to be exposed. You're a judge, meant to uphold laws and seek justice. How will that feel, Lewis, justice being meted out at last, your turn in the net?'

Clarence tilted his head towards the door. 'I don't need you as my lawyer, son. I'll get someone else. You go.'

Lewis looked towards his father, then to Amy. 'I can't do that.'

Clarence straightened. 'I don't want you here, Lewis. Go, please.'

Lewis stayed where he was, as if unable to work out his next move, before backing away and yanking at the door to the custody suite.

It was locked, only capable of being opened with the right security pass.

Lewis pulled harder. 'Open this door, now,' he barked, his cheeks flushed by panic.

The custody sergeant reached under his desk and pressed the security button. As Lewis bolted out of the suite, the sergeant shrugged and said, 'He wasn't under arrest.'

Just as the door started to close, three detectives entered. Two women and a man, the women tall and slim, one with long blonde hair, the other cropped and dark, with the man between them over six foot, his shoulders broad, the stress of the job written into the spidery veins in his cheeks and the permanent flush to his cheeks. They ticked all the boxes: lanyards, lilac shirts, dark suits.

'Ah, the cavalry,' Amy said.

'DC Gray, I think you ought to back away now, while you still have a chance.'

She dug her elbow into Clarence's back. 'This man threw a woman over a cliff, with my gaffer in support. I saw him do it. You can overlook it, or you can book him in. Your choice.'

The male officer stepped forward. 'We need to talk, now,' and he pointed to the door that would take them out of the custody suite.

The custody sergeant asked, 'Am I booking Clarence in?'

The detective frowned. 'Do it, for now,' he said, then followed Amy as she pressed her security pass against the sensor and went through the door.

She kept on going until she passed an empty room, one used for taking witness statements, windowless and bare, and went inside. They followed her in, the room now crowded.

Amy stood with her feet apart, her arms folded. 'MCU, I presume. I can see it in your egos.'

He held out his hand and spoke in a low voice. 'DC Gray, we might be the only friends you have right now. Park the attitude.'

The detective with the brunette crop stepped forward and tried a friendlier tone. 'Tell us what you know, Amy?'

'I'm sorry, I don't think I know you.'

'We know you,' she said. 'All about you. Please, for your sake, take a break. You've arrested your boss. Now, you've arrested the richest guy within twenty miles. Is this a career death wish?'

'I'm arresting murder suspects. Isn't that what we do? I watched that rich, old bastard murder a woman. I watched my gaffer there, helping out, but he kept on coming into work like it had been just a rough night down the pub, something he could shrug off by lunchtime.' She raised her eyes to the ceiling and blinked away tears. 'I watched my father do it too. So, there you go. Everything is as fucked up as it can be, but you have the people now.'

'Apart from your father.'

'And you want me to do that? Bring in my own father?'

'No, but you can tell us where he is.'

Amy slumped into a chair. 'How the fuck did it get to this?'

The woman sat in the chair opposite. 'We found Goldie. It looks as if the tide had taken her and thrown her back further along, snagged on some rocks. Crab fishermen found her. If what you're saying is true, help us, but you can't be involved in the investigation. Not if your father is a suspect, or your gaffer, or anyone you know. You need to step aside.' She looked back at her other two colleagues and said, 'Amy, I need to ask you something.'

'Go ahead.'

'If we bring in your father, you're the crucial eye-witness. Will you go that extra step and give evidence?'

'And if I refuse?'

'Your father goes free. But so does Clarence. Mickey Higham too.'

'You need me to sink my father?'

'You know we do.'

As she thought back to Goldie's terror as she knew her death was imminent, Amy knew she had just one answer, whatever it would cost her emotionally.

'I'll do it,' she said. 'I'm a cop. It's what I do.'

Eighty-Eight

There was a boisterous crowd outside Manchester Town Hall.

Sitting in front of an open square, the town hall was a statement of Victorian civic pride, with high, narrow windows set into sandstone arches, the roof broken by chimney stacks and decorative turrets, all of which surrounded a central clock tower. From a distance, it could pass as a miniature Houses of Parliament, although the setting was less serene. Restaurants and bars surrounded the square, and trams clanged and banged along one side.

There were two opposing groups of protestors clogging the square, the police forming a line between. Banners that proclaimed *End Racist Policies Now* clashed with those that said *Protect Our Borders*, both groups trying to out-shout each other.

Charlie and Isobel were both wearing smart jeans and jackets, t-shirts underneath and pumps on their feet, trying to look less like lawyers. Charlie had grabbed an old dictation machine from his desk. Isobel was carrying a notebook she'd bought at a newsagent. They had no idea how reporters behaved, but guessed that it was just about looking like they were bored, given the job of doing some dull report on an even duller announcement.

'If only the crowd knew what this was really about,' Charlie said. 'They think it's about immigration, but it's about money, nothing more.'

'Skimming from the top has always gone on,' Isobel said. 'At worst, it'd mean a few years on the backbenches.'

'But it's big money,' Charlie said. 'I can bet Willow LLC has invested heavily in this project. We're not talking about people being killed off because an old secret is going to cost them a few grand. This could be about millions of pounds, and it's all going to come crashing down, just because of an inconvenient missing woman twenty years ago.'

'These people are snakes. They care about no-one but themselves.'

'Which makes it dangerous,' Charlie said. 'Is there any point at which we back out?'

'Why should we?'

'I didn't say we should, but I want to know about the point of no return.'

'A hotel room in the middle of Manchester,' Isobel said. 'When I was stripped naked, drugged and photographed.'

A police officer in plain clothes was checking off names on a clipboard alongside identification checks. Some uniformed officers in the entrance tried to look impassive, but Charlie sensed the relish for a fight.

Charlie felt in his pocket for his driving licence, Isobel too. The officer looked at them, then at his list, before he waved them inside.

Jessica had done as she'd promised.

Charlie gasped as he went inside.

He'd never been in there before, there had never been a need. It was stunning. The entrance led to a sweeping staircase that rose beneath vaulted ceilings, painted blue and decorated by images of stars and suns. It was like an old Italian church, with granite columns and marble floors that bounced the light around.

The press conference was being held in one of the conference rooms, a rectangle of polished wooden panels and a latticed ceiling. The walls were decorated by images of old Manchester, with the sound deadened by thick carpets. There were reporters in clusters. Some were setting up television cameras, with journalists he recognised making notes. The killer-question, he presumed, because they had to have it, as the television news never showed the killer-question from another channel. The ones without cameras were chatting and laughing.

It must be like the local courts, Charlie realised, where everyone is in competition and on opposite sides, but friendships are formed when you see the same people every day. Charlie had gone out drinking with prosecutors after spending most of the day arguing with them. The ones who argued the hardest were the ones he liked the most. The political circuit must be the same.

There was a lectern at the front.

Charlie was wondering when it was going to start when the chatter amongst the reporters stopped. The camera operators went back behind their lenses as a door opened at the end of the room. A small group of people emerged.

As they got closer, Charlie realised that this was the opportunity. They were safe there, could ask whatever they wanted, because there was a large body of people around him who would witness whatever happened, and would record whoever asked the damning questions.

He felt Isobel's hand grip his.

As he looked down, he saw Isobel staring at someone in the group, her jaw clenched, tears of anger in her eyes.

'There he is,' she said, and wiped her eyes and took a deep breath. 'That's the bastard who drugged me and stripped me naked.'

Charlie followed her stare, to a man at the back of the group. He remembered him from the night before. Dougie McCloud.

'Don't let him see us,' he said. 'We want this to be a surprise.'

'Protect me, Charlie,' she said.

Charlie nodded to himself. He could only try his hardest, but with Dougie there, the circle was complete.

He felt his phone buzz. He checked the screen and read the text from Amy. *They're digging at the Buford House. That tree is coming up. We did it.*

He felt a jolt of excitement. He showed the message to Isobel, who gulped down a sudden tear and nodded, her eyes glazed.

They had him.

Eighty-Nine

Amy sat in her car outside Tammy's house.

It was her second stop after leaving the station, after swinging past Clarence's house, just to see the activity. Crime scene tape was stretched across the gate, attached to a metal spike so that it could be removed whenever someone needed to come and go. There were diggers and cranes on site, with officers in blue overalls holding spades.

She took little pleasure from it, because every turn of the spade would bring her father's demise a little closer.

Her time at the police station before then had been emotional, tears streaming down her face as she relayed her account of what had happened to Goldie, her story written down and signed by her on an official document.

It had the usual heading. *I make it knowing that, if tendered in evidence, I shall be liable to prosecution if I have wilfully stated in it anything which I know to be false, or do not believe to be true.*

Those words sealed her fate. Her father's too. If she tried to change her story to protect her father, she'd be in the dock for perjury. If she refused to co-operate, they'd compel her to attend court and threaten her with imprisonment. If she disappeared, they'd use the statement as admissible hearsay, on the basis that she cannot be found.

Whichever way she looked at it, as soon as she signed that document, she had thrown her father into jail, and discarded his reputation into the gutter.

As she thought about that, she felt no regret. Just sadness. For the cherished childhood memories that were forever tainted. For the events that will follow against a man she loved with every cell in her body. For the feeling that she had orphaned herself somehow. For the worry she felt for her mother.

She'd watched as Nancy Buford was led to a police car, frail and unsteady, gripping an officer's arm for support. She hadn't appeared as dishevelled as earlier. Her hair had looked well-groomed, and there were hints of make-up. Amy was sure that Nancy had smiled and nodded at her.

There could be charges for Nancy, but Amy doubted it. Sometimes, you need the bad people on your side, and Nancy would make a better witness than a suspect.

Amy had almost returned the smile, but instead was distracted by the appearance of a van in her rear-view mirror. It had the look of a media van, a logo on the front bonnet. Amy didn't want to appear on any footage. A big story was about to develop that involved her father. She wasn't ready for that exposé.

She'd turned her car around and headed back into Cookstown, knowing where she was headed.

Tammy's house had seemed quiet when she arrived. Amy knew things would change soon. Hopefully, for the better.

As Amy stepped out of the car, Tammy appeared in the doorway with folded arms, as always. 'Are you here to apologise?'

'In part,' she said. 'I think we've found her.'

Tammy's mouth hung open, then she leaned on the doorjamb in support. 'What do you mean? Alive?'

Amy shook her head. 'I'm sorry, no.'

Tammy slumped to the floor. She put her head back and let out a sob.

Amy went to her and put her arms around her, let Tammy cry into her neck.

Tammy pulled away eventually. She wiped her eyes. 'I knew it would come, but I don't know how I'm supposed to deal with it.'

'There's no handbook,' Amy said.

'Where is she?'

'I think she's on the Buford property, buried under a willow tree. We haven't found her yet, but we're digging.'

'So, it was Truman. The fucking bastard. What did he do?'

'It wasn't Truman,' Amy said. 'They made him take the blame because he didn't live up to their expectations. Something happened at the house, and it ended in Natasha's death. They buried her to keep the secret hidden. It's all coming out now. Those who did it. Those who covered it up. Including,' and this time it was Amy who choked a sob. 'Including my father.'

'Your father?'

Amy nodded. 'I'm not protecting him. Not now, not before. I didn't know. Once I did, I acted.'

Before Amy could say anything further, her phone rang. When she looked at the caller ID, it was her father.

Great timing, she thought, and debated whether to answer, but this was no time to hide from him.

When she pressed to answer, she heard him say, 'You've got to help me.'

'Dad, where are you?'

Tammy stood, recognising the panic in Amy's voice.

'Your father?' Tammy queried.

Amy ignored her. 'Please, hand yourself in,' she said.

'I will, with you,' he said. 'I can't do it alone.'

Tears clogged her throat. 'I'll be with you, Dad.'

'Come alone. I need to go in with my head held high. You've done the right thing. If I go in with you, they'll respect you. And me, perhaps. Let that by my last image.'

'I'll do that. I'll make it right.'

'If you come with anyone else, I'll run, I promise you. I'll make them kill me.'

'Please, Dad, don't. I'll come now.'

A pause, then he said, 'I'm where Goldie went over the fence. If I see that you're not alone, I'll go over the fence like she did.'

'I love you, Dad. Wait for me,' then she hung up.

Tammy put her hand on Amy's arm. 'What is it?'

Amy considered her options, then realised that she didn't have any. Whatever part she'd played in her father's demise, he wanted to feel some pride when he surrendered himself. She couldn't deny him that.

'The final piece,' Amy said. 'I've got to go.'

'No, wait, I can help.'

'Seriously, Tammy, you can't.'

Amy ran to her car.

As she turned the key, there were tears streaming down her cheeks.

***

Jessica stayed at the back of the room. Wendy was with Spencer, in close conversation, as always, although Jessica suspected it was an effort to make Spencer look engaged, the politician on a fact-find. Dougie went to the side of the room, always the detached observer.

There were a few camera flashes, temporarily blinding her, but when her vision cleared she saw that there was a group of around twenty reporters and three television cameras. Her eyes scoured the group for Charlie and Isobel, until she saw them, Isobel's red hair standing out.

She felt a moment of panic. Was it all a set-up, a scheme to catch out the disloyal? No, stay calm. Now was not the moment to get weak.

As Spencer moved forward and beamed for the cameras, Jessica whispered to Wendy, 'They're here, at the back.'

Wendy didn't say anything, just gave a slight nod to indicate that she'd heard, before she went through the reporters with a microphone and took up a position close to Charlie, but facing Spencer.

Jessica stared at the ground as Spencer gave a booming speech about the immigration system, how the government was trying to get the mix right, in that those people who want to come to the UK should be welcome if they're needed, but removed if they're not.

He'd decided to skirt the words *asylum seekers,* and instead use terms like *illegal entrants.*

The new detention centre was not a prison, he said, but a temporary home, so that those seeking to remain could be assessed fairly, and those who were rejected would be taken to a waiting plane. If they wanted to appeal, they had to stay in the detention centre until it was heard.

Spencer talked about improving borders, how a stronger border built a stronger country. No more people drowning in the English Channel, but a fair and humane system for those seeking legitimate help.

He was jabbing his hand forward, emphasising his point, his thumb prominent, because that's how politicians were taught. Emphasise with your hand, but don't point. Use the thumb.

Jessica remembered the meeting where Wendy had come up with that snappy soundbite, a stronger border builds a stronger country. Spencer had thought it sounded Churchillian, his pleasure shown in his triumphant smile, expectant of applause, but he was met with silence as the reporters held out their voice recorders or scribbled in pads, all of them veterans of political spiel. Some would champion it. Others would condemn it.

Had Jessica not discovered that the scheme was all about making money for Spencer, she might have been impressed, but she saw through it now. Once it was built, and Spencer made his cash, whatever promises he'd made about the quality of the detention centre would be forgotten. As Spencer had once told her, voters care more about locking people up than they do about the quality of the surroundings.

Once Spencer had finished his piece, hands started to go up.

There were the questions she expected to hear, Wendy going to the print journalists with her microphone. What about the burden on the taxpayer? Is it a sign that the current asylum system is failing? Should private enterprise profit from immigration? Wendy had prepared him, and he gave amended versions of the soundbite he gave earlier, ensuring that the same message played out on all the networks.

Jessica straightened to watch Charlie and Isobel. She detected some impatience.

Then, the moment came. Wendy handed the microphone to Charlie and said, 'Yes, you.'

***

Amy couldn't see him.

She'd parked in the same place as she had when Goldie died, expecting the area to be overrun with police and CSI, but the clifftop was deserted. She opened her car door so she could stand on the door edge and shout, 'Dad?'

She listened out for a response, but there was no answer.

As she made her way onto the clifftop, she buttoned her jacket. The wind was cold and strong, so that she was having to lean into it as she walked. The crash of the waves was a distant echo.

'Dad?'

Still nothing.

The lookout where Goldie had been thrown to her death was just ahead, where she'd expected her father to be.

Her phone buzzed. When she looked, it was showing as *private number*. When she answered, a voice said, 'Keep moving.'

She turned, trying to work out how he could see her. 'Who are you? Where's my father?'

'Do as I say. Keep moving. You'll see a building on the left. If I see you speak into your phone after I hang up, I'll kill him.'

Bile rose quickly in her throat.

'I said, keep moving.'

She set off walking again, her phone back in her pocket, more hesitant now, always looking around. As she went past where Goldie had been killed, the land sloped upwards, the path moving away from the cliff edge. The long grass strip walked by visitors and ramblers was replaced by farmers' fields, cattle grazing, bordered by wooden fences and topped by barbed wire. The grass-tops of the cliffs became gorse and bramble. There was a path that snaked through, one worn out by hikers, but this was away from the quick tourist thrill of the bird sanctuary.

Inland, there was a farm outbuilding, a barn the size of a small bungalow, prominent on a small rise. There were cows in the fields around it.

As she looked, she thought she saw movement inside, as if someone had moved away from one of the windows, just dark holes, no sign of glass.

She took off her jacket and placed it over the barbed wire, hoisted herself up onto the wooden fence posts and heaved herself over. She landed with a thump on the other side. She felt exposed, nothing between her and the building ahead.

As she made her way through the field, the grass got longer, brushing against her jeans as she weaved between the cow-pats. The cows huddled together as she got closer, before they moved en masse away from her, exposing the open doorway.

Amy hung back, wanting to keep an escape route, and peered inside.

She'd expected enclosures for cattle, or the shout of an angry farmer, objecting to her trespass. Instead, there was just an open space and a metal handrail visible. Then, she noticed the cattle grid in front of the doors. The cows weren't meant to go inside.

She lost the daylight as she went in. Her nose wrinkled at the smell of damp. The scrape of her shoes was loud, exposing her. The floor was covered in dirt and stones.

'Hello?'

'Keep coming,' someone shouted, the voice booming.

The metal handrail she'd seen from outside bordered concrete stairs that headed down, although some of the bolts holding it in place were loose in the concrete or missing, so that the rail wobbled as she went. Her stomach was in knots, not knowing where the threat was coming from, or what she would find when she got there.

She stopped as the stairs rounded a bend.

In front of her was an opening that was around ten-feet square, the way ahead all in darkness. She tried to peer inside, her hand over her eyes to block out the light that was making its way in, but all she could see was an all-enveloping blackness.

'Is that you, Lewis? Stop playing games. Where's my father?'

'I told you, keep coming.'

She pulled her phone from her pocket and switched on the torch function. As she shone it ahead, she gasped.

The opening was the beginning of a tunnel around fifty yards long, angling downwards all the time. Cables ran along the walls, although they were hanging down in places. Graffiti broke the long stretch of grey, just names and swirls in pink and yellow and red.

She realised where she was.

There was an old radar station built into the cliffs. She'd heard about it but never been in, put there to track Russian ships that once hugged the coast under the pretence of fishing the waters. It had been disguised as a farm outbuilding, but had fallen into disuse decades before. She'd heard talk of it, some place kids would go to drink and smoke, but it was far enough away from the town for it never to become a problem.

Until now.

But where was her father?

'Lewis, come out.'

'Keep walking.'

His voice was distant, but the tunnel would do that, she reasoned, his voice bouncing along the walls. She edged forward, her phone held out.

The tunnel ran for around fifty metres before it took a right-angled turn to the left, heading back towards the cliff-face. She knew no one could jump out on her as there were no breaks in the tunnel wall. Dust danced in her beam and made her cough.

As she got to the corner, she backed into it, to give herself the widest possible arc, and the best view of what was on the other side.

There was another corridor, except this time with rooms going off it. Broken glass peppered the floor. In one room, she could make out kitchen cabinets, the doors hanging either open or loose on broken hinges, decorated by more graffiti. In another room, there was machinery, large cogs and empty metal cases, with more broken glass along the floor.

Just as she was about to step forward, there was movement ahead.

A man appeared from one of the doorways. He was holding a shotgun, pointed down.

She gasped in surprise and stepped back, her arms out. 'Lewis, I'm here. Stop what you're doing.'

He reached back into the room he'd come from and began to drag something out.

Or rather, someone.

It was her father, pulled along the floor by his jacket, his hands bound behind him. Lewis jammed the shotgun against his temple.

'No, please,' Amy's stomach jolted, a sob stuck in her throat. 'You don't have to do this.'

Lewis kicked out, struck her father in the ribs. He groaned and coughed blood onto the floor. Lewis grabbed him under one of his armpits and hauled him to his knees. As her father's head hung down, blood streamed down his face. Lewis placed the shotgun against his temple once more.

She stepped forward, trying to keep the light on him, but not wanting to see what might happen.

'Lewis, please. Let him go.'

Lewis straightened. 'I can't, you know that. Not yet.'

'You can't shoot him, not in front of me. I'll be a witness. It's a shotgun. I'll get to you before you reload.'

'Do you think I'll care? Everything is gone now. You've taken all of it.'

'I haven't, Lewis. You have. This is all your doing. All I did was help to uncover it.'

'You can fix this.'

'It's gone too far now, you know that.'

'Bullshit. I know how the system works better than you, and it doesn't matter what you've said. You can undo it. You know how cases unravel. That's what you need to do. I'm not going to prison. I've sent too many people there. Can you imagine what'll happen to me behind bars? You can say how you've got things wrong, that you acted out of revenge, or because you weren't thinking straight. Just do whatever you can. Get rid of exhibits. Interfere with evidence.'

Her father shook his head and spat blood onto the floor. 'Be a cop,' he mumbled.

Lewis jabbed him on the cheekbone with the stock of the shotgun, making him in groan in pain

'Stop,' Amy said, stepping forward. 'You're not in the frame yet. Our fathers are, for what happened the other night, and there'll be some recompense for what happened to Sarah Marsh, because her murder is linked to this, but you're not part of that.'

Lewis grabbed her father by his collar and lifted him, so that his head was staring towards the light from her phone. He jammed the gun harder into his temple.

Amy felt sick. There was blood on his face, streaming from one nostril, and his cheekbone was swollen.

And she recognised the gun from the night Goldie was killed, with its varnished handle and grooves.

'Please, Lewis, stop. Not like this.'

'Are they digging, like my father said?'

Amy closed her eyes, wondering whether she was about to sign her father's death warrant.

She nodded. 'Yes,' she said. 'They're digging up the willow tree.'

***

Charlie took the microphone from Wendy. He coughed, nerves apparent, and glanced down at Isobel, who was staring straight ahead, her jaw clenched.

He needed her approval, because of the way this story was going to affect her.

She looked up and nodded. Her eyes told him what he needed. She wanted this as much as he did, so get them.

This felt like a whole different world to a criminal trial though.

In the courtroom, the witness doesn't get to decide when the questions have come to an end. Here, there was no one who could make Spencer answer the questions. He could simply walk out and buy himself some time to think of the answers.

And Charlie had no plan either.

That bothered him the most. During a trial, Charlie would know his roadmap, the journey he would take witnesses on, what he needed to expose. He'd know which questions to start with, either soft ones to make them relax, then catch them off-guard with the awkward ones, or to go in hard straight from the start, to unsettle them. He would know which questions would have the most impact, and which were best left until last. Here, he wasn't dealing with someone unused to the brutality of courtroom advocacy, but an experienced politician who was well-trained in avoiding the tricky questions.

But Charlie had one advantage: he had the information, and Spencer didn't know how much he had.

'Home Secretary,' Charlie said. 'Have you looked into the funding behind this project?'

Spencer's eyes flickered with recognition, and he tightened his grip on the lectern. He glanced at Wendy, as if to query why she had handed the microphone to him, but her expression was blank.

'We have secured the best price for this new detention centre,' he said. 'A model for immigration and asylum that will treat applicants humanely, so that we get the best people here, ones who will benefit our great country.' He forced a smile. 'A stronger border builds a stronger country, because we judge our homes on the strength of their walls.'

So far, Spencer had deflected with a different version of the same soundbite. He tried to move his attention to another reporter, but Charlie intervened.

'I'm sorry, Home Secretary, but that doesn't answer the question.'

Spencer cocked his head. 'Perhaps that says more about the quality of the question than the answer,' he said, drawing some chuckles from some of the journalists. 'Thank you for your interest,' then he pointed to reporter standing further along.

Undeterred, Charlie asked, 'Who are the investors behind the project?'

Spencer sighed and fixed his grin, although his stare was hard. 'I'm sorry, a lot of people have questions, so we must move on, but I know that we have the best price for a great project.'

'What about Willow LLC?'

Spencer faltered. He shot a glance at Dougie, who had moved away from the wall, his body tensed. The other reporters looked towards Charlie, wondering about the interloper, a journalist they hadn't seen before.

Spencer gestured again to the other reporter, but she wasn't rushing to ask a question, so Charlie continued, 'Willow LLC is a company based in Nevis. Has it invested in the company who won the tender for this detention centre?'

Spencer straightened, although Charlie detected a mild tremor to his voice. 'I applaud the private enterprise who are backing this scheme. It shows that they hold the same values that we do, that a stronger border builds a stronger country.'

'Yeah, yeah,' Charlie said. 'I hear the soundbite, but who is behind Willow LLC?'

All the reporters were now focussed on Charlie, sensing that something was about to unfold. The police officers acting as Spencer's security were getting twitchy, debating whether to intervene, but Wendy gave a shake of the head. Let it continue.

Spencer's expression hardened. 'As Home Secretary, I don't get involved in the company profiles of those smaller investors.'

'One last chance, Home Secretary,' Charlie said, a smile growing. 'Who owns Willow LLC?'

Spencer looked again to Wendy, expecting her to save him, but her gaze was fixed and set.

Charlie pulled some papers from his pocket, just some old witness statements he found in his office, but they were a good bluff. He waved them as he said, 'I have the information here, but I ask you again, Home Secretary, to be open and transparent. Tell everyone who owns Willows LLC. Who stands to gain from the award of this contract?'

Spencer faltered.

Charlie's smile widened. 'I'll help you. Willow LLC is owned by you, Home Secretary, along with your adviser, Dougie McCloud, an old university friend. He's there, by the wall. Come forward, Mr McCloud. Am I right?'

There were murmurs amongst the other reporters, now getting wind of something more interesting than a new immigration detention centre, their voice recorders turned towards Charlie more than Spencer. One of them was texting furiously.

'Has Willow LLC invested in any other government projects?' Charlie continued. 'There are journalists who'll go digging on my behalf, even beat me to it, but it appears that you, as Home Secretary, have awarded a contract to a company that is part-funded by your own company based in Nevis.'

Spencer was still silent, although the grin had gone.

'This is taxpayers' money, Home Secretary,' Charlie said, his voice rising, his own anger breaking through. 'Given out to those who pay you enough in bribes. And the irony is that you're keeping the money away from our borders, because Willow LLC is plain and simple tax-evasion. The company accounts are in Switzerland, keeping this swirl of money away from prying eyes. Tell me, Home Secretary, have you disclosed this in your register of interests?'

Spencer pointed at Charlie, but spoke to one of the police officers there to guard him. 'Eject that man. He is here to disrupt, nothing more.'

Before anyone could move, Charlie asked, 'Do you want me to read out your bank account number with Credit Monbijou?' He shook his head. 'I suspect not, but tell me this: why did you call the company Willow?'

Spencer had no idea what to say. He turned to look at Wendy, then the detectives, and even Jessica, but she merely glared at him.

'Can I turn to a different subject?'

Spencer nodded but stayed silent.

Charlie looked around, and saw that he had everyone's attention. 'What happened to Natasha Trenton twenty years ago?

***

The barrels of the shotgun wobbled as Lewis's hand tightened on the stock. 'That wasn't me.'

'What wasn't?'

'What happened to Natasha. I didn't start it.'

'Tell me.'

His grip softened on the gun. 'It was Spencer. It was always Spencer.'

'You need to tell the story.'

'Only when I know you've stopped everything.'

'No.'

'What?'

'You heard me. I'm not doing that.'

'I'll kill him.'

She swallowed to stop the bile rising in her throat. She stole a glance at her father, who gave the slightest of nods, a faint smile of encouragement.

'I've told the police already what Clarence did to Goldie, and the part he took,' she said, pointing towards her father. 'I've already killed him. Don't you get it? All you'll do is shorten the pain.'

Lewis's gaze shot from Amy to her father.

'The only one at risk now is you,' she said.

Lewis's arm shot out and pointed the shotgun at her.

She took a deep breath as she tried to stare him down. She took a step closer, making him squint as the light from her phone got nearer. 'You're not a killer, Lewis. You're desperate, but you're not cold-blooded.'

He stamped his foot in frustration and put the shotgun back to her father's temple. 'One step closer, just one step, and I shoot.'

'Tell me, Lewis.'

'He wanted her. What more is there to say?'

'Tammy deserves to know. Be a fucking human being, Lewis. Spencer is going down.'

'He won't. Don't you understand? People like Spencer never do. He wanted her. What part don't you understand? Don't you realise that what Spencer wants, he gets.'

'So, nail him. Tell me. If you don't, you'll all go down with him.'

Lewis stepped away from her father, who tried to shuffle away. 'You want to know how it happened. It wasn't my doing. You've got to understand.'

'Talk.'

'I tried to do the right thing.'

'I need to know.'

'I know, I heard you.' He took a deep breath. 'We'd all been into town, getting drunk. It was the Cookstown Fair. Spencer had been visiting for a few days, along with Dougie and Gerard, Ben too. Just university friends catching up in the summer. We shared a house in Oxford, and we were close-knit, but we were heading into our final year, so we were having a good weekend before our studies got serious. It was the last night, and Spencer had taken a shine to her, Natasha. She worked at the house. Lovely, sweet girl. Pretty, a bright smile, fun, really polite but with a glint, and Spencer was smitten. That was his thing, you see.'

'His thing?'

'The downstairs thing, if you know what I mean. Waitresses, shop girls, barmaids. Easily impressed, he used to say, so grateful, thought they'd brag about him.'

'He's insecure, I get it, doesn't like a strong woman.'

'It doesn't matter why. It was just his thing.'

'Of course it fucking matters, because that's the whole fucking point. He saw her as beneath him, disposable, a curiosity.'

'You can see it how you like.'

'I don't think you realise, Lewis, that I'm your best hope for redemption, so you better keep talking, because if I'm going to do what you want, I need to know what they'll find when they dig up that willow tree. And why.'

Lewis reached forward and grabbed her father again, yanking him back to his side, the shotgun jammed once more against his temple. 'Our bargaining position is pretty similar, I would say.'

Amy tried to read her father's expression. She expected fear, or resignation, or sadness, concussion even, but she saw anger. His arms were tensed, as if ready to strike, although the bindings on his wrist meant that he couldn't do much.

'Just tell me, Lewis, how none of it was your fault.'

'It was Spencer! We came back from town, worse for wear, high-spirited. Natasha was in the kitchen, cleaning. Spencer came on to her. He was just being Spencer, that's all. We'd just got back, and we were in a party mood. He grabbed her and wrestled with her, made out like it was playful, but she kicked out, which made him angry, so he wouldn't let go. The more she struggled, the more excited he got. He pressed her against the table, bent her over, and she fought. It all just got out of hand.'

Her father spat some blood out. 'Bullshit.'

Lewis looked down. 'What?'

'Out of hand?' he repeated. 'Bullshit, making out like it was a fight. Clarence told me all about it. That was the condition, remember, the full story. I would only help if you told me everything, and you did, crying and snivelling like a spoiled brat.' He put his head back and said, 'Spencer Everett raped her. Bent her over the kitchen table, Dougie pulling on her arms so she had no way to escape, until Gerard came in and tried to stop it. Except that he couldn't, because you held him back.'

'Stop talking,' Lewis said.

'She's got to hear this,' her father said. 'This has ruined lives. Gerard ran to get Clarence, to stop it, because he wasn't strong enough. Clarence told me all this, because I had to know.'

'Because it gave you a price,' Lewis said. 'Stop with the high and mighty. The worse it was, the more it cost my father, because it gave you power over him. For the first time in his life, my father wasn't winning, and you exploited it. Let's not pretend that you cared about that local tart.'

'By the time he got back in there, it was finished,' her father continued, 'Natasha was sobbing, curled up in the corner of the room as you and Spencer laughed like it was a joke. Then, she started screaming.' He spat out more blood. 'Do you want to finish the story?'

Amy stepped closer. 'Hand over the gun, Lewis.'

'He put her down,' her father said. 'That's how Clarence said it. He took her into the garden and shot her in the back of the head like she was nothing. That's how he made it sound, like he was killing a misbehaving dog, with the same shotgun now being held against my head.'

Lewis's arm was trembling, his eyes wide, his jaw clenched.

'They buried her deep under the lawn and planted a tree on top, so that she'd never be found.' Her father closed his eyes and tried to ignore the gun. 'He paid us to stay quiet. He told me it wouldn't bring her back, and he was right, but some good should come out of it. You, Amy. Get a good education. Get away from Cookstown. Do something with your life. I did it for you.'

'But I became a cop in your town, because I wanted to be like you,' she said, tears now streaming down her face. 'I looked up to you, but you did this.'

He sucked in air. 'You did the right thing, telling them about Goldie. It's almost a relief, you know. And I'm going to tell them everything. How we had to silence them, because Gerard wanted to talk. Ben Leech and Sarah too, because that journalist was about to report it, so Mickey killed Sarah.'

'Why Mickey?'

'He looked up to me and was young, but once he was involved, he had to protect himself. It's that simple. Some secrets had to stay buried. Sarah knew everything, but she protected you, Lewis, because she didn't want to lose you. Mickey spun the story about Truman, the family waster, because Clarence was prepared to see one son die to let the other one climb.' He laughed, mocking. 'In the end, we were all doomed. I'll tell the story, Amy.'

Amy shrieked as the shotgun went off, the blast deafening her, blood splashing her face.

She reeled back in shock, her ears ringing, smoke filling the space along with the acrid smell of gunpowder. She dropped her phone, plunging them into darkness.

She tried to focus, to see what had happened, but someone bumped past her, running.

Her father? Had Lewis killed himself?

She knew straight away though, even before she went to the floor and shuffled to his body. She scrambled on the floor for her phone, face-down on the ground, surrounded by a dim glow. Once it was back in her hand, she shone it towards the shape in front of her.

She let out a wail when she saw him.

Her father was slumped on his side, the concrete around him glistening with blood and tissue and portions of brain, pieces of his skull gleaming white in the light from her phone.

She screamed as reality hit her, long and loud, a sound dredged from somewhere inside her that was deeper than anything she'd ever felt before. As it subsided, she retched and sobbed as her mind whirled in disbelief. She felt her face. It was thick with his blood and brains.

There was the sound of someone running, the tunnel amplifying the noise.

She jumped to her feet, consumed by rage, and sprinted for the exit, running hard along the tunnel, the faintest of glows of the distant daylight showing her where the corner was, not caring about the threats underfoot. Loose stones. A hole in the floor. Trailing cables. Broken glass. She screamed as she went, her mind unable to function properly, but she was going to get him.

She slammed into the wall as she reached the corner, going too fast to take it smoothly, her shoes skidding on the grit, but she pushed herself away and kept going. Ahead, Lewis was bolting up the stairs, taking two at a time.

She followed, knowing she was younger, fitter, fuelled by anger, sprinting up the stairs until she was outside, back in the field, the breeze cooling the blood that glistened on her cheeks.

Lewis was running straight ahead, heading for the corner of the field that she hadn't spotted before, where there was a wall that would let him vault over the fence.

Her chest was desperate for air as she ran, her feet trying to stay upright as she bolted across the field, the ground uneven, deep ruts threatening to break her ankle. The line of the cliffs was ahead, the sea bright blue beyond.

Lewis made it over the wall and kept on running, jumping through the gorse and brambles, even as it got to knee-height.

Amy was gaining on him, grunting as she landed on the other side of the wall, before hauling herself up. The brambles tore at her clothes and scratched her skin, making her wince and grimace, but never enough to slow her. All she could hear was the pound of her feet.

She knew where he was going and gasped in shock, pausing her for a moment.

There was a path than ran through the gorse, the one she'd walked before, and she'd expected him to go that way, back to wherever he'd parked his car, but instead he was heading for the cliff in a straight line, not slowing.

He was going to take the easy way out and plummet to the rocks.

She wasn't going to let him do that.

Amy put her head back and increased her speed, leaping over brambles, trying to forge a way through them. The sea got bigger as she got closer, as the land started to run out. Lewis was twenty yards from the edge, no sign that he was slowing, but Amy was only a few feet behind.

The brambles ended and there was a patch of rough grass. Lewis kept up his line, heading straight for the drop. Once she was out of the brambles, she leapt in the air and flung out her hand.

She swiped at him and caught his ankle.

He tumbled forward, skidding on the grass. Amy was able to grab his trouser leg, but he kicked out at her, catching her in the nose, making her let go as she felt her own blood coat her lip, her eyes stinging from the pain.

He carried on his scramble to the edge on all fours, whimpering, desperate, so she rushed once more, pouncing forwards like a cat flying for a bird. She wrapped her arms around his waist and they both slammed to the ground, Lewis's head over the edge, Amy on top of him.

'It's over, Lewis,' she said, panting, tears streaming down her face.

He bucked underneath her, tried to throw her off, and for a stomach-churning second she lurched forward, and was looking to the rocks at the bottom, before she was able to wrestle herself back and land next to him.

He shuffled on his stomach and got his legs over the edge just as Amy grabbed his jacket.

'Don't go,' she said. 'No easy way out.'

Gulls wheeled overhead, screeching, and she saw the blood on her hands as she gripped him. Was it her father's? Or her own? Did it matter?

Her fingers went white as she tried to hold his weight, Lewis straining to get over the edge.

'Don't be a coward, Lewis,' she screeched.

'All this for her?'

'Come back up.'

He pulled against her. 'She wasn't worth this. She was nothing, the daughter of nothing.'

She leaned back to try to force him back up, her heels digging into the grass, but she could feel herself slipping.

'Let me go,' he said.

'No!'

'I can't face jail.'

She made one last heave, but he pushed back against her, making her lose her grip, fearful of going over with him, until he was over the edge, his arms on the cliff-top, his legs swinging below, his fingers gripping the grass fringe.

She sat back, panting, breathless, and watched as Lewis dangled.

His expression changed from desperation to fear. The anger from a few seconds earlier had gone, the adrenaline evaporated now that he was facing his death, the white heat of his emotions evaporated into the crisp air. This was cold-hard acceptance.

'I can't do it,' he gasped.

Amy hauled herself to her feet and went to the edge. She stood and looked down, her feet apart.

Lewis was scared.

'Pull me back,' he said, and he strained as he tried to haul himself back onto solid ground.

Amy's thoughts went back to her father, lying dead in the tunnel further up the cliff-face. She thought about Tammy, and her own childhood, the memories forever tainted by what her father did.

Lewis got one elbow onto the cliff-edge and was trying to swing one of his legs back onto the grass. The sea crashed onto the rocks a few hundred feet below, but the sound didn't reach them. It was just a constant back and forth, the waves and white foam, waiting for him.

'You said Natasha was nothing,' she said.

He was crying, sheer panic filling his eyes. 'Please, help.'

'Did she beg for help?' Amy's eyes were filled with tears too, but they were tears of rage. 'Did Natasha scream *no* as you cheered him on? Did she beg for it to be over with?'

He looked up to her, his eyes pleading. 'Please, I'm sorry. Just help me up.'

Her mind went back to her father again, to how he'd wrap her in his arms and tell her he'd protect her forever, how secure she'd felt in his love.

All of that was lost. Instead, he was lying in a cold tunnel, surrounded by his own skull and brains.

She screeched with anger as she kicked Lewis, her foot landing square in his face.

The impact knocked his head backwards, a tooth spinning out of his mouth, soon lost into the space beneath him. His grip on the grass edge loosened, so she kicked again, and this time he leaned back, as if suspended for a moment, his grip lost, his arms flailing.

His eyes opened wide in shock as he started to fall.

His face was filled with confusion as he went backwards, disappearing below her, until the air was filled by a scream, one that faded as he went, ended abruptly, cut off by his landing.

Amy sunk to her knees and took in deep breaths. She looked up to the sky, to the birds who flew in tight circles overhead.

It was over.

She stayed there for a few minutes, her chest pumping hard, trying to suck in air, before she hauled herself to her feet and started to walk away from the cliff-edge.

She pulled her phone from her pocket and dialled 999.

When the operator answered, she said, 'I want to report my father's murder.'

***

The atmosphere at the press conference changed.

Before, it had been mild curiosity at the interloper digging into backhanders, but now they were whispering to each other. More pictures were being taken. The cameras zoomed into Spencer. Reporters were doing internet searches for Natasha's name, the journalists looking at Spencer as they realised what the story might involve. Someone whispered, 'shit.'

Charlie stole a glance at Jessica, who was wearing the faintest of smiles as she glared at Spencer. She noticed Charlie looking, and gave him a nod.

Spencer's gaze darted around the group, but it couldn't find a place of safety. He looked at Dougie McCloud, but his jaw was set, his eyes dark and fixed on Isobel. He moved on to Wendy, imploring her to find a different reporter, but she stood next to Charlie, unmoved.

Spencer's voice had acquired a tremble when he asked, 'Natasha Trenton?'

Charlie could feel his own heat rising, his anger threatening to get the better of him. He had to stay calm.

'You don't remember her, Home Secretary? You should do. It was a significant event in your life, I would have thought, with the questions that must have been asked.'

'I remember the name,' he said, snapping. 'But enlighten me why her case has acquired renewed importance.'

Charlie knew that he was thinking exactly the opposite. He'd paled when Charlie had mentioned Willow. Now, his cheeks were flushed, his brow was speckled by perspiration, his fingers white where he clenched the lectern.

'Don't missing women matter?'

'They matter, of course they matter,' Spencer said. 'And, as Home Secretary, I am dedicated to ensure that those who harm woman will face the full wrath of the law.'

'And I hope that comes to pass,' Charlie said, with more bite to his voice. 'But you asked me to enlighten you, so I will.'

He glanced around at the other reporters, who were now turned towards him.

'Home Secretary, twenty years ago you spent some time at the home of an old university friend, Lewis Buford. This was in Cookstown, a small Yorkshire seaside town, just before your final year at Oxford. Am I correct?'

'Just tell your tale, man, so I can move on from your fantasies and get back to why we are really here. To talk about how stronger borders make a stronger country.'

'You'll know about Cookstown, Home Secretary, because it's the town where a reporter died just the other day. Nick Cassidy was his name. He was researching your past, and your connections to the company based in Nevis, and the Swiss bank account in your name, and who would benefit from the contract awarded for this new detention centre.'

The murmurs of the reporters got louder. One of their own, Nick Cassidy, was a victim now. Charlie could see that Spencer was looking for a way out, his mind working hard to decide whether to charm his way out of it, or just close down the press conference.

He went for charm.

Spencer grinned and spread out his arms. 'Ladies and gentlemen, I know you were here for a political statement about the exciting new development here in the north, part of our manifesto commitment to spread wealth throughout the countries of the United Kingdom, but now it's all got a little more exciting.' He pointed at Charlie. 'Please do not let this man become Chancellor of the Exchequer, because when he adds two and two, the answer is nowhere near four.'

Charlie ignored the jibes. He knew what was coming. And if Spencer was expecting a ripple of laughter from the press pack, it didn't arrive.

'This was just at the end of your restaurant-trashing phase,' Charlie said. 'But we know all about that, just youthful exuberance. The parents of your old university friend, Lewis Buford, are quite wealthy, so had a big house and staff. One of those staff members was an eighteen-year-old local girl called Natasha Trenton. Sounding familiar? Anything I've got wrong?'

Spencer cocked his head. 'I don't recall Miss Trenton, but I remember some questions were asked about her, and we answered the questions.'

'I'm glad you remember her, because she was working on your final night there,' Charlie said, and produced the photograph from his pocket. 'Here you are,' and he pointed at Spencer in the picture, then moved his finger across, turning so that all the reporters could see the image. 'And there is Lewis Buford. He's a judge now, His Honour Judge Buford, although you'll know that, as you've been in recent contact. The past has started to come back to bite you. Isn't that right, Home Secretary?'

Spencer looked across to Dougie, who hadn't moved, merely stood there with his fists clenched by his side.

'Whatever it is you have to say, Mr...,' Spencer said, then, 'I'm sorry, I didn't get your name.'

'Charlie Steele,' he said. 'We spoke last night, I gave it to you then, but well done for stalling. And like I told you last night, Gerard Williams was my client. That's him there,' and Charlie pointed at Gerard in the picture. 'He wanted to talk about what happened to Natasha, but he was killed, made to look like suicide.'

The reporters gasped.

Spencer held up his hand. 'I'm sorry to hear about my old friend, and I had read something about this, but Gerard's life hadn't turned out like it should. Now, if the police believe his death was suicide, today is not the time to discuss your wild conspiracy theories. From a lawyer, I expected more.'

'There is more.'

'And if you speak to one of my advisers, we'll discuss it in more detail, but we are here about a new detention centre.'

Charlie looked towards the other reporters. 'Do you want me to carry on, because there is much more, or do you want to ask about a new immigration detention centre?'

They exchanged glances with each other, murmuring their agreement, until one said, 'Please, carry on.'

'Home Secretary, it appears that the floor is mine,' Charlie said. 'Home Secretary, were you involved in the murder of Natasha Trenton twenty years ago?'

That brought a collective gasp from the reporters. True or not, they knew they were witnessing something newsworthy.

Spencer turned to Wendy, exasperated, but her gaze remained fixed ahead.

When Spencer didn't respond, Charlie asked, 'Is the name of your company just a sick joke, because Natasha Trenton is buried under a willow tree in the back garden of Lewis Buford's home?'

Spencer blinked, then shielded his eyes as camera flashes filled the room with bright, flickering light.

'A lot of people have died to protect this secret, Home Secretary,' Charlie said, holding the photograph aloft, his voice getting louder. 'Gerard Williams, the man on the far left, dead in a suspected suicide, but I think you know different. Ben Leech, the man on the right, another murder made to look like suicide. The woman who took the picture, Sarah Marsh, Lewis Buford's fiancée, was found dead on a Cookstown beach a week ago. What is the secret that was so serious that they had to be killed to remain silent?'

Spencer gripped the lectern harder, and for a moment Charlie thought he was going to faint.

'You are making very serious allegations that have never been made before,' Spencer said, his eyes darting from reporter to reporter. 'I must advice all the news agencies here that this is slanderous nonsense. If you repeat it or broadcast it, you will be as responsible before the courts as this gentleman.'

'They're digging up the tree,' Charlie said, and he waved his phone in the air.

Spencer went as if to say something, but stopped.

'That's right,' Charlie said. 'The police diggers are there right now. They're taking up the willow tree. Will they find Natasha Trenton under there, the tree planted to conceal her, the roots wrapped around her corpse? Is the name of the company you own, set up to drain the taxpayer of millions and keep the proceeds free from tax, a taunt at the death you played a part in? If they find her, will they find your DNA on her? Or inside her? Have you been silencing the people who threatened to expose you?'

Spencer appeared uncertain, looking around.

'Home Secretary,' Charlie said. 'What happened on the night Natasha Trenton went missing? Were you involved in her death? What will the police discover when they dig up the willow tree?'

The reporters craned forward. The television cameras zoomed in on Spencer. There was silence, everyone's attention focussed on what he would do next.

Spencer looked around the press pack, his eyes panicked, searching for a friendly face, silently imploring someone to intervene to help him, to change the subject. No one moved or said anything.

'Home Secretary, did you murder Natasha Trenton?'

Spencer closed his eyes and let out a small moan, then gritted his teeth and began to roar. Primeval, deep, the scream of a predator now frightened and cornered.

He bolted.

He pushed through the people who'd arrived with him, scattering them. He had no apparent plan, just a desperate sprint for an exit, his fight or flight instinct set on flight. Reporters shouted. Cameras clicked. Cameramen unscrewed them from tripods, desperate to go after him.

Charlie reacted first, Isobel close behind, except that she was after Dougie.

Spencer slammed through the doors, Charlie close behind. On the corridor outside, Spencer barged people out of the way. Someone shouted. A woman screamed as she went to the floor.

Spencer took the stairs two at a time, the entrance foyer and exit just ahead. Reporters were yelling as they emerged from the room behind them, the old building filled with noise. Security guards near the exit turned, but seemed unsure what to do, recognising Spencer as well as the threat.

Spencer was going too quickly to be stopped, his focus only on getting outside.

He rushed out of the main doors and into the square outside. Protestors yelled and chanted when they saw him, some pointing in anger.

He paused for a moment, looking around, suddenly uncertain of his next step, but Charlie appeared through the doors behind him.

Spencer ran again.

Charlie kept up the chase.

Spencer ran between the two groups of protestors. Charlie close behind. There were other people running, but Charlie kept up the pace. The protestors quietened as confusion spread.

Spencer was increasing the distance between them, fuelled by panic. There would be shopping streets ahead, with crowds he could get lost in. Perhaps taxis, black cabs he could jump into and be taken somewhere secret. Charlie wondered whether he'd always had a plan. An escape route. Money stashed. Contacts who would get him out of the country.

As Spencer rushed to the further corner of the square, the air was filled with the clunk and whirr of a tram, a snake of four carriages that would take the bend, then rattle along the roads of the city centre. It was coming towards him. Spencer ran in its direction, as if to cross the tracks behind it, taking the shortest route to wherever he had planned.

Charlie didn't let up.

But then, he saw something else.

Spencer's focus was on the tram heading towards him, wanting to run behind it, but there was another tram coming in the opposite direction, its noise hidden by the one closest to him. They would pass each other as Spencer got to them, both taking the bend, and Spencer wouldn't realise the other one was there, his mind in blinkered vision.

Charlie stopped and shouted, 'Spencer, no!'

Spencer didn't stop. His head was back, his legs pumping hard. He ran alongside the tram closest to him, the driver sounding a horn, but Spencer ignored it, the wheels right by him as he ran.

Charlie shouted again. 'Spencer! Stop!'

Spencer glanced back. He didn't slow.

As the last carriage of the tram passed him, he bolted across the tracks.

The air was filled with the loud blast of a horn as Spencer emerged in front of the second tram, now heading towards him on the track behind.

He turned towards it, but there was no chance for him to get out of the way. He raised his arms in futile defence.

There was a smack as it hit him, followed by the thud of his body as he was slammed into the road, trapped underneath the carriage, the weight of the tram crushing him, his clothes a blur of cloth and blood.

The tram screeched to a stop.

People screamed nearby, aware of what they'd seen. Charlie bent double and tried to draw in breath, panting hard. Reporters jostled him as they ran past, the bravest getting close to take some pictures, a couple stepping away with their hands over their mouths as they got a good view.

Spencer Everett was dead. There was no doubt about that.

Charlie felt an arm go around his shoulders. 'It wasn't your fault.'

It was Isobel.

Charlie straightened, sucked in deep breaths. He nodded, panting. 'It was the right thing to do.'

Ninety

'They must be Gerard's nieces,' Charlie said, as he gestured towards a group of people entering the churchyard, three tall and elegant young women leading the way, their poise oozing good education, their similarities marking them out as sisters. 'They've got a windfall coming their way, once I sort out the estate.'

Amy looked towards them. 'Their lives are one big windfall. Gerard must have been their interesting uncle.'

'Every family has a secret.'

'Yeah, I know that alright.'

They were outside a small church in a village on the edge of Manchester, with views along a valley, the grey sprawl of the city in the distance. Charlie, Amy and Jessica were on wooden benches in front of laurel bushes, the view towards the entrance.

The memorial service for Gerard had been arranged by his family. There couldn't be a funeral yet, the body hadn't been released by the police, but people were streaming into the church, the cars lined up on the road outside giving clues to Gerard's family background. Bentleys and Mercedes and Jaguars.

'I didn't realise he was so well-liked,' Charlie said.

'Some are journalists,' Jessica said, and she pointed to a small huddle by the entrance. 'I recognise them.'

'Yeah, now you say it, their suits look cheaper,' he said. 'It's still hot news. Are you looking forward to giving evidence?'

'No, is the answer,' Jessica said. 'I know the truth, but a lawyer will try to twist it into something different.'

'That's lawyers for you,' he said, then turned towards her. 'Where do you go from here?'

Jessica thought about that for a few seconds, before replying, 'Nowhere.'

'Really? I'd have thought you'd be valuable, a woman of integrity in politics.'

Amy laughed. 'That's her problem right there.'

'She's right,' Jessica said. 'Most politicians are a little dirty. They're scared I'll discover something and out them.'

'Join the police,' Amy said.

'How has it worked out for you?'

'Well, yeah, good point.'

'Do you ever wish we hadn't found out what we did?' Charlie said. 'We could have continued in blissful ignorance.'

Amy watched the crowd filter into the church as she thought about that.

'I don't know,' she said. 'For Tammy and Natasha, I know we did the right thing, but my father?' A tear escaped down her cheek. 'I can't process it. My father was killed, and partly because of what I did, but I tell myself that it wasn't me, it was him. He started this. Sometimes, I get angry with him, but I miss him too. Whatever he did, he was still my father. I try to think he was a decent man, deep-down.'

'How's your Mum?' Charlie asked.

'She won't talk to me.'

'She will.' Charlie reached across for her hand. 'You're all she's got left.'

Amy took a deep breath, as she tried to keep her emotions in check. 'How's Isobel?'

'She's fine, so she tells me. She hasn't told the police anything though. She figured that they had Dougie for enough. She didn't have to mention her time with him. The story would soon swirl around the Manchester legal circuit.'

A man split away from the group and headed towards them.

Amy glanced up. 'A copper?'

'DS Broome,' Charlie said. 'The last time I spoke to him was at the back of Gerard's house, when he was telling me it was a suicide.'

Amy nodded. 'So obviously a copper.'

'Mr Steele,' Broome said, by way of hello. 'And this is?'

'A friend,' Amy said.

Jessica spoke up. 'I'm Jessica,' she said. 'Another friend.'

'Thanks for believing me in the end,' Charlie said.

Broome smiled. 'We were both guessing at the time. It turns out you were right, but at least we got the right person.'

'Dougie McCloud?'

DS Broome leaned in and whispered, 'He thought he was clever. Destroyed his phone before we got round to him, but he'd hired a car. What he didn't know is that it had a tracker, so the hire company could find it if a customer tried to keep it too long. It put him right outside Gerard's house., tracked him right to the door.' He gave a nod of satisfaction. 'It's always the little things that get them in the end.'

'At least we found out the truth,' Charlie said.

'Agreed,' Broome said. 'I'll get in there, pay my respects. Are you coming in?'

'We will, soon.'

As Broome wandered off, Amy said, 'What next for you, Charlie?'

'A new start,' he said. 'I've found an apartment; I move in next week.'

'Hurrah,' she said. 'And the firm?'

'I'm using the higher rights.'

Amy frowned. 'Higher rights?'

'It means I can appear in the Crown Court and do jury trials. I got them a while ago, but never really used them.'

'You've got your mojo back.'

'I think you're right. I just wish it hadn't been because of this. What about you?'

Amy thought about that. 'I haven't worked anything out yet. I've been given extended leave from the cops, but I don't know if I want to go back.'

'You're a good cop,' Charlie said. 'Try moving. Give the big city a go.'

'Here? Is that an invitation?'

'Have you seen the prices of apartments in Manchester? I might need a lodger.'

'Be careful what you wish for,' she said. She held out her hand. 'Here, for the future.'

He put her hand over hers. Jessica laughed and joined in, all three of them bound together.

'To the future,' Amy said.

'The future,' Jessica said.

Charlie broke into a grin. 'Amen.'

Acknowledgments

I started writing this book quite a few years before I finished it, interrupted by Covid, then by long days in the courtroom as everyone slogged away to clear the pandemic backlog. Throughout that time, my fabulous agent, Sonia Land at Sheil Land Associates, stayed patient. My wife, Alison, didn't mind my endless returns to the same story, as I made continual changes.

I hope you liked it. That is the reason why I do it.

It is my thirteenth crime novel, so I would like to thank everyone who has been part of what has gone before.

To the great people at Avon, a HarperCollins imprint, you were my first adventure as a published writer, and my greatest time. My editors at Sphere were amazing, Jade Chandler in the main. Keshini Naidoo from Hera was an inspiration when she was my editor at Avon, much as she was when she tried her hardest for me at Hera.

For the people at BonnierZaffre, thanks for the cheque.

Liz Barnsley was a constant friend and supporter, so she'll always have my unending gratitude.

I write crime fiction. I practise criminal law. As you can probably guess, crime has always been my passion, from the rumble of the Johnny Cash prison albums as a child, and the adventures of the *Famous Five*, through to the great crime fiction I've read as an adult. I've met great writers, and I've met writers who thought they were great. My main inspiration, however, and my main fun, has always been those I met in my legal work, whichever side of the fence they've fallen on. I've met countless criminal lawyers over the years. They were always great company, even when we were falling out in the courtroom, and they worked hard. They sacrificed more evenings and weekends to help out their clients than I ever did writing novels. We weren't always on the same side of the argument, but we were always on the same side of trying to do the right thing.

Finally, to all the people who have read my books, thank you for everything over the years. It has been great fun being a published author. From loitering in supermarkets, the thrill of seeing my own books in one of the few slots they have, to spotting them in prominent positions at airports or in far-flung locations, as well as receiving the copies of the various foreign translations.

It has involved sacrifice too. Taking my laptop on holiday, or giving up weekends and evenings with editing and shaping and finishing off. Publishers don't care about other life commitments. They had deadlines, and I delivered.

As much as I loved being published, it is fun to write free of the demands of publishing houses. I can write what I like, when I want to, and it is a wonderful space to inhabit.

I just hope there are many more years to come.

Printed in Great Britain
by Amazon